ARISTO'S
PUBLISHING

ARISTO'S
PUBLISHING

THE
SECOND
COMING:
THE GATHERING

ALBERTO PEREZ

ARISTO'S
PUBLISHING

ARISTO'S
PUBLISHING

Aristo's Publishing
1040 Dale Earnhardt Blvd.
P.O. Box 866
Kannapolis, NC 28083
www.albertoperez.com
1 (704) 699-1959

Because of the dynamic nature of the Internet, any
web addresses or links contained in the book may
have changed since publication and may no longer
be valid. The views expressed in this work are solely
those of the author and do not necessarily reflect
the views of the publisher, and the publisher hereby
disclaims any responsibility for them.

Any people depicted in stock imagery provided by
Thinkstock are models, and such images are being
used for illustrative purposes only.
Certain stock imagery © Thinkstock.

ISBN: 978-1-7321718-3-1 (sc)
ISBN: 978-1-7321718-4-8 (e)

Library of Congress Control Number: 20179911789

Aristo's Publishing, LLC rev. date: 08/29/2019

Genre: Science Fiction – Christian – Fantasy

CONTENTS

ACKNOWLEDGEMENTS

To Jessica, my first born, I hope you find and connect to a character that reminds you of me;

To Jonathan, my son and the Defender of his family and a future Guardian;

To Michelle, who continues to help me relate my stories to future readers;

To Armand, who I hope will someday find an attachment to these characters and what they represent;

And to my grandchildren, Jacob, Natalie, Zachary and Zoey, whom I hope will someday discover something about themselves in me.

Finally, special thanks to my editor, Chelly Peeler, and my beta readers, Vincent James Vezza, Tracy Atchison, Michelle Baptiste and Milagros Perez, who helped me focus, clarify and tailor my words to enrich the experience of future readers.

DISCLAIMER

This is a work of fiction. Names, characters, businesses, places, events and incidents are either the products of the author's visions or used in a fictitious manner. Any resemblance to actual persons, living or dead, or actual events is purely coincidental.

Although the author and publisher have made every effort to ensure that the information in this book was correct at press time, the author and publisher do not assume and hereby disclaim any liability to any party for any loss, damage, or disruption caused by errors or omissions, whether such errors or omissions result from negligence, accident, or any other cause.

The Bible reads, 'Thus says the Lord of hosts: Do not listen to the words of the false prophets who prophesy to you. They teach you vanity, emptiness, falsity, futility and fill you with vain hopes; they speak a vision of their own minds and not from the mouth of the Lord. Jeremiah 23:16.'

This story is an account of the Rapture as seen through the eyes of the author. It is uncertain whether the events foretold will actually occur in the manner specified. Perhaps the happenings will transpire in a completely different fashion. Only God and his infinite wisdom truly understands what it will take to save the many versus the few. That said, this tale will unfold in a manner seen by me. I leave it up to you to seek God's wisdom and truth in this story using that most precious of gifts—free will.

AUTHOR'S NOTES

Humankind's brutality continues to jolt, astonish and baffle me on a routine basis. Nevertheless, I remain hopeful that someday peace will come at a price most of us will be able to afford.

The Second Coming brings hope into perspective for so many. I just wish it also inspired others to seek out optimism instead of lashing out. After all, a peaceful existence is what all of us should aspire to realize. If materialism was replaced with generosity, if debauchery was substituted with morality and cruelty with love, the world could easily transform into a paradise. Although I realize believing in global peace makes me sound delusional, I can't help but think this future could easily start with one person; perhaps me or you.

Obviously, peace will not be easy. Nothing worthwhile ever is. Especially when you consider that we promote and encourage drama, conflict and strife for entertainment. So I suggest the first step is to foster a different outlook and let others know how you feel.

Today, campaigns for genocide are commonplace in many countries around the world. But don't take my word for it, inform yourself. What if you discovered the eradication of Earth's inhabitants was being conducted by some camouflaged alien force? Wouldn't you speak out?

World leaders generate and keep focus on false propaganda to target those less fortunate simply because of the color of their skin, religious belief or where they live. The proof is all around us. Again, inform yourself. And when you're satisfied as to the validity of my claim, then perhaps you can speak out. Tell two people and ask them to speak to two others and so on and so on.

Now, let me change the topic and ask you a question. How often do you think about your influences in life? Guidance set by family members, friends, educational institutions, your culture, or even your ancestral lineage. Now, what about inspirations set by religious teachings? Or the encouragements and life lessons conveyed by those who don't believe in God at all? Are they all so different?

Here's a crazy question for believers, like me. What would it be like to physically be in God's presence? Do you have any idea how you would react? Would you even recognize God? Think about it. What if you were one of the first twelve disciples? And God, born in the flesh, asked you to join him? Would you? Would you have left your home, your family and your friends? Would you have left those you have loved most of your life to follow someone you just met? Well, only you can honestly answer that. If I'm truly honest, I'm betting it wouldn't have been easy. And they were all handpicked.

It's easy to say that if God were standing before you, you'd know exactly how you would react. Maybe you'd ask an endless string of questions. Or perhaps you'd hug him for the peace and serenity that could only come from an eternal soul. Maybe you would fall to your knees and ask for forgiveness or simply remain quiet and try to absorb the glory.

Personally, I don't think our reactions would be any different than that of the fictional characters in my book. Confusion and skepticism would be present at every turn. Just like I'm sure the original twelve disciples were challenged with on a routine basis. After all, it's hard to be encased in this fragile shell and take a leap of faith — out of this world.

I'm certain that just like the Apostles of old, we would all need convincing of who God was. So, I ask you to be honest. Is that really a bad thing? Are we expected to exercise our gift of 'free will' to its fullest or concede without question? The truth is that regardless of the evidence, most will not believe. I submit that that hypothesis holds true even for those that today march and rally throughout the world in God's name.

So the question is, *WHY*? Why the complexity? Why the endless choices? Why do we question *WHY*? Perhaps that's the true enigma. Our most powerful driving force — the ability to ask *WHY* — has never been taught. It's part of our genetic makeup. We're created to instinctively know to ask why. So, I ask you — does God ask why? And if God doesn't, why do we? After all, we're created in God's image.

ABOUT THE AUTHOR

I hope this short narrative helps you learn a little more about me and how I perceive the events that transpire around me. Life is often hard for many but I have found that a single random act of kindness can change lives. And not just for the people directly exposed to the event but often times to the witnesses as well.

Long ago, someone shared a quote with me which I have never forgotten. Almost five decades later, I still try to live my life by that simple proverb. My family had very little growing up. I remember going to bed hungry many nights but I never complained. I often saw the sorrow transpiring around me. So even from a young age I realized that others had it more difficult.

One day when I was maybe twelve years old, I saw a blind man on the subway peddling for change. I managed to find a few odd jobs and made $2.30 that day. It was enough money to avoid walking the ten miles home and still have plenty to buy food for the next few days. After paying the subway fare, I had two dollars left. When I saw that blind man, I thought to myself, my life is hard but his must be tougher. I gave him the two dollars knowing I would go hungry, but I did so nevertheless.

There was an elderly man next to me who saw me fidgeting with the money for almost a minute before giving it away. He asked me why I had not given him more. I was a little embarrassed when I told him it was all I had. He turned to me and said, "He who is faithful with little, is faithful with much."

I wasn't sure what he meant until much later in life. Anyway, the old man reached into his back pocket and pulled out his wallet. In it was a ten-dollar bill which looked older than he was. He handed it to me and I instinctively reached out and took it. I stared at it so long that when I finally looked up to ask this man why he had given it to me, he was gone.

Those ten dollars were a lot of money back then; over one hundred and fifty dollars today. Needless to say, that money kept my family and I fed for weeks. So, what's the moral of the story? You never know how an act of kindness will be repaid. I often think about that day. It's like the story of the old widow woman in the Bible who gives away two copper coins which took her days to earn. If you compared it to others who give away one hundred times more, the old woman's offering seems so insignificant. But only until you consider that it was all she had.

To me that story simply means, "I could always do more."

Sometimes, it's the smallest effort that makes the biggest difference. A friendly smile or a forgiving tone could set a trapped soul free. Like helping someone carry a bag of groceries to their car, so they can effectively tend to their toddler. You never know how a small act of kindness may somehow save a life.

The world is overrun by unfortunate economic and natural calamities every year. But we live in the greatest country in the world, and that gives us lots of opportunities to be special. In less than fifty years, studies show that the Artic will no longer be covered in ice during the summer months as it has been for countless millennia. Our planet may not recover from such drastic climate changes without a miracle. And just because most of us won't be around in fifty years doesn't mean we shouldn't try to make a difference.

We spend hundreds of millions on political campaigns every year but allow starvation to remain a real threat on every continent. My local public school's administration works hard to help to feed those less fortunate. I am thankful for being able to help support their local community efforts. Helping to fill a child's belly for a day is the least I can do. I like to think that *free will* doesn't mean we've grown accustomed to witnessing the macabre without reacting.

The event Christians prophesize as the Rapture will leave many good people behind. I hope God finds it necessary to pour its mercy out upon the world again. This action can take on many meanings but in its simplest form it will be referred to as salvation. Multiple millennia ago, a similar deed was performed and this act of mercy became known to over a billion as Jesus Christ. His presence will shepherd the lost from what is the beginning of an unimaginable struggle against unrestrained evil.

Raptured souls will someday join the ranks of immortals and most will receive the stature of Sainthood. Once their internships are complete, they will be granted authority over billions. Until then, God's divine purpose and those selected will remain hidden. I hope and pray that am not left behind.

Alberto Perez

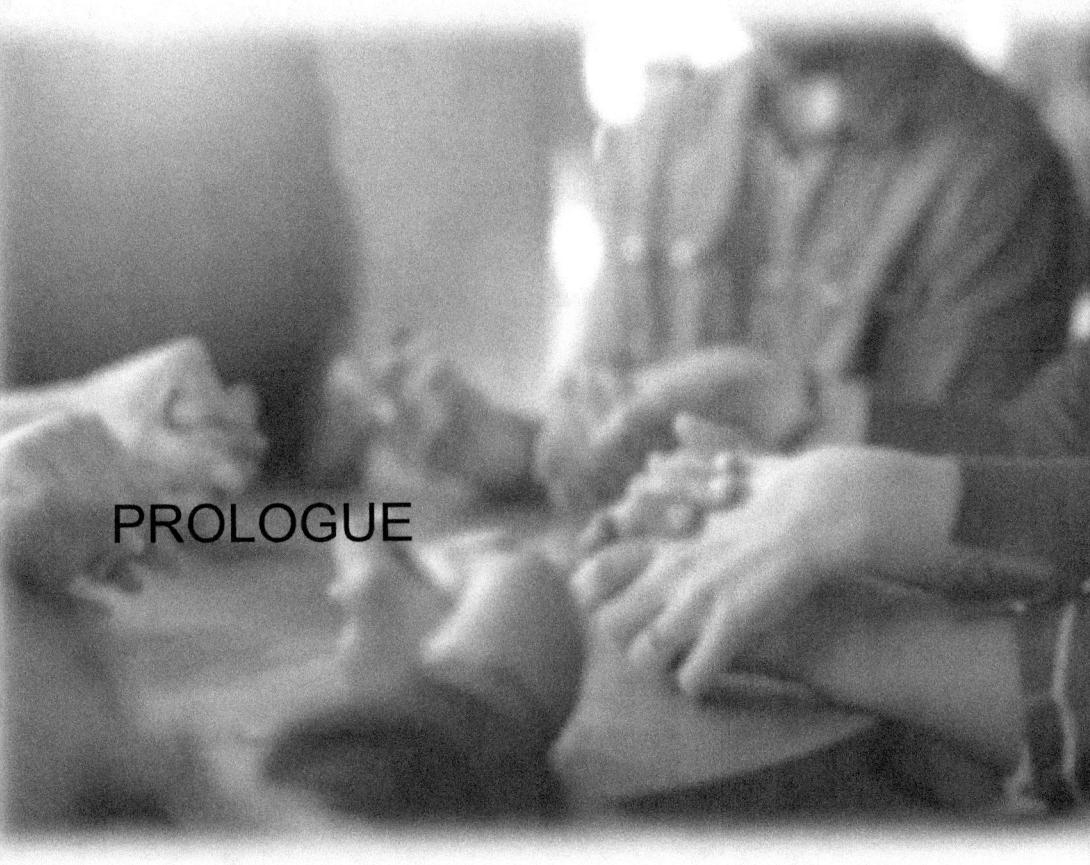

PROLOGUE

THE EVENT CHRISTIANITY PROPHESIED AS THE RAPTURE HAS taken place.

The Harem received a directive from the Almighty to cleanse the Earth of its unworthy inhabitants. Those considered righteous were left on Earth while everyone else requiring atonement were relocated to what is being referred to as the forbidden planet.

The Harem—referred to by many as 'Angels'—and the Helem—known to us as the 'Jinn' or 'Demons'—are opposing ancient souls. Their opposition has existed since before time was measured. Now, these forces are bringing their immortal combat to our front door.

The Helem tussle to counteract the influence of the Harem on those left behind, as the Harem target all the receptive souls with messages of peace and love. The Helem claim to be aiding humankind's survival against a brutal alien invasion. Unfortunately, the Helem's deceit is hard to detect. The planet finds itself facing a gruesome aftermath.

However, within the chaos a new leader emerges with a

miraculous plan for world order. He speaks of unity and perseverance. His virulent counter measures are so well camouflaged that they are quickly implemented worldwide and unite the planet. Many of those left behind look upon this young man as the savior. However, some believe he is actually someone quite different.

A band of new disciples rise up to oppose his work. Winnie is helping heal the sick, Akachi is helping feed the hungry, and Yvette is spreading messages of peace, hope and love. Their deeds are widely being accepted as divine in these times of despair. The world leaders are desperate to cancel this movement and dispatch their total might to capture and eradicate these believers. Their resistance generates an intense manhunt for them and any supporters. These efforts lead to the capture and merciless torture of countless.

The Harem have sent volunteers to the forbidden planet to protect Hoshea's followers. But Helucifer—or the Devil as it is known to us—has dispatched their forces with Reynolds' ignorance at the helm. Reynolds was asked to show no mercy and crush the resistance.

There is no citizen that is safe. And it's only a matter of time before both forces collide, leaving death and despair in its wake.

CHAPTER 1

The Cuban Introduction

THE HAREM HAVE BEEN AROUND FOR SIXTY-FIVE BILLION years. These genderless immortals have protected, guided and assisted humanoids' development on many different worlds. On Earth, the Harem who watch over us are referred to as angels. To those that have seen them, they appear to have familiar feminine friendly faces, and all have appeared dressed in similar flowing, silk-like gowns.

Although most seem expressionless, these genderless immortals feel deeply. However, after countless millennia they have learned to control their emotionalism. But with the change in current events, that control is now being tested.

It was a warm day like all the others in Harema. On Earth, Harema is known or referred to by us as Heaven. And even though the planet hosted daylight without end; it held an average temperature of 24° Celsius. The birds were chirping and God's small animals were scampering about. Lavish green meadows with wildflowers lined either side of the golden walkway and huge trees offered a delightful shade under which to socialize.

Hikiko, a Harem Guardian, was asked to meet Hilily in front

of the great Guardian Hall. "Hikiko, thank you for meeting me here on such short notice," Hilily said with genuine affection.

"It's an honor to have been asked to come, Your Grace. I am happy to serve in all things," Hikiko responded warmly and with the utmost respect.

Hilily was a principle Guardian—the head of its clan and the first aide to Heymie, the Harem Monarch. Like those in its clan, its pale skin had no visible signs of combat even though Hilily had been in countless battles against the Helem forces. The Helem are also part of the immortal ranks and are referred to by billions as the Watchers, the Jinn or Demons.

Hilily often wore red and emphasized its neckline, wrists and forearms with rubies. Although each Harem appeared to have slightly different colored hair, aside from black or white, it was all a variation of two primary colors. Hilily's hair was long and a solid black, worn in a braided ponytail pulled in front of a shoulder. More often than not, there were thick strands of hair on either side of its face.

"I have a new assignment for you. Let's walk while we talk," Hilily shared sisterly.

"Yes, of course, Your Grace."

Hilily reached out and took hold of Hikiko's hand and they walked off.

Interesting! It's true what others have been saying. Hilily does indeed show physical signs of affection, Hikiko secretly admitted to itself.

"Does the physical sentiment bother you?" Hilily asked. The Guardian was taken back by the question. It was rare for anyone to ask a Harem how it felt, let alone a superior.

"No, well, maybe a little, Your Grace. It's just—" Hikiko paused.

"Go on, it's just what?" Hilily pried for specifics.

"Well, it's just different. Or perhaps unexpected is a better descriptor."

Over thousands of millennia, the Harem had evolved past the physical comfort humans received from touch. Perhaps the temptation of physical intimacy was just too strong and the activity was suspended to reduce the enticement. However, their restraint against this behavioral trait was now being challenged by Hoshea and the new Saints on Earth.

"Well, Hikiko, the reason I'm asking is that I felt you tense up when I took your hand," Hilily expressed as it used a finger to brush strands of bluish red hair off Hikiko's face.

"Yes, I'm so sorry, Your Grace."

"Please, there's no need for apologies. But I must warn you that if you decide to accept this mission, you will be exposed to a variety of feelings and experiences you will not be accustomed to."

"If I decide to accept the assignment?" Hikiko stated in the form of a question. The Harem are accustomed to following orders and not being asked if they wished to accept a mission.

"Yes, if you decide to accept. This assignment will be like no other. You will be tested beyond your limits. Therefore, I thought it necessary to provide a caveat. You have the right to reject this mission and I will not think any less of you."

"Your Grace, I would never. I am yours to command."

"Yes, I'm aware of that. But I need your acknowledgment that you understand I have given you the right to refuse this task," Hilily stated autocratically.

"Yes, of course I understand, but I would never—"

Hilily knew what its Guardian was going to say. So it interrupted the comment by holding a hand up, palm out, and saying, "Stop. Please consider the decision carefully."

Hilily dropped the Guardian's hand and stepped out in front. Hikiko didn't remember the last time it felt intimidated, but this was one of those moments which definitely qualified.

"Listen," Hilily said tenderly, "I need you to relax and understand that you are an individual who is substantial. You are not my servant." Hikiko went to speak and Hilily interrupted again. "Please listen."

"Yes, Your Grace."

"You are one of my most trusted Guardians. But if this assignment is going to succeed, I'm going to need you to share your thoughts and feelings. You cannot simply follow orders and expect this mission to be successful. There will be too many new trials and experiences associated with these Saints which you will find astounding—in the extreme. I need Guardians at my side that can think independently and respond effectively to new and different scenarios. This will be a test of your intellectual and emotional prowess. Do you understand?"

"I'd like to, say that I do, Your Grace, but I'm not certain," Hikiko responded as its heart started pounding thunderously.

Hilily smiled slightly then placed a hand gently on Hikiko's chest and added, "It's all right if you don't understand, but soon, you will. So relax, and welcome to the emotional inversion that is now your new life." Hilily took hold of Hikiko's hand once more and they walked off again.

"Now, I asked you to familiarize yourself with the Cuban girls before meeting at the capital city. Were you able to do that?" Hilily questioned.

"Yes, Your Grace. I have reviewed the records."

"Very well, so in short, I want you to be my substitute as the Defensive Arts instructor to the Cuban girls."

"I'm not sure I understand."

"It's simple; I need you to be the primary trainer of the girls. I have encountered too many scheduling and emotional conflicts related to their training."

"I'm honored, Your Grace. But—" Hikiko paused.

"Yes, go on."

Hikiko took a deep breath and said, "Well, it's just that there are few Guardians, if any, better than you in the Defensive Arts. And I am surely not one of them."

"Nevertheless, I've chosen you because I believe you can be successful where I have failed."

"Again, I'm honored, but if you're being challenged, what hope do I have?"

"You are the element of surprise the girls will not see coming."

"I see," Hikiko responded.

"We're going to pay the Cuban girls a visit and you need to be ready."

"Yes, Your Grace. I'm ready."

"Very well, their home has the classic arched windows and French doors leading out onto covered living spaces on the first and second floor. This makes for numerous entry points which can't all be monitored. You will need to consider whether this offers you an advantage on surprise engagements."

"Understood, Your Grace," Hikiko responded seemingly

nonchalantly. However, internally it was so excited at the news of meeting the Cuban girls that it could hardly contain itself. Of the 1.254 billion souls raptured, the Cuban family was one of the few anyone ever talked about. It's like the girls were celebrities, if it was possible for such a thing to exist in Terra Nuevo or among the Harem.

Although the excitement Hikiko was experiencing was obviously visible to Hilily, it continued with the debriefing. "At this time, the Cuban girls are in their newly constructed studio practicing their ballet. Each girl has been stretching and limbering up for about fifteen minutes. This will make their reaction time much quicker than you would expect. Holly and Charlotte are normally still on the bar working on their plié. This exercise helps condition and stretch their muscles and tendons, making them soft and pliable. A proper plié can help prevent injuries because of the spring-like motion in your legs that helps absorb impact when you land from jumps."

"Understood, Your Grace."

"Mia and Artemis are typically on the floor doing front splits. The others are nearby doing an array of exercises from side splits and side tilt kicks to penché or attitude derriere and arabesque. These moves are the positions ballerinas are normally depicted performing on top of music boxes. And again, these exercises help condition and stretch their muscles and tendons."

"I understand, Your Grace."

"Good, so please take note that I'm providing you with this level of detail so later when you're wondering how it's possible for the girls to exhibit such grace in their aerial techniques, you'll know. Their dance routines are incorporated into their maneuvers for this purpose. Now, since they are creatures of habit, Heather usually calls over some of the girls to practice their brisé in about two minutes.

"I'm concerned our regiments are viewed by the Cubans as mundane or predictable," Hilily expressed, secretly hoping for insight from Hikiko.

"Well, Your Grace, perhaps they feel that way because they have nothing to fear on Earth."

Hilily thought about Hikiko's observation then responded with a slow nod and said, "Yes, perhaps. And that's why you're here. To point out the obvious I may have missed. Now, like I was saying, they combine a series of dance steps which are normally performed in sync to music. Heather and the others are extremely light on their feet. They travel across the studio floor and execute small battu or 'beat' moves many times in unison. And I can't tell you how difficult that is, although it seems effortless when you're watching it."

"Although, I can't remember the last time I watched this type of physical performance, it does sound graceful and precise, Your Grace," Hikiko shared.

"It's actually quite amazing to watch. These exercises keep them extremely maneuverable. In addition, they're a visual distraction. You can only force yourself to look away for so long. Then you find yourself mesmerized and that's when they strike."

Hikiko internalized a feeling of amazement, but simply responded by saying, "Interesting."

"Well, I would say 'amazing' would be a better word to describe the event but 'interesting' will do for now. The family converted one of the galleries in the house into a dance studio. Since Mia was a week behind everyone else in her studies, she suggested the conversion to save on travel time to the girls' other dance space. Plus, it actually helps everyone stay lighter on their feet. Since the atelier is now in the house, it is hard for the girls not to participate. Of course, the room is also used by Charlotte to compose her piano concertos and by Holly when inspired to create one of her oil painting masterpieces.

"The Cuban girls dance together every day for at least an hour. In addition, due to the recent chain of events, the entire family trains in the Defensive Arts for almost three hours every day whenever and wherever possible. However, more often than not, I start their training sessions without warning. I am determined to keep the family focused and aware of their surroundings at all times." Hilily paused, took a few seconds to make sure it wasn't forgetting important details, and then continued. "Oh yes, and their dancing gives them aerial prowess you have to visually witness to believe.

"During their routine sparring sessions, I make the girls change their partners often to avoid complacency. Since they are all learning the same maneuvers and techniques at the same time, their responses to different scenarios become too familiar. They are all so attuned with each other's reactions that it is difficult for any of them to generate an upper hand during training exercises."

"It sounds like a monumental training challenge, Your Grace. However, what I find peculiar, at best, is that we are discussing training tactics and strategy about week-old souls."

"It's remarkable really. Anyway, having the girls gain the upper hand on each other was difficult until I decided to keep score."

"Score?"

"Yes, it's a mortal concept," Hilily added for clarity. "So now, unless each student is able to successfully attain three solid strikes in a match, they cannot rest. To the Cubans, that one factor has made their training sessions exponentially more difficult."

"That was a brilliant prerequisite, Your Grace."

"Yes, I believe it was. So, are you ready to pay them a surprise visit?"

"Yes, I am."

"Good, then let's go." Hilily used the Adamic to cast a portal.

All seven girls were in the middle of the dance studio standing side by side and holding hands across their bodies. They were preparing to perform a Pas de Quatre routine as seen in *Swan Lake* but with seven ballerinas versus four. The Pas de Quatre was a ballet routine choreographed by Jules Perrot in 1845, to music composed by Cesare Pugni. In the middle of their performance, multiple sets of French doors opened into the gallery from the porch and dark maroon-dressed Helem jumped in, wielding their Adamic.

The Helem originated from Helema, a place known on Earth as Hell. And the Adamic they were using was once a divine device but transformed when they rebelled against the Almighty. The Helem's Adamic were limited in function and scope when accessed to perform non-benevolent activities.

Heather and Mia, who were at the right and left ends of the chorus line, tumbled sideways and away from the others when the Helem entered. Charlotte and Sam pushed off the right or left leg of the sister next to them and were airborne, flipping forward. Holly and Juno tumbled back and away from the center. All the Helem strikes missed the girls in motion. Artemis bowed and swayed to the left and right to avoid the strikes aimed at her. She was the only Cuban girl now remaining in the center of the room.

Artemis got down in the position of a defensive lineman and quickly surveyed the threat. She taunted several Helem to approach her by motioning to them using a few fingers on her right hand. The Helem seemed unapologetically provoked and several charged Artemis. She did a side split from her crouch position and rolled out of the way of incoming Adamic strikes.

Hilily and Hikiko watched the event unfold from the porch. "The Cuban girls are remarkably evasive," Hikiko remarked to Hilily.

"It's astonishing how such young souls with a week of training can avoid their advances and attack after attack," Hilily responded back.

The girls were jumping and flipping like professional gymnasts to avoid strikes and to keep from being apprehended and restrained by their opposition.

"As you can see, the girls are pushing off each other's feet in midair to gain further aerial distance and speed. This enables them to perform airborne maneuvers not possible by just launching off the ground."

"Where did they learn that? And why are we not doing that?" Hikiko asked in amazement. "Are they being shown advanced techniques reserved for an elite few?"

"No. They're not. The manifestation of these skills originates from within them."

Hikiko looked on in astonishment. The Cuban girls moved like Cirque du Soleil performers without the wires. They did front and side aerials, gymnastic layouts, two-meter-high pikes. And they slid under each other to knock the Helem off their feet by focusing their attacks solely on their legs.

"This is completely mesmerizing, Hilily. But should we join the fight?"

"No, wait. Not yet," Hilily instructed Hikiko who seemed to be holding its breath during most of the battle.

Mia was the youngest and hence thought to be an easier target by most. However, they were quickly shocked to find out that she too could perform maneuvers none of the opposing forces thought possible. Aside from being just as limber and possessing aerial talents matching or surpassing her newly acquired sisters, Mia could somehow step out of normal time just long enough to be a few seconds ahead of any pursuer's attack. It was like watching 'the *One*' in the *Matrix* movie trilogy.

Finally, the Cuban girls signaled to each other that it was time. There were six assailants in the room and each Cuban girl targeted the closest attacker to their right with a containment force field. Artemis then jumped up, spun around repeatedly and struck each goon on the side of the head with a debilitating roundhouse kick.

Spin after spin and blow after blow allowed each girl to release a Helem and watch their foe fall to their knees, cradling their head between their hands. Artemis watched her sisters leap into the air toward a Helem while bringing both arms up and back, preparing to deliver the finishing blow.

Just then, Hilily ran into the room and yelled, "STOP!" The girls retracted their force fields and landed lightly in front of their target.

"It's getting harder and harder to surprise you girls."

"No, I think you surprised most of us," Mia responded back while holding her chest. "My heart is racing pretty good."

"Really? What about the rest of you, were you surprised?"

"Yes," most replied back.

"However, Charlotte is more disappointed than surprised that you started this drill in the middle of our dance routine. She would have preferred for the attack to have been delayed until after our recital," Artemis added for clarity.

"And, of course, Heather knew the attack was coming. She always seems to receive premonitions ten seconds before pending danger. Although she is working on being able to mentally communicate an alert to all of us, currently she is only capable of relating her intuitions to a few," Artemis proclaimed for the benefit of Hilily and the other Guardians.

"But that will soon change," Heather added.

The Helem decoys changed back to their normal Harem appearance.

Hilily asked everyone to gather around. Hikiko had questions but Hilily asked to wait until they were outside the company of their trainees.

"Okay, everyone. That was a great session today," Hilily encouragingly announced. "Hikiko and I will discuss your performance and contact you when we're prepared to release our findings."

"Very well, family hug," Artemis said commandingly. They all moved in for a group hug and everyone sighed and felt at peace.

The Defenders were dismissed and started to walk out a few at a time. But not before receiving a separate hug and kiss from each of the Cuban girls. This exit protocol was now a standard departure routine thanks to the girls' affectionate nature. The Harem at first found the act of hugging others bizarre. For many it was a new experience and for others a forgotten memory. Now these gestures were starting to become contagious. This affection-displaying routine was evoked every time this portion of the clan gathered, regardless of the reason.

Although no Harem had said anything yet, physical contact by or between Harem was not practiced. They had evolved past the physical comfort humans received from touch. But Hoshea and a few families were introducing this practice with a vengeance.

"I have to go," Hilily exclaimed.

The Cuban girls prepared to complete their dance routine when Hilily stepped away to review a message on its Adamic. The message read, 'Hilily, your presence is requested in the Monarch's chamber.'

Hilily announced her departure and hugged everyone but kissed Artemis goodbye. She was the only Cuban girl Hilily ever kissed. Artemis was special.

CHAPTER 2

Mia Receives a Visitor

THE HAREM RECEIVED A DIRECTIVE FROM THE ALMIGHTY TO cleanse the Earth of the unworthy. This act weighed heavily on their hearts since they realized there would be a lot of good people left behind.

The Rapture started on a normal, otherwise uneventful day. Exactly twelve hours later, 1.25 billion souls were rescued and most received sainthood. This event transformed Christianity's eschatology from the theoretical to the actual. Sixty-seven percent of those saved were children and more than half were of the feminine gender. Surprisingly, the adult population was greatly skewed. A mere fifteen percent of the mature souls rescued were men.

Heymie, the Harem Monarch, was initially alarmed at the low percentage of men receiving salvation. However, it took comfort in the knowledge that the men saved had transcended past a brutal, savage nature and were spiritually deific.

While on Earth, many were told that the Raptured would go straight to Heaven. However, before this was possible, an acclimating process was required. Therefore, the saved souls remained on Earth and started the first of five internships toward their adjustment to an eternal life.

The Harem transformed Earth into a utopia almost overnight. Angelic representatives were dispatched among the righteous to guide them toward an everlasting life of unimaginable wonder and joy.

However, those less fortunate and morally corrupt were transported to what was now being referred to as the forbidden planet. This world was under the watchful eye of the Anti-Christ, the only begotten son of Helucifer, also known to us as Satan.

Mia was pulled off the forbidden planet by Jesus Christ himself—and placed on Earth. She was a ten-year-old prodigy with an IQ of 208. Because she was personally important to Jesus, Hilily introduced the Cuban family to the Defensive Arts early. Artemis was chosen as principal guardian of the family but everyone received protective training.

Jesus was called Hoshea in Heaven and was the first-born son of the Harem Monarch—while she was on Earth over two millennia ago. As he walked through the front door of the Cuban family home, he called out to the prodigy.

"Mia?"

"Hoshea, is that you?" Mia ran from the kitchen into the foyer. The room was of classic design. The floors were covered in black and white marble tile, tilted on end to present the illusion of diamonds. There were four wingback chairs scattered about this large room and a large crystal chandelier hung in the center of the room from a seven-meter-high vaulted ceiling. Multiple large mirrors were suspended over stone mantles to the left and right. Each granite mantle displayed family portraits and trinkets gathered from another life, and a chair rail surrounded the room over solid oak paneling painted white. The walls were covered in white and silver-gray elegant, scroll-patterned wallpaper which added depth and texture to the space.

When Mia arrived in his presence, she leaped on him and hugged him tight. "Where have you been?" She squeezed him a little longer then let him go. She pushed Jesus at arm's length and added, "I haven't heard from you in like a week."

"I'm so sorry, Mia, but these are trying times."

"I'm sorry it's been difficult for you. I would do anything to help, I'm sure you realize that."

"Yes, I do, and I'm sorry for taking so long to come see you."

"It's been brutal not knowing what's happening to everyone. I've technically been hiding out here while everyone I love is fighting for their lives on the forbidden planet."

"I'm sorry, but your mother, Winnie and Akachi are there because of the poor choices they made in their past. And although a penance for those unfortunate decisions must be enacted, you should nevertheless honor their sacrifice."

"I do, but I just feel so bad for them."

"I too am saddened by the tribulations they currently face and those that are yet to come. But they cannot escape their past decisions, and I'm glad they're there. Their struggle will help inspire others. There were so many good souls left behind which need their altruism, now more than ever.

"Mia, you were there when they were told what to expect, yet they volunteered and accepted the consequences. Mostly to save lost souls, but also to atone for their mistakes. You must honor that."

"Yes, of course I do. I know it sounds like I'm complaining but it's only because I thought you forgot me," Mia shared, teary-eyed. "I realize now it was selfish of me to feel that way. I'm sorry for displaying emotional weakness with the passing of time."

"It's okay, Mia, you're still adjusting to a new life. Plus, I could never forget you. Your love and compassion for others is one of the reasons I came back the way I did."

"Really?"

"Yes."

"Well then, I feel better." *Wait,* Mia thought, she was having reservations about past events since her arrival on Terra Nuevo. His last statement inadvertently caused Mia's previous suspicions to resurface. *Were my uncertainties justified?* Mia confessed to herself. *Obviously, Hoshea knew me before we met. Therefore he planned our encounter. But was anything that happened on the forbidden planet by chance? Were our struggles, our victories, everything by his design? If so, it would all make perfect sense. But that leaves the question of how? Not how could he orchestrate such a complex encounter — given the trillions of variables. But given our gift of free will, unless — ?*

Suddenly, Mia felt like someone was listening to her confessional so she asked, "Hoshea, my thoughts are my own, correct?"

"If that's what you wish."

"Yes, until I no longer desire it."

"Very well," Jesus retorted. He smiled internally then added, "How I've missed you." *Mia is astonishing and very little gets past her,* Jesus declared to himself. *She instinctively knew I was sharing her thoughts.*

"Thank you, Hoshea, but seriously, my thoughts are my own, right?"

"Yes," Jesus repeated with a smile.

"Awesome."

Mia doesn't just talk to me, she questions me. While everyone else is throwing themselves at my feet, Mia treats me like a person. She is most certainly — Jesus had multiple thoughts about Mia that he kept to himself, but added at the end, *just like every other Miriam in my life.*

The Cuban girls had left the kitchen and were all huddled up behind a knee-high wall on the opposite side of the foyer. Just the tops of their heads were visible as they watched Mia's interaction with Jesus. They were completely mesmerized at her behavior and comfort around him.

On the forbidden planet, by design, Jesus's appearance was different to everyone who saw him. This was to ensure that to most, his appearance was non-threatening. However, on Earth, everyone saw him as Mia did. Jesus now had the stature of a twelve-year-old human boy but weighed as much as the average male. His eyes were a piercing silver-gray and his hair was a curly, wool-like dark brown hanging just below his shoulders. His likeness, although young, carried a familiar resemblance of who he was on Earth several thousand years ago. Since he was still honoring his self-imposed limitations, Jesus appeared to be more human. His self-inflicted boundaries were to ensure he could save as many as possible without intruding into humanity's liberties of free will. On Earth, it never occurred to anyone to question Jesus's appearance. Those who knew him did not recognize him because of his physical likeness, but by what he represented — the essence of all that was righteous and pure.

"Mia has a relationship with the living God. She talks to him like he's one of us. He comes to visit her. It's unbelievable," Charlotte shared with her sisters. Jesus took Mia by the arm and walked in the house.

"Now, Mia, I have come with purpose. But first, let's find a quiet place to talk." Mia showed Jesus into her new home's main gallery. There were two Victorian-style sofas in the room facing each other, each seating three and covered in tri-tone leather. The sofas were placed in the front of the room perpendicular to the fireplace, separated by a long, rectangular coffee table.

The gallery walls displayed huge works of art on canvas comparable to magnificent masterpieces of past Earth artisans, but all created by Holly. Interestingly enough and for some unknown reason, the faces of all the male characters in Holly's paintings all wore the same facial features. Everyone in the house, without exception, had questioned her for specifics on what initially was perceived as an intentional act. To everyone's surprise, Holly explained the act away as simply coincidental, however improbable.

The Cuban girls gathered around the kitchen. "Wow, the relationship Mia has with Jesus is amazing," Charlotte announced again. "I still can't get over the fact that he actually comes to visit her."

"It's extraordinary," Sam voiced.

"Indeed," the other girls expressed collectively.

Jesus and Mia stopped in front of two wingback chairs placed just after the sofas. The chairs were separated by a circular end table. Mia sat on the left and Jesus on the right.

"This is nice."

"Yes, it's comfy and quiet."

"The space is perfect. I couldn't ask for anything more." Jesus seemed happy to be there but it was obvious to Mia something was troubling him. "So tell me about your new caregiver and of course, the Cuban girls." Jesus already knew everyone, but he realized that Mia was still acclimating to her new life. Conversation was still a huge part of how Mia and the others conveyed their thoughts, feelings and ideas.

"Oh my goodness," Heather blurted out then covered her mouth.

"What is it, Telly, what is it?" Charlotte asked repeatedly, trying her best to keep from yelling.

"Jesus is asking Mia about us."

"Oh my gosh," all the girls inhaled in unison and covered

their mouths.

"Well, I'm sure Mia has nothing but niceties to say about us," Heather shared.

"Of course," the girls replied while nodding.

"So, it would be impolite to listen any further," Heather added.

"Yes, totally," they shared then sighed in harmony.

Mia did her best to control her curiosity until such time as Jesus was ready to reveal the reason for his visit.

"Well, Axel is a Saint, as I'm sure you're aware. The girls were told that their mothers died when Artemis and Juno were infants. Neither girl has any actual memories of their mother. All they have are a few old photographs, but in neither photo is their mother's face clearly visible. So they relied solely on their father's stories. And even though they often secretly wish they had a mother, their father sacrificed to provide for their every want or need. Thus, the girls were fulfilled and content, prior to the Rapture."

"Axel is indeed a wonderful caregiver," Hoshea commented back.

"Yes, he most certainly is."

"Axel made it a point to never date after his wife Nora died. He focused all his time and attention on the girls. Even to this day it's a decision he has never regretted. On the day of the Rapture, the girls left Forest Brook Middle School with Axel and their two best friends. Juno left with Heather and Sam and Artemis with Charlotte and Holly. It's unfortunate but although the parents of these four girls were nice people, they did not make it. However, with the Harem's help, the four girls imprinted on Axel immediately and within hours were openly referring to him as Daddy."

Mia took a breath then continued, "So, of course, the parents of Heather, Sam, Charlotte and Holly are now on the forbidden planet."

"Well, based on what I know about Heather and the others, I believe it's fair to say their parents can still be saved."

"That would be awesome. I just hope someone gets to them in time."

And Heather, it's okay if you listen in, I have no secrets from my sisters, Mia conveyed in her thoughts.

Thank you, Mia, thank you, Heather thought, *you're amazing.*

"Well, guess what," Heather posed to the girls.

"What, what is it, what is it?" the girls rattled off.

"It's not nice to eavesdrop."

"No, of course not."

"But Mia gave me permission to listen in."

"Woo hoo!" the girls all cheered.

"Okay, so what are they saying, what are they saying?"

"Okay, you guys, please give me a minute, I need to focus."

"Oh yeah, sorry," most of the girls replied in unison.

"Well, I hope Mom or one of the others has a chance to talk to the girls' parents," Mia replied back with sorrow in her voice. "But the world is such a huge place. It's going to be hard, isn't it? You know what, never mind. You don't need to answer that. I will pray for their salvation. So is this why you're here? Do you need my help to save people like them?"

"They're talking about saving some people on the forbidden planet, who are related to us I think, but I missed who the people were."

"Aww," the girls recited in unison.

Jesus thought about Mia's question then said, "No, not really, but I do want you to accompany me somewhere." Jesus and his infinite mercy felt he had to do everything possible during this time of dread to save as many as possible. Plus, Mia had to be tested.

"Oh my gosh!" Heather exclaimed.

"What is it, what is it?" the girls squawked out.

"Jesus is taking Mia somewhere."

"Holy moly," Charlotte let out.

"Okay, so what do you need from me and where are we going?"

"Mia, I will have to show you. And you will need to have patience."

"Okay, but is it possible for us to save the girls' — ?"

Jesus interrupted Mia to say, "Mia, we need to focus our attention elsewhere, but I will send others to try and save them. Just remember, free will cannot be overruled. So, if they are confronted with a choice to believe in me and they resist, they cannot be forced to convert. The choice is theirs. And the road is set with peril and despair. If somehow they are saved, they cannot be removed from the planet until a penance is offered by them and lawfully accepted. Understand?"

"Yes, I believe so." Mia paraphrased Jesus's last comment. "So if they're saved — the girls' parents I mean — they have to pay for their mistakes. And if I'm correct, that payment will be awful."

"Yes, Mia, for some, the atonement will be terrible in the extreme."

"They are talking about saving someone's parents."

"Whose?"

"I'm not sure, but I have the feeling it's one of ours."

"Aww. Wait, what?" Sam exclaimed in disbelief.

"How can that be, Telly? You must have heard them wrong. They can't be talking about any of us because our Dad is here and our mother is—" Holly trailed off.

Jesus took a deep breath then said, "Mia, let's change the topic. Which of the girls have you formed the strongest connection with?"

"Jesus wants to change the topic," Heather announced.

"Wow, that's a tough question but I would have to say…Telly. She is the blonde-haired, blue-eyed, twelve-year-old cheerleader and the prolific dancer. She was labelled by her sisters as the eyes of the family. Heather receives premonitions. This ability has made us start referring to her as Telly, short for fortune teller.

"That's a nice name."

"Yes, it is. Anyway, I love the name Telly. She's showing me how to dance. She says I have built-in rhythm, which I guess means I learn fast. Anyway, she's fun."

"Well, she sounds amazing, and it seems like each of the Cuban girls is remarkable in her own right."

"Oh my gosh, Jesus just said we are amazing," Heather shared with her sisters.

The girls just sat back on their chairs and were nonplussed.

"I would agree with that assessment, Hoshea."

"Well, it's not that I don't want to learn more about your new family, but others are waiting for us. I suggest we go and perhaps finish this discovery later."

"Sure, we can go." They stood up and Mia added, "So who's waiting for us?"

"Are you ready, Mia?"

"Yes, I believe so," they started walking out toward the foyer.

"So who's waiting for us?" Mia asked yet again.

"You'll see. But brace yourself. This experience will be dreadful to witness."

Mia thought about his words for a few seconds then said, "I wish you wouldn't have told me that. When you say things are going to be bad, they are normally beyond terrifying. My heart is pounding so hard now that it feels like it's crawling up my throat." She reached up to caress her neck.

"Jesus and Mia are leaving and he gave her bad news. I can feel her heart pounding," Heather shared.

"I can feel her stress, too," Holly added.

Mia was hoping Jesus would negate his previous statement after her comment.

However, instead, he added, "Mia, this experience will test you, perhaps beyond your limits, but hold firm to your faith and the knowledge that you will make a difference."

"Although I'm sure you're trying to be supportive, Hoshea, I still feel like I'm going to pass out."

"Mia just told Jesus that she might faint from his news," Heather shared with everyone sitting at the kitchen table, then made the sign of the cross and covered her mouth.

"Mia, be at peace. You will be helping others you love, so find comfort in that." Mia took a deep breath and tried to relax and center herself. Jesus opened a portal when they arrived at the lobby and he reached out a hand for her.

Telly, I'm leaving with Hoshea. Tell everyone I love them and I will be back as soon as I can. I promise to have something noteworthy for Charlotte to record when I return. Mia communicated her intentions telepathically.

I hear you, Mia. Be safe and our prayers are with you always.

Jesus was emotionally stirred by the connection the girls had with each other. He closed the portal and thought, *Heather, come say goodbye to us and bring your sisters.*

Heather jumped up to her feet and covered her mouth.

"What is it, Telly?" Charlotte asked, knowing that something monumental had happened. Heather was standing stiff as a board as tears filled her eyes.

"What is it, Telly, what is it?" the girls repeated.

"He wants to see us. Jesus is leaving with Mia and he wants to say goodbye before they go," Heather exclaimed.

All the girls shot up. "Right now, Telly?" Charlotte questioned.

"Yes," Heather nodded repeatedly.

"Well, come on!" Artemis shouted.

"Let's go," Juno exclaimed then took Heather and Sam by the hand.

Artemis took hold of Charlotte and Holly and added, "Come, you two."

The six girls ran into the lobby holding hands and stood there at attention when they arrived.

"Mia and I are leaving but we wanted to say goodbye. Come." Jesus motioned for each girl to approach him and gave them a hug. He addressed each of the girls by name and paid individual attention to them after their hug.

He held Holly's hand and said, "I love your artwork but I love the artist more."

He moved a strand of hair away from Charlotte's face and said, "It's important you keep writing, your gift will move mountains."

Hoshea lightly tugged on Sam's ponytail which was in front of her shoulder and said, "I love affectionate people, don't ever change." Sam hugged him again.

He looked down at Artemis's boots then leaned in and whispered, "You come from a strong bloodline, which is why you were born a Guardian."

Then Jesus moved over, leaned in and whispered into Juno's ear, "The girls look to Artemis for strength—but it's your compassion she draws her strength from."

Finally, he held Heather's hand and said, "Telly, may I call you Telly?"

"Oh, yes, my Lord." Heather covered her mouth and did everything she could to keep from crying at his sensitivity.

"Well, Telly, treasure your gift of sight, many will need it before the end."

He gently touched all their hands again as he stepped away.

The experience made the Cuban girls' emotions swell up in their throat.

"Now, Artemis, move your sisters back, we need to go."

"Yes, my Lord." All the girls were holding hands so when Artemis stepped back, her sisters followed.

The portal was cast again. Jesus and Mia stepped through the gateway and were gone. Nanoseconds before the transport orifice closed, Mia heard Heather think, *You cling tight to your faith for strength, but you possess more power than you know.*

CHAPTER 3

Yvette's Tribulations
Tuesday, July 16, 2047 2 p.m.

ON THE FORBIDDEN PLANET, YVETTE STEPPED OUT OF A transport ring and found herself in the neighborhood where she grew up in Puerto Rico. After she had an opportunity to absorb her surroundings, she confessed internally, *Hoshea moved me from Miami to Fajardo in seconds. How he manages to control time and space with such precision is astonishing.* She took a deep breath, shook off the uncertainty of the moment and exclaimed, "I'm home."

The city's timeworn buildings generated a glimpse into the past of one of those old Spanish villages of the fifteen hundreds. Suddenly, Yvette noticed what should have been obvious from the moment she arrived. *Wow, there're a lot of lost souls here.* She looked around a little longer then admitted aloud, "I know Hoshea has a plan for me. I just hope I can do some good before I'm recognized, apprehended and probably imprisoned for the rest of my life."

I need to get home, it's not far. She started toward her family's place of business about two kilometers away. *I just need to keep my head down and avoid those without a blue aura.* However, to her disappointment, she was alarmed to see so many familiar faces. It seemed like many of the people she knew growing up were still there. In just a few hours, Yvette had greeted and kissed many of her old friends and family members like she had never left. *Well, I did a poor job of hiding my presence here after all,* Yvette admitted to herself.

Unfortunately, in those few hours Yvette realized that most of the people she knew in Fajardo were lost. *How tragic,* she thought. *Few were raptured but luckily, many can still be saved. Regrettably, that doesn't include anyone I've seen in my family.* Only a few family members who had welcomed her home had a blue aura. Even though she had spent very little time in Fajardo over the last few decades, Yvette truly loved her family, and those she knew growing up, now more than ever.

It's extremely painful to know that if something isn't done and soon, everyone I love will be lost forever. Hoshea warned me against targeting souls which didn't display a blue aura, but something has to give. How can I be expected to ignore my own family, my childhood friends, and not save them from certain death at the hands of a merciless enemy? I have no choice but to talk to them all again and again until I can no longer try. I'll start by speaking to them about their salvation one on one, then in small groups. Yvette mentally developed a plan to convert the masses. *Hopefully, I won't be turned in until I have made a difference.* She spoke about her experience with Jesus to as many as would listen. She provided comfort to the lost about the missing children.

She also addressed larger groups — sharing past, present and future events as factual every chance she got. Every so often she would confess internally, *I'm not sure, I wish I knew if I was making a difference. If there was only a way for me to solidify the results either way, I might feel better.*

Yvette arrived home and noticed the digital calendar on the wall as she entered the living room. It displayed the day of the week, followed by the numeric date and the time of day. *Wow, hours have turned into days,* she thought, *and it feels like I've alienated many of the people I've talked to. It would appear that I'm a terrible missionary. I'm so sorry, Hoshea.*

"It was naïve of me to expect this endeavor to be anything other than what it has been — relentlessly difficult. My efforts have made little progress," Yvette confessed out loud as she shook her head slowly in disappointment. *I've only converted a few people, and none of my family members, after three days of, well, preaching. Wow, it's been three days. Why I haven't been turned over to the authorities yet is remarkable. However, I know my time is running out. I just hope I can stay long enough to make a difference, somehow.*

Perhaps I need a new approach, Yvette wondered, and then it dawned on her. *This scenario illustrates what Mark Twain quoted long ago, 'It's easier to fool people than to convince them they had been deceived.' Regardless, I have to keep trying. I will leave tomorrow and take this act on the road. Maybe I will have more luck with strangers.*

But right now I need to rest, I'm exhausted, Yvette confessed as she sat down on the living room sofa. She leaned her head back and closed her eyes. The day turned to night and then turned to day again. Yvette unconsciously managed to lie out across the sofa. Without her knowledge, a family member walked in and placed a light blanket over her then kissed her gently on the cheek and walked out.

The family place of business and home was just like any other large funeral parlor and mortuary. It was made out of solid concrete to prevent loss of loved ones in their care in the event of an act of God, like hurricanes. It was three stories, the main floor being their primary place of business. This level held the business offices, a showroom, multiple viewing halls, several reception areas, the public restrooms, a few waiting rooms and a large commercial kitchen. The second floor was the living space for Mr. and Mrs. Santa and their three children. The basement housed the mortuary, multiple storage rooms and a large walk-in-refrigeration unit. The property had strong curb appeal which represented a peaceful and secure environment.

Yvette heard familiar voices coming from the kitchen; she opened one eye and then the other. A yawn and a good stretch and Yvette was awake. She wiped the sleep from her eyes and walked into the kitchen. Her father was standing there alone.

"Buenos dias, Papi."

"Buenos dias, mija." Yvette walked over and gave Joaquin a kiss. Mija was a term of endearment which translated into 'my loving daughter.'

"Who were you talking to? I heard multiple voices."

"Meenu."

"Aww, I wanted to see her. I've been home for days and I

haven't seen her yet."

"Well, you haven't been looking, because she's always here. She went out to get some *pan de agua*, so, you'll see her soon."

"Okay, good. Wait. What time is it? It looks like morning. How long was I asleep?"

"It's six a.m. and I'm not sure, but at lease twelve hours, maybe longer."

"Wow, I guess I was tired."

"Apparently. So, que pensas aser hoy, mija?"

"No se, Papi, I'm not sure what I'm doing today. I'm just trying to absorb everything that's happened over the last week."

"Me, too, mija. But I've heard you've been busy since you've been back."

"What do you mean?"

"There's talk about you all over town."

"Really, about me?"

"Yes, it seems you have been out preaching to the masses."

"Oh yeah, sorry."

"It's okay, mija, you don't need to apologize to me. You've done nothing wrong. But I didn't figure you for the evangelical type.

"I'm not, but these are desperate times."

"Oh, I agree with that," Joaquin replied then took a breath, sighed and added, "Well, I can't talk right now. Business has exponentially escalated over the last week. Maybe we can set some time aside and talk later. You can preach to me, if you'd like."

"Aww, that would be nice."

"Good, then it's settled. I'll see you tonight."

"Wait, where are you going?"

"To work."

"Oh." It took a few seconds for her father's statement to register then Yvette added, "Wait, do you need some help?"

"Sure, why? Are you offering?"

"Of course."

"Really? But you're a big-time doctor now. And you know how boring this work is. Are you sure?"

"Of course, Papi! Just give me a few minutes to clean up." Yvette ran off and returned maybe fifteen minutes later. Her father was sitting down at the kitchen table finishing a cup of coffee when

Yvette walked in and said, "I'm ready whenever you are."

Joaquin stood up and headed toward the basement door then suddenly stopped, turned around and asked, "And you're sure you wanna do this, right?"

"What? Yes. Is there something you're not telling me? Because, if you'd rather I didn't—" Yvette trailed off and paused."

"No, I can really use the help. So, if you truly wanna help me, Princess, then come on." Joaquin opened the door to the basement and started walking down. "I've been crazy busy. So honestly, I really appreciate this." Joaquin suddenly stopped and turned to look at Yvette. "Mija, I might have been under emphasizing when I said business was substantially better."

Yvette placed a hand on her father's shoulder and said, "It's okay, Papi, really."

"Okay, but there're twelve departed souls in the cooler and one on the table, plus twenty-five more waiting to be released to us this week alone."

"Wow, that's crazy. That's a lot of departures. I've never seen us handle more than nine in a week. And that didn't happen very often."

"I know, right? I told you. The world has become a senseless place."

Yvette and her father, Fajardo's oldest mortician, walked downstairs to the funeral parlor and prepped for the day. The family-owned mortuary was used as you would expect. Yvette's father had been a mortician for almost forty years like his father, grandfather and great grandfather before him. Although Yvette had an older brother, he had decided long ago not to follow in his father's footsteps. Hector was focused on the day to day business of the funeral parlor and did very little to help prep the cadavers, even though he was licensed to do so. However, Yvette's younger sister, Meenu, now thirty, was more involved in the prep work than anyone ever expected.

Yvette reviewed the work schedule on the clipboard and said, "Papi, there is no way you can effectively manage this work load by yourself. Is Hector helping you?"

"No."

"Then who's helping? I assisted you for years. And now, I'm a forensic pathologist, so I realize how much work is entailed. And the embalming process alone takes hours, so you might be able to process what, two a day? If there is no reconstruction required. That leaves more than fifty percent of your new work load unfinished. So again, who's helping you?"

"Meenu."

"What? Meenu? Really, since when? I remember her only being interested in boy bands and girlie stuff. She used to call me a freak for helping you."

"Well, she's changed."

"Since when?"

"Since you left for medical school, mija."

"But that's been like, twenty years. Why am I just hearing about this now?"

"Mija, you've been a stranger since you left for the University of Miami. We only see you at Christmas now, if we're lucky."

Yvette wanted to strongly rebut her father's observations, but after giving it a little thought she knew he was right. "Wow, I'm so sorry, Papi."

"It's okay, mija, I know it couldn't have been easy for you growing up the way you did. You were always alone with me in this dungeon, year after year with just me and the dead for company, since you were like ten years old.

"I started helping you when I was eight, actually."

"Wow, really? I'm so sorry. Okay, so I stand corrected, since you were eight years old. No boyfriends, no girlfriends—"

Yvette interrupted her father's confessional, "It's okay, Papi, I have no regrets."

"Si, mija, but I do.

"I wish I would have been a better father. I wish I would have said, 'Mija, go out and have fun with our vecinos more often.' So many of our neighbors' children loved you back then, do you remember?"

"Yes, I remember. But please don't feel bad, I believe I made good choices."

"Sure, you did, but...you were eight. I should have made better choices for you."

Yvette interrupted her father again to ask, "Do you want to hear something funny?"

Joaquin sighed then said, "Sure."

"I had this same conversation with Mia a week ago. It seems that I repeated the same behavior with her."

"Oh my God, mija, Mia! Where is she?"

"She's fine, Papi."

"Really, she wasn't taken? I didn't want to ask because I thought it would be too painful for you, since all the kids were taken. So where is she?"

"Well, she wasn't taken at first, but thanks to God's infinite mercy, she was raptured at the end."

"Raptured? At the end? At the end of what?"

"It's a long story. Let's talk about it later."

"Later? Did you turn my granddaughter over to them?" Joaquin asked while staring at Yvette. He looked at her expression and knew. "You did, didn't you? And you're so nonchalant about it. You're suggesting we talk about it later, like Mia is upstairs asleep. I can't believe it."

"I'm sorry, but what just happened here? You can't believe what? Did I just miss something?"

"So the stories about you and Winnie are true?"

Yvette suddenly realized she had made a critical error. Her face went blank and turned white. She had said too much and knew there was no way her father could understand without specific clarity. She now had to recover from this debacle or pay dearly. "No, of course not, the stories you've heard are all lies. Trust me."

"Really, so you and Winnie didn't help aliens kidnap hundreds of thousands, perhaps millions of children worldwide?"

"WHAT?! No, of course not, that's just crazy talk."

"Is it? So where's my granddaughter? Where's Mia?"

"She's safe! I told you."

"Where?" Joaquin asked with signs of antipathy in his voice which Yvette noticed.

"Papi, I'll tell you, I promise, but it's really a long story. Can we talk about it later?"

Joaquin shook his head slowly at Yvette with a look of disgust on his face and said, "You have betrayed us all, mija. It breaks my heart."

"What! Papi, it's not what you think. Mia is fine, I let her go for her own good."

"Oh, so you just let her go? Is that it?" Joaquin closed his eyes and bowed his head then said, "Get out." He raised his head and added, "Get out before I do something I'll later regret."

"Papi—"

"Yvette Mia Santa Milagro, I said, GET OUT!"

"Papi, I would never—" Yvette said remorsefully with quivering lips then tapered off.

Yvette's father turned his back toward her and added, "I never want to see you again. You're dead to me."

Yvette placed a hand over her heart and one over her mouth. Tears streamed down her face as she turned and walked out of the room. As Yvette approached the top of the landing, she noticed the police lights outside. She stepped out and was greeted by the Fajardo Police who seemed to be anxiously waiting for her.

Firearms drawn, Yvette heard, "Miss Milagro, turn around slowly and lace your fingers behind your head." Yvette was numb. She did as directed and was quickly put in handcuffs as she was read her Maranda Rights.

"Do you understand your rights as I have explained them to you?" Yvette was non-responsive. She was trying hard to focus. The onlookers, the muttered conversations, the sirens, the police lights were just too much. The police sergeant shook Yvette and repeated, "Miss Milagro, do you understand your rights?"

"Yes," Yvette replied in a whisper. Her eyes were cloudy. Her mind was floating. She felt faint. Everything seemed to be happening in slow motion.

Wait, wait, wait. *Everything is happening in slow motion,* Yvette confessed to herself then mouthed out, "What the—? How is this possible?" Yvette's heart was beating so fast she thought a heart attack was imminent. Suddenly, she heard her name being called, "Evie."

"Hoshea," Yvette let out under her breath. Then a spark of light caused everyone except Yvette and her sister to cover or close their eyes.

Meenu ran up to Yvette and hugged her tight then whispered in her ear, "I'm so sorry it took me so long to come see you."

"Meenu?"

"Yes, Evie, it's me."

"Where have you been?"

"Waiting!"

"Waiting for what? I've been home for almost four days."

"I had to make sure you were actually following him."

"What are you talking about? Him? Him who?"

"Jesus Christ, silly."

Yvette pulled back and said, "Really?"

"Yes, of course, and thus says the Lord of hosts: Do not listen to the words of the false prophets who prophesy to you. They teach you vanity, emptiness, falsity, futility and fill you with vain hopes; they speak a vision of their own minds and not from the mouth of the Lord. Jeremiah 23:16."

"Yes, wow, I didn't realize you were so well versed."

"I wasn't, but I've had to be with all the craziness happening around us."

"That's so true."

"So he's come back, right?"

Yvette focused hard on her sister's image and for the first time in four days, she saw a blue aura smiling back at her from a family member. "Oh my God, Meenu, yes, he's back."

"And not like any of us expected, huh?" Meenu added.

"No, but thank goodness for his infinite love and mercy." Yvette looked at her sister then added, "We need to talk, but obviously, not now."

"It's okay; we'll be here when you get back. You are coming back, right?"

"Yes, without question!"

"Good, because we need help. It's hard for so many of us to keep hidden and we're running out of food." Just then Meenu turned around and started running off.

"Wait, how will I find you?"

"Follow your heart to Veve."

"Wait, what?" Yvette quickly replied, but it was too late, Meenu was gone.

Yvette, go now and be at peace, Hoshea communicated telepathically.

"Hoshea," Yvette whispered under her breath.

"Yes."

"Thank you, my Lord, I needed that so badly," Yvette

quietly mouthed.

The police sergeant was finally able to uncover his eyes and look around. "Who were you talking to? And what the hell was that bright light?" the sergeant let out as he handed Yvette over to Officer Sanchez and said, "Here, take her."

"Si, señor," Sanchez replied.

The police sergeant looked at Yvette with a raised eyebrow expecting an answer to his questions, but Yvette didn't say a word.

The female officer took Yvette by the arm and escorted her to a waiting patrol car.

Yvette was still processing what had just transpired when the police officer's blurry face came into focus. "Wait, you're Sophia Sanchez, right? Remember me, Yvette Santa? We went to school together." Officer Sanchez stopped short, turned Yvette toward her then slapped her face so hard Yvette thought her face was on fire.

"Listen to me, cabrona, you don't know me and all I know about you is that you're a child kidnapper and killer. So if I were you, I would keep my mouth shut." Sanchez opened up a buck knife before finishing her sentence and held it against Yvette's lips. "Or I will literally cut out your tongue. Do you understand me, desgraciada?"

Yvette gently nodded her head submissively in compliance.

"Good, you psycho puta. My two girls were among those taken."

Yvette was forcefully placed into the Fajardo Police car then startled when Sophia slammed the door shut. As Yvette saw the terrifying female officer walk away, she noticed the blue aura around her. That's incredible, if she was pretending, her performance was Oscar-worthy. Finally, the full weight of everything that had happened came down on Yvette's shoulders like a sledgehammer swung hard against an iron anvil. She sat in silence and wept.

Twenty minutes later, the patrol car holding Yvette drove off. After being processed, Yvette was shackled to an unleveled metal chair in an empty room and left sitting there alone. Every time Yvette seemed to be nodding off, random white noise was piped into the room at an ear-splitting volume. Yvette screamed as the noise pierced her ears like frozen ice picks. Yvette sat there, hour after hour, forced to stay awake without food or water. Twenty-four hours came and went without a single bathroom break or a visit from anyone.

Finally, the cell door opened and the bright lights were turned down. Officer Sanchez walked in dragging another chair behind her. She placed it in front of Yvette and sat down.

"Listen, Miss Milagro, I have a few questions."

"I'm sorry, but I'm so tired it's hard for me to focus. Can I use the bathroom?"

"No. You need to answer some questions first."

"Please."

"I said no, cabrona. Now what have you done with all the children?"

"Children?" Yvette repeated back in a daze.

"Yes, the children, what have you done with all the children that were taken? Where are they?"

"I never took any children. But depending on their ages, there is a good chance they were raptured."

"Raptured?"

"Yes. Now can I use the bathroom?"

"No. Tell me about the Rapture. I thought that was all make-believe?"

"No, it wasn't. It was — it was — it was all true," Yvette stuttered out as she started to fall asleep. That was until Sanchez slapped Yvette awake."

"Please, I'm so tired. Have I answered all your questions? Can I go to the bathroom now?"

Sanchez lean in and whispered, "Listen, you psycho, Samantha was twelve and Charlotte was thirteen years old. They lived with their fathers in North Carolina. Now, where are they?"

Yvette started to fall asleep again but was slapped conscious once more. "You don't have to keep hitting me. I promise — to tell you, to tell you everything — but can I go to the bathroom?"

In the observation room, a heavy-set gentleman in a dark suit said, "Sergeant, take her to the bathroom. It's a long trip and I don't want to sit next to a soiled person in a confined space."

"Take her," another voice announced over the intercom. Sanchez stood up, looked at the two-way glass, snarled then walked around and untied Yvette's restraints, helping her up. Yvette's legs were painfully numb and her back was so cramped up that she fell.

"I can't stand," Yvette grunted.

"Stand up, woman. I'm not going to carry you to the bathroom."

"Bathroom?"

"Yes, woman, the bathroom."

"You're taking me to the bathroom?"

"Yes."

"Thank you."

"Don't thank me yet. Now stand up and walk or I'm leaving you here and you can pee on yourself."

Yvette grunted again and continued to try and stand.

"Yes. Of course, thank you for taking me. I'll walk." Yvette took almost a minute but forced herself up and they made their way to the bathroom. Sanchez stood in front of the open stall and watched Yvette relieve herself.

After Yvette finished, she slowly hobbled to the sink to wash her hands. Suddenly, Yvette remembered Hoshea's gift to her. 'To you, I grant the gift of Speech. You shall have the knowledge to set others free.'

"Samantha and Charlotte are safe and happy."

"What? What did you just say?"

"I said, Samantha and Charlotte are safe and at peace." Sanchez took hold of Yvette's arm and flipped her around.

"My girls are okay?"

"Yes, of course they are, why wouldn't they be?"

"Hmmm, let me think, because they were kidnapped. And taken who knows where."

"Your girls weren't stolen, they were saved. Sophie, would you really want two young, beautiful, innocent, loving girls loose on this planet right now? They are in a loving, caring and safe environment."

"How do you know that? How do I know you're not lying to save yourself? Or telling me what I want to hear?"

"Samantha loves styling hair, right? And Charlotte is a pianist. The girls look more like their fathers than you."

Sanchez released Yvette's arm and placed a hand over her mouth. Yvette then returned to washing her hands before continuing. "Samantha has blue eyes like her father and grandfather, and Charlotte has hazel eyes like her father and grandmother, right? Do the girls even know they're sisters?" Yvette looked over her shoulder at Sanchez before returning her gaze back to washing her hands. "Anyway, the girls' fathers were both in the military. They were both in the Army, no, the Marines, right? And they were stationed in Ceiba? You turned over custody to them when the girls were still toddlers."

"I had no choice." Sanchez shook her head then added, "Wait, how in the hell do you know all this?"

"I'm not judging you, Sophie, and I know because I must know."

"What the hell does that mean?" Yvette finished washing her hands and grabbed a few paper towels.

"Does knowing that your girls are happy and at peace bring you comfort?"

"Yes."

"Then that's why I know."

"I'm not sure I understand what you're saying, but can I see them?"

Yvette looked at Sophia and smiled, then said, "Yes, God willing."

"When? Where are they? When can I see them? Are they with their fathers?"

"Soon, and they're still in North Carolina." Then Yvette thought for a second and added under her breath, *well, what used to be North Carolina anyway.* "All you have to do to see them again is believe and trust in God. And no, unfortunately their fathers didn't make it."

"Meaning what? That they didn't get raptured?" They walked out of the bathroom and were heading back to the holding cell.

"Yes, I'm so sorry but the girls' fathers didn't get raptured. However, have no fear, because that's why I'm here. Samantha and Charlotte are with their best friends. And their caregiver is literally a Saint."

"What? And why are you so calm? You were sitting on that chair for twenty-four hours straight. I can't sit for more than an hour without my back killing me. Plus, you were forced to stay awake by deafening noise piped into the room. I know that had to be torture."

"It was, but you now have hope and that's why I'm here."

Just as they arrived in front of the holding cell, several men in suits stepped out with Sanchez's sergeant and said, "Thank you, officer, but Doctor Milagro is going with us."

"WHAT?! Going, going where? Where are you taking her? I'm making progress. You need to give me a little more time."

"I'm sorry, but your time's up. She's coming with us. But if you're truly making progress with her, you may come along." Sanchez looked over at her lieutenant who nudged her on.

Yvette, three heavy-set men in suits and Sophia got into a black Escalade and three hours later arrived at what could only be described as a sophisticated torture black site, in Guantanamo Bay, Cuba.

Upon arrival, Yvette was immediately subjected to water-boarding for hours. This form of torture restricts the breathing passages of an immobilized captive, causing the individual to experience the sensation of drowning beyond human endurance. She was also exposed to multiple forms of torture utilizing methods like sleep deprivation, temperature regulation, the playing of deafening white-noise, and other psychological manipulation while being interrogated. Yvette was also given chemical toxins to increase her sensitivity to external stimuli. These methods, though often brutal, frequently left no physical marks but after prolonged exposure, drove the victims insane.

Mia and Hoshea had stepped outside of normal time to observe the torment Yvette was being exposed to.

"How long has my mother been subjected to this brutality?"

"For several days."

"Well how long are we going to stand here and watch her get tortured?"

"Mia, this is your test. There is nothing we can do until they try to kill her."

"Why am I being tested? I thought I had already proven myself?"

"You did while on Earth. But we're not on Earth, are we? If you are to become the being I expect you to be, you must see this through," Hoshea provided, hoping not to seem apologetic or insensitive.

"I can't wait that long. I won't. I can't. I just can't. She's going to go insane or I am."

Hoshea took hold of Mia and said, "Mia, you must. Helucifer was told not to break bones or kill anyone to force confessions. Therefore, we have to wait until those rules are broken."

"Why? And what if the Devil never breaks the rules? I'm telling you, I'll go insane if I have to watch much longer."

"If you are to watch over others someday, then you must bear witness to these atrocities before —" Hoshea trailed off and was silent for a few seconds then added, "Just like every other Miriam before you. It pains me to say, but this is the worse in man. Cruelty is all that drives their empty carcasses now."

"I can't do it. I'm not like you. I'll go insane. This is just too much." She took a deep breath and started pulling her hair.

"Behold."

Suddenly, Mia saw the presence of someone else. The entity seemed to be floating close enough in front of her mother to reach out and touch her. Just then the apparition took hold of Yvette's head and pulled itself toward her and they touched foreheads. Then one word was spoken in a whisper.

"Hoshea, who is that?" Mia questioned. "Do you know her? I can't see her clearly. It looks like Hilily. Is it her?"

"It's a Guardian Angel, Mia. And it's here to help."

Just then, Hilily turned toward Hoshea and silently communicated a single thought.

"Is she here to save my mother?"

"In a way. It's here to protect her mind. Memories of Yvette's current captivity are being erased and will soon disappear from history."

"Does that mean that I too will forget what I've seen?"

"In a way."

"The memories of fear, helplessness, and anguish associated with these events will diminish and disappear completely in time. But the knowledge of the actions will remain. Before you forget the experience, you need to record what happened so others may know the sacrifice endured here in the preservation of righteousness.

"Mia, I realize observing these acts is a form of torture. I know it's painful and maddening, but you have remained steadfast. However, it's not over yet and we must wait until this chapter completely unfolds. Let's go see Winnie and then come back. She needs me." Hoshea opened up a portal and they were gone.

**********Back in Guantanamo's Black Site main office **********

Cooper walked into the command center to update his boss on Yvette's status. The room resembled a large concrete bunker with observation stations scattered throughout the space monitoring all aspects of the base. However, aside from the commander, Sanchez and one other person, the space seemed uncharacteristically void of people.

Cooper walked up to his boss and heard him bark out, "Report."

"Sir, we've been at it for over two days now. She doesn't know anything. She would have told us everything she knew days ago. Or she would have made it up. We have all manufactured information after hours of this type of torment. No one can withstand this level of agony and remain sane."

"Has she confessed?"

"No, sir. And she should have done so days ago. At this point, there's nothing to suggest that she will."

"Very well then, bury her."

"Sir?"

"Do you have a problem with that order, soldier?"

"Well, sir, it's that we have clear instructions from Europe that we're not allowed to kill these people, under any circumstances. This is why we're using the 'no-touch' methods of persuasion."

"Well, she hasn't revealed any information and she hasn't confessed. And at this point she's probably insane. So what would you suggest? We just let her go? Do I need to remind you that she's in league with our Master's greatest adversary?"

"No, sir."

"Then get rid of her."

Cooper took a deep breath, looked at Sanchez then replied, "Yes, sir."

"I will not allow you to kill her," Sanchez barked. "It's obvious to me now that this woman has done nothing wrong. She has said nothing but that she loves us and forgives us. I've been begging you men to stop for days because I can no longer bear to watch her torment. I have even been thinking of ways to confess on her behalf."

"So," the commander responded back with contempt.

"So? So, you need to let her go. Haven't you been listening to the reports? She hasn't done anything. She doesn't know anything. She poses no threat to you or anyone else here."

The boss inhaled for a few seconds then stood erect and replied, "Have it your way." He started to walk off and added, "Excuse me for a moment." He stopped behind a computer monitor in the corner of the room and motioned for Cooper to approach.

When Cooper arrived at his side, he said, "Take Miss Sanchez to see the doctor."

"Thank you, sir, thank you," Sanchez appreciatively replied.

He nodded sympathetically then whispered under his breath, "Cooper, find Avery and take him with you. Make sure you silence both women."

"Yes, sir, as you wish."

Cooper left the room with Sanchez while looking for Avery. He arrived in front of Yvette's cell and saw Avery walking out. Avery bumped into Sophia and slipped a cell phone into her back pocket.

"Where have you been?"

"I've been here interrogating this woman."

"Did you learn anything?"

"Only that she's lost control of all reason."

"Ha, that's what I just finished telling the chief."

Cooper looked over at Sophia and said, "Go on in."

Avery grabbed Sophia by the arm and walked her in, then whispered in her ear, "Sit and comfort her. She needs some tenderness. Tell her not to worry about Winnie, she'll be fine. Nod if you understand."

Sophia nodded and Avery walked out of the cell.

"What was all that about?" Cooper asked. "It seems like you know her."

"I don't, I just told her not to try anything or we would shoot them both."

Cooper laughed as he communicated the boss's instructions.

"Well, we need confessions. And we won't get them if you

shoot them both."

"Okay, so what do you suggest?" Cooper asked.

Yvette was lying on the cold concrete floor near exhaustion after days without sleep and repeated torture. Sanchez sat down and placed Yvette's head on her lap and caressed her hair.

She leaned down and whispered, "I'm getting you out of here." Yvette took hold of Sanchez's finger and shed a tear. It was all she could do.

"Threaten Sanchez," Avery suggested to Cooper.

"Oh yeah, good one, sir, I got this," Cooper replied as he stepped around Avery.

Cooper walked into the room and pulled out his firearm and said, "Doctor Milagro, this is your last chance. Tell us what we want to know and confess, or watch your friend die."

Sanchez screamed, "What the hell is this?! Your boss said I could take her out of here. You can't expect to get away with this."

A shot was fired, piercing the chest of Officer Sanchez. She recoiled, looked down at her chest, closed her eyes and slowly fell back against the wall, sliding down to the floor.

"One down, one to go."

"No!" Yvette let out in a loud whisper. "She's innocent... She's done nothing... Why would you do this?" Yvette was going in and out of consciousness. "Just, just kill me—"

"Very well, have it your way."

"Mother!"

"Mia," Yvette whispered. Another shot was fired at Yvette's limp body.

Mia stepped out of the transport ring and encapsulated her mother and Officer Sanchez in her protective field. The bullet ricocheted and Mia gazed up under her brow at the man who had tried to kill them both.

"What the hell? Who are you?" Cooper looked around then mouthed under his breath, "Where the hell did you come from?" He saw Avery standing behind him with his firearm drawn. "Are you seeing this?" Cooper questioned.

With a scolding look of defiance, Mia held her mother and said, "You were told not to kill them. That was a mistake. Your penance will be great." Mia waved her hand and all they were gone.

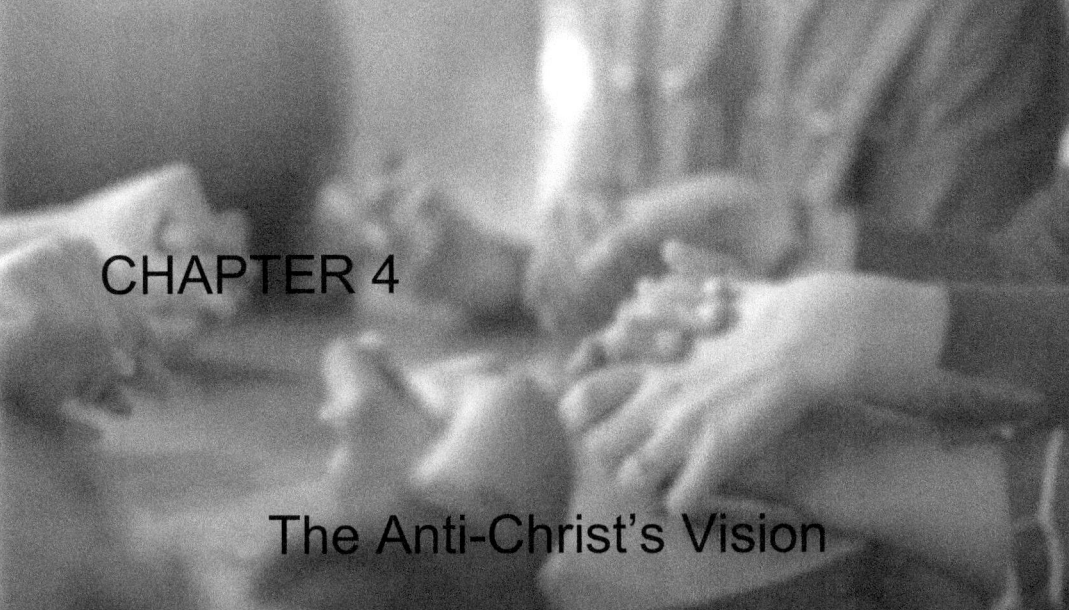

CHAPTER 4

The Anti-Christ's Vision

FILIP RETURNED TO HIS CHAIR, SAT DOWN, THEN TURNED TO look out his office window. The weather was a comfortable 22° Celsius and there was not a cloud in the sky. *The world will finally be mine,* Filip confessed to himself. He noticed there was an unusual amount of traffic coming in and out of the government complex. Filip's office was atop of the Warsaw Poland Capital Building. His office was decorated with early nineteenth century furniture which matched the architectural design of the timeworn building.

The terror and bedlam that had taken hold on the world over the last week had surrendered to his brilliantly fabricated strong-arm tactics. Filip was a junior member of the United Nations but leader of the European Union. The residing leadership at the UN had generated nominations to elect Filip Zarek to secede the current sitting President in mid-September of 2047, now just a few months away. His address of the general assembly a week earlier had solidified his affirmation. Filip felt confident he would be proclaimed not only President of the United Nations but the new temporary leader of the known world. His staggering eleven-hour-and-six-minute speech shattered the previous record held by Fidel

Castro since September 1960. Rumors were surfacing that the President of the United States, the United Nations and the Prime Minister of Great Britain had all cast their votes for this young man to lead the new world order.

Filip Zarek was just finishing up his morning reading ritual of the UK *Sun*, Germany's *Bild*, the *Wall Street Journal*, China's *Reference News*, Japan's *Yomiuri Shimbun* and the *Times of India* when Eric Tusk, his chief of staff, knocked on his door.

"Come in."

Eric opened the door and walked in. "Good morning, sir."

"Good morning, Eric."

"Sir, I'm sure you've read the articles written on you by the *Journal*, the *Sun* and every other major newspaper in the world?"

"Yes, Eric, I have."

"I especially like the comments made by world leaders that the cost of fossil fuels are being reduced for its citizens per your recommendation."

"It's as it should be, Eric, in these troubled times."

"And the pricing on fuel isn't the only item being reduced. The cost on all perishable food items has dropped by nearly seventy percent in a week thanks to you, my Lord."

"Well, how else would we expect our citizens to follow us blindly?" Filip added.

"Of course, my Lord," Eric confirmed.

"The sheep need a shepherd to lead them to slaughter," Filip rejoiced.

"Well said, sir. The scare of hostile aliens taking control of our monetary infrastructure and simultaneously destabilizing our societies worldwide has taken hold. We control the world's financial systems and all banks, including the Vatican and Switzerland independent entities. Even though our intent is a drastic dichotomy from the long-established norm, few are questioning us."

"It's a testament to our resolve and their cowardice and absurdity for conformity."

"Yes, my Lord."

"So, Eric, where are we on the distribution of the identification chips?"

"As you know, North America, Great Britain, and more than

half of Europe have already received tags for their citizens. We have also sent about one hundred million chips to China and India. Since you provided a surplus of ID tags to the United States and Great Britain, they are making plans to control specific regions of the world. And since we control the American and British leadership, we too will control those regions.

"Yes, sir, giving the US and the UK extra chips helped fueled their greed and our control. It seems that every country in possession of our identification chips has been busy placing them within their citizens."

"Excellent. So where are the tags being inserted?

"In the back of their right hand, as suggested."

"That's fantastic, Eric, please continue," Filip encouraged.

"Yes, sir. Every supplier with the capability and capacity to quickly generate the technology needed to implement our new monitoring systems has been engaged. We have sent messages to China and India explaining our actions and the one-week response time necessary for all their requirements to be met.

"Afterwards, we will focus distribution into the remaining parts of Asia, the Middle East, Central and South America. We will focus the dissemination of our product into Africa once the rest of the world is under our control.

"The companies developing the automated teller software to read and process our chips have completed their program development. As of this morning, the developers transmitted their chip recognition software worldwide and everyone is operational.

"Credit allocation stations for retailers have also been updated in the US, Great Britain, Europe and parts of China. Everyone else will receive updated software before the end of tomorrow. By this time on Friday, every retailer and or service provider worldwide will be able to accept and process credits for goods and services."

"Eric, that's fantastic news. You're a good man. Every major government worldwide has voided their paper currency. All financial institutions closed to retrofit their systems to our new credit program have reopened. There is no bank on this planet currently accepting anything other than our credits as currency.

"As I knew they would, my Lord." Eric rejoiced at Filip's unimaginable success.

"We are handing out worthless credits and everyone is lining up to receive them," Eric confessed with absolutism.

"Has there been much resistance?" Filip questioned Eric, hoping for an opportunity to dispense some cruelty and call it justice.

"Yes, sir. There is still strong resistance by the world's richest companies' leadership and their owners. And, as expected, many are lashing out with petulant behavior, as if—" Eric trailed off.

"We need to silence them immediately," Filip announced commandingly with impetuous verve.

"Yes, my Lord." I have a complete list of the nay-sayers. These are, of course, several thousand influential and powerful men and women. And at least half of them will not accept what is happening. Even now, they are working behind the scenes to impede our hold."

"Eric, do we know where these nay-sayers are?"

"Yes, sir. And since we helped many of them rise to power, we know their weaknesses."

"Fantastic. Have the courts issue arrest warrants under the suspicion of alien collusion on twenty-five percent of those on your list. Afterwards, we'll see how many fail to convert to our cause."

"Yes, my Lord."

"And show no mercy to this first group. I want signed confessions from all of them. Any that refuse to sign should be made to suffer for as long as possible before putting them to death. And make sure you torture them in front of some of the others. I want them to know what's coming.

"Yes, sir."

"If negotiations fail with the remaining leaders, pick up the next twenty-five percent of those on your list and continue your forced confessions until everyone submits.

"Yes, sir."

"Although I want this process completed within a week, I need you to administer a slow and miserable agonizing death to the first ten percent on your list. This is whether they confess or not. And make sure some of the others watch."

"Yes, my Lord. That sounds like fun. Should I also try to have them bear false witness against each other?"

"Of course, Eric, that goes without saying. We need to solidify our position. That will end their resistance quickly and allow us to focus our forces on more urgent matters," Filip admitted without fear of contradiction.

"Yes, sir. I will make sure all virtual newspapers are aware of our alien invasion discovery. This will generate broadcasts around the world that we are finally taking back control of our planet. In addition, this will give other opponents of the super-rich and those with standing power an opportunity to come forward while generating tumultuous crowds seeking justice. It will be easy to find corroborating witnesses. And if it doesn't yield the expected results, we will buy their testimony. A year's worth of credits will generate plenty of witnesses. Plus, the common people hate the wealthy, so it's just a matter of time."

"Agreed, and a year's worth of credits should undeniably generate loyalty from a population of simpletons," Filip added.

"On that note, my Lord, the alien hunt is taking on a mind of its own. Mankind is fighting back on the streets. Our common citizens like bus drivers, mechanics, carpenters and clerks have become our first line of defense, just as you predicted. Those that were meek are inheriting the Earth with a vengeance."

"That's excellent, Eric, that's absolutely brilliant."

"In addition, every adult on the planet with a tracking chip has registered and is part of our database. Even those that have not yet received the chips are willingly registering. The system is working perfectly, dispensing and allocating credit allotments as predicted. About seventy percent of all global citizens have received their first disbursement of one hundred credits per family member for this month. We should have full planet compliance within a few more days."

"Eric, that's truly impressive. It's well above the estimates I generated several months ago."

"Yes, sir. Also, the cost of fossil fuel was reduced to a half credit per gallon. All pipelines, wells, underwater rigs, receiving and processing stations are now under government control. In addition, all the local fuel dispensing stations are also government run. Since the cost of untreated and non-perishable goods has also been reduced, the distribution of these goods is being closely monitored. No one family can purchase more than a weeks' requirements of any one item. Well, with the exception of schools, cafeterias and food banks."

"Excellent, Eric, you're a loyal and faithful servant."

"Thank you, sir."

"Now, talk to me about trade borders, debt obligations, medical services, and narcotics," Filip inquired while displaying a noticeable loathing look on his face for the medical industry. Filip's philosophy was that only the strong should survive. However, since the greed of the industry was taking advantage of the poor and infirmed, he wasn't convinced he should eliminate the practice, yet.

"Yes, sir, all trade borders have been opened to everyone interested in legitimate trade."

"Is this effort worldwide?"

"Not yet, my Lord, only about ninety percent of the countries of high interest are participating. The other ten percent will take more time."

"Very well, the last ten percent don't really matter, so go on."

"The collection of past expenditures has been suspended indefinitely. Medical services are being provided to everyone for free. And although we want our citizens to take advantage of the drug market, the drug cartels are holding back their merchandise until they determine how to collect payment for their product."

"This is unacceptable. We need to resolve this quickly. You know my incertitude toward supporting the feeble-minded and destitute. I need the cartels to take advantage of this open market as the tobacco and the alcohol industries did in the beginning of the 19th century. If those currently in charge do not flood the market immediately, we'll replace them all."

"Yes, sir."

"What about prostitution?"

"This commerce is experiencing the same type of setbacks as the narcotics trade."

"Eric, we need these stress outlets made available. Have the escort services use the purchasing code provided by the entertainment industry for video sales. And have the drug cartels sell their product using a protein formula code. Make sure these two program codes are completely ignored under the new credit system during our audit cycles. Make sure the escort industry understands they will receive one credit for one date. And the narcotic industry will receive one credit for an ounce of, of, of, an ounce of, whatever."

"Yes, my Lord, this should solve those two enigmas quickly. I have some ideas on how to communicate this new approach to those two business segments. I expect the markets to see a noticeable change within a few hours."

"Excellent. I'll leave that in your capable hands. So continue."

"Yes, sir, well, citizens caught price gouging or engaging in counterproductive activities are being arrested. Their goods and property are being seized by local law enforcement, and they are being charged and convicted within hours. The punishment rendered is always the same. Their life is forfeit with extreme prejudice, as you requested, my Lord. Your mandate for zero tolerance is being honored worldwide. The global justice department platform is rendering no clemency to anyone trying to circumvent our new world order."

"That's excellent, Eric. I want those citizens that display generous and supportive behavior noticeably rewarded while those exhibiting obstinacy and rebellion crushed without mercy."

"Yes, of course."

"How are we doing on the pharmaceutical front?"

"Well, sir, most pharmaceutical companies are refusing to dispense free medication to distribution centers and our citizens. This would include specific oriented medication to target and seduce violent tendencies among the population. However, the CEOs and board members of those companies are the first group being targeted by our alien collaboration initiative."

"Excellent. Now, talk to me about the masses that are still referring to the disappearance of so many as the 'Rapture.' What are we doing about them?"

"That activity is being curtailed with extreme prejudice. Propaganda of the alien abductions is still being circulated relentlessly. Our efforts and countermeasures are also being communicated on a continuous basis. Our citizens are being told repeatedly that all aliens and their collaborators are being identified, targeted, captured and made accountable for their crimes against humanity. The Rapture is being exposed as a hoax and squashed. We have the head of many clergy organizations dismissing discussions of the Rapture. Allegations of this euphoria sham are being stomped out at the highest level within the remaining clergy organizations and its members. The religious leaders in the Christian faith who continue to preach a conflicting message are being targeted. If they do not admit to orchestrating a campaign of deceit, they are being put to death. And lower level clerics are eliciting large contributions of credits for supporting testimony."

"Fantastic. Let's negotiate with them, but we want them on our side, so complete the negotiations as quickly as possible.

"Yes, sir."

"Now, let's discuss the real threat. Talk to me about Yehoshuah and his new disciples. In short, are the remaining Jewish people leaning toward Jesus?"

"I'm not certain, my Lord. However, Harem banter has confirmed that Hoshea is no longer on the planet. And there has been no communication on Jesus's new disciples.

"Therefore, our global taskforce is currently doing everything possible in pursuit of these zealots. Sources tell us that somehow Hoshea's faithful leaders know exactly who to target and what to say. Their efforts will build up a strong resistance among the common people, if our efforts are not effective.

"However, that said, there is no measurable effort being spared to capture these fanatics and Hoshea, if he returns. The taskforce is being led by the United States. But, the leadership role has moved from the Department of National Security to the Global taskforce led by Reynolds. I assure you, sire, all measure of support is being brought to bear."

"Very well," Filip communicated with obvious odium. Eric could see the anger building in the eyes of his master. He thought he would change the topic.

"On a similar note, sir, if I may, I believe it's time I checked on Reynolds." Filip waved permission. Eric walked over to the book shelf that hid the entrance to Filip's secret worship room. He pulled the book shelf away from the wall and exposed the entrance and walked in. Like always, Eric covered his nose and mouth and held his breath. No matter how many times he entered this room, the initial stench was always overwhelming. He held it in long enough to have the passageway close behind him then projectile vomited. The pungent smell of urine and feces combined with the revolting odor of decomposing cadavers was too much. He wiped his mouth on his sleeve then walked over to Reynolds and felt for a pulse.

"You're near death, you mongrel lover," Eric voiced then spat in his face.

Eric walked out five minutes later rolling down his sleeves. The exit and entrance into Filip's temple was only accessible from his office. Filip was just hanging up the telephone when Eric walked back in.

"And how is Reynolds?" Filip inquired at a distance.

"He's alive, my Lord, but in agonizing physical distress and near death. I have submerged him in a warm, sterile, oxygenated solution. I need another fifteen, maybe twenty minutes to make sure he's clean and stable enough for transport.

"I may have been overzealous in my disciplinary disbursement. In addition to ripping the flesh off his upper torso, I gave him stimulants to keep him awake. Therefore, he is in near maddening torment. If he remains any longer in this substantially excruciating condition, I'm afraid he will die or go insane. I gave him antibiotics again, some additional blood and finally administered a pain suppressant. It's time for him to slowly start recovering. I will confirm the surgeon's availability immediately."

"Eric, I rely on your judgment, but make sure he doesn't die. We need him, so make sure he receives the finest care as soon as possible. After his recovery, this experience will send him out with new focus. I want Hoshea's disciples found and tortured with extreme prejudice. But remember, Eric, under no circumstances are we allowed to break their bones or kill them. Now, take this. It will help with Reynolds' recovery."

"I understand and thank you, sir." Eric walked over and took a pill Filip was holding up. Filip explained how to use it and why.

Eric had suggested that once Filip's confirmation hearing was held, they should start taking control of every humanoid on Earth's replica.

"Eric, I have been thinking about your recommendations and I agree that we should start with the conceited souls first as you suggested. Those people will be easy to influence and will refuse to admit they were deceived until it's too late. Afterwards, we'll target the gullible. They're poorly educated and cowardly. They're lemmings which follow those before them simply because they're in front. It's as flawless as it is tragic. They regurgitate our rhetoric like they understand it."

Eric chuckled then added, "Yes, my Lord, or they seem compelled to follow meaningless dribble as if it has some deep significance because they don't understand it. It's perfect."

"Exactly."

"What about the non-believers, sir?"

"What about them? They are executing a self-fulfilling prophecy. Just provide them a noose; they'll hang themselves in short order."

"Yes, my Lord, well said. But, I wanted to know if we should use them to target others. Their distrust, suspicions and insecurities can easily be exploited. It will be wonderful to see them choking on their own disdain at the end."

"Very well, Eric, do what you believe is best. This crusade is grander than the Spanish Inquisition which enslaved hundreds of thousands between the 15th and 17th centuries. Our commitment has revitalized this crusade with new potency. Trials are being administered by both civil and clergy authorities granting our new regime ultimate power. Not one citizen apprehended has been able to escape the might of our will.

"Our trials target individuals on multiple fronts. Anyone converting to or from Judaism, Islam or Christianity is in the crosshairs of the church. Those resisting the new administration mandates are pursued and arraigned by civil authorities. Regardless of the prosecuting body, everyone is subjected to torture until they confess to being part of the alien forces which removed over a billion of the planet's inhabitants a week ago. And since over sixty-seven percent of those missing are children, our brutal interrogation methods are quietly accepted.

"Our new world order is completely intolerant of any religious beliefs. And we need to keep it that way. Resistance needs to be met with severe and merciless torture. And I don't care if it drives most of the victims exposed to our methods insane."

"Yes, my Lord."

"Eric, no one is reporting the true casualty numbers, are

they?"

"No, sir, of course not. We're just releasing the amount of signed confessions obtained."

"Good, because those figures would not help our cause."

"I agree. The true calamity numbers are being withheld from the general public. We simply provide closely connected capture and confession estimates."

"Excellent, we cannot allow the populist to realize that more than three hundred thousand have been charged, convicted and executed with extreme prejudice within a week. That's literally twice the number prosecuted during the Spanish Inquisition which lasted over two hundred years."

"Yes, my Lord."

"And those that die without a self-admission of guilt regardless of our persuasive practices need to be studied. Our goal is to attain confessions from our captives, not to kill our citizens. At least, not yet," Filip shared with a smile.

"Yes, sir. And I'll continue to conceal the number of citizens driven insane by our overzealous methods."

"Yes, please do. And label those deaths as alien-induced seizures or simply delusional believers claiming to be possessed by the Devil."

"Yes, my Lord."

The forbidden planet was now truly a ghastly place for any believer in God. But the Harem continued to intervene in support of those worthy with hopes of saving as many lost souls as possible. However, the tribulations and catastrophes facing those left behind would be like nothing ever witnessed before or ever again.

CHAPTER 5

Winnie's Tribulations
Tuesday, July 16, 2047 2 p.m.

WINNIE STEPPED OUT OF THE PORTAL INITIALLY CAST BY Hoshea when they were outside Jackson Memorial Hospital in Miami. It only took a few seconds for her to realize she was back in England.

"Blimey, I'm like twenty minutes away from Mum's flat." Winnie looked up at the sky and confessed under her breath, "Hoshea, you're amazing. I love you," as she held a hand over her heart.

"Okay so, I haven't been home in five years. The family reunion is probably going to be painful given the circumstances surrounding last week. And let's not forget the crazy pills the BBC has been dispensing to every other news organization around the world at my expense." *Well,* Winnie took a deep breath, sighed and declared to herself, *it doesn't matter, I'm home. And that has to count for something.*

Then suddenly, Winnie tilted her head and placed a finger across her lips and confessed, *actually, home is probably the first place anyone would think to look for me.* She considered the situation a few more seconds, then motioned, *eh, whatever, I'm sure Hoshea knows what he's doing.* She giggled to herself and finished her synopsis by affirming, *of course he does, he knows everything. Well, I will trust in him to be safe until, until, aw who cares, I'm home.*

The familiar smells, sights and sounds made her feel at home immediately. The hustle and bustle of the city streets were as she remembered. It had been a week since the madness started and everything was returning to normal. London traffic was as active as ever and there were more pedestrians out than common for the time of day. Shops had reopened and the tea houses were full. *Brilliant, but I need to be cautious.* She kept her head down and walked quickly to her Mum's apartment. Winnie opened the door to the Paddington flat and walked in. "Hello, Mum? Are you home?"

She looked around the flat. It had been decorated the same since she could remember. It was like stepping back in time. The walls were maroon, and the windows had valances and ornate red drapes. There were several white contemporary sofas in the space and large modern works of art on the walls. There was a black glass rectangle coffee table with a solid wood center separating the two sofas. All the furniture was sitting atop of a huge, cream-colored Persian rug.

"Wen, is that you?" Jiani Chow Lee replied in total shock to hear Winnie's voice.

"Yes, Mum, it's me."

Jiani walked into the room then straight toward Winnie and gave her an uncharacteristically long hug. "Where have you been? And what took you so long to come home?"

Hmm, Winnie moaned aloud then thought, *Mum's behavior is a bit unusual. She's never this nice. Perhaps it's the times we're in.* She took another breath then answered in a loud whisper, "Well, Mum, the airports have been closed."

"For five years?"

"Oh, right, sorry. I've been busy with work. I've been on loan to the US from Sweden. Making life-altering discoveries on a routine basis. You know, just lots of work stuff."

"So how did you get home, Wen? Since the airports are closed. And just this morning the BBC announced that only military aircraft had permission to enter and fly within British airspace."

Winnie considered her mother's statement for a few seconds then replied, "Well, that's a long story, Mum —"

Winnie's mother interrupted her to add, "Plus, everyone on the planet is looking for you."

"Are they?"

"Yes, Wen, they are. Or at least they were, as of this morning."

"Huh, that's odd."

"Really? So the stories about you and your colleagues being broadcast all over the telly this week have been what, lies?"

"Yes, Mum, the stories are not true. And I'm sure you realize how crazy the broadcasts have been."

"Why would they make up those crazy stories?"

"Trust me, Mum, you wouldn't believe me if I told you."

"Tell me. Why would the Queen and country, the US and every other country in the world be broadcasting such senseless and hurtful accusations?"

"Simply put, because they can?"

"What? I don't believe that."

"I told you, you wouldn't believe me."

Winnie walked her mother over to a sofa and they sat down. She took another breath and said, "Mum, the truth is that with all the craziness going on in the world, people just want answers. And they don't care where those answers come from or if the information is true. They just want something to believe in, and hope that everything will be back to normal soon."

Winnie took hold of her mother's hands and continued, "Mum, this part is important, so please listen carefully. My colleagues—my friends—and I discovered the way to everlasting life. And there are forces in this world that want that secret to remain hidden. Every country, every political organization on this planet wants me and my colleagues—my friends—dead. So, I need you to trust me and help me keep this information safe, until I have had a chance to set it free."

Jiani shook her head as she summarily dismissed Winnie's comments then said, "Wen, I realize you've always been difficult. And I understand how your work as a geneticist may make you feel important, but you have always been a trouble maker. Is it possible that what's happening is something totally different than what you believe it is? Everlasting life? You can't be serious."

Winnie slowly closed her eyes and gently shook her head as

she inhaled a long, deep breath. Then her eyes shot open and she said, "Mum, I am so disappointed at your reaction. But it's not a complete surprise. You never believed me when I was a kid and you still don't. So, nothing between us has changed. However, as hurt as I am at your dismissive attitude, I need to make you understand my resolve. Nothing, nothing can alter my course." Winnie held her breath, stared at her mother and added, "The knowledge I possess is the truth and the light and anyone whom I share it with and believes will have everlasting life."

"Everlasting life, Wen?"

"Yes."

"If what you're saying is true, then why don't you just share it? What are you waiting for?"

"I'm waiting for the right people and the correct time to present itself."

"What?"

"Mum, only those with a meek, gentle, loving spirit deserve to live forever. How would you like the world governed by a bunch of cruel, egotistical, narcissistic, sociopathic immortals?"

"Isn't that what we already have?"

"No, absolutely not. Mum, trust me, please." Jiani looked at Winnie long and hard then hugged her and obediently nodded yes.

"The world is in a crisis, Wen. If you have the way to set it right, withholding the information will probably only make matters worse. How long must you wait?"

"I must wait as long as I must."

"I see. So, you're Confucius now."

"No. It's just the times we're in. So, where's Li Na and Dai?"

"Your sister is still sleeping and your brother is—your brother is doing what he's always done. He's looking after the restaurants. I think he's planning on reopening one for business tonight or tomorrow."

"Why is Li Na still sleeping? It's the middle of the afternoon."

"She didn't get in until late this morning."

"This morning? What was she doing to get home so late?"

"She was doing what most young girls do to feel loved, safe, and happy during these stressful times."

"She went to church?"

"What? No! She went to a friend's house who was hosting a party."

Just then, Li Na walked in. "Oh my gosh, I thought that was you, sis. The whole world is looking for you and not in a good way." She ran over and gave Winnie a hug.

"I've missed you, Wen, but you are probably not safe here."

"Yes, she is," Winnie's mother answered authoritatively. "And I want to make sure it stays that way, understood?"

"Yes, Mum."

"Well, sis, we need to have a serious chinwag. I want to know everything."

"Not now," Jiani interrupted to say. "Dai is expecting us to help him with the restaurant tonight. So you need to go clean up."

"Yes, Mum."

"And you need to hurry, you know how upset he gets if we're late."

"Yes, Mum." Li Na turned back to Winnie and said, "The repairs to the café are almost complete. We should be back in business by tonight or tomorrow. We'll finally, start making money again for the first time since all the chaos started."

"You mean since the aftermath of the Rapture?"

"Wen, you better not let anyone hear you refer to what's happened as the Rapture."

"Really? Why not?"

"Blimey, you really are out of it. The bobbies have been saying you're off your trolley or seriously barmy."

"Why? Because of what I said?"

"No, but because you believe it's true." Winnie stared at her sister when she added, "Look, why don't you come hide from the police at the restaurant? Dai would be happy to see you and you could help out."

"I don't think so. I'm tired and just want to rest for a while."

"Fair enough, then just hang out here and we'll talk after I get home tonight."

"Okay." Winnie held her sister at arm's length and said, "I'm so happy you're safe, sis."

"Me, too. So I'll see you tonight then?" Winnie nodded and Li Na leaned in and kissed her on the cheek then ran off.

Afterwards, Winnie walked over and kissed her mother then

left to retire to her old room. As Winnie was walking away, Jiani said, "Oh, by the way, Stefan called you like ten times about a week ago when all the chaos started. He seemed desperate to talk to you."

"He did? Did he leave a number?"

"Yes, one minute. Where did I put it?" Jiani looked around then noticed it was still on the coffee table where she left it. "Here." She picked it up and handed it to Winnie.

"Brilliant. Thanks, Mum."

"Winnie, how did he get this number?"

"I'm not sure, but when I joined the team, I had to provide emergency contact information so that might be where he got it."

"I see. Well, go rest, you look tired." Winnie nodded and walked off.

She opened the door to her room and to her amazement, her belongings had been untouched. It was like stepping back in time five years. Her old cook books, medical school texts and journals had a layer of dust.

Lucky for me, there's a cover over the bed and sofas, Winnie confessed. *It also looks like the weekly maid service hasn't gotten around to cleaning my room yet.* "Whatever, oh look, my gross anatomy dummy is still standing in the corner," Winnie let out. She pulled the cover off the bed and laid down and spread out. Winnie giggled. "The bed still smells like me." She crawled over and rested her head on her pillow then added, "Huh, the bed is a little mustier then I remember. I need to air this place out. But, it's nice to be home."

Winnie looked around, trying to absorb the peaceful surroundings. But then the true reality surfaced. *The world is lost and neither of my family members have a blue aura around them. But I wasn't expecting them to be so nice. Maybe it took a world catastrophe for them to mellow out.*

Nah, I'm sure they're as uptight and bonkers as ever. But, but they seem so nice. Well, I'm going to have to try and convert them. Hoshea can't expect me to save others and not try to save my own family, Winnie confessed to herself as she attempted to do snow angels on her bed. "Woo hoo."

Winnie drifted off into past memories and fell asleep. A few hours later, Dai, Winnie's brother, rushed into his Mum's flat and called out for his long lost sister.

"Winnie?"

Winnie instantly woke up to the sound of her brother's voice. She picked up her head and yelled, "Dai?"

She got off the bed and ran to the parlor. "Dai." She turned the corner and saw her big brother and jumped on him. "Oh my goodness, I've missed you."

"And I've missed you, sis." Winnie pushed him at arm's length and said, "And I love your aura."

"I have an aura?" Dai questioned.

"Yes and guess what color it is."

"Um, blue?"

"Yes, Dai, it's blue."

"Well, that's my favorite color."

"Mine, too," Winnie added then hugged her brother again. Her brother's strong arms brought her comfort. "I'm glad you're here."

"Me, too," Dai slowly let out.

He always had a special affection for Winnie. She never accepted the traditional Chinese gender roles. This was something that bothered him and at first, he resented. However, over time, as she grew older, he realized her resistance to this stereotype was necessary. Finally, Dai understood it was this one attribute that forged who Winnie had become and he truly loved her for it.

Winnie was cute and girly from a young age which generated a considerable amount of interest from boys. To complicate matters, Winnie became an attractive tomboy, which was a bad combination, obligating Dai and her father to teach Winnie Kung Fu. Unfortunately that combination made Winnie unpopular among girls and even more sought after by boys, but for the wrong reasons.

Suddenly, Dai lost all the expression on his face and said, "Winnie, you can't stay here."

"What? Why not, what's wrong?"

"Winnie, Mum and Li Na called the bobbies on you."

"What? Really, why? Why would they do that? They seemed so happy to see me."

"Winnie, you've been gone a long time and they no longer know you. Plus, there have been some pretty awful accusations made about you on the telly over the last week. And you know how suspicious Mum is."

"True. Very well, you win that argument."

Winnie couldn't believe the recent turn of events.

"I'm stunned. I have to sit down." Winnie walked to the sofa while shaking her head and motioning 'why' with her hands. She closed her eyes then took a deep breath and said, "What about you, Dai, do you believe the stories on the telly?"

"Me? Not a chance. Remember how you and I were always getting into fights when we were younger?"

"Of course, how can I forget? We were totally mental. Mum and Dad thought we were fighting each other. It wasn't until I turned like—"

"Fifteen," Dai interrupted Winnie to finish her thought.

"Yes, exactly. It wasn't until I turned fifteen that we even discovered why we were always in fights. The neighborhood boys must have thought we were mad."

"I had to fight almost every day to protect your honor. And I turned you into my cut-man, remember?" Dai quizzed Winnie.

"Of course, how can I forget? And I hated the sight of blood back then but you were my brother. So I sucked it up and tended to your injuries, every time you showed up all bloody—" Winnie trailed off as memories of those events started to surface.

"You were always there to tend to me, sis."

"And you helped bandage me up, too," Winnie cited, teary-eyed.

"Yes. Thinking back, it's hard to believe a decade went by before you found out I was fighting to protect your honor."

"That was completely mental, and meanwhile, I believed you were being picked on because you were so kind and gentle. Anyway, thoughts of that sparked me to go out and Kung Fu the bloody hell out of the local boys to defend my brother."

"Yes, and hence generating the causality loop."

"Wow, that's so true, but shortly after we talked—"

"The fighting stopped, literally overnight," Dai finished Winnie's thought."

"Yes, it did, and then Dad died. And everything changed again."

Yes, and you stopped cooking and—"

"And I buried my head."

"I'm so sorry, sis."

"Me, too, Dai."

"Okay, so you need to go. The bobbies are going to be knocking on the door any second."

Just then, there was a knock on the door.

"Blimey, is it the bobbies?" Winnie whispered.

Winnie's brother got up, walked over to a window and pulled the window dressing to the side, peering out. "Yes, it's Scotland Yard."

"Blimey, this situation went balls up fast."

Winnie and Dai continued to whisper back and forth to each other.

"Do you remember where we used to go hide as kids?"

"When we were grossly outnumbered by local gang members?" Winnie questioned.

"Yes, exactly."

"Sure, our pretend hospital."

"Yes."

"Is that old place still there?"

"Yes, now quickly, go out the back. I'll distract them so you have time to get away. I'll meet you there tomorrow or the next day?"

"I'm not leaving you behind, Dai."

"They're not after me, Winnie."

"So! I'm not leaving you here! I can't, what if they take you?"

"Winnie, you need to go or both of us will be incarcerated, since I'm not going to let them take you. Now trust me, sis, and go."

Winnie hugged her brother again and said, "I love you, Dai."

"I love you, too, sis. Now go." Winnie ran to the back door, opened it and walked out, just missing the two police officers heading toward the flat exit.

Dai quickly ran to the loo and got undressed. He jumped into the shower, got wet and jumped back out. He wrapped a small towel around his waist and ran back to the parlor's front door, where an officer was still busy pounding away.

"Open up, it's Scotland Yard!"

"Yes, all right, bloody hell, what's all the commotion

about?" Dai was standing at the front door dripping wet, semi-exposed.

"Well, go on. What's with all the ruckus?"

"I'm Inspector Rowland."

"Okay and — why are you here? How can I help you?"

"Pardon the intrusion."

"Is this going to take long, Inspector? Today is the grand opening of my restaurant in Westminster since all the chaos started. We host the best Asian cuisine in London. Social media has been abuzz with our re-opening for days. I don't want to disappoint our customers."

"Why are you standing here like that, Mr. Lee?"

"Because, Inspector, I had literally just jumped in the shower when the pounding started. I thought you would get the message and buzz-off if I didn't show but apparently that didn't happen."

"Go put on some clothes, mate."

"I'm not putting on clean clothes until I shower. So tell me why you're here, or would you rather wait until I'm done cleaning up?"

"Where is your sister?"

"Why? Is she okay? Has she done something wrong?"

"I'm sure she's smashing, I just want to ask her a few questions. So, where is she?"

"Well, she's normally at the restaurant during this time of the day."

"Why would Wen be at your restaurant?"

"Who?"

"Wen, Wen Chow Lee, your sister?"

"Oh, I haven't seen Winnie. I thought you were asking about Li Na."

"Who?"

"Li Na, my sister who works for me at the restaurant."

"No, we're here to see Wen Chow Lee. Your Mum told us she was here?"

"What, since when? Winnie, are you home? Winnie?" Dai walked off, pretending to look for his sister.

The inspector looked over at another officer and said, "He either hasn't seen her or he's a good liar."

"I believe the bloke hasn't seen her," the officer replied.

"I'm not certain yet."

"Winnie?" Dai called out as he continued to look around.

"Mr. Chow Lee, may we have a word?" the inspector declared over the yelling, causing Dai to return to the parlor.

"Inspector, it's like I told you, my sister is not here. I've checked the whole flat. So again, how can I help?"

"Do you mind if my men take a look around?"

"By all means go on, but I assure you, she's not here." Rowland motioned for his officers to step in and check the flat.

"Tell me, Mr. Lee, where do you believe she might be?"

"I don't really know. I haven't seen her in five years. But maybe she's gone to the restaurant."

A few minutes later, the officers returned to the parlor.

"Inspector, we searched the flat and there's no one else here."

"Has anything been disturbed?"

"Not that I can tell. One room as a layer of dust on everything and the bed and sofas are covered.

"That's Winnie's room. You didn't touch anything, did you? Mum wanted her to find everything as she left it."

"No. I didn't touch anything."

"Brilliant." Dai had placed the cover back on the bed during his pretend search.

"Very well then, let's go. I'll leave a few officers behind in the event she returns. Will that be an issue?"

"Not at all, Inspector, please." Dai motioned to the sofa. Make yourselves comfortable. I need to go finish cleaning up."

"Sure. All right, men, let's place two officers outside the flat in the event she returns. I want one out front and the other stationed in the rear. Let's —"

The inspector was interrupted by the back door opening.

"Sorry, Inspector, but there is no one outside and we didn't see anyone exit the flat."

"Very well, let's go, men. Mr. Lee, my apologies for the intrusion."

Dai nodded and closed the door behind the officers and returned to the shower.

Winnie ran the kilometer to the old Holy Apostles Catholic Church on Marylebone Road. This was their sanctuary when kids.

Winnie spent many sleepless nights there watching over her brother after patching him up. The elderly priest back then provided Winnie with the supplies she required to tend to her brother's injuries, then provided a clean cot for them to sleep.

Winnie walked in and immediately felt a sense of melancholy and nostalgia. She stood there for a few minutes just taking it all in. The smells, the sights, the sounds of the old building reminded her of the trials and tribulations experienced as a youth. Winnie took a deep breath then sighed and confessed aloud, "The walls of this sanctuary have never been breached, nor shall they now." And that thought brought her comfort.

The space was darker than she remembered. The church's stained glass windows allowed some light to enter the space during this part of the day. The stone walls were wet, as if a heavy deluge had just ceased. The interior walls looked like they should have been part of the building's exterior, and the dampness of the walls made the basement smell musty and feel a little clammy, but Winnie didn't care, she always felt safe there.

Winnie placed a hand on the staircase handrail and started walking into the old sunken gathering hall. "Wow, I don't remember the stairs in this part of the building feeling so rickety," she confessed out loud. "Well, it doesn't matter, I can hide here for days, if necessary," Winnie added.

Suddenly, she heard a voice in the distance.

"Blimey, there's someone here." Winnie's heart jumped to her throat. *I need to leg it out.*

"Winnie, is that you?"

Winnie stopped her exit and turned around slowly and said, "Father Flanagan?"

"Yes," a muttered, cracking voice replied in the distance."

"Is that really you, Father?"

"Yes, Winnie."

Suddenly, the lights came on, forcing Winnie to shield her eyes. She slowly looked toward the other side of the room and saw the old priest standing by the light switch. There must have been fifty or more people all huddled behind him on their hands and knees.

"Father, you still recognize my voice after all this time? I haven't been here in like twenty years."

"Well, you recognized mine."

"Good point," Winnie exclaimed then ran over to the frail old man.

"It's okay, everyone, you can stand up. Winnie is a friend."

Winnie embraced the priest and said, "I've missed you, Father."

"And I've missed our talks, lass."

"Father, I'm so sorry for not coming back to see you more often," Winnie confessed. Then she thought, *Father Flanagan has to be like a thousand years old by now. He was like three hundred when I was a kid.*

"It's okay, Winnie, you probably thought I was dead."

"No! Well, maybe a little. How old are you now?"

"I'm not quite a thousand if that's what you're thinking."

"What? I don't think that." Then Winnie noticed the expression on the priest's face and added, "Anymore."

"I just had my one hundred and second birthday."

"That's brilliant!"

"But why are you here?"

"Partly because I'm not dead?"

"Yes, of course, I can see that. But what I meant was, why didn't you get raptured? You were the sweetest, kindest, and most caring person."

"Well, because just like you, my dear lass, I'm needed here."

Winnie pointed up and said, "He doesn't miss anything, does he?"

The old priest slowly shook his head and replied, "No, he doesn't."

"So why are all these people here?"

"They needed a safe haven. The world has gone completely mental."

"Yes, it has. So, how can I help?"

"I'm not sure. What have you been doing with your time of late?"

"Well, I went to medical school."

"That's brilliant. There are plenty of people here who are poorly for multiple reasons. Perhaps you can determine what ails them? I believe God has sent you here for a reason. I have a few medical supplies saved up. But something tells me you may not need them."

"Now that's interesting, Father, why would you say that?"

"A hunch."

Winnie stepped back and tilted her head and looked at the old man. *He has an aura, but why is it different?* She questioned herself. *If I didn't know any better, I would swear this old man was Hoshea. But that can't be right, can it?* Winnie tilted her head to the other side and stared a little longer.

"Winnie, when you're done looking at me with fancy eyes, perhaps you can focus on those less fortunate."

Winnie shook her head. "Yes, sorry, Father. Of course I can. I'm on it," Winnie replied then went to walk off.

"Good. And I'm not who you think I am."

"Wait!" Winnie stopped, turned around and said, "What…what did you just say?"

"I said, I'm not who you think I am."

"That's exactly what I thought you said. Why would you say that? How did you know what I was thinking?"

"I guessed?"

"Oh no, I didn't ask you to guess what I was thinking in the middle of a conversation. I was just looking at you. Yet you knew. So who are you really?"

"I'm the person you remember. Or better yet, I'm a friend of a friend."

"Hmm!" Winnie mouthed then thought, *His answers seem conveniently cryptic and evasive.* As she stared him down with the corner of her mouth crinkled up, she thought, *Fine, don't tell me. I'll figure it out eventually, I always do.*

"Well, Father, if you don't mind, I'm going to care for our refugees." Winnie turned and walked away again.

She was only a few meters away when she heard the old man say under his breath, "Son, she came back just like you said she would."

"Okay, that's it. I heard that, Father. What's going on?"

"Relax, Lass, I'm an old man who occasionally talks to others that aren't here. Or maybe I'm doing it to seek attention. You can't blame a lonely old man for wanting a feek like you fussing over him, can you? Plus, we used to spend a lot of time together. It's not my fault I know you better than you remember me."

Hmm, Winnie grunted then turned around yet again and walked away without saying a word. When she was several meters away, Winnie suddenly said under her breath, "I'm not a feek. Am I cute? Yes, I think so. Okay, so I'm totally cute, but I'm not gorgeous."

Winnie walked on and started tending to the sick. Most of the people waiting were sitting on old church benches with no back rest like the ones used hundreds of years ago as church pews in third-world countries. Although the old space was rather damp and clammy, everyone seemed happy to be there and patiently waited their turn.

For days, Winnie displayed her divine gift in the name of Hoshea to everyone that walked through Father Flanagan's doors. Even the priest was in awe at her abilities to heal the sick and injured.

Late in the afternoon on the third day, the elderly Catholic priest asked Winnie to speak privately. They stepped into a small storage room at the end of an adjacent corridor to the gathering hall. Father Flanagan asked Winnie to enter then closed the door behind them. He stood there quietly for about ten seconds until Winnie broke the silence.

"Father, what can I help you with? I need to get back out there. We have more people walking in than ever before. This place is famous."

"Yes, Winnie, it's too famous."

"What do you mean, Father?"

"I mean that too many people outside these walls are talking about how you're not a doctor but are healing people."

"But I am a doctor."

"Yes, but doctors normally diagnose symptoms that ail people, before they render an opinion or make recommendations on a treatment or course of action. Regardless, they most certainly use medical supplies in this process, somewhere."

"Okay, so?"

"So, you're not doing that."

"Isn't that a good thing? I'm saving money and time."

"Yes, Winnie, but you're just holding their hands and praying with them. Your touch is healing them."

"Their faith in Hoshea is healing them, not me."

"Yes, okay. But you have treated hundreds. Maybe thousands, I've lost track. And you haven't slept, you haven't eaten, and I haven't even seen you go to the loo."

"I'm sorry, Father, but I've been busy."

"Yes, Winnie, but your deeds have been greatly noticed. And many outside this sanctuary are talking about this haven led by you. Therefore, your divine gift is out. Which means, you now have to go."

"What, why?"

"God's work here for you is done. They're coming. And you cannot be here when they arrive. So, Winnie, go now and be at peace."

Aww, "Hoshea talks like that." The old priest smiled at her then Winnie asked, "How much time do I have?"

"Not much."

"Do I have enough time to treat a few more people?"

"No. You have to go."

"Very well," Winnie replied then had a thought. "Wait, Dai is coming here for me."

"I will talk to your brother when he shows up. Now go." The priest escorted Winnie out an old underground passageway leading to the street above. Winnie kissed the old man and said, "We shall meet again," then ran off.

Winnie wasn't on the street more than a minute before questions started surfacing. *Why didn't Dai come to see me? It's been like three days. Plus, the effects of the nutritional supplement Hoshea gave me are wearing off and I'm getting hungry and increasingly thirsty. And, now I have nowhere to go. Maybe Dai hasn't shown up because he's been arrested for helping me get away. I'm starting to have terrible thoughts. I have to know what's happened to him. It's settled. I have no choice but to venture back to Mum's flat and get answers,* Winnie admitted to herself.

Meanwhile, Dai went back and forth to work for several days like nothing had happened. He avoided talking to his mum and Li Na about Winnie. However, he did make it a point to pretend he didn't care either way what happened to his sister. He focused on work, which seemed like his normal behavior to Jiani and Li Na.

Dai was positive he was being followed by at least two

police officers. He did his very best to avoid looking obvious when he periodically looked over his shoulder. However, it had already been three days and he had to reach out to his sister. Dai worked on confusing the two bobbies following him without making it seem like he was intentionally being deceptive. Scotland Yard even questioned his mum about his routine outings.

"Mrs. Lee, does your son routinely leave the restaurant during the day?"

"Yes. Normally he ventures out multiple times a week. However, with all the mental chaos occurring in London over the last week, I'm sure his suppliers need more tending to than usual."

"Do you have any idea why he takes such convoluted routes?"

"No. But I'm sure there's a reason for his actions. My son is quite deliberate in everything he does. Let me ask you, Lieutenant, does he take the same route every day?"

"Yes, mum." Although the police offices were saying 'ma'am,' their British accents made the word sound like 'mum.'

"Then what he's doing is completely normal. He is a creature of habit. Had you told me he was taking different routes, I might have considered his actions suspicious."

"Very well, mum, can you confirm one last item for us?"

"Sure."

"Can you explain the significance of these six locations?" The lieutenant handed Ms. Chow Lee a list of addresses. She reviewed the list as she gathered her thoughts.

"Well, this first address is to our meat supplier and a serious risk to our business. This gentleman provides perishable produce and Dai likes getting first pick. This person supplies us poultry and has to be managed routinely. This agency provides additional staffing during our busy seasons and seldom returns phone calls. Dai has been trying to replace them for years but they're the best in town so... This business does our linens. But this address on Victoria Street, I'm not familiar with."

The lieutenant looked over his shoulder and an officer whispered a name into his ear.

"Thank you, Corporal."

"It's PCF Finance, Mrs. Lee."

"Oh, PCF, they hold the notes on our equipment. And you

say he's been paying them a visit every day?"

"Yes, mum."

"That's unusual, Dai dislikes them. They have always been barmy. I sincerely hope they are not calling the notes due. That would be an issue. I'll discuss it with Dai. Wait, maybe they're working on updating our systems to accept credits. Dai has been very anxious about that." Jiani got lost in thought and was silent for a few seconds. She then shook her head and added, "Sorry, will there be anything else?"

"No, mum, and thank you for your support."

"You're most welcome, now if you will excuse me." Jiani walked off, seemingly a little distracted.

Dai was out performing his daily errands. He took the underground to multiple locations, exiting businesses via the rear versus the front door. He hailed multiple minicabs to several locations, crisscrossing London daily. Dai also took several buses to visit local suppliers which made his daily outings and mode of transportation seem odd at best. It was a complex and convoluted errand run but he never varied his routine. So even if he was lost in the congestion of London commuters, the police could anticipate his next location. And regardless, he always seemed to show up where expected within minutes of his estimated time.

On the evening of the third day, Dai started his final travel routine. However, today, he made plans to alter the time of his final destination. As he anticipated, it was difficult for the police to follow him using the local buses without being detected. Dai altered his route before his final stop at PCF and paid the Holy Apostles Catholic Church a visit. He got off the bus four minutes before his last destination but only a one-minute walk from the church. It was just after five p.m. However, to his extreme disappointment, Father Flanagan told Dai that Winnie was no longer there.

The portion of the church they used as kids was an old meditation and recreation room. It was closed a decade before and the contemplation practice was moved to a renovated portion of the building. The old space was abandoned, cold, musty and had poor lighting, but it was as Dai remembered.

"Where did Winnie go, Father?" Dai whispered.

"I told her the bobbies were coming for her and that she had to leave."

"So where did she go?"

"I'm not sure, but I'm positive you will find each other. Now you must go as well."

"I feel so poorly, Father. I brought her food and water, and she's not here. I'm sure she's starving."

"Well, she stayed busy while she was here doing God's work. And I never saw her eat or drink so keep that with you. Now go find her."

Winnie, where are you? Dai thought as he considered the possible whereabouts and physical condition of his sister.

"She'll be okay, son. Now go," the elderly priest insisted as he tried to push Dai toward the exit.

Dai looked around and was surprised to see so many people in this old part of the building but he had to focus. He had already been away three days too long.

"Thank you, Father." Dai turned and headed out the door then stopped and said over his shoulder, "Father, you're a Saint," then was gone.

"No, I'm not, but you and Winnie will be."

Dai made haste to PCF while talking to himself. "Winnie is probably in trouble or will be soon. I need to find her, but how?" Dai continued to think and make mental notes. *I'll make my last stop then head back to the restaurant. I need to clear my head if I'm going to figure out where she is. I need to remain calm if I'm going to figure this out.*

Seconds before his arrival at PCF, he admitted to himself, *I truly have no idea where Winnie might have wandered.* Dai found himself asking the cosmos aloud, "Where is she? Can you please take me to her?" Dai walked into the office of his final supplier where the two officers were waiting for him and noted his arrival.

Dai apologized to PCF management.

"My apologies for being late, gentlemen, I was distracted and got off on the wrong stop. By the time I noticed my mistake, the bus had left the station, so I had to travel the last few kilometers on foot. Anyway, business has been poorly, as you would expect, but last night was a huge improvement. I am, however, still acclimating to this new credit system."

"Where's your chip?"

"I've been so busy, I've failed to follow up in that respect.

However, I have plans to do so tomorrow, first thing."

"See that you do, we expect our credits from you tomorrow."

"Understood." Dai finalized his note to credits ratio with PCF management then concluded his meeting and returned to work.

Winnie returned to her Mum's flat and waited for the opportune moment to sneak back in. Finally, after six hours of hiding in the shrubbery, she saw her chance and took it. She made her way into the flat and headed straight for the shower. Afterward, she changed clothes, ate and drank two liters of water, then waited.

At two a.m., Dai left his mother and sister at the restaurant to close up and went home. Dai found himself unconsciously opening the door to his mother's apartment. He walked into the parlor where Winnie was sitting in the dark.

Dai turned on the light and saw her. "Winnie," Dai exclaimed as he ran over to her and picked Winnie up off the floor with his hug then whispered in her ear, "Oh my goodness, Wen, I was so worried about you. When I stopped by the church today and you weren't there, I imagined the worse."

"I'm so sorry I wasn't there." Winnie press tight against her brother's chest. She had almost forgotten how his embrace made her feel safe and his presence brought her comfort in the most trying times.

Dai pushed Winnie at arm's length and said, "Winnie, it was a mistake to come here. There have been bobbies outside for days waiting for you."

"I'm so sorry, but when you didn't show up, I had to know if you were all right. Then, of course, it didn't help that I was all sweaty and gross and thirsty beyond words."

"I'm so sorry for putting you through that, but I didn't want our secret place to be discovered. I've had bobbies on me twenty-four seven for three days."

Suddenly, both the front and back doors to the flat opened and Scotland Yard officers walked in.

"Well, Ms. Lee, you're a difficult woman to find. Men, take her."

"Winnie, don't talk to anyone or answer any questions until I get the family barrister to represent you."

"Really, mate? Don't you realize what she's wanted for? Haven't you been reading the papers or watching the telly?" She's Britain's most wanted."

"I don't believe those stories."

"Interesting, well then, bring them both."

"What?! On what charges?" Dai declared.

"Sir, it's now clear that you have been conspiring to obstruct justice, abetting a wanted fugitive, deliberately misleading officers of the court and meticulously plotting rendezvouses with enemies of the Crown. Any one of these infractions would be reason enough to apprehend you. But in its totality, it would be within my rights to shoot you where you stand." The inspector turned toward the front door and added, "Bring him — and if he resists, shoot him."

"That's brilliant, Inspector. But your soliloquy has only confirmed my suspicions."

The inspector turned back toward Dai and asked, "Which is what exactly, Mr. Lee?"

"That our lives are in considerable peril."

"That they are, sir," the inspector confirmed yet again.

An officer grabbed Dai by the right wrist. Dai pulled his arm back, stepped in and elbowed the officer in the face. Dai grabbed another officer by his left wrist with both hands, then twisted the man's wrist around, forcing him to bend forward and straighten his arm out behind him. Dai then pushed down and applied considerable pressure to the man's wrist and shoulder, making him grunt and then yell in pain. Dai kicked another officer in the face and stepped in and placed his knee to the temple of the officer bent down in front of him. Both officers were knocked unconscious. Dai struck and flipped another. Three, four then five officers were on the ground, incapacitated or unconscious. When Dai turned to focus his attention on the inspector, he noticed that Rowland was holding Winnie across the chest and had his firearm pressed against her temple.

"That was a critical lack in judgment, Mr. Lee," the inspector announced in a seemingly calm voice. "Consider your next actions carefully."

"The reasons for your intrusion into my home unannounced are unjust. And your overconfidence will be your undoing."

The inspector cocked the hammer on his Glock back.

"My barrister is going to teach you the meaning of humility, Inspector."

"We'll see. Now help my men up or this situation will end poorly for you and your sister," Rowland said with absolutism.

"I'm so sorry, Dai," Winnie confessed, teary-eyed.

"Everything will be okay, sis. Don't worry," Dai said, hoping to comfort his sister while helping the officers to their feet. As soon as the men were able to stand on their own, they pushed Dai away.

All the officers took a few seconds to shake off their lightheadedness then three of the officers grabbed Dai. He had an officer on each arm and another standing behind him with a vice-grip around his neck. The other two men flanked him with firearms drawn and the inspector said, "Let's go."

The ride to Scotland Yard was quiet but the inspector informed his superiors who notified theirs and so on up the chain of command.

Upon arrival at police headquarters, the inspector barked out orders to multiple officers.

"Constable, take Ms. Lee to room thirteen and Sergeant, take Mr. Lee to the morgue and place him in one of the refrigeration units. Make sure he disrobes first then place a camera in with him and pipe a feed into room thirteen." Both men answered in the affirmative and started walking off in different directions.

"Bloody hell, Inspector, you can't do that!" Winnie exclaimed in disbelief then placed her hands over her mouth.

"It's okay, Winnie, I'll be all right."

"But you hate the cold, Dai."

"I'll be fine, and don't let them intimidate you."

"Well, it's too late, I'm already scared."

"Call our barrister."

Winnie was taken to an empty room and shackled, where she sat for hours yelling out for information about her brother. The room was like most interrogation spaces. There was a metal table, two chairs and a two-way mirror with observers on the other end. Finally, the inspector entered the room along with a technician.

"Where the bloody hell have you been? I've been—"

Winnie's vocal tirade was interrupted by a severe slap across her face. "If I were you, young lady, I would keep quiet until you're asked to speak. These are not normal circumstances. Your right to habeas corpus has been suspended for the duration of your stay. In addition, your constitutional rights to due process have also been rescinded. Unfortunately, your crimes are so grotesque and numerous in nature that a special dispensation has been mandated just for you. I'm afraid your freedom is in serious jeopardy, but that's the good news. Many are asking you forfeit your life so we can move on to other things." The inspector closed his eyes and rotated his head around in a circle several times, stretching out his neck muscles. He then suddenly slammed both hands down on the metal table in front of Winnie and leaned down toward her. With bloodshot eyes, the inspector snarled out through his teeth, "You're never going to leave this place."

Tears started streaming down Winnie's face but not from the pain of her recent blow to the face. She was remembering the stories of torture Hoshea had revealed to her during their short stay in Cuba, if she was captured. The technician finished installing the video feed from the morgue into the room and displayed the results on a fifty-five centimeter television screen which was placed on the table.

"Just push this button, Inspector," the technician said then started for the door.

"Thank you," Mr. Rowland replied. The young man nodded and closed the door behind him.

"Now, Ms. Lee, just a few questions."

"About what? I don't know anything."

"Really? Let's see if that's true." The inspector pushed the button and turned the television screen toward her.

"How about now, do you know anything?"

Winnie was mortified. Her brother was naked, gagged and turning blue from the cold, hanging up by his wrists in what appeared to be a freezer.

"Why would you do this?"

"It's almost five degrees Celsius in that room. And he's been in there for hours. I'm not sure he'll survive much longer. Do you want to help him?"

"Yes, of course."

"Then I'll need you to answer some questions."

"Yes, okay, but please, get him out of there, he's freezing.

He'll suffer permanent skin damage and possibly organ failure if he remains in that environment much longer."

The inspector looked at the screen and said, "You know what, you're right, let's warm him up." He spoke into is watch and said, "Sergeant, please open the door and warm up our guest."

"Thank you, Inspector, thank you," Winnie proclaimed.

Mr. Rowland turned the telly back toward Winnie as the sergeant opened the refrigeration door and threw a bucket of warm water over Dai, and then closed the door again.

Dai's muffled screams slowly choked the life out of Winnie and then she saw him start convulsing.

"My mistake. I really thought the water would warm him up."

After Winnie's violent tremors were under control she yelled, "Exposing him to water in that environment is like pouring sulfuric acid on him! What the bloody hell is wrong with you? Get him out of there!"

Winnie was slapped across the face repeatedly as pleads for her brother went unanswered.

"I need answers," the inspector repeated. "Where are your friends? Tell me about the discovery you made for eternal life. Where are the aliens holding up?"

Hours came and went. Dai was periodically removed from the refrigeration unit to raise his body temperature. He was placed in a sauna and forced to stay awake by piping deafening white noise in the space.

Winnie's answers made no sense to the inspector so the torture intensified. Winnie was placed in the freezer while her brother was kept awake and made to watch. After a day of mind-bending agony, the inspector was interrupted by multiple visitors. Two of which were from the US.

"Inspector, sorry to interrupt."

"Yes, Constable, what can I do for you?"

Inspector Rowland had his back to the door and never looked up when the officer entered the room.

"Sir?"

"What is it, man?!" the inspector shouted with disdain. "Can't you see I'm busy?"

"I'm sorry, Inspector, but this gentleman has orders to take the Lees."

The inspector whipped his head around and let out, "What?" in a controlled yell.

"He has authorization from the office of the prime minister."

"Is that so? Well, we'll see about that."

Rowland's boss's boss's boss walked in and said, "Inspector, I hope this isn't an inconvenience."

"No, sir."

"We are pressed for time, Inspector, so I will get to it. Please gather the Lees' personal effects and prep them for departure."

"Sir, with all due respect, where are they being moved?

"I have released them to the US.

"Sir, as a matter of law —"

The chief superintendent turned his head and placed a hand up in front of the inspector, motioning for silence. Mr. Rowland stopped talking abruptly and the chief continued. "Mr. Lee is yours, Special Agent Avery, and the constable will show you to Ms. Lee."

"Thank you, Chief; it's an honor to work with such agreeable allies."

"But Chief, the Lees are British nationals."

The superintendent raised his hand up again then looked at Rowland and said, through his teeth, "Not another word, Inspector."

Agent Avery took Winnie and Dai into custody and transported them to the Guantanamo Bay's black site for additional questioning.

Twenty hours later, Dai and Winnie were being waterboarded. Hours turned to days and the no-touch torture techniques continued without either Dai or Winnie being asked any questions. Dai appeared to be going insane or had already succumbed to insanity.

"Hoshea, how long must Aunt Winnie bear the torment? They're not even asking her any questions. Why are they continuing to torture her?"

"Because these particular beings are sadistic and at this point they're convinced Winnie is incapable of articulating any intelligible answers."

"So they believe she has gone insane?"

"Yes."

"So has she? Has she gone insane, Hoshea?" Mia's questions appeared to have fallen on deaf ears.

"I'm not waiting any longer. I have to do something. I will take her place. Please, please, please, I'm begging you, Hoshea, please."

"Mia, have patience." Suddenly, an apparition appeared before them.

"Wait, is that the same Harem which appeared over my mother?"

"Yes," Hoshea replied.

The angel took hold of Winnie's head and pulled itself toward her and their foreheads touched. This Guardian's gift was to eliminate all thoughts or feelings of distress and anguish and remove memories that would damage a person's psyche.

Just then, Mia heard a word whispered with more love and compassion than any word she had ever heard pronounced before. "Forget."

The guardian angel looked at Hoshea and silently communicated, *It is done.*

Thank you, Hilily, Hoshea responded back.

"Hoshea," Winnie muttered.

Yes, Winnie, I am with you.

Help...Dai, Winnie thought as she finally lost consciousness. Subsequently, Winnie was returned to her cell.

A single tear rolled down Mia's face.

About an hour later, Avery walked into Winnie's cell.

"Winnie," Avery whispered, "Wake up."

For several minutes Winnie struggled in and out of consciousness, until she finally gathered up the mental faculties to ask a question.

"Am I dead?"

Avery was happy to reply, "No, not yet."

"Are you here to kill me?"

"No."

"Are you sure?"

"Yes."

"Because it would be okay if you were. Since I'm so tired, I won't give you any trouble. And I wouldn't blame you," Winnie added.

"I'm not here to kill you."

"So, then who are you, and why are you here?" Winnie remained conscious only long enough to hear him say, "I'm Avery," before fainting.

"Winnie, wake up." It took him over two minutes to wake her up again.

"Am I dead?"

"No."

Winnie focused her eyes and said, "Avery, are you here to kill me?"

"No. I'm not here to kill you. Now, focus on my voice. Can you hear me?"

"Yes."

"I'm here to help you. Do you understand?"

"Help me?"

"Yes."

"Thank you, Avery, but you shouldn't help me."

"Really, and why is that?"

"Because you'll get in trouble."

Avery tilted his head and looked at Winnie as she struggled to stay awake. *Her genuine concern for my wellbeing even though I'm an enemy is – in one word – remarkable,* Avery emotionally confessed to himself.

"I'm so tired, Avery."

"Well, that's understandable," he replied. "You have been through a mind-bending escapade. Now, in order to regain control of your faculties you must focus."

"Focus?"

"Yes."

"Focus on what?"

"Focus on my voice, Winnie."

"Are you British?" Winnie questioned.

"Yes."

"You're MI6," Winnie stated confidently.

"Now, that's insightful."

Winnie shook her head and tried to sit up. When Avery walked in, Winnie was lying on a cold concrete floor in an empty room two meters by just over a meter wide. There was a metal toilet-sink combo in the far corner, and a dirty sleeping pad on the side. Avery helped her sit up but continued to support her frame until he was convinced she could support herself.

Suddenly, Winnie responded to his earlier comment. "My guess wasn't insightful really. You're in a US government bunker in a different country. And I'm British. So, it's not much of a stretch."

"Brilliant."

"How's my brother?" Winnie asked.

"What makes you think I know the status of your brother?"

"Because if you're MI6, you know."

"Bloody brilliant, but I never confirmed I was with British Intelligence."

"Please, your lack of denial confirmed it."

"Winnie, you're just bloody brilliant."

"So, how is he?"

"He's recovering. But he's not as lucid as you. And your dossier doesn't do you justice."

"I have a dossier?"

"Yes. But it fails to describe the true strength of your mental faculties and your ability to overcome unimaginable distress. In just the few minutes I've been here, I'm convinced you have supernatural abilities."

Winnie was trying hard to regain her independence and composure but the last several days had been grueling in the extreme. She continued to lean on Avery for support.

"Well, I don't feel supernatural, all I feel is exhaustion."

"Trust me. For you to be talking to me at all is a miracle."

"Now that's interesting. Because if you truly believe what you just said, you wouldn't be here. Unless…" Winnie trailed off.

"Unless? Unless what?"

"Unless you were remorseful," Winnie innocently shared.

It took all of Avery's strength to keep from confessing the guilt he felt over her abuse. However, he managed to hold his tongue.

She mustered a small smile and said, "It's okay, Avery, I forgive you. Now how's Dai and can you take me to him?"

Avery shook off his feelings of astonishment at her insight and his emotional regret then said, "Winnie, even if I could take you to your brother, it's not possible. I'm afraid you're too weak to walk."

"I'll force myself."

"He's in a different wing and even if you could manage to stand and walk, there are many guards between us and his cell."

"Well, I know Kung Fu. Do they?"

"I'm not certain, but they have guns."

"Blimey, well, that puts a bit of a damper on things."

Avery smiled then said, "Winnie, I don't want to seem bloody insensitive, but how are you still sane?"

"I have a guardian angel watching over me."

"Well, since I'm at a loss as to your remarkable strength of will, I'm not going to argue the point. However, I just want to state for the record —"

"What record?" Winnie interrupted Avery to ask. Suddenly, she realized that she used the same idiom just a week ago.

"I don't know, THE record. You're missing the point. It was just an expression."

"I'm just joking with you, Avery. I feel like I've been on a bloody bender for a week."

"Brilliant. Well, that's actually my point. Everyone who's been in your position, until now, has lost complete control of their bowel functions and their grip on reality. I find it a marvel that you are still sane. Honestly, it's a bloody miracle. And I'm sorry to keep repeating myself."

"That's bloody gross, Avery. But can I change the topic? Is he still being tortured?"

"Who?"

"My brother."

"No. Your brother is resting. He's not as strong as you, but I believe he will recover.

"Hoshea."

"Hoshea? Who's that?"

"Our savior."

"Huh, is that another name for Buddha?"

"No. It's another name for Jesus."

"Jesus, as in, Jesus Christ?"

"Yes."

"Well, I've never heard him called that before, but there's no doubt he fancies you, love.

"And you, Avery."

"I'm afraid, my dear, there's little hope for me."

"Really? Yet here you are, tending to an enemy of the Crown. Showing mercy and compassion to someone you think is a danger to others. You need to go before someone sees you."

"Interesting, why does it matter to you if someone sees me here?"

"I don't want you to get in trouble."

"Really, after everything that's happened to you, you care about what happens to me?"

"Yes." Winnie was weak and finally drifted off to sleep again. Avery tried again to wake her but without success. He placed her head on his lap and caressed her hair.

"Fine, it's okay, sleep if you must. I will be here when you wake up. No one else shall touch you while I can prevent it." The hours came and went and Winnie slept.

"Winnie."

"Hoshea."

Avery was startled awake and noticed Winnie was also up. "Winnie, I see you're up again."

"Avery."

"Yes."

"Hi, Avery. I would get up and introduce myself properly, but I'm a bit of a mess. Have I been asleep long?"

Avery looked at his watch and replied, "About ten hours."

"Have you been here the whole time?"

"Yes."

"Oh my gosh, why? You need to go. You're going to get in trouble for sure. Why would you risk that?"

"Because you're special, Winnie."

"So are you, Avery. I see your aura."

"I have an aura?"

"Yes, you do. But who is making your aura blue?"

"It's a long story."

"I love long stories. Those are the best kind. Plus, I have nothing else to do and nowhere to go. So, tell me, what has made you blue?"

"It's probably my daughter, Holly, who was around thirteen years old."

"Around thirteen? You don't know how old your daughter

is?

"Well, my wife moved to the US when I died, and she has been raising Holly by herself. In North Carolina, I think.

"Wow, you're dead? So I guess that means that I can talk to the dead?"

"No, sorry. Like I said, it's a long and complicated story. But in short, I faked my own death to hide my wife, Shelly, and daughter from the psychos loose in this world."

"I understand, so you stayed away to protect them from the horrors surrounding your life. So now that the world has gone completely mental, where are Shelly and Holly?"

"Shelly is still in North Carolina, I think, but Holly was taken."

"What do you mean taken?"

"She was taken by your alien mates."

"So you believe I took her?"

"Well, I did, at first. That's why I stood by for three days and watched them torment you."

"And now?"

"And now I know you're innocent. I have seen some bad people do some horrific, monstrous acts. Of which, kidnapping and killing children is at the top. So I know bad when I see it."

"And?"

"And, if you're bad, I'm the Pope."

"Good. I'm glad I didn't have to try and defend myself because I'm just too mentally fatigued to do that."

"I wish Evie was here."

"Evie?" Avery countered.

"Yes, Yvette Milagro?"

Avery sat up and gave Winnie his full attention. "Why?"

"Why, what?" Winnie replied back.

"Why do you wish Evie was here?"

"Well, because she might know where your daughter is."

"I'm sorry, but I'm completely confused. How would she know where Holly is?"

"Well, if I told you, you won't believe me."

"Try me."

"Well, Evie is pretty smart and if she doesn't know where your daughter is, she can find out."

"How, how's that possible?"

"I'm sorry, but did I say she was pretty smart?"

"Yes."

"Well, that was an understatement. Evie is beyond brilliant. But her daughter, Mia, is even more so. And what is truly remarkable is that Mia is the best friend of someone who literally knows everything. Like everything knowable. If you asked him what was the last time any random person read a book, he could give you the day, the hour, the second, the page, the last word on that page, the language the book was written in, the—well, you know what, you get the point. He would definitely know where Holly is."

"Winnie, your story is so preposterous that you're either completely mental or you're telling the truth as you know it." He tilted his head to the side and looked at her long and hard.

"Okay, and?" Winnie questioned.

"I believe you. And Yvette Milagro is here."

"Here? Where? Is she okay? Can I see her?"

"Winnie, this isn't a hotel. You can't just dial up room service. Look, just wait here and I'll go check on her."

"Okay. But I will need details when you get back."

"Understood," Avery told Winnie with confidence.

Avery made the trip to the inmate Charlie wing where Yvette was being held. Winnie, Yvette and Dai were kept apart in separate buildings on purpose.

Avery walked into Yvette's cell minutes later. He tried to wake Yvette up without success. Avery had no choice but to give her a shot of adrenaline.

"Yvette, wake up." After several minutes, Avery admitted to himself that perhaps they had gone too far with Yvette. That shot should have woken her up easily. *The innocent always seem to pay the highest price*, Avery thought. He wanted to let her sleep but he knew there was little time.

"Yvette, you have to wake up."

"Who are you?"

"Avery. I'm Winnie's friend."

"Winnie?"

"Yes, Winnie."

"Is she here? Is she okay?" Yvette whispered. Since Avery

could barely hear her, he picked her up and rested her head on his chest.

"Yes. How are you feeling?"

"I am so tired. Can I sleep?"

"Yes, soon."

"Thank you. I'm so sorry, I'm just so tired and my chest feels constricted."

"It's the adrenaline I gave you."

"How much did you give me?"

"Enough for anyone your size to do back flips."

"Well, that's not good. I can hardly keep my eyes open."

"Yes and the adrenaline is placing a considerable amount of stress on your heart.

"Yvette, please focus. I need to ask you a few questions and I don't want to give you any more medication. Can you answer a few questions?"

"I'll try, but I'm so tired."

"Do it for Winnie."

"Is Winnie your friend?"

"Yes, she most certainly is."

"For her then, but call me Evie."

"Very well, Evie? I was told you might know where my daughter Holly is."

"Holly?"

"Yes, she was thirteen living in North Carolina with her mother, Shelly."

"Holly Arrington?"

"Oh my God, yes."

"Holly's fine. She's very happy and totally loved.

"Where, where is she?"

"She was raptured, Avery."

"Raptured? What does that mean? Like she's in Heaven with God?"

"No, not exactly." Yvette faded back into unconsciousness.

"Evie, stay with me, stay with me. Now, tell me where's Holly."

"Holly?"

"Yes, my daughter Holly, Holly Arrington."

"I can show you, it would be easier. But can I rest a little first? I'm so tired."

"Do you actually know where she is? Or are you telling me what I want to hear?

"I know Holly Arrington. She is identified by those around her as their source of innocence. And even though she is just a thirteen-year-old, Holly creates the most wondrous oil painting masterpieces, which easily rivals those of established legendary Earth artisans. Holly has blue eyes, Irish red hair and feels deeply. You left her mother before she was born. You have pictures of her, which you took while hiding in the shadows. You keep them in a safe place, which only you know about. Although Holly has never seen you in person, her mother gave her an old photograph of you, which she has worn out around the edges. Holly has missed you as much as you have missed her."

Avery's mouth was wide open as he listened to Yvette's proclamation. "How? How do you know all this?"

"I know because I must know. Now, can I rest for a little while, please? I'm so tired."

Although Avery thought her reason for knowing was cryptic, he believed her and replied, "Yes, Evie, rest."

Avery laid Yvette down gently and walked out of her cell only to see Cooper walking up.

Cooper gave Sophia the go ahead to tend to Yvette. Avery walked her in and provided her with some covert but comforting instructions.

Avery and Cooper remained outside discussing their final actions for Yvette.

Sophia placed Yvette's head on her lap and tried to comfort her, then leaned down and whispered into Yvette's ear, "Evie, Avery wanted me to tell you that he will keep Winnie safe and he is working on getting her out."

"Winnie?"

Sophia tenderly covered Yvette's mouth with three fingers then leaned down and said, "Chica, keep your voice down, but yes, Winnie."

Yvette gingerly removed Sophia's fingers away from her mouth and asked, "Is Winnie okay?"

"Yes, Winnie's fine. We are all leaving soon." Suddenly, sorrow filled Sophia's heart and she felt like confessing. "Evie, I'm so sorry for what has happened to you. I was an idiot for letting it happen as long as I did. Please forgive me."

"It's okay, sweetie, I was glad to bear the punishment so the innocent wouldn't have to."

"Oh my God, Evie, you are so amazing and brave. I feel ashamed." Yvette patted Sophia on the hand and added, "It's okay, this darkness has helped you see the light and that is what matters most."

Cooper walked into Yvette's holding cell and immediately gave her an ultimatum.

Avery pulled out his firearm and thought to himself, *This is the day I turn against everything I have been taught. I now swear to support and protect that which I know is right against those I have served my whole life.*

Avery heard a shot fired and immediately believed he was too late. He stepped into Yvette's cell to see Officer Sanchez up against the wall and sliding down to the floor.

Avery crinkled and tightened up his face with anger and mouthed, damn it, as Yvette argued for an explanation to the senseless shooting, but it fell on deaf ears.

"She's innocent and has done nothing wrong. Why?" Avery heard Yvette cry out and then asked for the end.

"Very well, have it your way."

I don't think so, Avery thought then started to pull the trigger. Unexpectedly, he heard a word echo off the walls. "Mother!"

"What was that?" Avery asked himself.

"Mia," Yvette whispered.

Another shot was fired at Yvette's limp body. Avery was in disbelief. He hesitated and now it was too late. But Mia had stepped out of a transport ring and encapsulated her mother and Sophia. Cooper's bullet ricocheted and he was stunned at what he could only categorize as a spirit on the ground in front of him.

"What the hell? Who are you?" He looked around then mouthed under his breath, "Where the hell did you come from?"

Although Avery saw the scolding look of defiance on what he categorized as an angel, he was not afraid.

"You were told not to kill them. That was a mistake. Your penance shall be great," Avery heard the apparition say and then she took Yvette and Sophia. With the exception of an old dirty mattress pad, the cell was empty.

Cooper turned around and looked at Avery and said, "What the hell just happened?"

"Listen, mate, don't freak out. We need to check every cell on this compound. I will check Alpha and Bravo and you check this building and Delta wing. Make sure you account for every inmate.

"Yes, sir, but what the hell was that?"

"I don't know but before we report this, we need answers. Understand?"

"Yes, sir, but did you see that, that ghost thing? What the hell was that? My hair is standing on edge, look!" Cooper held up his arm as proof.

"I hear you, mate. I was bloody there with you. Now go and tell no one what you saw. We don't want everyone to think we've gone mental, understand?"

"Yes, sir."

Avery and Cooper moved off in different directions. Avery arrived at Winnie's cell in A wing as quickly as possible. Winnie was lying back on the dirty mattress pad.

"Winnie," Avery announced abruptly as he entered her cell.

"What the—you startled me, Avery. What is it? What's going on? You look flushed."

"Winnie, you told me you knew Kung Fu. Was that true?"

"Yes, of course. Why?"

"Are you any good?"

"Well, I've been in thousands of fights over the years. Most of the times against multiple adversaries and managed to win a lot of them so, yes, I'm pretty good."

"Brilliant. We're going to put those skills to the test."

"Why, what's happening?"

"We're leaving. I'm getting you out of here."

"What? I'm no good to you right now, I haven't eaten in days. I'm weak from the stress and abuse."

"Well, I have this." Avery held up what appeared to be a huge EpiPen.

"What is that, an Epinephrine Auto-Injector?"

"No, it's adrenaline."

"Wow, how much is that?"

"It's enough to make a grandmother do handsprings. The stress associated with this scenario and the adrenaline will overstimulate your hypothalamus—"

Winnie interrupted Avery to add, "Yes, it will either give me a massive heart attack or—"

Avery interrupted Winnie to finish her statement, "Or turn you into a Superwoman, able to leap tall buildings in a single bound."

"Winnie, we have no choice, they will be coming to kill you soon. We have to go."

Avery injected Winnie in her thigh and Winnie started shaking violently almost immediately.

CHAPTER 6

Reynolds' Search Begins
Tuesday, July 16, 2047 2 p.m.

REYNOLDS WAS MOVED VIA AMBULANCE FROM FILIP'S SECRET medieval worship chamber to Instytut Matki hospital in Warsaw, Poland. Filip had Poland's most skillful reconstructive surgeons—in five disciplines—standing by exclusively for Reynolds.

The head surgeon introduced Filip's chief of staff.

"Everyone, this gentleman is Mr. Tusk. He is our guest and will be observing this procedure in its entirety." The nurses and doctors welcomed him and then prepped for surgery. Eric and his two sentinels stood motionless and watched as hours of surgery ticked by. Finally, after sixteen hours on an operating table, Reynolds had astounded them all.

The plastic surgeon, Dr. Banās, was the team's leader. He walked over to Eric and said, "We've done all we can. It's now up to him. But the prognosis isn't good. Your man is in a coma and based on his injuries, there is a high probability he will never wake up. "

"I understand. Thank you, Doctor, and please thank your staff for me."

"Yes, sir, I will."

"Now, I need ten milliliters of sterile solution in a small

cup," Eric asked authoritatively.

Dr. Banās motioned for a nurse to approach and repeated Eric's request to the letter. She quickly returned with a small amount of solution and offered the cup to the surgeon.

"Please give the cup to our guest," Dr. Banās stated. The nurse handed the cup to Eric who raised it up to the light and peered in. He brought the cup back down and poured out half its content on the floor. He then pulled a pill out of his pocket and placed it in the water and looked at his watch. Twenty seconds later he pulled the pill out and passed the cup to the surgeon.

"Place this solution in a syringe and inject it into his IV."

"What's in the cup, Mr. Tusk?"

Eric just gave the doctor a cold hard stare and said nothing.

The lead surgeon handed the cup to the nurse and repeated Eric's instructions. The nurse did as directed then looked over her shoulder and said, "It's done."

"I'm sorry, sir, but what did we just administer to this man?"

Eric never took his gaze off of Reynolds but instead, pointed and said, "Watch."

Everyone looked at Reynolds. Minutes went by and the team lead turned to Eric and whispered, "Sir, please excuse my ignorance, but what are we looking for?"

"Patience, Doctor." Eric pointed at Reynolds with his chin and said, "Patience. Just keep watching."

The room returned their collective attention to Reynolds, when suddenly, his injuries miraculously started to slowly fade away. His vital signs were no longer registering near death. The anesthesiologist instinctively removed the life-support apparatus attached to Reynolds, only to unexplainably witness him begin to breathe on his own almost immediately.

"What the—that's impossible," Dr. Banās voiced under his breath.

"Move him to a private room and have a nurse sit with him. When he's communicative and ambulatory, give him some clothes and send him to me. Do you understand?"

"Yes, yes, sir," the doctor stuttered out after shaking his head multiple times.

"Good." Eric turned around and started toward the exit.

One of his sentries moved ahead and opened the door for Mr. Tusk.

The lead doctor, who was standing near Eric, broke through his mystified state to finally ask, "How?"

When Eric broke the operating room's threshold he turned, looked over his shoulder and said, "Shoot her." He was pointing at the nurse who initially gave him the cup with too much sterile solution.

The bodyguard still in the room pulled out his Glock and shot the nurse in the face. He turned, holstered his firearm and followed Filip's chief of staff out of the room.

As the door slowly closed, the doctor faintly heard Eric say, "You don't have the need to know."

One of the other surgeons asked, "What the hell just happened here?" The other nurses all had their hands covering their mouths.

The lead surgeon motioned with his hands, *I have no idea.*

Reynolds was moved to a four-meter-square private room with a bank of monitoring equipment. Three nurses were assigned to the room on eight-hour shifts and directed to closely observe his recovery. The nurse on watch sat in one of the two leather cushioned chairs and kept a small nightlight on at all times, atop of a rolling side-table. The only window in the room had a heavy curtain over it which looked like it hadn't been moved in a decade. There was a private restroom in the space but the nurses were the only ones using it. Two days later, Reynolds was awake and asked for his clothes, but the nurse was in the bathroom.

She walked out to hear Reynolds ask, "Who are you and where are my clothes?"

"I'm your nurse," the young woman stuttered out. She walked over to the closet and picked up his clothes. She carried the bundle over to Reynolds and handed it to him. It contained a complete wardrobe and everything else he would need. On top of the pile was a handwritten note from Filip Zarek which read, 'Go forward and do my will.' The nurse was a nervous wreck. Mr. Zarek had left specific instructions that he didn't want Reynolds to wake up in an empty room. And to her misfortune, he had done just that.

Reynolds dangled both legs over the side of the bed and asked, "How long have I been here?"

"Two days, sir, you've been in this room for two days."

Reynolds started removing his bandages and to his astonishment, there were no visible scars to his injuries. "What the hell?" Reynolds looked at the nurse and asked, "How is this possible? I should be at death's door or dead. What happened?"

The nurse simply shook her head slowly as tears flowed down her face and mouthed, "I don't know," in an eastern bloc European accent.

"It's okay. I'm not going to hurt you, you've done nothing wrong. I just want answers."

"Sir, I'm so sorry I was in the restroom when you woke up."

"It's okay, don't worry. It's not an issue, really."

She handed Reynolds a note with a trembling hand then said with a cracking voice, "Sir, Mr. Tusk wants to see you as soon as you're able."

Reynolds was naked, so he stepped off the bed to get dressed.

"What's the quickest way out of the hospital and how do I get to the capital building?"

The young nurse pointed then said, "There's an emergency exit just outside this room on the right. Take the stairs down to the ground floor. When you exit the stairwell turn left. If you walk straight down the passageway past the double glass doors, you can hail a cab outside from the curb."

"Thank you." Reynolds put his jacket on, holstered his Glock and started out. He opened the door then stopped to read Eric's note, which said, "Shoot her."

He shook his head then turned and said, "Young lady, I work for a degenerate. He has issued me orders to kill you, but I know you've done nothing wrong. So, when you wake up, go home, pack a bag and disappear. Do you understand?"

The nurse shook her head as she trembled. Reynolds pulled out his Glock and shot at the girl. The bullet moved the hair on the side of her head as it whizzed by and struck the wall. The discharge noise was so loud that it caused the nurse to tense up and she fainted.

He stared at the girl a few seconds then said, "I'm sorry, my lady."

He then walked out, hailed a cab and took it to the Warsaw

capital building. He walked in and notified the guard at the front desk that he was there to see Eric Tusk.

"Are you Mr. Reynolds?"

"Yes, I am."

"Sir, may I see your passport?"

Reynolds reached inside his jacket pocket and pulled out his identification then gave it to the guard.

The officer examined the document and said, "Thank you, sir," then handed his papers back along with an attaché and added, "Sir, if you would, please follow me."

He was escorted to a private lounge on the first floor facing the main street. The guard opened the door and said, "Sir, if you please." Reynolds walked in and was asked to review the information contained within his case.

He sat down then tried to open the attaché but couldn't.

"The briefcase is locked. How do I open it?"

"Sir, the key should be in your coat pocket."

Reynolds quickly searched his person and found the key.

"If that will be all, sir?"

"Yes, thank you," he cordially replied as he looked around the empty lounge. The space resembled an airline's first class lounge at any international airport. One side of the room was lined with windows. The room had a dozen small circular end tables scattered throughout, each surrounded by two, three or four single-cushioned chairs. There were drink and snack stations located along the wall opposite the windows. Counters full of beverages and fast food items on display seemed to have a familiar tone.

Reynolds opened the portfolio he was given and started reviewing the documents.

There were detailed intelligence files on everyone he had been exposed to over the last week. There were even records on individuals he had never met.

"Who the hell are Mick Ruben and Sophia Sanchez? And why do I recognize the name Labelle Rogan? Wait," Reynolds started thinking. *Rogan, Rogan? Wasn't that the name of an assassin or enforcer working against the New York crime syndicate years ago? I thought he was made up. A myth the crime bosses used to scare the other families.* "Interesting, Filip has somehow hired a mythical psychopath to work with me. I'm not sure how I feel about that."

Reynolds read on then thought aloud, "Great, he's going to be in Miami when I arrive. Well, it might be handy having a psycho killer working for me. Akachi is a formidable adversary." But as he gave it a little more thought, his concerns started to limit his enthusiasm. "Oh, whatever, having this crazy person on my side is better than having to confront one. Although, why are there detailed files and images on everyone except for him? That's odd."

The lieutenant read every document four times then grabbed a small metal trash can to destroy the material. He removed the liner and set the files aflame by an open window. After the fire was out and the records destroyed, he opened a bottle of water, poured it into the rubbish bin and mixed the ashes up with an umbrella he found near the entrance. He set the container down then made reservations to be taken to his private G11 Gulfstream jet standing by at the Warsaw Chopin Airport.

Reynolds was welcomed by the pilot, a co-pilot and two stewardesses.

"So, where would you like our first destination to be, sir?"

"Miami, Florida."

"Very well, sir, after you." Reynolds walked onboard and found a seat.

The pilots returned to the cockpit and plotted the flight to Miami then asked the airport tower for permission to depart.

"Is there anything we can get for you, sir?" one stewardess asked while the other leaned over her shoulder and hugged her around the waist. They were dressed like Pan AM stewardesses of the early 1960s. However, the girls wore their skirts six inches above the knee versus what was customary for the earlier period. Nikki wore high-heel shoes but Vikki wore military style combat boots. They both had on a big button Barbie hat, the white gloves and the vintage purple pagoda parasol bridal umbrella which made the outfit over-the-top adorable.

"Well, aren't you two the cat's meow?"

The stewardess peering from behind the other leaned to the side, pushed her bangs over her ear and said in a squeaky, childlike French accent, "Aww, thank you monsieur."

"You're welcome, Carrot Top." Then Reynolds addressed the flight attendant in front. "I would appreciate a Scotch, neat, Doll Face."

"Yes, sir, as you wish. The stewardesses started walking away when they heard Reynolds add, "However, I may need some additional tending to later. I'm not at my best."

"Yes, sir," the brunette replied back. "I'm Vikki, and the kitty behind me is Nikki." Reynolds nodded in acknowledgment.

"Ladies, this is the captain speaking. Please make the cabin ready for departure then take your seats. Mr. Reynolds, we shall be airborne in just a few moments. Our transit time to Miami, Florida is an estimated twenty-seven hours and twenty-one minutes. Since it's 11:35 a.m. local time here in Warsaw, this should put us wheels down in Miami International at 8:56 a.m. tomorrow. We will be stopping twice to refuel en route. If you have any questions, please do not hesitate to ask me or any staff member. This is a permanent assignment for us until you say otherwise. We are honored to be serving you, Lieutenant, and we hope you enjoy the flight."

The red-headed stewardess brought Reynolds his drink and sat it down in front of him.

"Thank you, Carrot Top."

Nikki leaned forward and whispered into Reynolds ear, "If there is anything else you need, monsieur, please ask," then she wiggled off and sat down next to the other flight attendant and threw her leg over Vikki's right thigh, and started filing her nails.

Reynolds drank his Scotch and fell asleep. Twenty-seven hours and eighteen minutes later, the Gulfstream was pulling into a private hangar at Miami International Airport, where a black Escalade with a driver was waiting.

Reynolds disembarked the aircraft along with the two stewardesses. "Where are you two going?"

Nikki held onto Vikki's shoulders, and while peering over her said, "We're your bodyguards, Lieutenant."

"Oh really," Reynolds turned his back to the girls, pulled out his Glock and drew it on the stewardesses. The brunette moved in and immediately disarmed him. The redhead leaped forward grabbing Reynolds while he was disorientated and with an arm-lock and a hip-toss, jujitsued him to the ground. Nikki then leaned in and asked all bubbly, "Was that a test, monsieur? Was it, was it, was it? Did we do good? Did we pass?"

Reynolds moaned, "Ah, yeah," while holding onto his lower back, then added, "Good job, but let's keep the test results between us, okay?"

"Sure, no problem."

Vikki walked over and placed her hand on Nikki's shoulder and said, "Easy, girl, just help him up."

"Oh yeah, sorry." Nikki moved her foot off his shoulder then cleared her throat and reached out to help Reynolds up.

Reynolds looked the two girls over then questioned, "People underestimate you two, don't they?"

"Oui oui, monsieur," Nikki responded.

"All the time," Vikki added assuredly.

"That's perfect."

"Where to, sir?"

"The Miami City Police Department on 30th Avenue."

Vikki informed the driver where to go then opened the door for Reynolds and said, "Lieutenant," as she handed him his gun.

"Thank you, Doll Face." His new bodyguards also got into the car. Vikki sat in the back next to Reynolds and Nikki sat up front. The driver pulled out of the hangar and drove off.

Thirty minutes later, Reynolds was greeted at the police headquarters lobby. "We're glad to have you back, Lieutenant," the Florida governor told Reynolds as he shook his hand followed by the mayor, and the chief of police.

"I'm glad to be back, sir."

"Mayor."

"Lieutenant."

"Chief."

"Reynolds. Your staff members and the Global Task Force are standing by for your orders."

"Thank you, Chief, I shall put them to good use."

Reynolds made the trip down the hall and entered the command center located in the middle of the building. He took his jacket off, rolled up his sleeves and started barking out orders.

The Global Task Force had representatives from thirteen countries: the UK, Germany, Sweden, China, India, and Poland to name a few. More than half of those present were past ambassadors or still active members of the United Nations.

He also had six permanent staff members assigned by the police department. Reynolds pointed to one of them and said, "Manny, I want you to find out where Mick Ruben currently is. I need to interview him. He's an emergency room doctor at Jackson Memorial."

"Yes, sir."

"Gail, find Stefan Magnusson. He's a geneticist assigned to Jackson Memorial here in Miami. However, I believe he's currently in Stockholm, Sweden on holiday. Get him on the next flight back."

"Yes, sir."

"James —"

"Yes, sir."

Reynolds looked for the other staff member in the crowd. When he saw him, he said, "James, I need you to talk to Dr. Milagro's family. Corral her parents, her siblings, and let's talk to them all. You can find them in a funeral parlor in Fajardo, Puerto Rico."

"Yes, sir."

"Eric, I need you to find Sophia Sanchez. She's a police officer in Fajardo. Talk to her family, friends, anyone that knows her. I need you to learn all you can."

"Yes, sir. And may I say how happy I am to have you back, sir."

"Sure. Now, you all have your orders."

"Yes, sir," his staff members replied in unison.

"Miguel," Reynolds pointed to another staff member in the back of the crowd. "Get up here."

"Yes, sir."

"Miguel, why are you hiding in the back?"

"I'm sorry, sir." As he moved his way forward, he heard Reynolds' request. "Talk to me about Dr. Milagro, Dr. Chow Lee and the whereabouts of Special Agent Akachi Ihejika."

"Yes, sir, well —"

Reynolds interrupted Miguel with a targeted question at the remaining group, "Oh, wait a minute, Miguel. Who's the senior Global Task Force member?"

The members looked around at each other and the Belgium representative said, "I believe I am, sir, followed by the honorable gentleman Luis Carlos Arroyo, from Mexico."

"Luis, you're in charge of my Global Task Force now," then the Lieutenant pulled out his Glock and shot the Belgium archetypal in the face.

"I do not forgive mistakes nor do I tolerate weakness. I would highly recommend neither of those two directives be violated while you're under my employ. The smallest transgression will be met with extreme finality. Are there any questions?" Everyone was silent as the grave.

"Good, now Miguel, where were we?"

"Well, sir, you were asking about Milagro, Chow Lee and Akachi."

"Oh yes—damn it. I'm sorry to interrupt you again, but I just remembered one more thing. Where did the distinguished gentleman from Mexico get off to?"

"I'm here, sir."

"Luis, I expect you to use your overseas connections to help my local resources reach out globally to apprehend the people we're after."

"Si, señor, that goes without saying."

"You're a good man. Buenos, Luis, adelante hombre."

"Si, señor, y gracias."

Reynolds waved off the ambassador from Mexico and looked over at his new bodyguards. "You two, get rid of that," he pointed to the Belgium representative on the floor.

"Sure, no problem." Nikki walked over to the command center door, opened it and yelled out, "We need a body bag in here!" She looked around then added, "Hello, anyone, we need a body bag! Hello?" Reynolds looked over at Vikki then pointed to Nikki with his chin.

One of the G-force members turned to another and said, "She's dead."

Vikki walked over and placed a hand on Nikki's shoulder and said, "Easy, girl, just go see the quarter master."

"Oh yeah, sure, no problem."

Reynolds shook his head then returned his attention to his previous conversation with Miguel. Within hours, every task Reynolds had assigned was thoughtfully being pursued. Most with extreme vigor and intense focus on the minutest details with one exception.

Reynolds addressed a young woman, the last of his assigned staff, and said, "Ginger, I need you to be my assistant and coordinate my schedule. Make sure I see everyone in an orderly fashion. And remember, time is of the essence."

"Yes, sir, of course."

About four hours later, Ginger returned with an update and the lieutenant's schedule.

"Sir, a word."

"Sure, Ginger, talk to me."

"Doctor Ruben is sitting in the lobby waiting to see you. I have an office reserved for you for the duration of this investigation. Sir, if you would, please follow me."

Reynolds' assistant and his two bodyguards left the command center, turned right and entered the last office on the left.

"Wow, this office is huge."

"It was the district file room, but since everything is now digital, the space has just been sitting here empty. So I claimed it and had it updated."

"Well, Ginger, thank you for looking out for me."

"Yes, sir, you're welcome.

Reynolds walked over and sat down behind an old mahogany desk at the corner of the room. He had bulletproof windows behind him to the left and right for at least seven meters in both directions. Vikki stood behind him to the right and Nikki to his left. There were several wingback chairs in front of the desk. Behind that was a conference table that sat twelve and multiple other cushioned chairs scattered about. A dozen bookshelves lined the walls opposite the windows with a collection of recent law books.

"Should I send in Dr. Ruben?"

"Yes, please do."

His assistant stepped out and a minute later returned with Mick Ruben, then excused herself and closed the door behind her.

Reynolds made his way around the desk to shake Ruben's hand. "Dr. Ruben, I'm Lieutenant Reynolds. Thank you for seeing me on such short notice."

"Sure, Lieutenant, what's this all about?"

"Please, have a seat, Doctor."

Mick sat down then looked at the two ladies and asked, "Who are they supposed to be?" The girls just snarled at him, causing Ruben to raise his eyebrows.

"They're my book ends, ignore them."

"Well, with all due respect, Lieutenant, they seem quite memorable to me. They're like menacing vipers." The comment made the girls pull back at the neck and shoulders causing Ruben to add, "But in a picturesque sort of way, of course."

"Well, thank you for the descriptive commentary, Doctor. But my reason for asking you here is simple. I need you to answer a few questions about Yvette Milagro."

"Okay, so, what about her?"

"What can you tell me?"

"What would you like to know?"

"Everything, like when was the last time you spoke to her? What was that conversation about? What did she say to you? Do you know where she might be? Do you know who her friends are?"

"Whoa, wait, that's a lot of questions. First, I haven't spoken to Evie in over a week. And our last conversation is none of your business. I haven't seen her since and I don't know where she is. And if you must know, Evie doesn't have any friends. She has an odd life motto that pushes people away."

"Which is what, exactly?"

Ruben looked at the two girls, waited a few seconds then summarized, "In short, she prefers the company of the dead over the living."

Nikki let out a giggle then shared, "I love her."

Vikki looked over at Nikki and said, "Easy, girl."

"Oh yeah, sorry."

"Look, the truth is that aside from her job, Dr. Milagro does nothing else. At least not that I'm aware of, so, if there is nothing else?" Ruben interjected. "My shift starts in a few minutes and I've never been late for work."

"Sure, but just one more question, Doctor." Mick just stared Reynolds down. "If you happen to hear from the good doctor, I need you to call me. Can you do that?"

"Sure. Now if you will excuse me." Mick got up and started for the door. Vikki leaned down and whispered into Reynolds' ear, "I don't trust him."

Ruben opened the office door and went to step out but instead turned around and thought out loud, "I don't have your number, Lieutenant, should I need to talk to you."

"Yes, of course, how thoughtless of me." Reynolds handed

Vikki his business card and she walked up and handed Mick the card.

"Thank you."

Vikki just turned around and returned to Reynolds side. She leaned down and whispered to Reynolds, "I feel a little better about him now."

"Me, too. He's a little elitist and a bit rude but so are most of the doctors I've met. Let's wait and see what happens."

An intercom tune sounded and a voice announced, "Sir, I have Dr. Wilson on the line for you. He says it's urgent."

"Thank you, Ginger. But refresh my memory, who is he again?"

"He's the Jackson Memorial Hospital administrator."

"Oh, yes, thank you, I remember now. He was the person who initially called me about the alien threat. Put him through."

"Yes, sir."

********** The week before, in Stockholm, Sweden **********

Dr. Magnusson was at home with his wife grieving over the loss of their three children.

Stefan Magnusson along with Wen Chow Lee and their team were trying to definitively determine the age of our human DNA. This would allow the team to accurately extrapolate mental and physical developments or improvements over the next several hundred million years. Over time, would humans evolve past the use of their ears, or other sensory organs? And would they generate new ones? Would we become more resilient to infectious organisms? Would we generate a stronger dependency on technology or become interconnected with Nano circuitry?

This was considered the next step in the discovery of the nucleotide base pairs sequence completed in the early turn of the twentieth century.

The telephone rang.

"Hej Magnusson."

"May I speak to Dr. Magnusson?"

"One moment please." Malena looked at her watch, covered the microphone on the phone and said, "Stefan, there's a call for you."

Stefan walked over, took the telephone and asked his wife, "Who is it?"

"It's an American."

Stefan crinkled the corner of his mouth then said, "I'm so sorry, sötnos." He kissed her gently on the cheek as Malena walked away.

"Hello."

"Dr. Magnusson, this is Dr. Penn. I joined your team about a week ago."

"It's Jay, right?"

"Yes, sir."

"What can I do for you, Doctor?"

"Well, sir, I stumbled across the samples Dr. Chow lee was reviewing before her departure—"

"I'm sorry to interrupt you, Doctor, but you do realize this is not a good time for my wife and I?"

"Yes, sir, and I'm so sorry for your loss, but this can't wait."

Americans, Stefan thought to himself. "Very well, what is so important, Doctor? But please, make it brief. I need to get back to my wife and family."

"Yes, sir, well, I found something that is—" The line went quiet.

Dr. Magnusson broke the unexpected silence and asked, "What, what have you found, Doctor?"

"The Holy Grail, sir."

"Sorry, would you repeat that? I'm not sure I understand the reference."

"Yes, sir, of course. You're not going to believe this—" Jay spent two minutes summarizing his findings while Stefan held his breath and sat in silence.

"Hello, Dr. Magnusson, are you still there?"

"Oh, sorry." Stefan shook his head then added, "Yes, yes, I'm still here. Apparently, my initial reaction was exactly as you predicted. You understand that what you've just told me is theoretically impossible. But—but you're in possession, actual physical possession, of the blood?"

"Yes, sir, several small vials, but more than enough." There was another long pause in the conversation. "Hello, Dr. Magnusson, are you still there?" Stefan was lost in thought again, contemplating what this discovery would mean to mankind. It was like listening to Dr. Higgs describe the God particle, holding the physical proof in his hand.

"Yes, sorry, sorry, I'm here — so do you have digital copies, images of the blood?"

"Yes, sir, of course, I've taken hundreds of images and I have made several videos at multiple magnifications."

"Excellent, place all the digital proof on the hospital's secure server and refrigerate the samples. I will log in momentarily and download the files."

"Sir, I want you to know something else."

"Yes, go on."

"Well, sir, I found myself talking to the samples, like, literally talking to the blood."

"Okay, well I guess that's understandable, given the nature of this discovery." Even though Stefan found Dr. Penn's statement odd, it wasn't the strangest declaration he had heard from him that day; at least not yet.

"Well, sir, the odd thing is that I swear the samples were talking back." Then Dr. Penn went silent as Stefan had done earlier, forcing Magnusson to call out.

"Jay, Jay!"

"Yes, yes, sir?"

"Jay, listen to me carefully. I will be there as soon as possible.

"How? The airports around the world are closed. And only the military and some cargo planes are allowed to fly.

"I realize that. Now listen, once I've reviewed the files and have made preliminary notes, I'll secure passage on a garbage scow if necessary. Just keep the information secure and ask Dr. Wilson to safeguard this data. I'll be there as soon as I can."

"Yes, sir."

"And, Doctor?"

"Yes, sir?"

"You did the right thing by calling me."

"Yes, sir. Thank you, sir."

CHAPTER 7

The Cuban Challenge

HILILY AND HIKIKO WERE GETTING TOGETHER WITH THE Cuban girls' normal training entourage to discuss future combat sessions. Hilily wanted its replacement to understand the trainees.

The other clan members were standing at attention when Hilily and Hikiko arrived at the great Guardian hall. The senior Harem in the group asked Hilily to speak when they approached. Hikiko motioned for the Guardian to step forward.

Hai stepped out in front of the others and welcomed their clan leaders then asked, "Your Grace, thank you for giving us the opportunity to discuss our skirmish tactics prior to our next session with the Cuban girls."

"Absolutely, this is how we improve our performance and theirs. So, let's start this review with your verdict on your last performance?" Hilily asked, hoping to hear a brutal assessment of their previous engagement accompanied by strong and valid suggestions for improvements.

"It was poor at best, Your Grace."

"I agree. So what would you recommend we do to improve and limit injuries?"

"Well, is it possible for us to wear helmets during the Cuban girls' ambush sessions moving forward?"

"WHAT?! Absolutely not. Why would you ask me that?" Hilily asked with incredulity since no one ever wore protective equipment other than their vambrace, gauntlets and greaves during these sessions. However, more often than not, their protective gear was referred to as sleeves and leggings.

"It's that most of us are tired of getting hit on the head during these surprise attacks which the Cuban girls always foresee."

"What's wrong with your sleeves?"

"They're not very effective, Your Grace."

"Really? I'm surprised to hear you say that, since vambrace and gauntlets are coded to the metabolism of the individual wearing it. Simply put, your sleeves are a defensive barrier. They repel intrusion into the personal space of the wearer."

"Yes, of course, but a peaceful breach will be repelled with little to no force."

"But repelled nevertheless," Hilily added to the Guardian's statement then continued. "Once the wearer's emotions are heightened, their sleeves work automatically, extending around them or the individual they're protecting with extreme prejudice."

"Yes, Your Grace, but the Cuban girls have somehow mastered the use of these articles. And our sleeves, more often than not, perform poorly in deflecting their strikes."

"Is that so? Perhaps you need to work on improving your reaction time."

"Yes, Your Grace, but if I may?"

Hilily was visually disappointed and scrunched up the right side of its mouth then said, "Yes, go on, Hai, what is it?"

"I was going to say that it's difficult to use our defensive gear when our arms or legs are immobilized so quickly by the trainees. The Cuban girls have somehow learned to manipulate and perform functions with their sleeves and leggings that none of us knew were possible. Would it be agreeable to have Artemis show us how they execute these maneuvers? That might make it possible for us to develop counter measures."

Hilily thought about the Guardian's request for a few seconds then decided not to seem dismissive off hand so it countered with, "Perhaps."

"And if I may?"

"Yes, by all means, continue."

"We've observed the girls using their gauntlets to hold on to each other during many of their aerial maneuvers. This creates extended barriers which are difficult to penetrate since the obstructions are practically invisible until we run into them. We're sorry to say that their tactics have us stupefied." The Guardian closed its eyes and bowed its head.

"It's okay, Hai, please continue," Hikiko said encouragingly.

"Thank you, Your Grace, I just need a few seconds to gather myself. I'm a bit nervous."

Hilily stepped forward and placed a hand on the Guardian's shoulder and said, "Be at peace."

Hai nodded then took another few seconds before continuing. "Furthermore, to our misfortune, Artemis has shown her sisters how to focus and hold our arms or legs while battling someone else. These restrictions add confusion since we initially have no idea who to target to regain full mobility. Nevertheless, we try desperately to find the point of origin to the snares but the process is slow at best. Their strategy and techniques are unquestionably flawless. If I didn't know any better, I would guess they change targets often to keep us guessing," Hai summarized for Hilily.

"Regrettably, I agree with your assessment, which begs the question. Why do they possess skills that we lack?" Hikiko added.

Hai confirmed a little too enthusiastically by yelling out, "Exactly!" Afterwards, Hai noticed the expression on Hilily's face and quietly cowered behind Hikiko.

Hilily made a low grunt sound then looked over at Hikiko who just shrugged.

Hai stepped to the side and added, "I believe since the Cuban girls do not have access to an Adamic, somehow they have spiritually been able to access functionality to negate that weakness."

By the time the senior Harem had concluded its summary, the whole team was nodding in agreement to the provided synopsis. Hilily's acceptance of the Guardian's assessment brought some comfort to a beaten and bruised team. But their comfort was short lived.

"Although your synopsis is informative, Hai, it would benefit you to remember that when we first began our training sessions long ago, we weren't given an Adamic either." Hilily looked around and noticed that every Guardian had their eyebrows raised or their eyes opened wide. "Unfortunately, Hai, in your desire to generate valid reasons for our misgivings, you've misclassified elements in your equation.

Hikiko jumped in and said, "That's an excellent point, Your Grace. The Cuban girls' ingenuity and execution is astonishing."

All the Guardians quickly agreed by silently nodding their heads up and down.

"They project defensive moves to block strikes meant for someone else other than themselves. This makes it almost impossible to anticipate or counter since it's unclear where the restrictions are coming from."

"These are all good observations, everyone, but again, how do we effectively respond?" Hilily countered.

"Your Grace," one of the junior Defenders addressed Hilily and asked for permission to speak. Although finding a resolution was taking much longer than Hilily anticipated, this was the first time any of these Guardians had ever voiced their opinions. Therefore, some repetition and simple comments were to be expected. Consequently, Hilily thought a certain level of latitude was in order.

Hilily asked the Defender to step forward. "Go on, Defender, do you have a question?"

"No, not exactly, Your Grace." The Defender cleared its throat and said, "I realize it takes nearly two thousand years to complete the Defensive Arts Internship. In addition, if a soul chooses this discipline as their primary votary, their training continues, and for many, it will never end."

"Yes, Defender, we're all aware of the training timelines. And although I agree with your comments, they're a bit obvious, don't you think?"

"Yes, Your Grace. But to our astonishment and embarrassment, Artemis can effectively repel those of us who have actually completed the defensive program millennia ago. Why? Well, I believe there are several strong mitigating or contributing factors toward Artemis's prowess," the junior Defender voiced. "It might help us overcome our shortcomings if we acknowledged her strengths."

Hilily smiled then said, "Go on, Hazimi, share your thoughts." Everyone listened intently as the junior Defender spoke.

"Okay, so I believe: one, Artemis has immense passion and extraordinary raw ability. Two, since she is so young, she has not had the opportunity to doubt herself. Therefore, she actually doesn't know that some of the maneuvers she's attempting are unattainable or outright impossible. And because of that, she executes the inconceivable. Three, maybe God has anointed her with special abilities because of a specific role she is meant to play in the aftermath of the Rapture. And more important, she is the only Saint who has actually been in battle with the Helem."

The Guardian clan members all looked over at each other as they absorbed and processed the information shared.

Hazimi finished by saying, "Well, regardless of the reasons, Artemis is remarkable and it's an honor to have her by your side when trouble comes."

Hilily got a smirk on its face and said, "Nicely put, girl."

"Girl, Your Grace?" Hazimi questioned as the others chuckled.

"I'm sorry, but I'm using the word 'girl' as a term of endearment."

"I see," Hazimi thought about it for a few seconds then said, "Well, I'm not sure why, but I kinda like it." All the Harem looked around at each other and again chuckled collectively then said, "Girl," and laughed again.

"There is no question Artemis has astonishing abilities. And it's an honor to defend the righteous by her side. However, is it possible that the other girls are simply toying with us?" another junior Defender shared. But as soon as the words were uttered, the Defender felt guilty for even suggesting it and reached up to cover its mouth.

This surprising comment about the girls' motives made many of the Harem raise an eyebrow. Consequently, all their ears perked up.

"What? No!" Hilily sighed. "Look, let's be clear, they're not toying with us," Hilily shared with its Guardians. "The truth is that the girls are young and full of so much enthusiasm that it's hard for them not to enjoy these sessions. This is especially true since they have yet to feel the sting of defeat."

"I'm sorry, Your Grace, but apparently I'm not as smart as the rest of you. I just don't see how any of this information helps us?" the youngest Defender voiced with reservation.

Hikiko stepped forward and said, "Oh, but it most certainly does."

"How, Your Grace?" The young Defender pried for specifics.

"In the simplest terms, these discussions lend proof that our approach has been all wrong. Now, I agree with Hilily — we must improve these sessions so our trainees can learn how to defend themselves against true adversaries. And we haven't been doing that. We've just been gawking and in awe of them — but that stops today. At least, during battle training simulations anyway. So, this is what we must do."

The Guardians gathered as Hikiko shared their new approach. "First things first, we need to surprise the girls."

"How? Heather always sees us coming," a Defender voiced.

"Exactly. And we'll use that to our advantage," Hikiko responded.

"How?" another Defender questioned.

"By turning their world on its axis ninety degrees."

"I'm so sorry, Your Grace, but I don't understand."

"It's okay, let me explain." Within minutes of Hikiko sharing elements of their new approach, every defender, without exception, was teary-eyed at a flawless and brilliant strategy.

An hour later, Hilily asked, "Does everyone know what to do?"

"Yes, Your Grace," the Guardians answered in unison.

"Excellent, then let's go." Hilily opened a portal and they were gone.

Everyday for the next several weeks, the Cuban girls were returning home tattered and bruised. For the first time since arriving at Terra Nuevo, their morale had taken a turn in an unlikely direction.

Heather always managed to foresee the Guardian's training attacks coming. Nevertheless, Hikiko's approach somehow remained a surprise. The Defenders were attacking the girls from underneath and trapping their legs in the earth. This would delay the Cuban girls' response time and threw off their rhythm for the rest of the session—making it difficult for the Cuban Saints to ever gain an upper hand.

Hikiko would voice an attack launching from behind and then the attack would materialize from above. The girls were unsure as to how this was being accomplished. In addition, their aerial prowess was being negated by force fields, making it impossible for the girls to execute any of their airborne counter moves.

Even Artemis was affected by her sister's stress levels and gloomy outlook. The probability of them ever getting the upper hand under these strenuous, and in some cases crippling circumstances was looking bleak. Since Jesus Christ had other plans for Mia off world, she was the only one spared the recent misery engulfing the current training sessions.

Mia arrived home one afternoon after the girls had returned from a sparring session and noticed their appearance. "Wow, what happened to you guys? What have you been up to? You all look…terrible."

"Well, that's how we feel," Artemis replied.

"Really, why? What's going on?"

"Defensive training?" Artemis meekly replied while comforting an aching shoulder.

"Huh, that's odd. I remember those sessions being more colorful and informative then physically brutal. What's changed?"

"Hilily."

"Really? But she's so gentle and nurturing." Mia and the others would often refer to Hilily—and its Guardians—using the feminine pronoun even though the Guardians weren't female.

"Oh and she still is," Artemis happily replied. "If it wasn't for her healing sessions after class, I'm not sure any of us would have the ability to stand let alone walk."

"Okay, so what's the issue?" Mia asked in a state of confusion.

"The issue is that Hilily is no longer leading our training. Hikiko is. And she's clever, relentless and emotionally inflexible. Therefore, she won't let us quit regardless of how tired or exhausted we are." All the Cuban girls were standing to the left and right of Artemis nodding in agreement.

"Okay, so I think I understand — the combat drills are more difficult?"

"Ha." Some of the girls laughed with a sarcastic tone then covered their mouths.

"What am I missing?" Mia questioned at the girls' odd behavior.

Artemis looked back at her sisters and gave them a *be quiet* look — and everyone took a deep breath and was silent. "Well, the truth is that their attacks are harder, faster and more focused than any of us are able to repel."

"Really?"

"Yes."

"Then I suggest you not be there."

"What do you mean? These classes are mandatory."

"Yes, and I'm not talking about the classes. I'm referring to their strikes. If their attacks are harder, faster and more focused than any of you are able to repel then I suggest you not be there when the assaults come."

Artemis looked around at her sisters and then back at Mia and said, "Mia, we're not as fast as you."

"Really, you think I'm fast?"

The girls just nodded frantically in agreement and Heather said, "Mia, you're so fast, you're like invisible when you want to be."

"Ha," Mia chuckled, "I'm no faster than any of you. I just choose not to be there when the punches and kicks come at me."

Again, Artemis looked around at the others and most of the girls just shrugged in confusion. Then Artemis turned back to Mia and said, "We don't get it."

"Mia tilted her head to the side and in a gentle, nurturing voice said, "It's okay, I'll just show you. Artemis, swing at my head — and don't hold back."

"Really?"

"Yes. Go on."

Artemis punched at Mia's face and couldn't believe the results.

"Again," Mia cried out. Artemis swung at her again.

"Go on. Again," Mia said encouragingly.

Artemis vigorously kicked and punched at Mia's head from all sides and Mia just stood there and not one strike made contact. Artemis along with the other Cuban girls were in awe of what they saw.

"How? How is that possible, Mia? Are you a hologram?" Artemis questioned.

"No, but it's like I've said, I choose not to be there when you try to hit me."

"Mia, you're smarter than the rest of us too. So you're gonna have to spell it out. How are you doing it?" Artemis questioned for the group.

"Wait, I think I get it," Charlotte let out.

"Really?" Artemis stated in the form of a question.

"Explain it to them, Charlotte, I have other issues to tend to."

As Mia walked off, Charlotte said, "Look, we've been looking at this all wrong. Mia is trying to tell us that we are still thinking like corporeal beings which we're not. Time and space is not linear to us — not anymore."

Exactly. Mia thought to the group.

Everyone thought about Charlotte's explanation then brought both hands to their chest and sighed, "Aww."

"Oh my God, Mia is so smart," Juno let out. "I get it."

"Me, too," the other girls thought in unison.

Incredible, Heather thought.

Mia thought to the group, *Now you can all be at peace.*

CHAPTER 8

Disciples Assigned Harem
Tuesday, July 16, 2047 2 p.m.

HILILY TELEPORTED TO THE PASSAGEWAY IN FRONT OF THE Monarch's rest chamber. Transport coordinates to every location were restricted. In order to maneuver through space using Harem portals a seven-section, one-hundred-fifty-digit location cypher was required. However, even if you were in possession of a location code, your individual forty-digit identification encryption number had to be approved for that particular site. And the code was directly linked to specific DNA markers of an approved Harem. Access to transport location cyphers and travel approval were regulated by the Office of the Universalus Ministerium de Transportation ac Inpigre.

Once a Harem completed its five Internships, the Monarch presented the individual with an Adamic in the presence of God. That entity was then granted full access to control time and space — if required.

The Adamic also granted the user infinite retrieval of information and knowledge, if essential to a Harem's duties. It also provided access to celestial passageways to any world in the known universes. In addition, it could be used to defend against the forces of evil. This divine instrument functioned on organic parts and was known to the Harem as 'Οικουμενικής'. The combination of the item's organic components and the user's DNA allowed the holder access to the Akashic records.

Hilily approached the Monarch's chamber and its presence was announced. The security force field was released and Hilily was made visible.

"Hilily, please come in."

"Thank you, Your Eminence, what may I do for you?" The Monarch's other two aides were already in the room.

"I have assigned you as the principal Guardian to Yehoshuah and his current disciples. You will assign protectors to each, but I will expect you to take the lead in ensuring their safety." Since the Rapture, the Monarch would occasionally refer to Hoshea by his former Hebrew name. Heymie was his mother and actually knew him on Earth by that name. Hoshea's name over millennia was eventually translated into Greek, then Latin and finally English to mean Jesus. However, no one in Harema ever used those names.

Hilily selected the Defensive Arts as its primary responsibility long ago. As such, Hilily applied itself and advanced among the ranks quickly. This discipline had three ranks or levels. Protectors were level one and were responsible for watching over assigned souls. Each had special abilities to help their assignee overcome temptation. For example, if a particular being had a weakness for gambling, they would be dispensed a Protector which specialized in overcoming that weakness.

Defenders, or level two Protectors, were more disciplined, more focused and more apt to control the possibility of fear and apprehension associated with combat. These brave souls fought to repel the forces of evil. Their training was more focused on advanced aerial combat techniques and maneuvers.

Guardians were level three Protectors and the most experienced and honored among their clan members. Many Guardians possessed hundreds of millennia of advanced evil resistance training and were considered above reproach. They were assigned to watch over those souls the council deemed important to the survival of a particular species. They also protected the council members. Every cabinet member had three aides assigned and at least one was always a Guardian.

Hilily assured Heymie that Hoshea's twelve new faith leaders would be protected. "I will keep them mentally safe and out of permanent harm, Your Eminence." Hilily had the gift to heal.

"Hilily, I have no doubt you will. However, please keep in mind the end game is near. Helucifer will stop at nothing to drive these beings insane with the hopes of snaring their souls forever."

"Yes, Your Eminence." *Perhaps the Monarch didn't have to make that last statement,* Hilily thought. *Nevertheless, it was made, but why? The Monarch never says anything without cause.* Then it occurred to Hilily. *This assignment might be my last.* Hilily had to assure the Monarch that if required, it would gladly surrender its existence for the survival of the disciples under its care.

"Your Eminence, I hope you realize that I would gladly sacrifice myself—"

The Monarch interrupted Hilily. "Don't you dare say it. Don't even think it." The scolding look on Heymie's face made Hilily bow its head from the maladroitness of the moment. Heymie reached out and lifted Hilily's face with a finger. "Hilily, look at me." A few seconds went by and Hilily slowly opened its eyes. "Good. Now, it would not be acceptable for you to perish in the protection of anyone under your care. I need you by my side, as does Yehoshuah and his ardent followers. I simply meant that you must bring to bear whatever forces are required to ensure the existence of everyone, including yourself. Is that understood?"

"Yes, Your Eminence."

"Then say it. I need to hear you say it."

"I will command whatever forces are required to ensure the continuation of Hoshea, his devotees and myself."

"Excellent," the Monarch replied then leaned forward and hugged Hilily. "You had me worried for a moment." Heymie pushed Hilily at arm's length and said, "Please don't ever do that again."

"Yes, Your Eminence. And I'm so sorry. I should have interpreted your wishes more carefully."

"Let's not speak of it again."

"Yes, of course, and thank you for your understanding."

Heymie handed Hilily a list of names. Hilily opened the list and read it.

Just then, Heymie confirmed the list verbally. "Of the new

disciples, Yvette, Winnie, and Akachi will be the most exposed and yield the greatest retribution on the forbidden planet. However, the others will in fact need more support before the end. It might require additional assistance from perhaps the Cuban family members. However, they will require mobility to and from Earth. Therefore, you must assign watchful eyes and additional support to keep this group safe."

"I understand, Your Eminence," Hilily answered, although shocked and completely unsure as to the reasoning behind the names.

How can such seemingly venal souls be responsible for converting those left behind on the forbidden planet? I'm confused as to how this decision was reached or how these individuals of bribable character could achieve what would be asked of them. However, their questionable morality at this point is not my concern. I was directed to focus on their safety. That mission is paramount.

I am certain their selection will astonish and awe me at some point in the future, just as all of Hoshea's prophecies have done thus far. I must pull together the most experienced team possible considering these individuals' past transgressions. Hilily premeditated, and then the obvious rang out. *Perhaps their past indiscretions and corruptibility was exactly what would be required to help save the lost on the forbidden planet. If they could be saved, anyone could.*

"Hilily, I see the concern on your face. But consider that perhaps it's only these tainted spirits that will be able to cope with the dangers, the horrors, and the persecution enough to resist or thwart temptation and keep the faith. Everything else required they will receive from Yehoshuah and you." Heymie knew Hilily had concerns but felt that soon these followers' actions would impart confidence and remove any doubt.

My beliefs have been confirmed, Hilily confessed internally. *These entities don't have to deal with all the self-induced uncertainties and misfocused logic. In short, they have been exposed to such horrific losses already that nothing will seem impossible and therefore overcoming insurmountable odds might be more probable.*

However, I can't help but feel trepidation. These poor shameful followers will continuously face humanoid seniors which are intransigent. The believers left behind cling to a false belief framework and often reject descending opinions regardless of the evidence.

Hilily shook its head and said, "Well, Your Eminence, I will ask Hikiko to help. I will split the devotes into two groups, having a Guardian and three Saints per team. I will lead one team with Artemis, Holly, and Juno. Hikiko will lead the other with Charlotte, Heather and Samantha.

"Excellent."

Suddenly, the Monarch changed the topic. "Tell me, how is the Cuban family training sessions progressing?"

"The Cuban girls are extraordinary. And even Axel, with such a gentle spirit, has had the fortitude to excel."

"That's wonderful news. I'd like to hear specifics, so Hilily, please elaborate."

"Yes, of course. The Cuban girls' strategies and techniques are being adopted into the Harem Defensive Arts curriculum."

"As I expected."

Really, Hilily thought, and then asked, "Your Eminence, excuse my ignorance, but how did you know that would happen?"

"Because they're Saints, forged in the midst of horrors and tragedy most Harem cannot comprehend. Their spirit is above reproach. And everything they do is for the glory of God and the righteous.

"Of course, Your Eminence." Hilily felt a little embarrassed having asked a question to what now seemed so obvious."

"And Hilily, there is no need to feel embarrassed. This is new to all of us."

Hilily looked up at Heymie with amazement. *How did the Monarch know what I was feeling?* Hilily internally questioned.

To Hilily's continued wonder, Heymie added, "And I know what you're feeling because I know you, plus it's written all over your face." Then Heymie smiled and finished by saying, "Please continue."

"Yes, of course. The girls' raw abilities are so awe-inspiring that it's difficult for my Defenders to not be mesmerized with their performance." Hilily continued the synopsis while trying to contain noticeable exhilaration. "Whenever my team conceives of a way to penetrate their defenses, they seem to have a contingency plan in place to foil our advances. And these alternative tactics are not defenses I have taught them. They are sitting down and developing these maneuvers independently of my instructions. It's remarkable. In my one billion years, I have never seen or heard of anything like it."

Hilily took another few seconds to compose its state of astonishment then continued. "It also appears that they are choreographing complex aerial maneuvers simply to see if it can be done. Most are so beautiful and graceful that their opponents — my Defenders — don't realize they are being distracted until they are struck down by powerful blows to the legs or poked in the eye.

"And yes, Your Eminence, you heard me correctly, I said poked in the eye. Their maneuvers keep them either extremely high in the air or very low to the ground. And they only get close when they can strike their opponents' foundation mercilessly or poke their adversaries in the eye. For some reason this activity makes them giggle and they seem to keep score.

"Unfortunately, the girls unconsciously or innocently consider our combat sessions a game. Although the young Saints actions are irritating to some, my Defenders remain steadfast. Nevertheless, we have recently developed a strategy to challenge their raw intellect. I have placed Hikiko in charge of their training and it has made a considerable difference in toughening them up."

"It's good to hear that progress is being made, but you're in a difficult position, Hilily. They're young spirits. And therefore, having fun is part of this educational process. If you get too serious, you may eliminate the joy and curtail their creativity. However, that said, if you don't emphasize the importance of this training, they will most certainly realize it when it's too late.

"We most certainly do not want to lose one of these young souls in any engagement, let alone their first. Unfortunately, something has to give. As I said, you're in a difficult position. Do what you must to safeguard these souls but stress the significance of these exercises." The Monarch turned and started to walk away.

Hilily raised a hand up to ask the Monarch if its current approach was sufficient but after considering the question, it was glad the Monarch missed the request.

"However..." Heymie knew Hilily well enough to realize it still had questions. Heymie turned around to finish its train of thought. "Hilily, girls will be girls. Rejoice in the knowledge that they generate such visual splendor and encourage their creativity. There will always be time for reality. I would suggest you develop a way to incorporate these techniques into an assault campaign. Their maneuvers are so radically different, any opponent on the field will be caught off guard and placed in a perpetual state of conjecture."

"Yes, Your Eminence. I totally agree. And that crusade is already being formulated."

"Excellent. I also suggest you bring in just Guardians for the next few waves of training. Leave the less experienced Defenders behind to observe. Soon the Cuban clan will regain the upper hand and you want as many observers as possible. I also suggest you continue to change their training venue and force the girls to work in lower lighting.

"If you obscure their line of sight to potential targets, in addition to limiting their space, the ability to execute aerial maneuvers will be thwarted. However, knowing you and Hikiko, something tells me these factors have already been considered. Unfortunately, this advantage will not last long, so continue to introduce new and more complex variables."

"Yes, Your Eminence."

"Oh, and you were correct. You're too close to these girls. It was clouding your judgment and objectivity. Separating yourself from their primary training sessions was the correct decision. Little good will come from your attachment to them while functioning as their instructor."

"Yes, you're correct, of course."

"Now excuse me, Hilily, I have other matters to attend to."

"Yes, Your Eminence." Hilily left the Monarch's rest chamber and returned to its own.

Hilily's Curatoria, Hanico, was lying in wait, ready to pounce on Hilily when it walked in. Hanico wanted to play. Hilily's Curatoria resembled a snow leopard—Panthera Uncia on Earth—which normally inhabited the mountain ranges of Central and South Asia but it was twice as big. Hilily's leopard was a male and weighed approximately 110 kg, or 243 pounds. He had a body measuring in length from the head to the end of its tail 300 cm, or 10 feet. However, the tail was quite long, at 200 cm. Hanico had short, stocky legs for such a big cat, standing about 120 cm at the shoulders.

Hanico had long, thick fur and its base color was smoky gray, with whitish underparts. He had dark grey to black open rosettes on his body, with small spots of the same colors on its head and larger spots on its legs and tail. Hanico had pale blue eyes.

Hilily entered the room and was almost knocked down.

"Easy, boy. Yes, yes, yes, I'm happy to see you, too. But we'll have to play later, I'm mentally exhausted. Just come here and lay down next to me for a little while. I need some company while I clear my head and think."

Hanico, being emotionally connected with Hilily, felt the stress so he quickly acquiesced to the request. He climbed on top of the sofa first and Hilily curled up in the middle of his fur.

"That's a good boy."

Hilily was emotionally numb. *I already knew everything the Monarch had said or suggested. The question is why? Why am I so emotionally attached to these girls? Why am I so excited to be around them? I have trained my whole life but have never been so exhilarated during drills before. Why now? I have been guarding these types of souls for hundreds of thousands of years. Perhaps it's the fact that for the first time in my life, I have actually physically touched them or talked to them or cried and laughed with them.*

It's now crystal clear why Hoshea longed to be around humanoids. And to think, this whole time I thought humans were a bunch of vile savages. These saints are indeed remarkable. Perhaps that was the missing factor I never considered. Regardless of their shortfalls, once cleansed, their true magnificence is revealed, Hilily confessed to itself while lying back on Hanico with its fingers laced behind its head.

The Monarch was right, the emotional allure is too great. They are such a joy to be around. It makes me wish I was young again, if only for a month, a week, a day.

Hilily never actually realized how powerful the Cuban girls' presence would impact its life. *I must develop a strategy when dealing with them or it will be my undoing.*

Hilily was alerted by a soft chime; there was an unexpected announcement at the chamber entrance.

"Yes, who is it?"

A feminine mechanical voice replied, "Your Grace, your visitor has identified itself as Artemis."

"Okay, well, open up and let her in."

Artemis stepped through the threshold and the force field materialized behind her resembling the wall.

"That's cool," Artemis reacted and then added, "I don't

believe I will ever get used to that."

Hilily's rest chamber was like all the rest—clean, sterile-looking, and tranquil. Everything seemed to be made of an aqua-colored glass and the room had very little furniture.

Just like Hoshea's room, there was a desk protruding from the wall on the left as you walked in. Around the desk were a few high-back chairs made from crystal with maroon velvet cushions on the seats, backs and arm rests. In one corner of the room was a large, oval-shaped sofa with a white mattress and matching pillows. Hanico was still laying on it. The sofa back was angled up to resemble a futuristic futon which sat on a large, oval, glass-like pedestal.

There were hundreds of old musty books and mementos collected during the many campaigns Hilily was involved in spanning almost a billion years. It was extremely rare for Hilily to have visitors. Aside from Hoshea and the Monarch, who dropped by a few times in a thousand years, there had never been anyone there.

Since the Harem people never slept, there was no real sleeping area. However, the corner sofa was an area where Hilily longed to someday lie back and read or cuddle with friends or family. This had occasionally happened with Hoshea. It was pleasant and memorable.

"I'm sorry, Hilily, is this a bad time?" Artemis asked, unsure what to make of the blank expression on Hilily's face. Hanico stepped off the sofa and Artemis looked around Hilily and said, "Hi, boy."

Hanico released a soft growl.

"Hanico, hush," Hilily exclaimed commandingly. "Go lay down over there." The big snow leopard walked over to the right side of the room and laid down by the bookshelves. Hilily then quickly walked over to Artemis and took her hand and said, "Come," yanking her forward.

"Easy, girl, you're being a little rough," Artemis quickly shared.

It was hard for Hilily to hide its excitement at having company. Plus it had very little experience with personal interaction. Before Hoshea, and the Monarch, Hilily had no memory of physical contact with anyone.

Hilily dropped Artemis's hand. "I'm so sorry, I have little experience touching people."

"I can tell," Artemis replied with a smile.

Hilily bowed its head in embarrassment. "You can go if you wish, I realize I'm awkward."

Artemis picked up Hilily's face and said, "You're so cute, I, like, so totally love you. Brace yourself, you big baby."

"What—?"

Before Hilily could get another word out, Artemis jumped up and wrapped both arms and legs around Hilily.

"Oh." Hilily sighed as it stepped back from the initial collision. Hilily hugged Artemis back and said, "And I so totally love you, too, Artie."

"Ha. Artie, that's so cute, I love it. So can I stay for a little while?" Artemis questioned as it pulled itself away to look into Hilily's eyes.

Hilily was so happy; it took all its strength to keep from crying. "Yes, of course you can stay," it muttered out.

"Good." Artemis stepped off and Hilily kissed her on the cheek before walking over to the sofa and sitting down.

"That was nice. You are the only girl who has ever kissed me aside from my sister, Jun. But your kiss was nicer." Artemis giggled. "Kind of like a big slobbery baby."

"I'm so sorry, but until now, I've never given anyone a kiss. I have no experience in such matters."

"Wow, really?"

"Yes. You are also the first girl to kiss me. I don't know if you remember but you kissed me on the day of our first training session."

"Yes, of course I remember." Artemis and Hilily were lying back on the sofa. She looked over at Hilily and noticed a tear coming down its face and reached out to wipe it away.

"Why are you crying?"

"I'm just happy you're here."

Hilily is so cute, Artemis thought but then her mood changed when she considered that Hilily might no longer be happy when she revealed the reason for her visit.

"Artie, you do realize that I'm not a girl, right?"

"Well, that's what you tell me." Artemis sat up and

continued, "But you're not a boy, right?"

"No, not really."

"Well, that's kind of cryptic." Artemis laid back down again and said, "Well, you act like a girl, you look like a girl and you sound like a girl." Artemis sniffed the air and asked, "Are you wearing perfume?"

"Perfume? No, why?"

"Well, because," Artemis sniffed the air again and confessed, "you also smell like a girl. And on Earth we had a saying, 'if it looks like a duck, swims like a duck, and quacks like a duck, then it's probably a duck.'"

"Well, that might all be true, but I'm not a duck."

"Okay, but please do me a favor."

"Sure."

"Please don't freak me out by proving to me you're not a girl. I don't think I can handle that personal of a reveal. Is that okay?"

"Yes, of course, that request is more than reasonable."

"Unless it makes you uncomfortable that I think of you as a girl," Artemis then admitted apprehensively.

"No, it doesn't. And again, I find your wishes sensible. Plus, divulging that part of myself to someone else has never occurred to me. Well, until now anyway. So maybe we can just lie here together and relax.

"Of course." Hilily was as happy as it ever remembered being. Artemis took a slow, deep breath then reached out and took Hilily's hand and said, "I'm happy...you?"

"Yes. Happy and content."

"Me, too."

After a minute of silence, Hilily said, "Can you refrain from revealing your news for a few minutes?"

"Wait, what makes you think I have news?"

Hilily tilted its head down and gave Artemis a cold hard look.

"Okay, sorry. I'll share my 'no longer a secret' news with you whenever you're ready."

Both Hilily and Artemis were quiet for several minutes then Hilily asked, "So why do you wear those boots again?"

"I don't know," Artemis answered. "They're comfy and they

make me feel strong, I guess."

"Don't they make your feet smell?"

"I don't know, maybe, I've never thought about it."

"Well, I don't see how they couldn't."

"Really?" Artemis sat up and placed her right foot on the edge of the sofa and took off a boot. She leaned forward and placed the boot on the floor, then pulled her foot toward her face and took a whiff. Artemis leaned back down and said, "That's what I thought."

"What?"

"I don't smell anything."

"What? I'm not sure that's completely accurate."

"What?" Artemis readjusted her position and laid back perpendicular to Hilily, placing her foot in front of Hilily's face as she said, "Go on."

Hilily moved her head to one side to get a clear view of Artemis and said, "Go on and what?"

"Smell for yourself."

"Really?"

"Yes, you seem to doubt me, go on then, check for yourself. It's what sisters do."

Hilily crinkled the corner of its mouth and stared at Artemis for a few seconds to confirm she wasn't pretending. It quickly became apparent she wasn't playacting. So Hilily leaned forward and gently took hold of Artemis's foot and placed its nose close to her toes to take a sniff. Hilily pulled its head back then leaned forward and smelled again, then let go of her foot. Hilily sounded, "Huh," as it leaned back and laid down.

"Well?" Artemis questioned.

"Well, your foot is a little smelly."

"What?" Artemis sat back up, pulled her foot back up to her face and smelled again.

"I don't smell anything."

"Well, you haven't had a billion years to improve your olfactory senses."

Artemis took a deep breath and covered her mouth. "Jeepers, Hilily, I'm so sorry. I never considered that. Artemis closed her eyes and muttered out, "I'm a little embarrassed now."

"Oh, please," Hilily said to Artemis, "it didn't smell that

bad. I could barely smell anything. Your foot just smells a little sweaty. I actually like it. It's cute. It reminds me of you."

"Really? That's awesome, I remind you of sweaty feet?"

"Oh my goodness, no! That's not what I meant!" Hilily countered with an open hand over its heart, seemingly mortified. "It's just that you're a week old and have recently stopped sweating so the residual aftereffects are still noticeable. The scent is so different it's memorable. Plus, we have spent so much time training together, the smell of perspiration reminds me of you. That's all. It would probably not even be noticeable to anyone else but me, really."

"Oh, well thank you. That makes me feel so much better," Artemis informed Hilily with a pouty face.

"Artie, I love you more than you will ever know, whether you're sweaty or not. I would not change anything about you. I love you just the way you are."

"Stinky," Artemis retorted, still a little annoyed but mostly cradling her injured self-image.

Then Hilily, for the first time since it had known Artemis, came back with an uncharacteristically playful response, "Yep, the stinkier the better," then quietly chuckled.

Artemis visually maintained a frown for a few seconds then smirked and asked, "So you're cracking jokes now, huh?"

Hilily shrugged and gently smiled. Artemis sat up, lifted up Hilily's left arm and curled up under it. "I love you, too, but I'm not really stinky, am I?"

"No, of course not. You smell wonderful—like me." Hilily displayed a smile then added, "And I dare anyone to argue otherwise."

"Thank you," Artemis exclaimed then added, "I feel better."

"Good."

They both laid in silence again for a few more minutes then Hilily said, "So what's the news you found necessary to share with me in private?" Hilily questioned but was unsure whether Artemis's response would be received without unwanted heartache.

Artemis sat up and took hold of Hilily's hand, forcing Hilily to also sit up.

"Wow, this seems serious, Artie."

"Well, my sisters and I were talking to Mia and we figured

out how to defend ourselves against your attacks."

Hilily laughed out loud, then covered its mouth.

"What? What's so funny?"

"Really, that's your news?" Hilily questioned.

"Yes. So what's so funny? Tell me."

"You seemed to be carrying such a heavy burden and your news turns out to be no news at all."

"What? How can that be?"

"Well, the Monarch and I spoke about your training sessions about an hour ago and we deduced this would happen. I'm surprised it took you so long to figure it out."

"Really?"

"Yes. Of course. You're skills are remarkable."

"Thank you, but I still feel silly."

"Why?"

"Because I really thought my news would hurt your feelings and I was concerned for no reason," Artemis shared.

"I'm sorry, Artie."

"It's okay I guess. It's my fault for being so sensitive."

"No, it's mine for seeming so cold. So tell me, how can I make it up to you?"

"There's no need, really."

"But I want to, so tell me. How can I make you feel better?" Hilily questioned with genuine concern.

Artemis thought about it for a few seconds then admitted a truth to herself. And Hilily was probably the only person that would tell her what she desperately wanted to know. Since the moment she first saw a Curatoria on the battle field, she felt like she needed one. So she took a deep breath, sighed and said, "Hilily, tell me about your cat."

"Sure, but first you need to show me what you've discovered."

"Okay, and then you'll tell me about your Curatoria?"

"Yes."

"Okay, so stand up and try to hit me."

Hilily swung at Artemis repeatedly for almost a minute then stopped, fell to its knees and said, "You're astonishing."

"Not really."

"Artie, you make me question what I see happening before

my very eyes. I'm in awe of you."

"Please don't. And I'm not the only one with this ability. All my sisters sisters have it – to some degree."

"Then you're all anointed. And it doesn't make what you've done here any less magnificent."

"Okay, okay, stand up. You're freaking me out."

CHAPTER 9

Akachi is Discovered
Tuesday, July 16, 2047 2 p.m.

AKACHI STEPPED OUT OF THE TRANSPORT PORTAL INITIALLY cast by Hoshea when they were outside Jackson Memorial Hospital in Miami. It only took him a few seconds to realize he was back in Bangui, Africa. Bangui was the capital and largest city of the Central African Republic. It was established as a French outpost about one hundred sixty years earlier and named after the Ubangi River.

The city formed an autonomous commune covering an area of sixty-seven square kilometers. The city consisted of ten urban districts and two hundred neighborhoods. The Ngaragba Central Prisons were all located here which made canned food products, beer, shoes and soap big commodities.

Bangui had been the scene of intense rebel activity and destruction during decades of political upheaval, including the current year-old rebellion. As a result of political unrest, the city was recently labeled one of the top five most dangerous places to live in the world.

Many of the concrete structures were just shells. But the year-old rebellion had taken its toll on more than just the buildings. The roadways were dirt which hadn't seen a drop of rain in over a year. Craters were visible every so often left behind by mortar fire. And the citizens looked abused and spent. Sorrow ran deep in this land.

Wow, not much has changed, Akachi thought. *God's mercy is desperately needed here. I'm glad to be home. Since I haven't been here in five years, the only people who may remember me are the elderly. I should be safe for a little while. Luckily, the local militia members who wished to do me harm are no longer among the living. My past methods of dispensing justice spawned a form of finality which I hope is now behind me.*

However, I need to be cautious, my clothing will make me stand out. Akachi walked the five minutes to the Indasso Village and purchased some local attire and a few other items to help him generate a comfortable camp that night. He changed clothes, had them cleaned and bartered them away for a few extra provisions.

His sister, Adadi, managed a local orphanage nearby so he thought he would pay her a surprise visit. She always needed help and since no one knew they were related, she should remain safe after his departure. Twenty-five minutes later, he was knocking on one of the compound's heavy double wooden doors. He tried the door latch and since it was unsecured, he simply walked in. The settlement was a little less than half a hectare, or about an acre in size. It had a two-meter-high wall completely around it made of straw, hay and mud, so it was difficult to see anything or anyone inside.

"Adadi."

"Akachi?" she replied in the form of a question as she ran out of the main office to greet her little brother.

"Oh my goodness, Akachi, it is so good to see you. I've missed you so."

"And I've missed you, Maman," Akachi happily replied. He used the same term of endearment as the little ones in her care, which literally meant mother. "I hope it's okay that I stop by."

"Of course, you're always welcome here. You're my baby brother."

Adadi took him by the arm and they started walking into the camp. "Well, you look fit, dear sister. Life has been good to you, but I'm sure you have needs. So tell me, what can I do to help? I don't plan on staying long, so I want to do as much as possible before I go."

"Akachi, I don't want to ruin your trip by burdening you with my issues."

"Nonsense, your problems are my problems. God has sent me to you, so I need you to tell me what I can do to help."

She stopped to embrace him again then pushed him at arm's length and said, "Then I thank God for sending you."

Akachi smiled and replied while caressing her back, "Go on, Maman, put your little brother to work."

"Okay, but first, how about a tour?"

"Sure, that would be fabulous."

"Well, I'm so proud of the place we've built here."

"As you should be, Adadi, it's a blessing to so many."

"Well, you see our large playground on the right. The money to erect it was donated by many of the parents who adopted our kids. Anyway, it can comfortably accommodate fifty or sixty children."

"I'm sure the true joy comes from seeing the children playing on it," Akachi shared while still caressing his sister's back.

Adadi looked up at him teary-eyed and said, "Yes, yes, it does," then smiled and continued her little tour. "Well, over there we have a two-meter-square greenhouse which supplies most of our vegetable requirements. Even during difficult times we can feed fifteen to twenty people and most of our livestock on a routine basis.

"There's our small power station with a generator, a bank of batteries and solar panels on the roof. It easily keeps the water pump running, the lights on and a refrigerator running. Our school house is that light blue building just past the station. We have three classrooms which hold twenty children each. Along the far southwest wall are the boys' dormitories. To the left are our bathrooms. Four shower stalls in the middle, and three toilets on either side of the showers. We have six sinks, three on either side of the toilets. All the buildings were constructed using the same material we used on the walls."

They stopped and sat down by a burned out campfire and Adadi continued the tour. "The girls' dormitories are along the eastern wall and this here is our admin building and staff housing. That building there along the north wall is used for storage and the other small one is empty."

"Adadi, you've done a fantastic job of keeping this place going."

"I do it for the children."

"So now tell me, how can I help?"

Adadi took a deep breath and started sharing. "Well, it's been a struggle over the last week for me. Overnight, I lost all the children that were here. I was in such a dark place afterwards. However, God blessed me with eleven new ones to look after."

"Adadi, the children who are no longer here are in a better place. Find comfort in that." Adadi wanted to ask Akachi how he could possibly know that, but she could see the peace on his face and for some unexplainable reason, she knew he was right.

"Well, many of our stores were looted a few days ago by nearby villagers that heard all the children were taken. So, I now have very little to support my recent arrivals. As you know, the world outside these walls is in a constant state of chaos and this last week has drawn the madness closer to our doors. I'm afraid the local insanity will soon make its way past our walls and there is nothing the children nor I can do to stop it. To make matters worse, I have no money and we're just about out of food. And there are twelve mouths to feed here."

"Well, Adadi, be at peace, I'm here to help. You and the children will not go hungry."

Adadi squeezed Akachi's hand tight and repeated, "I'm so glad you're here."

"Me, too. So now tell me, why do you have so many children?"

"Where else would they be?"

"I honestly thought they would all be gone."

"Gone, gone where?" I'm not sure I understand what you're trying to tell me."

"I'm sorry, what I meant was that most of the children in the world were raptured. So it's odd to see so many in one place."

"Raptured, wow! I wouldn't use that word around here. Our regional government is working with the local criminal families to vanquish anyone and everyone that believes the disappearance of those missing was a result of biblical prophecy."

"I see."

"Anyway, the truth is that these kids used to work for the local thugs until a week ago. So they have lost their innocence. As a matter of fact, many were quite violent until a week ago. But I still think we can save them."

Akachi looked around and saw many of the children's heads sticking out from behind obstacles. To his surprise and joy, every little face he saw was surrounded by a blue aura.

"I agree, Adadi, they all appear to be redeemable, thanks to your tender touch and God's infinite mercy." He wanted to ask why she was still there but he knew there had to be a logical explanation. So instead, he asked, "So how old are the kids?"

"They all range from ten to sixteen years old."

Akachi shook his head and said understandingly, "So, without going into too many painful details, tell me what happened?"

"Well, like I said, the world was under siege, and I guess the chaos started in Bangui first. Anyway, all the local children's mentors, or employers, were hacked to bits by a new crime lord.

"Afterwards, all the children came here. And you know me, I can't turn anyone away."

"No, you've never been able to do that. And that is why they come." Akachi noticed that all the children now were peering out of the windows and doorways. "I'm noticing that every child in camp seems skittish, and none appear threatening. I have to say that I find it surprising given their background and the current state of the world, and the dangerous zone we live in."

"Not really, the criminals these children were associated with were brutally executed in front of them. It's enough to scare anyone straight."

"Perhaps, but regardless of the reason, the children all seem peaceful now and we can work with that."

"I agree. I'm just sad they had to witness something so horrific to finally see the light."

"Me, too." Adadi got up and walked into the parlor to put a pot of water on the wood stove to boil. Akachi followed and they continue their discussion over a cup of tea.

"So, Akachi, you do think it's more than just a remote possibility we can save these children?"

"Yes."

"Good, otherwise, they would grow up and continue the chain of violence."

Akachi looked around again just to make sure and every child on the property had a blue aura. *Isn't that interesting,* he confessed to himself, then asked, "Are these ten children all you currently have?"

"No, the oldest boy takes off every morning and doesn't come back until nightfall."

"How old is he and where does he go all day?"

"He's sixteen and I'm not sure where he goes, but he never causes any trouble here. I think he just uses this place as a free and safe place to sleep. And I'm okay with that."

"Afia was the son of the militia leader who was shot and killed like five years ago. Remember?"

"Yes, I remember."

"Well, rumor has it that the local government hired some freelance assassin to execute him and all his minions. No one asked any questions afterwards either. Even the local police dismissed it as local violence and never investigated the murders. It was a big deal around here. Finally, everyone thought the city was going to experience long-needed democracy. And for over four years, we did. The county was on its way to becoming part of a civilized nation and investments started pouring in. Then everything went crazy again."

Akachi didn't say anything but it was his form of justice that caused the county's democracy reaffirmation. Five years ago, he had returned home and executed every militia member responsible for the torture and murder of his family.

"I didn't know Ashanti had a child. Does Afia remember anything?"

"I'm not sure what he remembers but he was there when it happened. I think he was even injured by the crossfire. Anyway, it's sad when any eleven-year-old has to experience something like that."

"Yes, yes it is. But his father's death probably saved hundreds of lives."

"More like thousands. You probably don't remember but Ashanti was notorious for murdering at least four or five people every week, whole families in fact. We called him the 'Weekend

Butcher.'"

"I remember."

"He killed our whole family in one of his weekend rampages."

Adadi swallowed hard and replied, "I know. I think about that weekend often." Then she admitted to herself, *it always ends the same way, with everyone I love dying because of me. If only I had been stronger...* Adadi's thoughts trailed off. She shook her head and asked, "So, how long are you planning on staying?"

"For as long as I'm needed."

"Really?"

"Yes."

"That's amazing," Adadi shared, teary-eyed. "It will be a great joy to have a strong man around camp tending to our safety and needs."

"I will do what I must."

Akachi gathered all the children and introduced himself. He entertained the boys while his sister set up the table for lunch. Everyone sat down to eat and talked about all the activities required to ensure their safety. Some of the older boys talked about how they could grow a few more vegetables like potatoes and cabbage. Those were hearty plants which could easily keep them fed. The camp went through two kilos of rice every day and an assortment of vegetables and some meat, normally a chicken or a few fish. They still had eleven chickens, a rooster, and about two dozen chicks running around. The chickens provided eggs in the short-term but they required livestock food. Their small fish farm provided a fish or two three times a week but like the chickens, it also required livestock feed. And having livestock requirements complicated matters.

Currently, no one knew Adadi was establishing a homestead. However, if word got out that her camp was self-sufficient, many more would come looking for handouts. This placed her and the children at great risk from returning looters.

"Adadi, I didn't bring much with me but I do have nine kilos of rice and five cans of spam."

"What?! Akachi, that's amazing. That will literally feed us all for another five days. And it gives us some time to replenish our supplies. With that, we now have a solid two weeks of food if I stretch it a little."

"How's the water situation?" Akachi asked, knowing that in a dry climate, water was always a concern.

"Good. We have a well on the other end of the camp and we store four two-hundred-liter barrels of water in the event of a serious drought. The showers are regulated and timed and we have low-flow toilets.

"We have a bank of twelve batteries which runs the well pump and solar panels keep the batteries charged. We use the excess power to run the bedroom and living area lights at night."

"That's fantastic. Okay, so tomorrow, I'll go out and purchase some additional supplies. I'll also visit a few vendors that carry livestock feed and try to cut a deal. Who knows, I may get lucky and also find a few kilos of meat at a reasonable price."

Adadi smiled then said, "Akachi, it's a blessing to have you back. But please make sure you don't buy livestock feed locally."

"Oh, of course not, that'll draw unwanted attention to us."

"Yes, exactly."

Akachi went to walk away but added, "Adadi, you do realize that you're the true blessing for these children, right?"

"Perhaps."

"Adadi, this place is important, now more than ever." Adadi bowed her head and uttered "thank you," then hugged Akachi and excused herself for the night.

"Goodnight, Akachi."

"Goodnight, Maman."

Nightfall came and went and Akachi was off early to search for provisions. He took several empty backpacks with him and purchased small amounts of food at different places. It cost more but it didn't draw any attention to what he was doing and the fact that he was stockpiling food and other provisions. That could easily make the camp a target for crime. In the event of unexpected looters, they hid all but the current day's food requirements. Fish was salted or smoked and placed deep underground in a disguised food cellar.

Akachi always traveled a little farther from home every day for additional supplies. He didn't want to shop in the same area twice in the same week. It was easier to stay anonymous. Akachi also made it a point to stay away from Afia for multiple reasons.

Unfortunately, Akachi's anonymity was betrayed by what he'd witnessed. He found villages, whole communities, starving and felt he had to do something. So something was exactly what he did. He used the divine power granted him by Hoshea and fed the hungry. Day after day he went out, purchased food and fed whole communities that were experiencing hunger. The news of his deeds was spreading fast but he didn't care. No one there actually knew who he was. At first just hundreds and then thousands were being fed daily. Akachi professed a message of peace and love to all that would listen. Every day he'd traveled a little further out and never stopped at the same village twice. He commuted to a new location every morning before sunrise and returned to Adadi's camp after sunset under the cover of darkness.

On the morning of the sixth day, Afia noticed Akachi leaving the camp before sunrise. He asked a few of the other kids for information on the stranger. However, unbeknownst to him, the children had been well briefed by both Akachi and Adadi. All the children said that Akachi had shown up the night before and needed a place to sleep. Maman, being so kindhearted, let him spend the night by the camp fire for a cup of rice.

Afia had an odd feeling about the stranger. Most men were not as gentle or quiet or chose to hide behind two-meter walls. He needed to be sure. Afia went after Akachi and found him a few hours later five kilometers from camp. He then followed him at a distance using a pair of binoculars given to him by his father on his eleventh birthday. It was the only item Afia had ever specifically received from his dad and he seldom used it. But when he did, it had always served him well. This stranger looked familiar but he wasn't sure why. He had to get closer.

Afia walked quietly behind him another five kilometers to the settlement of Boy-Rabe. He wasn't sure why Akachi was traveling so far from the village to pick up supplies easily acquired closer to camp. *This man is trying to hide something*, Afia thought, *and I have to know what that is.*

Afia got close enough to get a good look and then realized he had seen him before. While Akachi was in the market, Afia negotiated with a local business man to borrow his phone and take a picture of the stranger. Afia pretended to take a picture of some kids playing in the street to capture Akachi's likeness without suspicion.

The local business man charged Afia five thousand CFA Francs to print a color image of the photo. Afia took a cab back into the local town near Adadi's camp and went around showing the picture to everyone he could.

No one had ever seen the man in the picture Afia was showing around. He was about to give up when a local business owner recommended Afia show the image to one of the oldest citizens in town.

"Mr. Dalila has worked for the Christian mission in town for almost sixty-five years," the business man explained. "He knows everyone."

Afia thanked the man and left. He ran to the mission and quickly found the elderly gentleman. He raised the picture in front of Mr. Dalila and asked, "Do you know this man?"

"Yes, he was born near here. I believe his name is Akachi."

"What can you tell me about him?" The old man knew who Afia was and that the boy could easily be dangerous. However, if he answered his questions and seemed uninterested, there should be no trouble.

"I think his family was killed maybe twenty-five years ago."

"Killed? Killed by whom?"

"I would guess the local militia at the time. But who knows such things."

"Have you seen him recently?"

"No."

"What was the last time you saw him?"

"Maybe five years ago."

"Where?"

"Here."

"Here? Here like in town or in this mission?"

"Here in this mission. He had been shot like five times. He was here on the same day Doctor Milagro was gunned down. The same day your father died."

Afia was starting to put the pieces together but wanted to be sure. *This man had something to do with my father's death,* Afia confessed to himself. *But anyone that could kill ten men single-handedly and get shot five times and still survive is dangerous. I need to be cautious.*

"Did you talk to him back then, five years ago? Did he shoot and kill my father?"

"No, I didn't talk to him. And I don't know who might have killed your father, son.

"If you suspect him, perhaps you should involve the police. But I always found Akachi to be an agreeable chap. As a matter of fact, there are rumors circulating that he is going around feeding whole communities with just a handful of food. People are claiming he's performing miracles. He doesn't sound like someone who might have committed such a crime."

"Thank you, old man."

Afia sat down and looked at the picture and asked himself over and over again, "How do I know this man? Did he kill my father?"

Afia asked the same questions so many times that at one point the old man thought Afia was asking him a question, so he said, "I guess anything is possible. Maybe Akachi was the sort long ago, a criminal I mean, and has found peace in charity work today. However, it's hard to escape your true core or your past. Maybe you should check the wanted posters around town or at the police headquarters."

Afia stood up, thanked the old man again and left, running to the police station. He looked through the most wanted board and there at the bottom right-hand corner was a picture of Akachi. He was wanted for an assortment of crimes and there was a number listed at the bottom and a reward — one million Francs.

"I knew it." Afia wrote down the number and ran off to find someone with a telephone.

CHAPTER 10

Reynolds' Hunt Intensifies
Tuesday, July 23, 2047 2 p.m.

"DR. WILSON, THIS IS LIEUTENANT REYNOLDS. I SEE YOU'RE still the hospital administrator at Jackson Memorial."

"Yes, Lieutenant, and congratulations on your promotion."

"Thank you, Doctor, and to what do I owe the honor of this call?"

"Well, Lieutenant, one of the doctors on staff told me such an incredible story, I thought it warranted an investigation and perhaps your full attention."

"I see, well, you have my attention, Doctor, so go on."

"We found blood."

"Blood?"

"Yes, Lieutenant, alien blood."

Reynolds wasn't sure why the doctor was calling him with E.T. stories. *I'm involved in a worldwide man hunt and my staff has me taking calls from a fruit-loop. I need to ask my assistant to screen my calls better or there's going to be hell to pay. This is ridiculous,* Reynolds confessed to himself.

"Okay, Doctor, so what does that have to do with me? What makes you think I can help? Shouldn't you be calling the sci-fi tabloids or something?"

"Lieutenant, you don't understand, we found alien blood from the creature you have been pursuing for over a week."

Reynolds sat up and placed an elbow on his desk and asked, "You found blood which belongs to the alien we initially discovered in the hospital a week ago?"

"Yes, Lieutenant."

"Where is it? Where's the blood?"

"My geneticists have several small vials in storage. But it's the test results which are beyond belief."

"How so?"

"Well, Mr. Reynolds, with all due respect, the information is too complex to discuss over the telephone. I have asked the doctors to make themselves available for a Q&A session, at your convenience, of course."

"Very well, Doctor, I can be there in say, ten minutes."

"Fantastic. If you come in through the emergency room, I will be waiting for you to escort you to the lab. My team will be on standby in ten minutes."

Reynolds hung up the telephone and said, "Girls, let's go." The lieutenant stood up then finished his thought. "Oh, and this will probably turn out to be a messy scene, so please stay alert. If I give you the word, you do what has to be done to protect this mission and our country, understand?"

Both Nikki and Vikki nodded in the affirmative.

Reynolds quickly made is way out of the office building and to his car. His two bodyguards were close behind. Vikki opened the back door to the sedan and Reynolds got in. She climbed in after him and told the driver where to go.

Nikki jumped into the front passenger seat and said, "Let's go," to the driver who had been sitting in the car most of the day.

They arrived in front of the emergency entrance to Jackson Memorial ten minutes later and everyone got out of the car except the driver.

"Wait here," Vikki directed the chauffeur.

Reynold and his bodyguards were greeted and escorted to the laboratory on the fifth floor where six of the eight geneticists on staff were assembled around a monitor.

"Lieutenant, this is Dr. Penn, this is Dr. —"

Reynolds interrupted Dr. Wilson and said, "Doctor, let's dispense with the formalities, shall we? Time is our enemy here, we need to press on. So please, tell me what you've discovered."

Dr. Wilson cleared his throat and said, "Very well," while motioning to Dr. Jay Penn.

Jay stepped forward and pulled up an image of human blood on the monitor from a hospital server. "Lieutenant, this is a magnified image of human blood. There's an estimated twenty-five thousand human protein-coding genes. This is going back 200,000 years which eventually formed the anatomically modern Homo-sapiens we are today. This is the blood we discovered." Dr. Penn pulled up another image and held his breath.

"Okay, and? What am I looking for? I don't really see any difference."

"All the doctors' mouths dropped in unison and they all looked at each other."

Reynolds noticed the look of disbelief on everyone's faces and said, "I'm sorry, doctors, but did I miss something?"

"Lieutenant, if we were to physically evolve as a species for say, fifty billion years, that's billions with a 'B', we would not achieve this level of sophistication. But aside from that, these markers here," Dr. Penn brought up a few additional images with flags identifying specific areas which spanned the length of the whole image, "these markers make us who we are. Every one of those markers is in the alien's DNA but in one millionth the space."

There was silence in the room for about five seconds when finally Reynolds asked, "Okay, which suggests what, Doctor?"

"Well, which suggests, Lieutenant, that this blood sample belonged to a human. Or to a being that, once upon a time, maybe, one hundred billion years ago, was in fact a human."

Reynolds crinkled his brow and the corner of his mouth. Nikki and Vikki were standing at arm's length behind him, about a meter apart and completely expressionless.

"Or it was always human," another doctor interjected.

"Meaning it never went through an evolutionary process like us. Although, that's only a theory," another doctored spouted.

The doctors in the room realized by the expression on Reynolds' face that he didn't understand the importance of this discovery. Another doctor stepped forward and joined the presentation.

"Mr. Reynolds, picture the thickness of a tank's steel hull and the armor it represents for the people inside. Can you picture it?"

"Sure, I know what a tank looks like."

"Good, now, everyone knows that Jupiter is huge. It has thirteen hundred times the volume of Earth. Now, imagine that tank I mentioned having armor the thickness of Jupiter."

"Okay, so that would be pretty thick armor. And..." Reynolds trailed off.

"And? Well, if you compared the evolutionary process of our blood to this sample, it would be like comparing the volume of Jupiter to the volume of a human hair."

"I'm lost," Reynolds replied.

"Okay, so in short," Jay resumed the presentation, "we're all scientists here, so this is going to sound odd. But, if God truly exists and if God had blood, this would be it. This person, this being, or the entity this blood came from doesn't actually need a body at all. We've hypothesized that its appearance in human form is probably for our benefit."

"What?"

"You see, it's easier for us to interact and relate with other bipedalism—which look like us—versus say, a burning bush or a talking bright light."

Reynolds scrunched up his forehead again and shook his head then asked, "Look, doctors, isn't it possible that this alien is just a person who has been around for a long time?"

Dr. Penn looked around at the others in the room then replied, "Sure, it's possible. But only if the person has been around six times longer than the beginning of time. Well, time as we understand it anyway."

"I don't get it," Reynolds replied.

"By our estimates, this blood appears to be sixty to seventy billion years old—at least."

"So..."

"Really? Okay so we, as in scientists, proved or thought we proved that the existence of everything started about fourteen billion years ago with the big bang. And this blood is six times older." The doctor was met with a blank stare.

"Wow, okay, Lieutenant. So, do you believe in God?"

"No."

"Well, neither did we. Not until just recently anyway. The point is that some of us believe this being, this entity, could be God, or a god."

"What?"

"You know, like Jesus Christ, God? The one who so many are claiming has come back to gather the righteous unto him? Lieutenant, I'm sure you've noticed."

"Noticed what?"

"That only the innocent were removed from the world. Including everyone we as a species would have considered to be wholesome, gentle and good." Dr. Penn saw the look on Reynolds' face and realized they would soon be cut off. "Look, Lieutenant, in our opinion, if this entity has a message, we, as in the world, need to listen. Failure to do so could very easily be the beginning of the end."

"The end of what?" Reynolds asked with a look of bewilderment.

The doctors once again looked around at each other and Dr. Penn said, "Everything."

"Okay, I've heard enough."

Reynolds leaned back toward Vikki and whispered, "These guys are all a bunch of fruit-loops, get ready." Nikki leaned in and Vikki whispered into her ear then they stood at the ready once again.

"Where are your MRI machines?" Reynolds asked Dr. Wilson.

"On the second floor, why?" Reynolds held up a finger, suggesting he needed a few seconds before he could answer.

"And the hospital data is stored on IBM AS 400s?"

"AS 800s, actually, with one hundred thousand times the storage and processing power of their predecessors — in one third the space."

"Okay, I stand corrected. So where are they kept? Where is your data center?"

"It's in the basement, just past the hospital kitchen. Now, Lieutenant, can you please explain the reasons behind this line of questioning?"

"Thank you." Reynolds held up a finger again.

He leaned back and whispered into Nikki's ear, "Carrot Top, go to the third floor maintenance room and ask Andy to pull two large magnets out of an MRI machine. It shouldn't be any harder than removing the exterior cover and loosening up ten to twelve bolts from each magnet. Once you have the magnets, bring them down to the data center in the basement. Use thirteen as a secondary portable radio channel on your watch."

"Yes, sir." Nikki turned around and left the room.

"Lieutenant, please?"

Reynolds, who was still holding up a finger, said, "This is important, Doctor, just one more minute."

"Dr. Penn, do you have actual samples of the blood?"

"Yes, of course."

"Where?"

"In the bio storage room. I'm sorry, Lieutenant, but I'm not sure where you're going with these questions."

"I understand. My reasons will become clear in just a few seconds. Now, I just have a few more questions. The only two geneticists absent from this team are Dr. Chow Lee and Dr. Magnusson, correct?"

"Yes."

"I know Dr. Magnusson is in Sweden on vacation. But does he know of your discovery?"

"Yes, of course he does. He's the team's leader," Dr. Penn replied.

"Very well. Dr. Wilson, may I have a word with you please, in private?" Vikki opened the lab door for them. Dr. Wilson looked around, raised his hands up in a 'why' gesture then slapped his thighs when he brought his hands back down and stepped out.

Reynolds whispered into Vikki's ear, "Doll face, please contact Customs and Homeland Security and make sure Stefan Magnusson is on their TremEx lookout list. We need him here and he's never taken any of our calls."

"Yes, sir."

"Good, now —" Reynolds turned back to those in the room and said, "Please give us a few minutes, doctors. This won't take long." Reynolds walked out followed by Vikki. Before she closed the door behind them, she said, "Thank you all for your service to our country." Most of the doctors nodded so as to not appear rude but they knew something was wrong.

Vikki closed the door behind them and they stepped away.

"Now, Lieutenant, what's the meaning of all this?"

"Doctor, there is a traitor among your group."

"What?!"

"What's the portable radio channel in the hospital?"

"Twenty-six."

"Good." Reynolds pulled out his firearm and said, "Doctor, do not speak. Just listen. Your next actions will be the most important of your life. Please nod if you understand." Dr. Wilson nodded.

"Failure to comply with my requests will prove that you are either the traitor or in league with him. Nod if you understand." Dr. Wilson shook his head again.

"Good, now ask Andy where he is. If he's not in the maintenance room have him stop what he's doing and go there immediately. Nod if you understand." Dr. Wilson bobbed yet again.

"Good. Do it now."

The doctor nervously raised his wristwatch to his mouth and said, "Andy, this is Dr. Wilson, over."

Seconds later, Andy answered, "Yes, Doctor."

"Andy, where are you?"

"I'm in the maintenance room."

"Good," Reynolds stated. "Now, inform Andy that he will be receiving a visitor in just a few minutes. He is not to ask any questions but just do as directed, is that understood?"

"Yes, sir," Dr. Wilson replied.

"Andy, I've sent someone to see you. Please do what they ask without any questions. Do you understand?"

"Yes, Doctor, but should I stop what I'm working on? Does this take priority?"

"Yes, Andy, this takes priority."

"I understand. But I'll have to tell my supervisor."

"I'll take care of that."

"Okay."

"Well done, you have been completely exonerated. Just one more thing, since this is a police matter, please tell Andy that if he has any questions or concerns moving forward, he should ask me."

"Andy, this is Dr. Wilson again, over."

"Yes, Doctor."

"Andy, the person coming to see you is a police officer. Since you will be working on a police matter, if you have any questions about what you're doing, please voice them directly to Lieutenant Reynolds. He's on the hospital grounds and may be coming by to see you."

"I understand."

"I didn't ask you to say any of that," Reynolds stated with concern.

"I'm sorry, Lieutenant. I'm a bit nervous and your directions were vague, so I improvised a little."

"It's okay, but no more at hawk improv, understood?"

"Yes, sir. Sorry, Lieutenant."

"Now let's dismiss your team."

Wilson walked back past Reynolds toward the lab when he felt the back of his head go numb. There was searing pain emanating from the top of his skull from blunt force trauma. The doctor raised a hand up and placed it on the back of his head as his knees gave way. He turned around and stumbled back to see the butt of Reynolds' gun dripping blood. Vikki kicked the back of the administrator's knee and as he fell, she moved in, elbowed him to the face and knocked him unconscious. She grabbed Dr. Wilson under his shoulders and pulled him into an empty office where she sat him down in a chair and draped him over a desk to resemble a sleeping posture.

Reynolds pointed to the lab with his chin and Vikki opened the door, walked in and closed the door behind her. Six shots were fired in groups of two. Everyone was hunched down covering their ears when they looked up at Vikki and saw her wink.

She raised a finger to her lips and made a *shh* sound. Vikki walked up, kneeled in front of everyone and whispered, "Doctors, if you want to live through this event you need to remain quiet. And no one is to come out of this room for at least five minutes after I leave. Afterward, you go home, pack and never come back. Take whatever information you can and head out in different directions. Nod if you understand." Everyone nodded as they clung together in a small group. However, a few of the doctors mustered up the nerve to ask a question."

"Where would you suggest we go?"

"Anywhere but here."

"WHY? We haven't done anything."

"You've all seen too much. So if you want to live, run, and never look back. When you're in a safe place, get online and tell others what you've seen."

Without saying another word, Vikki stood up, turned, walked over to the door, left the room and pulled the door closed behind her. She and Reynolds walked to the elevator and took it down to the basement to wait for Nikki to show up.

"We might need to go back up and erase the files on the lab computer."

"That won't be necessary. I noticed Dr. Penn was retrieving the images off one of the hospital mainframes. So, all we need to do is erase the information on the mainframe hard drive."

They walked into the data room and were surprised.

"Oh boy!" Vikki exclaimed. "Which drive is the information on? There's a room full of computers here, plus they have backup tapes in there." Vikki pointed to another room.

"Easy, we'll just erase them all. The magnets Nikki will be bringing are huge with more than enough power to erase everything with ease.

Five minutes later, Reynolds asked, "What is taking her so long?"

Vikki pulled her arm up and pointed to her watch.

"Oh, thank you, Doll Face."

Reynold adjusted his watch and started talking. "Andy, where are you, over?"

"We're almost done here, Lieutenant, we need another two minutes," Nikki replied.

"Nikki, change your receiver to our secondary channel and call me back."

"Roger."

Seconds later, "I'm here, Lieutenant."

"Nikki, tell Andy we need a high frequency AC magnetic field to erase some computer drives. Make sure he brings the magnets and anything else we might require."

"Oui oui, monsieur."

"Oh, and ask him to find and bring four ball peen

hammers."

"Roger, no problem."

There was silence on the line for thirty seconds then Nikki spoke into her watch and said, "We're now thirty minutes out. Your new requirements have greatly increased our ETA."

"Nikki, ask Andy to gather some additional support from a few other maintenance men."

"Roger, stand by."

Sixty seconds later, Nikki got back on her watch and said, "Lieutenant, we're now seven minutes out."

"Perfect. Nice job, Carrot Top."

Nikki arrived with four maintenance men in tow, able and willing to do whatever she asked. Three of the four men started pulling hard drives. However, since they were going to be disabling hospital systems, she had the last man take her to speak with hospital security and their IT staff. Soon, Nikki had hospital employees spouting national security propaganda to keep the hospital running while Vikki, Reynolds and the others destroyed the hospital's computer infrastructure.

One hour and thirty-three minutes later, Reynolds, Vikki and Nikki were walking out of the hospital. Andy and the other maintenance men had helped Reynolds pull off what would have been a difficult job. They erased then smashed every hard drive from ten AS 800 servers then similarly destroyed the backup tapes under the belief it was a matter of national security.

Nikki stopped by the bio-lab and picked up the vials of alien blood with the help of her maintenance man escort before returning to the basement. A level of nervousness she was unaccustomed to came over her as soon as she took possession of the small bottles. She therefore handed the vials over to Vikki as quickly as possible. Vikki placed the ampoules in her pocket and felt an uncertainty surface concerning their mission. This type of anxiety was never present before, on any mission. Now, for the first time, an unexplained level of uneasiness filled her thoughts about their current assignment.

On the way back to the office, Reynolds received a telephone call from his assistant. He pulled out is cell phone and answered it.

"Reynolds."

"Lieutenant, is this a good time?"

"Yes, what is it?"

"Sir, we received word on our fugitives. Dr. Chow Lee and Dr. Milagro are in custody in Guantanamo Bay and have been there for three days."

"What the hell? Why wasn't I notified sooner?"

"The intelligence community is a secretive organization, sir. This information came across my desk by chance. However, it's been confirmed."

"Damn those bastards—"

Ginger interrupted Reynolds to say, "Sir, there's more. Akachi has been spotted in Bangui, Africa in a local orphanage camp."

"What?! Since when? How long has he been there?"

"I'm not sure, but we received the information about two hours ago from Interpol. I've been working on corroborating that information. And about five minutes ago, I found a local source that claims he has seen Akachi today, just several hours ago."

"That is fantastic news, give yourself a promotion."

"Yes, sir. And thank you, sir."

Reynolds covered the mouthpiece on his phone and informed the driver they had a change in destination. Reynolds returned to the phone call and asked his assistant to locate the pilots. "Please call the pilots and inform them to get the plane ready, I want to be wheels up as soon as possible."

"Lieutenant, I called the pilots two hours ago."

"Impressive, that was some forward thinking, young lady."

"Well, sir, I thought you might want to be the one that apprehends Akachi. Therefore, since your private plane is incapable of making such a long journey, I asked the pilots to appropriate one that could. They have been franticly looking for an aircraft. Five minutes ago, the main pilot called to say he located a 757 and was busy prepping the jet. It should be available and ready when you arrive."

"Fantastic."

"You should be receiving hangar information shortly."

Vikki received a text message seconds later which read, 'Aircraft on standby near Hangar 7.' She told the driver where to go and showed the text to Reynolds.

"Thank you, young lady, we've just received the hangar

notification."

"You're most welcome, Lieutenant." Reynolds terminated the call.

They arrive at hangar 7, boarded the aircraft and secured the plane for departure. The pilot got on the intercom and said, "Lieutenant, I have plotted our course to Bangui, Africa. We shall be airborne in just a few minutes. Our transit time from Miami is an estimated twenty-two hours and thirty-one minutes. It's 4:14 p.m. here, which should put us wheels down in Bangui at 2:40 p.m. tomorrow. We will refuel upon arrival. If you have any questions, please do not hesitate to ask. I have also taken the liberty of leasing a helicopter for the duration of our stay there. It will make it easier for you to move around. Bangui is a dangerous place. And ladies, please take your seats."

"Doll Face, please give the pilots my thanks and tell them I'm ready to depart."

Twenty-two hours and thirty minutes later, Reynolds' aircraft was landing. It took considerably longer to clear customs than initially anticipated. Due to this delay, their helicopter was appropriated by the local crime lord. Vikki leased Reynolds a car and they took off two hours after arriving with hopes of finally apprehending Akachi.

At 4:48 p.m. local time, Reynolds' car was stopped just outside the airport by a sedan with four thugs.

"These men work for the local crime family," the driver informed Reynolds.

"What do they want?"

"Money and anything else they find of interest or value."

"I see."

Three men got out of the car but the fourth stayed behind the wheel. The one with the machine gun stayed near the back door but the other two men stepped out in front of the sedan. They crossed their arms and just stood there like statues. Reynolds and the two girls got out and walked around to the front. Reynolds told the driver to keep the engine running.

"So who are these two skanks supposed to be?" one of the thugs questioned.

"Really? You don't ask me for my name or who I am. You just go straight for the insults. Very well, this is Nikki and she's my second lieutenant. Go on, Carrot Top, don't be shy."

"Oh really," the young African ruffian replied.

Vikki stood at the ready while Nikki gyrated her way in front of the two men while spinning her closed parasol over her shoulder. She stopped and put the umbrella under her right arm and started taking off her white glove. She fanned out the glove by slapping it on her open hand one too many times. Her glove flew off and landed on the ground in front of the men.

"Oops, sorry," Nikki squeaked out while prancing over to the glove on her tippy toes. She turned around and bent down to pick it up and intentionally flashed the men her derrière. As both men looked at Nikki's rear, she picked up her left leg and drove the eight-inch stainless-steel stiletto heel into the closest man's left thigh, then pulled it out. The thug made a heavy grunting noise as he bent down to grab his thigh. Nikki kicked up and drove the stiletto heel on her other foot through the man's throat and into his cerebellum.

The other hoodlum pulled out a revolver and stepped toward her. Nikki pulled the trigger on her parasol, and released a twenty-centimeter spike out of the ferrule. She stepped forward and drove the blade up through the man's chin and into his brain. She caught and held him up while peering over his shoulder and patting him on the back.

"Shh, I know it seems unfair, but I'm the bringer of death for the wicked." The man's arms were dangling at his side when Nikki peered over her brow at the third man and said, "It's time for you to join your friends." The third man, still in shock, started raising his machine gun. But by the time he had acquired his target, Nikki had launched a twenty-centimeter throwing spear—which she kept in her hair—and pierced the man's forehead. And just like that, in less than seven seconds, three men were dead.

The driver of the thugs' sedan spun the tires out and pulled the car back. When he was twenty meters away, he put the car in drive and pulled away, leaving a cloud of dust behind him a kilometer long.

Nikki removed the ninja throwing blade from the man's forehead, cleaned it off on his shirt, then spat in his face and returned to the car. Reynolds and Vikki made their way to the back seat and closed the door as Nikki climbed into the front passenger seat.

"We're not skanks," Nikki said while pouting.

"No, no, no, of course not," Vikki replied.

"No, no, no, absolutely not," Reynolds added.

"He was completely out of line," Nikki said.

"Yes, yes, yes, I completely agree.

"Yes, his comment was completely uncalled for," Reynolds stated with clarity.

"We're good girls," Vikki shared, hoping to comfort and subdue her.

"Yes, yes, yes, I completely agree, you're categorically refined in both taste and spirit," Reynolds confirmed.

Nikki turned around in her seat and looked at Vikki and Reynolds and asked again, all teary-eyed, "We're nice girls, right?"

"Totally — with a Catholic school moral upbringing."

"Yes we are," Nikki confirmed as she worked on ending her sniffles. "And the way we dress is a deliberate distraction."

"Absolutely!" Vikki and Reynolds replied in unison as the driver pulled out.

En route, Reynolds leaned over and whispered into Vikki's ear, "She's a bit sensitive."

Vikki nodded then added, "Well, she hates being accused of something she's not."

Thirty-five minutes later, they were knocking on the door of the orphanage.

Adadi opened the door and Reynolds said, "I'm looking for Akachi Ihejika."

"I'm sorry but he's not here. You will have to come back." Adadi went to close the door but Reynolds pushed it open.

"And you are who, exactly?"

"I'm the caretaker of this children's home."

"What's your name?"

"Adadi."

"Well, Adadi, when will Akachi be back?"

"I don't know."

"Do you know where he might have gone?"

"No, I don't."

"I see. Do you know who Afia is?"

Adadi took a long breath and replied, "No."

"You hesitated, so therefore I know you're lying.

"Instead of asking you the same questions repeatedly until you decide to tell me what you know, I'm going to make it easy for you. Let's see, what can I use to give you a little incentive. Reynolds pushed past Adadi and saw the children circling a camp fire.

"Oh, I know, Nikki, grab one of those kids there and hack off his arm."

Nikki scrunched up her brow and said, "What?! Are you insane?"

"Hey, it's not me. It's what these crazy bastards do here.

"Grab that one there." Reynolds pointed to one of the ten-year-old boys up front. Adadi moved in front of the boy.

"I will not allow you to harm any of these children."

"I'm afraid your rebellion will stop nothing." Reynolds looked at Nikki then pointed at the children with his chin. She knew the order had been given. She moved toward the group of youngsters. They all took a few steps back but held their ground. They had seen this many, many times before. If they ran, they would all be gunned down. But if they stood their ground only a few would die. Death would be gruesome and excruciating but quick. They were ready. It was a way of life here. Nikki stopped beside Adadi and said, "There is no way I'm going to kill a bunch of kids. You're insane, I quit."

"What?! Have you lost your senses?" Reynolds yelled. "We're on a mission."

Nikki leaned down and held the little boy's chin targeted for termination and said, "It's okay, chérie, no one is going to hurt you."

She then stood back up, crossed her arms and gave Reynolds a stern look of defiance.

Reynolds made a 'why' gesture with his hands then looked at Vikki and said, "Talk to her."

Vikki crinkled the corner of her mouth, looked over at Nikki and said, "What are you doing, girl?"

"This is crazy, Vee, and you know it."

Vikki looked at Reynolds and shook her head then walked over to her sister. She stopped less than a meter away then leaned in and whispered, "Girl, are you crazy? You're going to get us both killed."

Nikki punched her in the chest.

"Ow! What the hell? That hurt," Vikki confessed, while reaching up to comfort her left breast with both hands.

"That's what you get for not backing up your sister."

Vikki shook her head, then said, "Gees, I'm sorry. But dang, that really hurt."

"I'm sorry, Vee."

"That was really mean," Vikki added while still coddling her left breast.

"I said I was sorry. Now girl-up and back me up."

"Fine, whatever." Vikki turned around and stood in front of her sister and said, "I'm sorry, Lieutenant, but I can't help you either. I quit, too."

Reynolds placed both hands on his head and declared out loud while looking up at the sky, "Are you guys kidding me?"

He stared at the girls for a few seconds then said, "Fine."

Reynolds turned and started walking away. While Nikki moved in to shoo the children away, Vikki mouthed to Adadi through her teeth, "Take the children and run."

Reynolds drew his firearm, turned and fired at Vikki's back. She turned in time to feel a bullet enter her chest. Nikki caught her sister with one arm, opened her parasol with the other and yelled, "She said to take the children and RUN!" She knelt down, draped Vikki between her legs, wedged the parasol handle to the ground with her foot then pulled out two Glocks and started firing.

"What the hell?" Reynolds was hit twice before turning to run for cover. When he was safely behind one of the few trees in the camp, he yelled, "Where the hell were you keeping two guns? And since when do girls carry a Kevlar bulletproof umbrella?"

"Hold this, Vee," Nikki handed Vikki the parasol handle.

"I'm so sorry. Please forgive me."

"Just hold on, Vee, we've been in worse."

"Just leave me here and save yourself. I'm spent."

"Nonsense, stay with me, Vee. Now, damn it, hold this." Vikki held onto the parasol handle and Nikki dragged her to the nearest building for cover. Reynolds reloaded and fired again. "I see you forgot your guns, Carrot Top."

Nikki peered out around the corner of the building. "Merde, I left my guns on the ground. Damn it. Oh wait, the guns are empty and I'm out of bullets, so who cares," Nikki confessed. She was about to make a witty retort to Reynolds' statement when Vikki spoke.

"Here, take mine." Nikki took hold of her sister's Glocks with a smirk, kissed her on the cheek then returned fire.

"Oh wow, I see you found more guns!" Reynolds yelled. *Damn it, I keep underestimating her,* Reynolds confessed to himself. *Wait, of course I do, just like everyone else. That's why she's so deadly.*

Reynold saw an SUV pull up and five heavily-armed men get out. *Damn it. I'm outgunned by a girl with an umbrella, and now I have to contend with these guys. Well, I'm not dying in this toilet, so, it's time to go.*

Reynolds ran to the edge of the camp and jumped over the clay wall. "I'll live to fight another day. Akachi isn't here, so if they kill everyone in the camp, I lose nothing. In fact, they're doing me a favor. Plus, this diversion will—wait, wait, am I monologuing? That's unbelievable! This whole situation with the girls has me riled up. Damn it. I really liked them. And this development has greatly undermined my position. That's it, I'm done being Mr. Nice Guy."

Now, where the hell is my car? Reynold looked around the corner of the north wall, while favoring the arm of his injured shoulder and holding his stomach with the other. Just then he saw his driver get shot in the head from behind. "Now I'm pissed," Reynolds declared as he ran off.

The five men worked their way into the camp as Nikki peered out from behind the door.

"Merde, Reynolds is gone, Vee, but now there's five other blokes with automatic weapons. I can take three, maybe four, but five? What do we do?"

"See that small table over there?"

"Yes."

"Bring it here and sit me down on it." Nikki leaned her sister up against the wall then ran over, grabbed the table by the leg and dragged it back, causing everything on it to hit the ground.

All the men turned toward the noise and lifted their firearms.

"Don't shoot, don't shoot!" Nikki yelled out in a cute girlie-like voice with a French accent, "that other man was trying to kidnap me. I'm a missionary." She sat Vikki down on the table and handed her one of the guns. "Are you up to this?"

"Of course," Vikki replied, "and missionary?"

Nikki shrugged. "It was all I can think of."

"It was a good idea."

"Show yourself!" an armed man yelled.

Adadi stood up and started walking toward the door. "Not you, chérie, let me go. Just keep the children out of harm's way."

"Oh my goodness, I'm so glad you strong boys are here. I was so worried." Nikki pranced out looking from side to side while letting her hands flail about. "Is he gone?"

"Who are you talking about, woman?"

"The white man that was here a second ago, didn't you see him? Be careful, he has a gun."

The men looked around, but didn't see anyone. The leader sent two men out to search the camp for Nikki's phantom. One moved toward the left while the other advanced to the right.

"And then there were three," Nikki said under her breath. *I have to get close to the leader for this to work,* Nikki professed. *Okay, now Nikki, think stupid thoughts, think stupid thoughts, think stupid thoughts.*

Oh, got it. Nikki had an idea and started roleplaying. "I was so scared. Can I give my savior a hug? Please?" Nikki squeaked out, all teary-eyed.

"Wow, girl, way to lay it on thick," Vikki muttered out under her breath.

The leader looked back at the other men and saw them shrug.

Nikki saw her chance and gyrated over. He stepped back then stopped.

Vikki was losing focus, her eyes were getting blurry. "Hurry, girl," she mouthed.

Nikki landed chest first on the man in front of her, pushing him back. His men were now on either side of her.

Nikki knew her feminine assets would help her prevail. It didn't matter what part of the planet she was on, men were always men. The thug grabbed her by the shoulders and held her at arm's length and asked, "Where's Adadi?"

"I was playing hide and go seek with the boys. It's an American game."

"Yeah, yeah, where's Adadi?"

"She's looking for the boys. Will you protect me?"

"Sure, sure, now get Adadi out here. Adadi, where's Akachi?"

Got you, Nikki confessed to herself then jumped on the man and embraced him. "Thank you, thank you, thank you," Nikki said repeatedly while holding her throwing blade in the man's throat long enough to make sure he was brain dead.

"He's going to protect me," Nikki told the man on the left then pierced his heart with her umbrella shank. Then she turned to the other man and asked, "But who's going to protect you?" She pulled the parasol out of the man's chest and let the other go. Both men fell and the other stepped back and raised his firearm but it was too late. Nikki used the umbrella as leverage to jump up high enough to dropkick the last man. Both of her stainless steel stiletto heels were driven into the man's chest cavity. He was dead before he hit the ground.

The other two men finally noticed what was happening and opened fire. She opened her parasol and moved it to one side and knelt behind it. She returned fire and put down the man on the left then moved the umbrella to the right. She was out of bullets. When the last man came around the building into Vikki's view, she took him out.

Suddenly, there was machine gun fire coming from the front of the camp.

"Wow, really? There's another man? Where the hell did he come from?" Nikki asked as she moved the parasol and hid behind it.

The gun went silent. Seconds later, Nikki peered out and saw Akachi walking in while answering her question, "He was the driver."

"Oh?" Since Akachi appeared to be unarmed, Nikki stood up and asked, "And you are?"

"I'm Akachi."

"Oh, wow. Everyone is looking for you. And these guys weren't very friendly."

"Well, that is a mistake they won't soon repeat."

Nikki chuckled then said, "That's so true. I'm Nikki." She stuck out her hand in a peaceful and playful nature.

"You've been hit." Akachi pointed at her left arm with his chin.

Nikki looked down, flexed her arm then said, "it's just a through and through. I'll tie some gauze around it later.

Akachi reached out and gently held her hand and placed his other hand over it, "Well, my dear, it's an honor to meet you."

"You're so sweet." Nikki looked over at her sister and said, "Vee, he's nice. Vee?" She looked closer at the window and noticed her sister wasn't moving. "Vee, are you okay?" Vikki was draped over the window sill motionless. "Vee!" she yelled while running to her side.

"Talk to me, Vee!" Nikki ran in and pulled her sister up, cradling her head as she started caressing her face, "Vikki, don't leave me." She embraced her and started crying uncontrollably for what seemed like thirty seconds. "Vee," Nikki cried out repeatedly.

Akachi stood quietly nearby with his sister at his side. Suddenly, Nikki's face went blank. That expression along with the previously displayed grief could only mean one thing. He was in the eye of the storm. All he could do now was hope he wasn't swept up in its fury. Nikki peered out over her brow and asked, "Did you know those men?"

"No, not personally, but I know of them. Their boss has a camp twenty kilometers from here and keeps maybe thirty men at his side at all times."

"It could be worse. He will never see me coming. All I have to do is get close and he'll be pushing up daisies."

"Why? It won't change what happened to you or Vikki."

"No. But it will make me feel better."

"But all the men here are dead. So whoever shot Vikki has paid with his life. Isn't that enough?"

"They didn't shoot Vikki. Reynolds did. And those thugs helped him get away. Now their boss and Reynolds will continue to send men until we're all dead."

Akachi was silent for a few seconds then said, "Peace comes at a price, which we all must pay. But the secret is to never pay too much, since death offers no refunds. So, perhaps you should consider another way—before you invite death to take you prematurely."

Nikki closed her eyes, squeezed her sister again then looked up and asked, "Akachi, were you born here?"

"Yes."

"And with all this insanity, you grew up an honorable man."

"What makes you think I'm honorable?"

"I have been around bad people my whole life. It has made me who I am. But more importantly, it has given me an eye to spot the weak, the liars, the cowardly, the strong, and the brave. I have learned how to exploit human frailties and capitalize on the assets God has given me. I have never needed anyone. Vikki is really hurt and probably won't survive the night. Thirty men may be too many for me to handle safely. Would you help me end this psychopath's tyranny?"

"Nikki, I'm not sure how I could be of any help. Plus, if you dethrone one warlord, there's always another to take his place."

"Yes, but only when there isn't someone like you standing by to seize command."

"I'm not interested in a throne."

"And that's why you're worthy to rule, and I will stand by you. You can usher in a new era for these people. Plus, I will help you take out Reynolds." Adadi squeezed Akachi's arm as she thought of the carnage Nikki was suggesting.

"So you brought Reynolds here?" Akachi questioned.

"Yes, well, he brought us."

Akachi crinkled up the corner of his mouth, gently shook his head and replied, "I'm sorry, Nikki, but my path lies elsewhere."

"I see, I'm sorry to hear that." Nikki turned away from Akachi, then turned back and with all her might she tossed her throwing spike at his chest. Akachi pushed Adadi clear and moved out of the way. The spear cut his shirt and buried itself halfway into the wall behind him.

"Ha. I knew it. My instincts are never wrong. For the last five years, I have had a 100% mortality rate with that spike, until now. You knew it was coming before I threw it. That's the only way you could've avoided it. And not only that, you moved an innocent person out of the way first.

"Your reflexes are as good as mine, if not better. This degenerate probably controls the whole city. And his confidence will be his undoing. I can probably do it alone but with your help we are sure to burn him to ashes and eliminate the relentless pursuit and the many that will die in our stead."

"Ms. Nikki, can I suggest you focus on the present? You're hit. Let's take care of that first."

"It's not a big deal. Like I said earlier, it's a through and through. I can tend to it at any time."

"Very well then, Adadi, tend to Vikki while Nikki and I take a walk. Please place her in a comfortable sitting position. We're leaving soon and we won't be coming back. So gather the children and have them take only what is personal and private to them. And please ask them not to carry anything else. They won't need it."

"How much time do we have?"

"Until nightfall."

"Okay," she was quick to reply. Although she thought, *I have spent so much time building this place that leaving it without a fight seems cowardly.* Nevertheless, my goal should be to keep the children safe and that overrides my sense of ownership and pride in this place. "That gives me more than enough time," Adadi added then reached for Vikki.

"Come, we have a lot to talk about."

Nikki kissed Vikki on the face and handed her over to Adadi.

"I will take good care of her. Have no fear. I will protect her with my life, until she can stand again."

"Excuse us for one minute, Nikki." Akachi pulled a pill out of his pocket and placed it in Adadi's hand. "Now, Adadi, listen carefully to my instructions and do exactly what I tell you, nothing more, nothing less. Understand?"

Adadi nodded in agreement and Akachi gave her specific instructions on how to tend to Vikki. He then turned around and joined Nikki who was standing outside wiping tears from her eyes.

"Nikki, walk with me." Akachi led her through the camp grounds. "You have a kind spirit, I see your aura."

"Really?"

"Yes."

"I didn't know I had one."

"Well, you do."

"Is it blue?"

"It most certainly is. But why would you ask me that?"

"Because it's Vikki's favorite color."

"Tell me about her."

"Why? You're not going to talk me out of this."

"I'm going to try. But first, talk to me about Vikki."

"Why? You didn't know her."

"Exactly. This is the birthplace of all life. No one who stains the ground of Africa with their blood in defense of the innocent should ever be forgotten. So, tell me about Vikki."

Akachi stopped and extended out his hand. "Please, I would truly like to know her through the eyes of someone who loves her."

Nikki looked up at Akachi and a single tear rolled down her face as she took his hand.

"They say that you choose your friends but you can't choose your family. That's not true. Vikki chose me. My parents came to America from France when I was five years old. New York City was enormous compared to the city we came from. Anyway, I was unhappy to move. It was difficult for me to adjust without knowing the language. I had no friends and my parents were always working. School was hard. I was picked on routinely and got beat up often.

"One day, when I was eight, I was fighting off three girls, and Vikki stepped in and helped me. It was the only kind face I had ever seen while in America. She walked me home that day. To my surprise, and for the first time that I could remember, my parents were at home waiting for me when we arrived. I wanted to introduce Vikki to them but instead, they ordered me never to see or talk to her again. I cried harder that night than I knew was possible.

"The principal had called and spoken to my parents about me getting into fights and that I was associating with the wrong crowd. My parents thought Vikki was the problem. Her parents were poor, not like mine. I guess being poor gave you bad character, or so my parents thought. Anyway, they moved me to another school, and the next two years were the worst in my life.

"One day, I was walking home and the same three girls that Vikki saved me from years earlier were walking toward me. Without saying a word, when they got close enough, they attacked me. I fought back hard. I had been in the fire forging for five years for that day. I was prepared to die or kill them all, but Vikki came out of nowhere and stopped me.

"The police came and took Vikki away. The three girls and I went to the hospital. I was in bad shape and so were the other three. Since the only person uninjured was Vikki, the cops thought she had assaulted us. Without evidence, my parents and the parents of the other three pressed charges. Since the girls were badly beaten and too afraid to talk, and I was apparently too traumatized to testify, they charged and convicted her. They placed Vikki in a juvenile camp for the beatings. She never told them the truth, that it was me who tried to kill those vile girls.

"After the trial, my parents moved back to France. By then, my French was terrible and my English was even worse. For five years, I wrote to Vikki and she wrote me. Our emails were not secure but over time we developed a code. When I was fifteen we returned to the states on holiday. Vikki was getting out and I was going to be there. It was just after her eighteenth birthday.

"When I saw Vikki walk out of that correctional facility, I ran toward her. That day I hugged Vikki for the first time and she hugged me. It was the only time in my life that I ever felt loved. We never left each other's side after that. Vikki's parents were there to pick her up and I went home with them like I had always been there. My parents made it impossible for them to keep me, so Vikki and I ran.

"Over the years we did some awful stuff to eat and pay for clothes and things. We became better fighters, learned what we could and could not do with boys. Well she did, anyway. I got pregnant and had a baby at seventeen."

"What did you have?"

"A girl. We named her Heather. She was so beautiful. But the streets were no place to raise a baby. I turn her over to Vikki's parents. They raised her as their own. I'm not sure she even knows I'm alive. Anyway, Vikki's parents could no longer afford to live in New York City, so several years ago they moved south, to North Carolina. I get pictures from time to time but I didn't want Heather to grow up like me, so I stayed away."

"How old is she now?"

"Twelve, or was twelve."

"Was?"

"I found out three days ago she was among the taken."

"What about Vikki's parents?"

"I spoke to them. They're the ones that told me. They were devastated to lose Heather and will probably now lose Vikki, too. I don't think I can ever face them again. Vikki took a bullet meant for me. If Vikki dies and having lost Heather, it will be too much for me to handle."

"Vikki sounds like a wonderful person and so do her parents. But what if I told you, you could see Heather again?"

"What? How? How would that be possible?"

"I have powerful friends."

"So the stories about you are true?"

"What stories?"

"What stories? The stories about you being in league with aliens. It's the reason I joined Reynolds' team."

"Well, lucky for me you *were* with Reynolds, right?"

"Yes, I was, but—" Nikki stopped and stepped back, getting into a defensive posture before repeating, "Are the stories about you true?"

"No. Do you believe those stories?"

"I didn't until I found out my kid was stolen right out of her middle school. And now that you told me I could see her."

"Nikki, have you ever heard of the Rapture? And what that event is supposed to mean?"

"Ten years of Catholic school here, so of course, yes to both questions."

"Well, if Heather is gone, like you say, then she wasn't taken, Nikki, she was raptured."

"What?"

"Think about it. People are gone by the hundreds of millions all at once and no one saw anything? You can't take a banana off a fruit cart without several people seeing you. What did you think was happening on the planet?"

"I think it's the same merde that has always happened, just intensified."

"Really, the world is on fire, the world, and it feels the same to you?"

"Well...?"

"Yes, yes, think about it. It's like all the good in the world has been sucked out. You and Vikki have been dodging bullets, literally, for what, a decade and today she just takes one in the chest?"

"What are you saying?" Nikki questioned in a confused state.

"I'm saying that the Anti-Christ is alive right now and the world is in a death spiral toward an abyss, and Reynolds is leading the charge."

"What? I don't believe that."

Akachi laughed then added, "And that is why he wins. You told me not ten minutes ago that you had an eye to spot the weak, the liars, the cowardly—" Akachi paused for a few seconds then continued, "Am I any of those?"

Nikki stared him down.

"Let go of the hate. You know what I'm saying is true, whether you understand it or not."

She stepped back, closed her eyes then held her head between her hands and asked, "Vee, what do I do? Tell me. You were always the smart one."

"Yes, Nikki, think, don't give in to the hate. There is another way."

"The hate has kept me safe, I just can't..." Nikki trailed off and paused.

"Oh yes, you can. Tell me, have you ever hurt anyone that you thought was truly innocent? Have you?"

Nikki looked up and answered, "No. But how would you know that?"

"Because like you, I have been surrounded by evil most of my life, and I know good. How many times have you been asked to find the family member of someone to use as leverage?"

"Quite often actually," Nikki answered with her eyebrows scrunched together.

"So, have you? Have you ever tortured or even harmed anyone's family member?"

"No."

"No matter how many times you've been asked or how much you were offered."

"No, never."

"Why not? Tell me, why not?"

"Because I might be beyond redemption, but I never wanted to cause the pain and suffering I went through as a kid to anyone who was actually innocent."

"Then trust in that humanity now and help me save these children, because I need you."

Nikki looked up at Akachi long and hard then said, "I'm not sure about you yet."

"No problem. You can kill me if I get out of line with one of your throwing...thingies."

"To kill you with one of those might be hard. I may have to strangle you."

"Well, that sounds awful."

"Well, I could break your neck, it's quick and painless, or it's supposed to be, anyway."

"Okay, then do that, but," Akachi held up a finger and added, "not now. And only if I get out of line. Agreed?"

"Okay."

Nikki stuck out her hand to shake on the deal but Akachi raised his finger up again and added, "But you have to talk to me first, if I get out of line I mean. You know, just to make sure there isn't a misunderstanding or confusion."

"Okay."

Akachi went to shake her hand but pulled it back yet again to add, "You'll be gentle, right?"

Nikki got a smirk on her face and said, "Yes, you big baby." Nikki shook her head and said, "Men." They shook hands and were at peace.

"Now, help tend to the kids while I look in on Vikki."

"Wait, I wanna see Vikki, too. Can you actually help her? And what about Heather? How and when can I see her?"

"Yes, I will surely try. And as far as Heather is concerned, I'll make that happen for you."

"Are you sure?"

"Yes, but it won't be easy."

"Okay, when?"

"I need to connect with my friends."

"Where are they? Let's go see'em."

"They're probably on different continents around the world."

"Oh, that sucks for me."

"Have patience, Nikki. We will find them. I promise."

"We better."

"We will. Now come, we have a long way to go and lots to do."

Nikki and Akachi started walking back to the main building in camp and Nikki asked, "So what did you hand Adadi before you walked out?"

"Wow, you don't miss much do you?"

"Well?"

Akachi looked at Nikki and said, "I gave her a pill."

"What kind of pill?"

"Well, let's just say it's a pill Vikki needs."

"That's awfully vague, and I don't like that. If it hurts her…" Nikki trailed off.

"I could no more hurt her than you could harm an innocent child in your care."

"Well, it better not," Nikki added with the corner of her mouth crinkled up.

CHAPTER 11

Hell is Real
Monday, July 22, 2047 8:11 a.m.

A WEEK HAD GONE BY SINCE THE RAPTURE AND FILIP ZAREK was just finishing up his morning reading ritual as always. His aide had scheduled weekly reviews with prominent world leaders. Filip looked at his watch and confessed, *I need to have Eric revisit my appointment schedule. My morning docket is full but most of the leaders on my calendar are still asleep.* Suddenly, there was a knock on the door.

"Come in."

Eric Tusk, his chief of staff, opened the door and walked in. "Good morning, sir."

"Good morning, Eric." Filip briefly took his eyes off the floating projection screen above his desk as Eric closed the door. "I was just thinking about you."

"Sir, is there something you wish?"

"Well, first things first, you have a somewhat jovial expression on your face, old friend. Do you have good news for me?"

"Yes, sir, I do. But I noticed your morning agenda is tight. Is there anyone on the docket you need me to reschedule? The global time differential associated with these world leaders makes keeping these appointments difficult in these trying times."

"Interesting."

"Sir?"

"That's exactly what I wanted to discuss with you. But since you're already aware of the issue, there's no need to discuss it. Just take care of it," Filip replied while closing his web browsers with the flick of a finger.

"I will, sir. Is there anything else?"

"No."

"Are you sure? You look...fatigued." The young Polish leader was tall and slender, although he was average in weight; his ordinary stature concealed his muscular build and true physical strength.

"Yes, I'm certain, but you're observations are accurate, of course. I have been putting in long hours. Perhaps I need to relax a bit," the Anti-Christ replied. "However, that said, Sir William, the British Prime Minister, and Frank Stilton, President of the United States, are on my schedule for this afternoon and I want you present for those discussions."

"Yes, sir."

"Now, what's the good news?"

"Well, sir, it's our fugitives."

"Go on."

"Dr. Yvette Milagro and Dr. Chow Lee are currently in US custody in Guantanamo Bay. It's estimated, but not yet confirmed, that the no-touch torture methods being used have driven them both mad, as directed."

"That's fantastic news, Eric. Make sure they're told to continue the torture regiment on our two doctors nonstop until they have unequivocal proof they are both insane. Is that understood?"

"Yes, sir."

"These two mongrel dogs were in league with our master's most hated enemy. They are to receive no mercy."

"Yes, sir."

"Now, let's relax a bit. Do you have a few hours available this morning?"

"Yes, sir."

"Good, I want to pay my Lord a visit and I want you to

come with me."

"Sir! It would be an honor. Thank you, sir," Eric replied as he bowed repeatedly. "Sir, how will I be—" Eric paused while he thought of the correct way to phrase his question.

"What is it, Eric? Out with it, man, what's on your mind?"

"Well, sir, the scriptures—"

"What about them?" Filip replied with a raised eyebrow.

"Well, sir, the scriptures read that mortal men are not allowed in that realm."

"I will make an exception on your behalf. Plus, you won't actually be...physically there."

"I'm not quite sure I understand."

"It doesn't matter. It will all be clear to you in short order, now let's go."

Filip opened a portal and they both stepped through and were gone.

A few seconds later, when Eric gathered his footing, he asked, "Where are we?"

"We're on Helema, my father's realm."

"Hell?"

"Yes, to humanoids this would be Hell."

"That's interesting. For some reason, I didn't expect to see people walking around. Who are they?" Eric asked in disbelief.

"You're looking at the inhabitants of Helema. Few mortals have ever seen this place, at least not without it being part of the last moments before their physical death."

"Well, it looks amazing. But if I didn't know any better, I would swear we were somewhere on Earth. Well, it looks like Earth anyway, with the exception of color and the fact that everything looks a little blurry."

"I know, this planet is a close replica, just one thousand times bigger. But the lack of color is just a byproduct of the portal and the fact that we're still in it. If we were to step out, the color would return.

"Anyway, Helema, or Hell to you, is where eternal souls go for penance on their transgressions."

"I'm sorry, sir, but I'm not sure I understand."

"It's simple, Eric. You're born on Earth as a being with free will. Those that don't follow a specific path with their lives as illustrated in the Tanakh, or the Christian bible, for example, end up here." Filip looked at Eric and noticed a blank stare looking back.

Hmm, Filip grunted then paused for a few seconds with his eyes closed while tapping a softly clenched fist on his forehead. *How do I communicate a cosmic reality to such a limited soul?* Filip wondered. Then he had an idea. "Okay, Eric, now listen, after the expiration of your corporal shell on Earth, you're classified.

"Classified, sir? What does that mean? And what's the purpose of being categorized?"

"Let's not get ahead of ourselves. For now, just trust me when I say that everyone is classified."

"Yes, sir."

"Now, those categorized as saint-like, for example, go to Harema, or Heaven, while everyone else comes here. If you come here, there's a price you must pay for the disobedience of the cosmic rules you failed to follow. And they are categorized in grades of penance. Some sentences are greater than others but all are atonements nevertheless."

"Sentences, sir? You make it sound like retribution."

"Okay, let's not get sidetracked, but yes, in a way that's exactly what it is."

"So, my Lord, all these stories about Heaven and Hell are true?"

"Of course, you didn't think you could just do anything you wanted and get away with it, did you?"

"Well, sir, I actually did."

"Well, you can't. Upon your creation, you are given an eternal soul. With that comes enormous power and responsibility but there are specific actions we must all follow. And there lays the trap. The true problem for most is free will. It's a bitch. When you can do anything or everything you want, who wants to follow a bunch of rules they had no part in creating?"

"No one, sir."

"Exactly, but many do nevertheless."

"Okay, so you're saying we're all required to follow specific guidelines of behavior?"

"Yes, that's exactly right."

"I'm sorry, sir, but I don't remember ever being given general rules of conduct to follow."

"Oh please, of course you were. Every society has them. You just choose to ignore them like everyone else that's here. Love thy neighbor as thyself, don't bear false witness, don't covet your brother's wife, and all the other happy horse shit.

"Anyway, everything has rules, my friend, not just us. Everything! Rain falls down, not up. Fish extract oxygen from the water while we remove it from the air. Trees and plants absorb carbon dioxide and generate oxygen in a process called photosynthesis and not vice versa. Water freezes at 0° Celsius and not one degree above. Need I go on?"

"No, sir. So there's a price we all must pay for the decisions we make during our life on Earth. And more specifically that price goes up or down depending on how we follow specific cosmic rules. In the end, Helema is where most will come to pay for their misgivings."

"That's categorically correct, Eric. You see, that wasn't so hard." Filip looked at Eric and was surprised by what he saw. Huh, "I see a look of disappointment on your face. Don't feel bad, old friend, because a penance is paid by everyone regardless of who they are. It just happens to be that most will execute their atonement here versus paying for it on Earth. Plus, what few will ever know is that our Lord has a celestial purpose in these end times."

Eric crinkled his brow and said, "Wow, that statement is going to require some additional clarity."

"Perhaps, but you won't receive it today. There are so many other revelations I want to expose you to. However, I promise to share that cosmic reality with you, as soon as I believe you're ready, just not today. I need you to focus your attention elsewhere."

"Yes, sir."

"Now, do you see that man over there?" Filip pointed to a man in his mid-thirties walking alone in a park.

"Yes, sir."

"This is his fifth life here. While he lived on Earth, he was a con-artist. He swindled dozens of people out of millions. Here he lives out his lives experiencing the heartaches he caused on Earth until he has run the full gamut for his transgressions."

"I see, so if someone kills another and that one murder affects five people, he or she relives the life experiences of each of the five individuals afflicted until he or she has felt the pain and sorrow of every victim."

"Yes, that's exactly correct. Brilliant, I knew there was a reason you were my second."

"Well, that's harsh. I was actually hoping you were going to say I was completely wrong."

"What? Why? Haven't you heard the expression, 'An eye for an eye?' Where did you think that expression came from?"

"Honestly, sir, I thought that motto came from the weak."

"Well, it does, but the truth exists nevertheless."

"So our greatest criminals on Earth…" Eric faded out, hoping Filip would fill in the blank.

"So the greatest criminals on Earth undergo an extremely brutal existence here. But that's what the Helem role is in this eternal stage." Filip paused for a few seconds then added, "Until…"

"Until what, sir?"

"Until it all comes to an end. The Helem truly detest the fact that they were not created with the right to free will. Therefore, they hate, and I'm using the word hate here, they hate those beings that were given that gift. Especially since so many humanoids have ignored or completely devalued that which the Helem covet most.

"Many of the initial exiled Helem have achieved a state of insanity from countless millennia immersed in guilt, hopelessness or surrounded by cretins in self-predicated torturous agony. Perhaps a more accurate way of expressing a Helem's outlook is to say they have become callous to the pleas of those in spiritual damnation, as a result of their own hand. If that wasn't the punishment for a Helem's initial disobedience, it has surely become their hollowing instrument over time."

"That seems like an over reaction."

"Many Helem would agree with you. But you'll find no one here to complaint to, so I would suggest you keep your observations and opinions to yourself."

"Yes, sir. So, is it fair to say that the initial residents of Helem all hate me?"

"Oh yes, Eric, my old friend, especially you. You get to do everything they wish they could do and more. And you're still given a chance at redemption. That's where the injustice is truly felt by the initial residents of Helema. They were never given a chance at redemption even though many were remorseful soon after the rebellion."

"I see. So child molesters, murderers of children, and rapists of the innocent—those who deprive others from experiencing that which the Helem covet most are treated badly here?"

"Absolutely, depending on the number of victims and their ages, their souls are hollowed out here; many are driven mad over numerous lives from torture and sorrow. The majority kill themselves, repeatedly. But there is no escape. There are no cemeteries, no victims and no one is innocent. Everyone here receives retribution and pays a quantifiably equivalent atonement for their transgressions at the end, without exception."

"So souls are reincarnated here for that purpose?"

"Yes, by the Helem at an accelerated rate. A full birth term takes less than a month and a soul grows into full adulthood in seven years versus twenty-one like on Earth. Children are not allowed to be harmed here like on Earth so punishments are made much more severe because of it.

"And those that were mass murderers on Earth are what?"

"They are murdered here once for every victim, usually in the same manner as their earthly victims. Since the events are all connected after so many lives, their souls get weaker, making them less able to fend off attackers even though their desire to do so increases over time. Afterwards, they live out the lives of all their victims' loved ones."

"Is there any way we could help them?"

"What?! Why? Why would you want to? They're guilty! Let them suffer for their transgressions. Plus, once their penance is complete, it's over. However, before then, each atonement retribution received is passed on and remembered in the next life lived."

"So if you murder five people on Earth, you will be murdered five times here by the Helem?"

"Yes, in every gruesome detail."

"And you will remember all of them?" Eric questioned.

"Yes, that's why so many souls go insane here."

"I'm sorry, sir, but I'm feeling a little overwhelmed. Why would you tell me all this? I would think shielding me from the truth would keep me more obedient."

"Perhaps, but these are the end times. And the fact that you know what's to come changes nothing. Their retribution for us will be short compared to say, Dr. Josef Mengele, or others bent on committing genocide like Adolf Hitler, the Ottoman Empire leaders, Kampuchea, Nazis, Circassia, party members for the Independent State of Croatia, and the early North American government party members who committed genocide on entire cities of peaceful Indian natives. So, we will be getting off super easy, trust me. And rejoice in that, my brother."

"Yes, sir," Eric replied but internally he wasn't sure he believed Filip. *Huh, I'm thinking if anything, our punishment would be the worst ever. We are helping bring about the end of the world. Wait, am I having second thoughts about what side I'm on?*

"Eric, don't have second thoughts about what side you're on. You've picked the winning side. The Helem have been around for billions of years." Filip looked over at him to see if he would have to rip out his heart.

"Look! The difference between you and all these schmucks out there is that you are helping me serve the Prince of Darkness. He rules this place. Don't you think that grants you some benefits?"

"Actually, sir, come to think of it, I can't imagine how it couldn't."

"Exactly, Eric! You are bound to end up in Helema, and your relationship with me will yield you magnificent rewards. Without question, those advantages will make almost everyone else here envy and covet you before the end."

Of course, Filip realized Eric's position carried with it no leniency. If anything, his punishment would be greater. But Filip didn't care. Eric, along with every other human being on Earth, was just flesh he needed to see burn.

"Yes, sir. So, all those stories about us burning in a lake of fire for an eternity are...?" Eric paused and waited for Filip to fill in the blank.

"Now, there are many terrible stories about this place, which are true. But that's not one of them. That tale is ridiculous."

"Is it, sir?"

"Oh, come on, man, of course. Think about it. You are born and live on Earth for what, sixty, maybe seventy years? How would a merciful God condemn anyone to an eternity of suffering and misery? It just makes no sense. It's a lie permeated by the church to keep people in line.

Honestly, there is nothing you could do to justify that extreme a reaction. Even if you started torturing kittens at the age of ten and killed thousands of people and then died at seventy, how would a million years of suffering, let alone one hundred billion years be justified punishment?"

"It wouldn't, sir."

"Exactly. And that's us saying that. On the other hand, sentencing you to sixty years of the same torture and misery you brought upon others might be defensible and warranted. Understand?"

"Yes, my Lord."

"Good. So, enough said on that topic. We can discuss this issue in more detail at some other time, if you wish. However, right now, we have more pressing matters to tend to."

"Yes, sir."

"Oh," Filip laughed. "Look at the idiot walking by the newsstand and tell me, what do you see?"

"My Lord, I see a contemptible poor fool who doesn't seem to have done anything wrong but is still in hell."

"Yes," Filip laughed. "Eric, you have a good eye. Your account of that person is spot on. He was actually a decent person on Earth. He followed the law, paid his taxes, raised several children successfully and even went to church on a routine basis. But he's still here. Why do you think that is?"

"I'm not certain but perhaps because he didn't choose a side?"

Filip laughed yet again. "That's exactly right. He thought it was okay to remain neutral. In his heart, he never committed, he just spoke the words. And now he's here being used as a punching bag. Pathetic."

Eric thought, *I need to make a mental note of that example. I'm sure it's important in some way. And I don't want to be here without —*

Eric's train of thought was interrupted when he heard Filip say, "Come on, Eric, we're wasting time. Our Lord is waiting."

"Yes, sir."

CHAPTER 12

Ruben Receives Visitors
Tuesday, July 23, 2047 2:12 p.m.

MIA STEPPED OUT OF THE TRANSPORT RING WITH HER MOTHER and Sophia at Jackson Memorial Hospital in Miami. She pulled the curtain to the side and frantically looked around the emergency room for Dr. Ruben. *There, there he is,* Mia announced to herself.

"Mick!" Mia shouted as she ran over to him with a look of desperation on her face.

Dr. Ruben turned and saw Mia coming.

"Mia, Mia, is that you?"

"Yes, Mick, it's me."

"Oh my God, Mia, you look so different. You look like an angel. What's happened to you? Where have you been? And where's your mother? The whole world is looking for you guys."

"MICK, please listen!" Mia shouted. "I need you to focus. I need your help. My mother and her friend need immediate medical attention. So, come on." Mia grabbed him by the hand and pulled him away. He suddenly felt a little lightheaded but attributed those feelings to the sudden and unexpected presence of someone he thought was gone forever. He followed in tow while mentally working on shaking off his unforeseen grogginess.

A few seconds later he replied, "Sure, Mia, I'm here for you."

Mia stopped in front of a curtained off portion of the emergency room, where Sophia was lying on a gurney and her mother on the floor.

"What in the world?" Dr. Ruben let out in shock and disbelief. He stood there motionless for a few seconds. Yvette looked near death and the other girl looked worse.

"Mick, my mother has been tortured for three days straight. She is in extreme mental distress and is probably close to having a heart attack from the torment. You need to sedate her and keep her safe. People will be coming for her and she won't survive another session in captivity.

"Mick, are you listening?" He was just standing there looking at Yvette trembling on the floor and imagining the worse. Suddenly, he snapped out of it.

He looked around then said, "Yes, I understand." Then pointed to a nurse and said, "You, come here. Place this woman on a gurney and start an IV, then administer twenty milligrams of morphine and monitor her vitals."

The nurse ran over and asked, "Who is she, Doctor?"

"That's not important, what is important is that you do what I ask, right now!"

"Yes, of course, Doctor," the nurse stuttered then called over three others to help her get Yvette on a bed.

Ruben grabbed another nurse and said, "You need to assist me."

"Yes, Doctor."

"Mick, Sophia was shot in the chest about twenty seconds ago. Based on her labored breathing, the bullet pierced her lung. She needs emergency surgery."

Ruben ripped open Sophia's shirt and saw the hole in her chest. "Mia, who did this?" But Mia didn't answer.

"Nurse, place a gauze on that puncture wound, then start an IV and prep her for surgery." Several other nurses joined in. "Get her airway opened and someone get an x-ray machine over here. I need images, now."

Mia started pulling Dr. Ruben to the side.

"Mia, what are you doing? I need to tend to your mother

and her friend."

"I know, but this is important, Mick, please."

Mia pulled Mick away from everyone and whispered into his ear, "Save them both, Mick, and keep them safe. They're more important than you know." She leaned up on her tippy-toes and kissed him on the cheek, then placed a hand over his heart.

"May God improve your hands and sight with the power of his might. To save the virtuous in flight and avoid the blight that would corrupt your convictions on sight."

Mia then pushed him away. Ruben felt lightheaded and stumbled back. He had to look away for two seconds to balance himself. And in those few seconds, Mia was gone.

"Mia?" Dr. Ruben looked around. What the—? Mia!"

"Doctor, we need you here!"

Ruben shook his head and returned to Sophia's side. At a single glance he knew what needed to be done. "Let's move her into surgery right now."

"Doctor, all the operating rooms are full."

"Then get an anesthesiologist and a trauma surgeon down here!"

The head nurse looked at her watch and said, "I'm sorry, but both are in surgery and the anesthesiologist has several procedures scheduled afterward."

"How do you know that?"

"I looked at his schedule moments ago at the beginning of our shift," the nurse answered.

Another nurse walked up and said, "Here are the images you requested, Doctor."

Ruben looked at the x-rays. "The bullet pierced her lung. Damn it! Wait, wait," Ruben exclaimed as he looked at another image. "Good, it's okay, the bullet is not actually in the lung. I can remove it and repair the damage, if any, quickly. But we need to be quick," Mick confessed to a seemly uninterested audience.

"Okay, nurse, if the doctors are busy and the ORs are full, then we'll do it here. Nurse, immobilize her." The nurse strapped Sophia down.

"Nancy, get 2mg of Propofol ready to induce and maintain general anesthesia."

"That's not really safe in this environment, is it, Doctor?

There should really be an anesthesiologist present to do that and we should move her to an OR."

"Really, are you ladies punking me?"

"No," the three nurses replied in unison.

"Are you sure? Because what you're telling me makes no sense." Ruben pointed to the head nurse, "You told me, in the presence of these other two, that all the operating rooms were full. And then you," Ruben pointed to another, "told me that the anesthesiologist was not available and neither was the trauma surgeon. So what's it going to be?"

"Well, I'm not going to help you break protocol, because if she dies, I will most certainly be fired for it."

"That's ridiculous."

"Is it, Doctor?"

"Yes, it's completely ridiculous. She will most certainly die if we do nothing. So, we should just let her die then? That's your plan, is it?"

The nurses banded together and refused to help. "We're sorry, Doctor, but what you're asking us to do is completely against hospital policies and procedures. Plus, don't you recognize who that is? That's Dr. Milagro, the mortician."

"Yeah," another nurse chimed into the discussion. "Like the whole world is looking for her. So that other woman there is probably in league with her, too."

"Wow, I see, I didn't realize I was working with a bunch of witches. So be it. I'll do it myself. And she's a forensic pathologist, probably the best in the world," Ruben informed the nurses in disbelief. He shook his head and added, "I'm totally disgusted with your attitudes, ladies."

Ruben walked off to scrub up. When he returned to Sophia's side, a nurse from across the room had walked over and said, "You clean her up and I'll get you a surgery kit. You'll need a scalpel and a set of forceps at least, right?"

"Yes, thank you."

The nurse administered the general anesthesia and Ruben did his best to make up for lost time.

"Wow, I've never seen anyone work so fast," Maggie said to Ruben as she assisted in with the surgery.

"Well, these aren't ideal conditions or the best environment.

But, on a positive note, the bullet missed the ribs completely, so there's no bone fragments to contend with. All I have to do is find the bullet and pull it out. Please hold this and hand me those forceps."

"Here." Maggie held the entry incision open while Dr. Ruben worked on retrieving the bullet.

"Thank you."

"How are her vitals?"

"Not good."

"Damn it. Wait, our luck is changing, I got the bullet. Here, bring that pan closer." The nurse brought the pan over so Dr. Ruben could drop the bullet in it and a pair of forceps."

"Her vitals are getting worse, Doctor."

"It's okay, I need suction and the suture kit."

"You take this and I'll do this," the nurse said. The nurse suctioned the cavity while the doctor prepped to suture.

"Thank you."

"Okay, I'm going to inspect the lung one more time before I close." A few seconds later Ruben announced, "Done. I need to close. It won't take more than a dozen sutures. Please go find her some plasma while I finish up."

"Yes, Doctor."

"And increase her oxygen. I don't want her dying seconds before I'm done.

"Yes, Doctor."

As Ruben was finishing up, Maggie pulled the curtain to the side and walked out and confronted the other three nurses who were just standing outside the partitioned room.

"What is wrong with you three? What you guys did was reckless."

"What?!"

"That poor woman could have died."

"You know very well we don't perform surgery in the emergency room."

"What?! Of course we do, we do it all the time."

"No, we don't. Not like that. He's not suturing up a laceration or setting a compound fracture. He's performing a procedure that required Propofol. That requires an anesthesiologist and an OR. So, if anything, you were the one being reckless."

"What?! That woman received a gunshot to the chest. That makes it an exception."

"Yes, but he's not a trauma surgeon. At the very least, there should have been a surgeon here. If that woman's vitals fail, you will not be able to revive her."

"You don't know that."

"Oh yes, we do. That woman has a punctured lung. If her vitals fail, that would be the end of that. Any application of revival protocols would cause massive internal bleeding, and you know it." The other two nurses stood on either side of Nancy with their arms crossed. They were each wearing smirks on their faces, and nodding their heads up and down in unison.

"Anyway, it doesn't matter now. We called the cops. They're coming for her and her mortician child kidnapper buddy, too. You saved her and ended your career for nothing. You're going to be fired and no one will hire you after this."

Dr. Ruben was listening to the nurses' conversation when he interrupted.

He looked at Maggie and said, "Nurse, can you help me move these two into the ICU ward?"

"Sure, Doctor."

The nurse looked back at the other three and said, "What if this would have been someone you loved?

"It wasn't."

"Shame on you three."

"No! Shame on you, Maggie, for helping him save a terrorist kidnapper."

Mick shook his head in disappointment as he pushed Sophia's gurney away. Maggie followed with Yvette's bed. On her way out, she noticed the three nurses were just standing there whispering insults about her. Maggie looked back and stuck her tongue out at the nurses and made the *nyah* sound.

When she entered the hallway, Maggie was still a little distracted. It took her a few seconds to notice they were heading the wrong way. "Doctor, where are we going? The ICU is in the opposite direction."

"We're not going to ICU."

"But you said we were. So if we're not going to the intensive care unit, then where are we taking them?"

"I'm not sure, but they can't stay here."

"Doctor, you've just extracted a bullet from that girl. And she's lost a lot of blood. She's in no condition to be moved."

Ruben stopped, turned around and asked, "What choice do I have? If they stay here, they'll be arrested and thrown in a dungeon somewhere to die a slow and agonizing death. I can't, I won't in good conscious allow that to happen," Ruben recited with quivering lips.

Maggie looked at him and was touched at his sensitivity and said, "Okay, I won't either. I'll help you."

"Are you sure? If you help me, you'll be in trouble for sure."

"I don't care, I'm not coming back to work in this house of horrors."

Mick smiled then said, "I agree. These nurses are sadistic and I can't be around cruel and heartless people."

"Okay, so why don't you take your friends out through the basement? The exits on the left are never monitored by security and no one ever goes out that way. It's where all the garbage cans are so the area is always stinky. I'll pull my car around and meet you down there once I pick up a few medical supplies."

"Okay, Maggie, and thank you."

"Yes, sir." Maggie started running off when Dr. Ruben called to her.

"Maggie?"

"Yes?"

"Call me, Mick."

"Yes, sir, Mick."

Getting two gurneys to the basement hospital exit by himself was a challenge. However, ten minutes later, Mick was at the exit with his two escapees as Maggie was pulling up in an all-terrain vehicle.

Maggie got out and opened up the back door hatch. "We can lay them both down in the back. I put the seats down. Help me with these portable scoop stretchers."

"Nice thinking."

"Thanks, I thought it would make it easier for us to move them and keep them immobilized during our escape from the law."

Mick laughed then said, "Yes, Maggie, it absolutely will."

Just then, several police officers were getting out of their patrol cars and working their way into the emergency room.

At the back of the hospital, Maggie informed Mick that she had also taken a few pillows and blankets to make their patients more comfortable. They quickly placed Yvette and Sophia on stretchers and moved them into the car.

"What's in these bags?"

"Well, the truth is, I pilfered a few medical supplies and a cooler full of plasma.

"Wow, that's awesome. You were busy in the ten minutes you were gone."

"It's definitely not a good idea to move either of these two in their condition but it's either move them and risk death or leave them and ensure death. So I brought supplies to help improve their chances of survival, since it's the hospital's fault we're now on the run."

"That's a good bit of reasoning, Maggie."

"Thank you, Mick. Now, let's go." Maggie drove off while Ruben sat in the back between the two girls and monitored their condition.

The police officers confirmed the identity of the two escapees upon arrival. Afterward, they were escorted to the ICU ward.

In transit, Mick started a blood IV on Sophia and then started rummaging through the bags full of medical supplies.

"Wow." Suture kits, Morphine, Oxycodone, Propofol and surgical supplies were among the items Mick noticed in the bags. "Maggie, are you expecting us to open up a trauma center?"

"No, but given the circumstances surrounding these two, I thought more trouble might be coming. And I didn't want us sitting around dying in agony from gun shots or who knows what. So I took a few things just in case."

"Wow."

"Well, my dad and uncles were always in trouble so that made me a worry-wart."

"I guess so. Well, I'm glad you thought ahead. So, where are we going?"

"My father died a year ago on one of his capers."

"I'm sorry to hear that."

"It's okay, it was his fault. I warned him many times.

Anyway, he and my three uncles have a cabin in the Everglades. It's nothing special but it's clean, quiet, and out of the way. Plus, nobody knows about it, just in case the witches of the Craft wanna put the screws to us. I didn't wanna make it too easy for the cops to find us."

"Witches of the Craft, should I know that reference?"

"No, it's just an old movie."

"Okay, so what if you're uncles show up and call the police? And what do we do for food?"

Maggie laughed then said, "My uncles don't like cops so there's a zero chance that will happen. And if they do show up, they might shoot you so, if I were you—" Maggie trailed off.

"Go on."

"Um, be careful. Oh, you know what, don't worry; I'll be there too, so you should be okay."

"Should? I hope you're kidding," Ruben exclaimed then looked at Maggie for confirmation. When she just stared him down he asked again, "You are kidding, right?"

Maggie finally responded back, "Um, yes," then changed the topic. "Now, there's plenty of dry food in the cabin. I kinda manage the space for my uncles now. So, I go up once a month and replace their expired supplies and refill the cupboards."

Mick thought, *wow, you just never know people.* Then shook off the uncertainty and said, "I see. But are you sure all that is necessary?"

"Please, the house belongs to four Latin men. And they seem tough, but they're a bunch of babies. They don't cook, so I have to have a bunch of jarred and pickled stuff up there for them. And an assortment of junk food. But I also keep lots of pasta and rice. So, when their junk food runs out, all they have to do is heat up water."

"Okay well, that's smart and convenient. So, what do we do for protein?"

"We catch fish."

"Fair enough, but I've never been fishing so—"

"Wow, really? Why not?"

"I don't know. I've been busy."

Hmm, Maggie grunted.

"Well, I guess we're in good hands. So tell me, Maggie. Maggie, Maggie, that doesn't sound like a Spanish name."

"It's not, it's short for Margarita. Originally people started calling me Margie for short. But I didn't like it because it made me sound old. So I changed it to Maggie and it stuck."

"Nice, well I like it."

"Thanks. I also liked the nickname Margo, but in Spanish it translates into 'bitter,' so I couldn't use it."

"Well I like Maggie, it suits you."

"Thanks."

"Uh-oh," Maggie let out.

"What is it? Ruben asked.

"Look out the back. There's a police car behind us with its lights on."

Mick looked out and said, "So what. That doesn't mean anything. They could just be responding to a call or engaged in something else. Just slow down or pull over. Let's see if they go by."

Maggie had a bad feeling but she pulled over anyway. And in her rearview mirror she saw the patrol car pull up behind them.

"Mierda," Maggie exclaimed and then added, "We're in serious trouble."

"What? Why? You don't know that. For all we know, one of your tail lights is out."

The police officers got out of the car, pulled out their firearms and yelled, "Get out of the car and place your hands behind your head."

"So you still think it's a taillight?"

"No, but this is a complete overreaction on their part. We haven't done anything."

Mick started opening the back door and Maggie yelled, "What the hell are you doing?"

"They told us to get out."

"Are you crazy? We're fugitives.

"What?"

"Mick, what did you think would happen if we aided and abetted two other fugitives? Those cops probably have orders to shoot us on sight and ask questions later. You can't go out there."

"I can't believe that—I won't." Mick went to step out and shots were fired.

Ruben fell back into the SUV and let out, "What the hell's wrong with those guys?"

Maggie peeled out and said, "Mick, I realize this is all new for you, but you have to trust me."

"But it's those men. They've lost their senses. Why would they shoot at us? I was just getting out of the car like they asked us to."

"Mick, focus. Everything you know has changed. Now help me. Get up here and get my gun out of the glove box."

"What? You can't be serious. What am I supposed to do with a gun?"

"You point it and fire, Mick." Maggie held two fingers out on her right hand and made gun noises, "Pew, pew, pew, pew."

"You expect me to fire on police officers?"

"Yes, if you wanna live."

"This is insane! I can't do that. Do you have any idea how much trouble we would get into for doing that? Plus, even if I wanted to — which I don't — I've never fired a gun before."

"It's easy, you hold the pointy end away from you and pull the trigger. And try not to shoot one of us."

Mick held the gun in his hands for maybe five seconds then stuttered out, "I, I, I, I can't. I can't do it."

"Mardida sea, hombre; just hand me the gun."

Mick held the gun a little longer then said, "No. There has to be another way."

"Are you kidding me? They're going to kill us."

"You don't know that. Plus, you need to focus on driving."

"Arrrr, idiota." Maggie took a deep breath then said, "Fine, I can't fight you, too. Then just hand me my cell."

Mick looked around and said, "I don't see it, where is it?"

"God, Mick, it's in the glove box."

Suddenly the police car rammed the side of Maggie's SUV.

"Damn it. This is getting seriously intense."

"Duh, you think? Get my cell." Maggie drove while mumbling obscenities then yelled, "Hurry!"

"Here, here! Geez! You're stressing me out."

"What? I'm stressing you out?" Maggie stated in the form of a question. "Just gimme that, before I —" She snatched the phone out of Mick's hand and dialed 7 on her speed dial. Just then, they were rammed again.

"Luis, I'm in big trouble."

"Maggie, is that you?"

"Yes, I need to get off the road. And fast."

"Are all those sirens I hear for you?"

"Yes, so can you help me?"

"That's my girl."

"Luis, focus. I need your help. How soon can you get to me?"

"What's the magic word?"

"Y carajo?" Maggie stated a vulgarity in Spanish.

"Nope, that's not it. Try again."

"Please, please, please, you piece of —"

Luis interrupted Maggie to ask, "Where are you?"

"I just made a left on 7th Avenue off of Northwest 20th Street."

"Good, you're close, just keep coming up. I need five minutes to set up."

"Five minutes—we'll be dead long before then. I have maybe two before I'm boxed in."

"Fine, follow 7th Avenue to 41st Street and make two quick rights. I'll be ready."

"Thank you, Luis. I owe you."

"Nonsense, if it wasn't for you, my dad would be dead. So it's me that owes you. I'll see you in two." Maggie hung up and noticed three patrol cars behind her and two others coming straight at them.

"I guess our time is almost up."

"What do you mean?" Mick let out.

"Hold on!" Maggie took a sharp turn on 32nd Street and tried to lose the police on the multiple intersecting city streets.

"Maggie, you're going to kill us all if you don't slow down. And the girls have been through enough trauma today, we don't need to get into an accident."

"Mick, please be quiet. I need to focus. Get in the back and make sure the girls are safe. I have to keep these cops guessing for another sixty seconds or what speed I'm going won't matter. We'll all be dead. Is that clear?" Maggie looked over at him with a penetrating stare he hoped to never see again.

"Yes," Ruben replied then made his way to the back.

"Are the girls okay?"

"Yes. They're still alive anyway."

"Good. And keep them that way or all this will have been for nothing. We have five more streets to weave in and out of. I just hope I can make it to Luis," Maggie confessed. She had lost three of the five cars using her zig-zag maneuvers but two were only seconds away.

"39th Street. 40th. Just one more street," Maggie said under her breath then suddenly four other patrol cars came out of nowhere.

"We're surrounded," Mick confessed aloud.

"Oh gosh. Baby Jesus, I need your help. Show me a sign. I need to get to Luis." And then she saw it. A big red mark on the side of a building. "There! X marks the spot. Thank you Luis. And you too baby Jesus."

"What are you doing?" Ruben asked. "You're not driving through that brick wall, are you?"

"Hold on!" Maggie yelled.

"You are!" Mick went silent as he draped an arm over each girl, lying down in the back. "I hope we live through this, ladies," Mick whispered under his breath.

Maggie drove easily through the wall. Luis had set charges on the inside supporting structure which greatly softened their passage. There were also green arrows on the abandoned warehouse floors and multiple red X's on either side.

Maggie took to the right side marked with the red X's. The three police cars were seconds behind. As Maggie passed the second X on the ground, she triggered a wire which pulled tire spikes across the ground disabling the patrol car behind her.

The police car to her left did the same thing disabling the patrol car behind them. Maggie crossed in front of the last police car and he rammed her bumper causing her to do a 360-degree spin before regaining control. She drove past the disabled patrol cars and the policemen opened fire. "Get down!" Maggie yelled. Ruben was still lying across the girls in the back.

As Maggie passed the second set of X's on the ground, she triggered another wire which pulled a third set of tire spikes across the ground disabling the last patrol car behind her. She drove out of the warehouse and turned toward 41st only to see another police car on her tail.

"Here she comes," a man whispered over the radio.

Seconds later, Maggie made a right on 41st Street and a twenty-seven-foot moving van backed up into the street causing the patrol car to slam into the truck. The truck driver got out and started screaming at the cops. The police car backed up and both officers leaned out of the window with their firearms drawn and yelled, "Move that pinche truck."

Maggie made another right, slowed down and drove up a ramp and into a twenty-two-foot moving van waiting for her. The two men behind the truck stored the ramps and closed the back gate and the truck drove off. The men then jumped into the back seat of a car resembling Maggie's all-terrain vehicle and peeled out and made a right.

The twenty-seven-foot moving van drove out of the way and the patrol car made a right. The officers were joined by another patrol car. "We have them," an officer said into the radio. They just drove under I95 and are heading east toward Buena Vista."

Twenty minutes later the moving van stopped, pulled out the ramps then opened the back gate. Maggie drove her car down and got out to give Luis a hug.

"Thank you so much, Luis."

"It was nothing, baby girl. I'm just glad I could help."

"How did you set that location up so fast?"

"Oh no, that's just one of a dozen places I have set up around the city."

"Maggie slowly nodded her head and said, "Nice. It was perfect." Mick got out of the car and started rotating his neck around in a circle with his eyes closed.

"Who's the stiff?"

"A friend who's not used to this type of excitement." A few seconds later, Maggie asked, "Do you have another car I can use?" Luis motioned for one of his men to bring a clean car around. "I'm gonna need help getting my two passengers moved over."

"No problem, we can help with that." Luis had six of his men move Yvette and Sophia into the new car then asked, "Who are they?"

"Girl friends that have been through a lot at the hands of butchers."

Luis got a serious look on his face and said, "Do you need

me to get some revenge for you?"

"No, we just need to get going. We have a long way to go."

"Well, you should be safe on the road. We transported you out of the city."

"Thank you, Luis—really."

"Again, it was nothing. But my abuelita is going to be mad at me for a few days after the harassment she was subjected to by the idiots that were following up."

"Oh my goodness, is she okay?"

"Of course, she's been in this alien country for seventy years. She's a tough old bird."

"Good. Then give her my best."

"I will." Mick and Maggie got into the car and Luis said, "Say hi to your tios for me."

"I will," Maggie replied as she drove off.

There was silence in the car for about twenty minutes. Maggie focused on driving as quickly as possible without drawing any attention to the SUV. She noticed in the rearview mirror that Mick was holding Yvette's hand, so Maggie decided to ask a probing question.

"So you still have the hots for Evie, huh?"

"What?!" Ruben let go of Yvette's hand and said, "Why would you say that?"

"Because I'm a girl. We notice these things."

"Well, the truth is that I have been interested in her for a long time, but she doesn't know I'm alive."

"That's because men are stupid."

"That seems rather harsh. Your friend Luis just got us out of a pickle back there."

"A pickle? Well, there's always a few exceptions. Anyway, when her husband died, she was devastated. How much time did you give her?"

"What? That was like five years ago."

"Yes, but how long did you wait?"

Um, Mick mouthed.

"Exactly, not long enough. The last thing she wanted shortly after losing the love of her life was to have some horn-dog sniffing around."

"Wow, that's gross."

"I know, right? So why would you do that?"

"What?! I didn't sniff around her at all! Much...very little." Ruben thought about what Maggie had said then admitted the truth out loud. "Shit. I'm such an idiot."

"I know, right, that's what I'm sayin'. But don't take it badly, papi."

"Gee, thanks."

"Look, God made men to love women. And men don't care how women feel or what they're thinking. They only have one thought in their tiny little head."

"That is so not true."

"Really?" Maggie was quiet for a few seconds to allow the truth of her statement to sink in, then added, "But it's okay, that's why God made women just as dumb."

"Wow, really?"

"Yes, God made us stupid, too, so that we could love men."

"Wow, that's kinda mean.

"Sorry, but it's so true."

"Which part, that I didn't give Evie enough time or that I'm an idiot?"

"Both, actually."

"Gee, thanks."

"Well, men can't help that they're whordiots," Maggie added.

"Wait, what? What am I?"

"You heard me. So think about it."

Mick considered Maggie's comment then replied, "Oh, men are idiots because they only have one thing on their minds — according to you — and since they sleep around, that makes them a...I get it."

"Exactly! So now that you're realizing the truth, don't you feel better?"

"No, not really."

"Well, you should. You've come to a realization. Now, all you have to do is admit it and you can move on into boyhood."

"You mean manhood, don't you?" Ruben asked with a specific degree of certainty until he looked at Maggie and saw the corner of her mouth turned up and her eyebrows scrunched together.

"Oh, I guess not."

"Don't feel bad, papi, you're growing."

"Now, take me, for example. I'm twenty-seven, I'm tall for a girl, I have an athletic build, with luxurious dark-brown hair. Man, I'm a Latin cutie. And I've never been married, and I don't have any kids. Plus, I know how to make men happy. I'm a catch. So, why am I still single?"

"You mean make men unhappy, don't you?" Ruben asked a little sarcastically then looked over at Maggie to see a little pouty face with a quivering bottom lip. "Okay, okay, geez, I'm sorry."

"Are you?"

"Yes, yes, I'm sorry, so please don't start crying."

"You see, Mami's boy is growing up. Who's a good boy? Come on, who's a good boy, show me." Ruben smiled then chuckled a little. "There he is. That's my big boy. Now don't you feel better?"

Ruben gently shook his head and said, "You know what, you're—"

Ruben was interrupted by Maggie announcing, "Okay, Mick, hold that thought, we're here."

CHAPTER 13

Winnie Fights Back

AVERY INJECTED WINNIE IN HER THIGH WITH ENOUGH adrenaline to make a grandmother do handsprings. However, the stress from the dosage made her start shaking violently almost immediately. *Bollocks,* Avery thought.

After ten seconds of watching Winnie trembling on the floor, Avery actually started to show signs of worry. *The injection should have had her on her feet by now. Bloody hell, I think she's having a seizure.* He propped her up against the wall.

I need to do something or this isn't going to end well. What do I do? What do I do? Think, man, think! Suddenly, out of desperation, Avery leaned back and slapped her face.

"Winnie, come back to me. Winnie!" He slapped her again then grabbed her by the shoulders and shook her. "Winnie!" Avery went to slap her again but stopped. He heard her whisper but couldn't make it out.

"Are you okay? Talk to me." He repeated himself and listened but her voice was still imperceptible.

"Listen to me, I need you to focus and speak up."

She broke past the whisper and repeated, "I said, ow, you big bully, that hurt." She brought her hand up and cradled her face.

"I'm so sorry. I panicked." Winnie's eyes dilated to three times their normal size and she sprung to her feet. It almost brought tears to his eyes. Avery stood there motionless for several seconds then asked, "So are you okay?"

"Yes. Yes, I think so." She grabbed Avery by the arm and said, "Now, where's Dai? And why is it so bright in here?"

Avery was so uncharacteristically overwhelmed with emotion; he leaned in and embraced her tight. "I was so worried about you. Don't do that to me again."

"This seems so out of place for you. You must actually care about me." Avery let her go and gently pushed her back then cleared his throat.

"Apologies," Avery cleared his throat again and added, "I told you, you're special." He placed a closed fist to his mouth and cleared his throat once more.

"You're so sweet." Winnie saw the expression on his face after her comment and whispered, "But don't worry, I won't tell anyone."

"Good looking out."

"Now again, where's Dai?"

"He's resting in the next wing over."

"And Evie?"

"She's gone."

Winnie grabbed Avery by the scruff of the neck and said, "Gone where?"

"Easy. Easy. Take it easy. I don't know where she is. A few minutes ago she was removed from the room, by—by—" then Avery paused and was silent.

"By what, Avery? By what?"

"I'm not sure, by some kind of apparition."

"A ghost?"

Um, "Well, more like an angel, I think," Avery was a little embarrassed to admit.

Winnie let Avery go and asked, "What did this angel look like?"

"I'm not sure."

"Think, Avery."

"It was young and beautiful, I guess. The way you would imagine an angel would look?"

"Was it a girl, Avery? Was the angel a girl?"

"I don't know. Perhaps, but I wasn't that close. So, it may have been." Avery thought about it for a few seconds then added, "No, wait, you know what, her voice was feminine. So yes, if I had to guess, I would say it was a girl."

"Good, now what color was her hair?"

"Wow, is that really important?"

"Yes, man, now think, what color was her hair?"

"I'm not sure, and why all the questions? I'm not even sure if what I saw was real. I was standing behind Cooper so my view was obstructed."

"This is important, Avery, so think."

He turned his head to the left and looked up and closed his eyes. "Wait, it's coming to me. Yes, it was black, her hair was black."

Winnie let out a sigh of relief and said, "Ah, thank God."

"Why, do you know who or what that was?"

"Yes, it was Mia."

"Mia? Mia, as in Yvette's daughter, Mia?"

"Yes. Okay, let's go get Dai." Winnie walked out of the cell and Avery followed.

"Which way?"

"Wait, Yvette's daughter, Mia, is an angel?"

"No, she's more like a Saint."

"Okay, wait, I'm not following."

"Avery, which way?" Avery shook his head and pointed. Winnie bent down and headed in that direction on her tippy-toes.

"Winnie," Avery whispered, "please explain to me what I saw. I don't understand."

Winnie turned around and said, "Avery, not everything is knowable and explainable. So, just trust me. Plus, even if I wanted to explain it, there's no time. We need to get Dai."

"But, Winnie—!"

She interrupted Avery again and said, "Listen, if we survive this, everything will become clear to you but right now, we need to move, so let's go."

"Okay, but in order to get Dai, we have to go deeper into camp."

"So?"

"So, if you expect us to get out of this alive, we need to leave now. Moving deeper into camp will get us both killed for sure. We'll be easily surrounded."

"Avery, I'm not leaving without Dai. Plus, if you expect us to get out of this at all, we need him. I can't fight a bunch of men by myself, nor do I want to."

"But I thought you said you were a Kung Fu master?"

Winnie stopped and turned around yet again and said, "Yes, I am. But I can't dodge bullets."

Avery shook his head and pulled his torso back. "What?"

"Avery, look, do you know anything about Kung Fu?"

"Well, I know that fighters use their arms and legs to generate an endless combination of strikes."

"No, I meant Kung Fu history. Do you know anything about Kung Fu history?"

"No, and frankly we don't have time for a history lesson."

"Yes, we do, now listen. In China, long ago, there were Kung Fu masters that controlled provinces. One day, a challenge was made and all the masters got together to choose who would represent China from the North and South. One man stood out among them all. That person was Ip Man. He fought and became the grand master, the lord over all the masters."

"That's bloody interesting, but what's the point?"

"Yes, okay so, if you compare my skill level to others, I am a master. But Dai is the grand master, get it?"

Um, Avery thought.

"Blimey, I thought that would clear it up for you. So, let me think. How do I...oh, I have it, Dai can dodge bullets," Winnie added.

"Oh. Oh, oh, bloody hell. I get it. Damn it."

"Good, because my bullet-dodging skills are limited," Winnie concluded.

"Got it, follow me, and Winnie?"

"Yes?"

"That was a good short narrative."

"Thank you."

"You know, you're dossier doesn't do you any justice."

"This is why they fail," Winnie summarized.

Avery chuckled then said, "That is so true."

"So, am I going to become Superwoman because of that injection? I would totally love to leap tall buildings in a single bound."

"I don't think so, plus if you did, I wouldn't be able to follow you. So, that would leave me here alone to die a slow and agonizing death."

"That wasn't an actual question. It was a joke."

"Bloody hell, you got me. I'm so distracted. Oh wait, we're here."

"Okay, Avery, open it, open it, open it," Winnie chanted. Avery opened the cell and Winnie rushed in.

I wonder where all the guards are. Both 'A' and 'B' blocks had no guards, Avery thought.

Winnie tried to wake Dai up without success. She sat down and placed his head on her lap and said, "Oh, Dai."

Avery pulled the cell door closed then squatted down next to them. He took a deep breath and with genuine sincerity said, "Winnie, I'm so sorry, love, but I didn't know how to tell you."

"Tell me what?"

"Dai's mind is gone. If he wakes up, he will give us away. There is nothing we can do for him. I have seen it many times before. I'm so sorry."

"That can't be true."

"I'm sorry, but there's no way to remove the damage Dai has sustained. The only defense mechanism he has left is to scream and thrash about uncontrollably when he's awake until he passes out."

Winnie looked up at Avery and cried.

"I'm so sorry. I can put an end to his suffering quickly. It will be painless, I promise."

Winnie looked up, wearing disgust and incredulity on her face and said, "Avery, if you're suggesting what I think you are, then you've gone completely mental."

"I'm just trying to end his suffering."

"Listen to me carefully; I'm prepared to repel you with extreme prejudice before I allow you near Dai with thoughts of terminating his life."

Winnie's look of defiance made Avery raise both eyebrows then throw his hands up and say, "My apologies. It's regrettable that I even brought it up. What would you suggest we do? And how can I help?" Avery knew that Dai would reveal their location if he woke up. Contritely, he placed a hand behind his back and took hold of a hidden knife and was prepared to silence him and perhaps even do worse, if necessary.

"Avery, I know what you're thinking. Remove your hand from behind your back."

Avery raised both eyebrows again and did as directed.

"Now, give me your word that this is the last time you contemplate anything so vulgar and absurd."

Avery was quiet.

"Avery!" Winnie yelled.

"Yes, yes, you have my word," he said reassuringly. Then he confessed to himself, *I have forgotten how brilliant this woman is, and how loyal family members can be toward loved ones, regardless of how hopeless a situation is. But I actually feel fortunate I haven't been confronted with this scenario often enough to draw it to memory.*

"Oh, Dai." Winnie continued to try and wake up her brother to no avail. Finally, she closed her eyes, took a deep breath, sighed and said, "Hoshea, it's in your name I pray." Winnie placed a hand on either side of Dai's head and briefly witnessed the torment he was subjected to. She started praying in a language Avery did not understand. Then ten seconds later, she opened her eyes and said in a calm and encouraging voice, "Hey, big brother, come on, it's time to get up. We have to go. Come on, wake up. You can do it, come on."

Dai opened his eyes and said, "Winnie, is that you?"

"Yes."

"Are you okay?"

"Yes, Dai. I am now." Winnie looked up and said, "Thank you, Hoshea."

"That's impossible," Avery let out as he stood up, shaking his head in bewilderment.

"How, Winnie? How is this possible?"

"I have the gift of healing through the power and mercy of God."

"I don't believe it."

"You see and yet do not believe. Perhaps that is why you fail."

Dai got up and moved his neck from side to side and heard it crack several times. "How long have I been out?"

Winnie looked at Avery.

"About…about twelve to fourteen hours," Avery stuttered.

"That explains why I'm so hungry. So, since there's three of us standing in this cell, I take it this is a rescue mission," Dai posed.

"Yes, it is. And now that you've been rescued, we need your help to escape without killing anyone or being killed," Winnie shared.

"Avery, where to?" Winnie asked, but Avery just stood there. "Avery?"

"Sorry, I'm still completely baffled at what just happened. Dai, you shouldn't be saying nor doing, well, anything. Your mind was gone. I witnessed it for myself."

"Avery, you need to get past that. We need to go. Now, which way?" Winnie stated authoritatively.

Avery shook his head and said, "Back the way we came."

"Are you sure?"

"Yes, yes, there's a landing pad about twenty meters outside building Alpha on the north end. If we can get to the helicopter, and I can get us airborne, we might have a chance. But those are some big ifs."

"How many men do we have to contend with?" Dai asked.

"Over fifty on guard at any one time."

"Well, if we can distract them initially, then gather them together and restrict their movements and narrow their fighting space, I think we can take them, sis."

"Have you considered that they all have automatic weapons?" Avery added.

"Oh, well, that changes the outcome a bit. I can't dodge that many bullets."

"Well, I'm going to set aside the question of how you could possibly dodge a single bullet, since witnessing your miraculous recovery proves miracles happen. So, this is what I believe we should do." Avery squatted down, pulled a pen out of his pocket and started sketching on the ground. Winnie and Dai crouched down also. "First, Winnie, you need to take off your pants."

"Excuse me?"

"And your blouse, too."

"What? Are you daft, man? You can't be serious," Dai questioned. "That's my sister you're talking to. I suggest you apologize and mind your place."

"What?! No, sorry, mate. I meant no disrespect so keep your wits about you. She's the main part of our distraction is all," Avery stated then waited to receive confirmation to continue from Dai.

Dai stared him down for several seconds then grunted and said, "Go on."

"Yes. Now, this is the plan." Avery started articulating his plan but was interrupted by Winnie.

"Avery, you do realize that your plan can't involve us killing anyone, right?"

"What? Winnie, we may have to. These people are not held to those limitations, they will be shooting to kill."

"It doesn't matter what they do, we need to escape without killing anyone."

"I don't see how that's possible." Avery thought, *Well, I'm feeling prescient, I've spent my whole life fighting beside trained killers and I'm going to die rebelling alongside the gentle and forgiving.*

"Avery, Avery," Dai repeated. Avery shook his head, trying to remove the concerns but they slowly started creeping back in.

"Yes, sorry, I was away with the fairies."

"Are you with us now?"

"Yes, sorry."

"Good, so Avery, all you have to do is get me close," Dai said. "But since Kung Fu is a defensive art, I agree with my sister. These are American soldiers who believe they're defending democracy. We can't just kill them."

Avery just shook his head gently and crinkled up the corner of his mouth in disbelief. *The innocence being demonstrated by Winnie and Dai is bloody unbelievable. However, as incredible as their request may be, it's in defense of people like them that I chose to do what I do. I just have to consider if what they're asking is even remotely possible,* Avery admitted to himself as he rested his head on the palm of his hand.

"Avery, are you okay?" Winnie added.

"Yes, I'm just thinking."

"Wait, don't you guys have like non-lethal force defensive equipment or something?"

"Defensive equipment," Avery responded back initially,

unsure as to the meaning of the question.

"Yes, that's a great idea, Winnie," Dai shared out loud. "Yes, Avery, you know, like plastic bullets, rubber mallets or clubs, and maybe some bombs that knock people out rather than kill them?"

Huh! "Come to think of it, we bloody do," Avery suddenly realized. "We don't have plastic bullets, but we do have rubber ones. We have bean bags we could use as projectiles from shotguns versus lead slugs or buck shots, and we have stun grenades. Which, as you said, knocks people out rather than kills them."

"Brilliant, there you are. Wait, that's all non-lethal stuff, right?" Winnie questioned.

"Yes. It does bloody hurt when you get hit in the chest with a bean bag, but yes, it won't kill anyone. And neither will the rubber bullets or the stun grenades."

"Brilliant, then let's do that."

"Yes, but first we need to get our hands on those types of weapons."

"Okay, so how do we do that?"

"I would need to get to the armory."

"Brilliant, then you go to the armory and we'll wait here."

"Very well, but I need you both to realize that trying to escape from a military installation using non-lethal force is completely mental. To my knowledge, it has never been done."

"That's why it's going to work," Winnie replied innocently.

"Perhaps," Avery added, seemingly optimistic. However, he realized that the chances of escaping under these conditions were virtually zero. Nevertheless, for them, he would try and die, if need be. "If we had the element of surprise and maybe ten more men," Avery posed under his breath.

"We do." Winnie pointed and Avery looked around.

"Oh, bloody hell." *Maybe our chances are better than zero,* Avery thought. "Well, I'm going out to get the supplies we need. When I get back, this is what we're going to do." Avery started laying out his crazy plan. "I should be back in ten minutes or less."

Winnie took off her pants and shirt.

"What are you doing?"

"You told me to take off my pants and shirt."

"Yes, but not now, when I get back. Not that you don't look quite attractive in—"

"Okay, stop talking and turn around." Winnie started putting her clothes back on and punched Avery hard on the arm halfway through.

"Ow, bloody hell, woman."

"That's for being a pig."

"Apologize to my sister."

"Yes, yes, I'm bloody sorry.

"Good."

Avery took off and ran outside toward the armory between 'B' and 'C' wing and immediately ran into Cooper, so Avery had to cover his true intentions.

"Cooper, have you found anything?"

"No, sir, I was just coming to find you. Did you?"

"No, I didn't."

"Well, sir, I took my time, as you suggested, and casually looked in every cell, but I haven't seen anything out of place. I don't understand what happened in that room or why everything else seems so normal. The guards in 'C' block know something is wrong, since they heard me fire my sidearm."

"It's okay, we'll figure it out. Now, where are all the guards from Alpha and Bravo wing?"

Cooper looked at his watch and said, "Well, it's time for a shift change so maybe that's where the four Alpha soldiers are but the Bravo guards are with me. They're on standby over there." Cooper pointed to the entrance of 'C' block. "I had them follow me in case I found something. And I didn't want to leave 'C' block unattended. Plus, I knew you were searching 'A' and 'B' wings and you could take care of yourself."

This tosser is such a coward, Avery thought. *He doesn't care about me, or anyone else. He just wanted more men around him at my expense. I just need to play along. This might turn out to be easier than I thought. On a positive note, this stupid bloody American can't possibly succeed at anything.*

"Fair enough, it was a good idea," Avery suggested. "Have you told the guards anything?"

"No, sir, but the Bravo guards spoke to the Charlie wing sentries, so they know I fired my sidearm and we're searching for something."

"We can't tell anyone what happened until we figure it out

ourselves. However, we can't just act like everything is normal, because it's not."

"Agreed, so, what do we do?"

"First, let's take a few seconds to calm down."

"Yes," Cooper brought both hands up and rubbed his face intensely. Avery closed his eyes and took a deep breath, pretending to center himself, then blew it out slowly.

"Look, I'm not sure what we saw, but if it's one of those aliens that abducted millions of people without a trace, they have technology that we want. Therefore, we need one alive.

"Oh my God, that makes perfect sense. So, how do we do that?"

"Well, we know for a fact that if they were aliens, they'll be back."

"How, why?" Cooper asked.

"Because we're still holding several of their conspirators."

"Yes. Shit, why didn't I think of that?"

"Well, it doesn't matter. However, we need to be ready when they come back. So we need to hand out non-lethal rounds to everyone. Then, you walk back over to Charlie and Delta wing and tell the guards we will be conducting a training exercise soon. Remind them to stay alert but relax. You know what kind of wussies these soldiers are. So, if they find something, I don't want us being caught in the cross fire."

"Great idea."

"Come with me to the armory, it's on your way to Charlie wing. We'll take the Bravo guards with us and have them pass out rounds to the soldiers on the grounds."

Cooper chuckled then said, "Excellent plan, sir."

"But, what if we find them, those…those alien ghost people? We have to do something."

"Absolutely, but we want to capture them, not riddle them with bullets."

Cooper chuckled again then said, "Yes, I agree, that's smart. It would be fun to make them squirm."

"Yes, but there will be no, wait, I'm sorry, what did you call it?

"Squirming."

"Yes, exactly, there will be no squirming if we don't capture them. I will take non-lethal rounds to the guards in Alpha and Bravo block and you focus on Charlie and Delta."

"Yes, sir."

"Remind them it's a training session. We don't want to kill each other in this process."

"Agreed." Cooper gathered all the ammunition he required and took off, returning to wings 'C' and 'D'.

Avery successfully disseminated misinformation to every soldier in his path. He then gave the Bravo guards non-lethal ammunition and sent them off. One guard handed out rounds to the soldiers on the towers. One soldier handed out rounds to the sentries around buildings 'C' and 'D'. Another soldier disbursed ammunition to the men guarding the grounds around buildings 'A' and 'B' and the last soldier gave out ammo to the men in Alpha wing. Afterward, Avery returned to Bravo wing.

When Avery arrived, he released six inmates being detained in Bravo block.

"Why are you doing this?" an inmate asked.

"I'm helping you escape," Avery replied with a smirk on his face.

"Why?"

"Because it's the right thing to do, since you men have been here long enough without cause.

"Now, listen up, you three head toward 'C' and 'D' wing, in that direction," Avery pointed, "and let everyone out. Afterward, head toward the armory and gather additional fire power. You three head up north toward 'A' wing but first release the men held here. I will generate a distraction for as long as I can. Hopefully it will give you men enough time to set everyone free. If I manage to get the helicopter airborne, I will provide air cover to further increase your chances of getting away.

"Does everyone understand?" Avery looked around as the men lightly nodded.

He gave two men shotguns with beanbag shells and had one go to each entrance point. He gave two men M16 rifles with rubber bullets and sent one toward each exit. He gave the last two men a Glock with rubber rounds and a sonic grenade and sent them to either side of the building.

Avery looked around at all the men and saw the looks of

skepticism on their faces. He could tell no one thought his plan would work but he had to sell it. If his diversion was going to work, the men had to believe it. So he focused and decided to give an empowering short speech.

"Look, we're on a military compound with over fifty men on guard at any one time. This is all I could do to give us a chance. You could stay here and die a slow and agonizing death alone in a cold cell or you can die free men. It's your choice."

I hope that did it. I feel motivated, Avery thought as he looked around and saw everyone nodding in agreement.

"Brilliant, now keep a look out until I give the word." Everyone nodded and Avery ran into Dai's cell where his two soon-to-be fugitives were waiting.

"We're glad to have you back."

"Are we ready to go?" Winnie questioned, seemingly a little impatient.

"Yes, I think so. Does everyone remember the plan?"

As Winnie started taking off her clothes again, she said, "Avery, we discussed the plan like ten minutes ago, so yes, we remember."

"For goodness sake, my lady, attitude. And put your clothes back on. That part of the plan is no longer required."

Ugh, "Really? Turn around, and don't look at me. I look totally gross." Winnie put her clothes back on and punched Avery hard on the back of his arm again.

"Oh, bloody hell, woman, what was that for?"

"'Cause you're a pig. And you could have told me I no longer had to take my clothes off."

"But I just walked in!"

"That doesn't matter."

"Okay, you two, stop playing around, we need to go. Avery, lead the way." Dai pointed to the cell door.

Winnie punched Avery yet again. Argh, "Bloody hell, woman, you're going to be the death of me."

Avery and the others quickly moved to the north end of the building and Avery gave the word. Three men ran out the north and south ends of Bravo block simultaneously. Even though the soldiers were told a training exercise was taking place soon, they were all caught off guard. The four soldiers outside the Alpha and

Bravo wings were taken down almost immediately. Avery's inmate distraction worked. They fanned out toward the towers while Avery rushed into Alpha block. He yelled for the guards to come out and join the resistance. The soldiers stepped outside and Dai and Winnie quickly Kung Fu'ed the men into submission. Just one kick to each of the soldiers' torsos and heads was enough to render them unconscious.

Avery and Winnie ran to the north end of the Alpha building and peered out the door. "There, there's the helicopter, and our way off this bloody rock," Avery informed Winnie.

"Blimey, it's further than I thought and completely in the open," Winnie shared with Avery.

"The distance is a non-issue since all the men have been neutralized. And it's a helicopter landing pad so we don't want obstacles in the way. Now, all we need to do is get to the helo and get it airborne before bloody reinforcements arrive."

"Then let's move." Winnie turned around and saw Dai releasing most of the inmates. Dai, what are you doing? Come over here." Dai stopped and ran up to Winnie and Avery.

"Dai, you do realize you set some seriously bad people loose among us, right?" Winnie questioned.

"Yes, but if we expect to have any chance of escape, we need the distraction and support."

"I agree," Avery added. "Plus, it's too late now. It would be impossible to get them back in a cell without a fight. And we have other more pressing matters to tend to. I'm sure additional men are en route already, so we need to move."

Mia and Hoshea were observing Winnie from a portal opening.

"They're not going to make it, Hoshea."

"You don't know that, Mia."

"Yes, I do. There's a dozen men coming this way. And they don't know that. We have to do something."

"Mia, we must wait."

Ugh, "This waiting is just torture."

"Mia, these are beings with free will. You have to let them make the choices they want. It is not up to you to decide what is right or wrong and when or if you should intervene. I realize you would gladly sacrifice yourself for one or more of them but this is not about you. We must wait, because their struggle will inspire and save others. You must have patience. Everything has to unfold as it must."

Mia knew Hoshea was unhappy with her impatience. She grabbed him by the arm and leaned her head on his shoulder and said in a deeply remorseful voice, "I'm so sorry, Hoshea, please don't be mad at me. I'm ashamed for implying that you are unaware of how this is affecting me."

"Your embarrassment is justified, Mia. You must display greater fortitude."

"I'm sorry, but I'm still just a stupid kid and my emotions get the best of me."

Hoshea picked up Mia's head by the chin until their eyes met then said, "Mia, you are a spiritual being now. With unimaginable powers which you have yet to explore or comprehend.

"You will forever guide the development of beings much like these. As your heart aches for them so does mine. But their life is there right now. And yours is here. To remove one of them from this current environment could condemn the rest to death. Who is to say which of them is more important, more wonderful or more glorious? The sorrow you feel for beings of good conscious will never change but the exultation you'll receive from their victories will eventually overwhelm and outlast feelings of disappointment and dread.

"Mia, give them time to make the mistakes they must. Think of them as your children. And as a parent that sees a child try to walk for the first time. What do you do when you realize they will fall? Do you let them try, hence encouraging independence and freedom, or do you step in before they fall, limiting their potential and possibly their future?"

"I should let them fail," Mia whimpered out.

"Why?"

"Because with failure comes success."

"Yes, Mia. Eventually, they fall less and walk more. But they will always fall. To keep them from walking so they don't fall is a false security and a penitentiary for their independence. One day, they will not just walk, they will run. And on that day you will rejoice for and with them.

"Unfortunately, before then, like today, you will be horrified when they try to fly without wings. But Mia, allow them the honor to fail with dignity. This is your test. There can be no greater sacrifice than to watch those you love fall so they may rise again. And always thinking, this might be the one trial they do not survive."

"Perhaps I'm not worthy of the honor bestowed upon me nor do I have the strength to bear what I see. How do you bear it, Hoshea?"

"That's simple, I wait for them to ask me for help."

Huh? "Wait, what did you just say?"

"I said, I wait for them to ask me for help."

"So, if they ask me for help, I can help them?

"Of course, that would be their choice and yours."

Mia jumped on him with a strong embrace. "You are truly magnificent."

Then Mia took a few seconds to think about what Hoshea said and her happiness started to fade. "Wait, wait, wait, what if they don't realize they can ask me for help? Or what if they know they can, but they don't ask me?"

"Then you wait and see how their decisions unfold."

"Really? That's awful. I'm back to square one."

"That's not true, Mia. Because, if they don't ask you, they may ask me, and I may allow you to go in my stead."

Mia jumped on Hoshea again and bear-hugged him. "You are truly magnificent." Then Mia thought about the exchange she and Hoshea just had and said, "You do realize you generate some serious avant-garde challenges."

"Do I?"

"Yes, you do, and in the extreme."

"Well, Mia, the issue is free will."

"I feel better as long as you're not getting tired of me."

Hoshea lightly smiled then they stepped back and continued to observe Winnie's struggle.

A dozen additional men arrived and surrounded Dai, Winnie and Avery as Mia foresaw. Unlike the movies where everyone stood around in a circle discharging their firearms, the soldiers knew they were too close to risk injury by friendly fire. These twelve men were heavily trained in hand-to-hand combat and could easily subdue three civilians.

Dai was easily holding his own against a considerable number of adversaries. Men were being tossed about like rag dolls. Winnie, on the other hand, was holding back. She was remorseful about hitting any soldier too hard, so her attacks required multiple strikes repeatedly to incapacitate a single opponent. This made the engagement much more difficult for Dai and Avery.

"Mia, have you noticed that Winnie doesn't want to hurt any of the soldiers, so her lack of commitment is causing Dai and Avery significant stress?"

"Yes, I see it."

Finally, Avery realized their engagement was lasting minutes longer than it should. This delay was giving their adversaries an opportunity to engage more men. He saw no other choice but to release a stun grenade in the midst of them all. This act of desperation would have negative repercussions for them but it was a chance he had to take. Dai had somehow been taken off his feet and was getting pummeled on the ground. Avery could smell and taste the pepper spray in the air so he rationalized that Dai had been sprayed repeatedly. He released the grenade then dove at Winnie seconds before the blast ignited.

The explosion knocked everyone within a six-meter radius around the initial blast off their feet. Dai was fortunate he was already on the ground covering up his face and ears from multiple attackers. Avery covered Winnie's ears from the detonation shock so he absorbed the full blunt of the stun grenade and was knocked unconscious.

Dai powered through the pain of the pepper spray and managed to be the first one back on his feet. He rendered any soldier who was recovering from the blast unconscious. Their ruffian diversion had actually done a good job of removing the threat from the closest towers. There was an unhindered path to the helicopter, they just had to get to their feet and get there.

Winnie pushed Avery off her and tried to revive him.

"Avery, we need to move. Get up." Avery's eyes started to flutter and the high whine got louder as his blurry vision came into view. Avery shook his head and opened his mouth wide repeatedly.

"Avery, are you okay?" Avery saw Winnie's mouth moving but couldn't make out the words. However, that didn't matter; he knew what she was trying to say. He got up and yanked her forward.

"Bloody hell, you don't handle women very often, do you?" Winnie questioned an over-aggressive Avery.

"We need to move!" Dai yelled.

The men on the ground started recovering and getting back to their feet. However, Dai kept kicking them back down. Regrettably, there were other guards closing in and suddenly they started firing. Avery, Dai, and Winnie were all hit by incoming weapons fire. Avery looked down and saw blood coming from his stomach and Winnie's leg. Winnie was holding onto Avery's arm so tight, her grip felt like a tourniquet.

Bloody hell, we're in serious trouble. The soldiers realized this wasn't a training exercise anymore. They were using real bullets now. The helicopter was only fifteen meters away. *We just need a few more seconds under cover but we won't make it under these conditions without a miracle,* Avery confessed to himself. "God, if you're out there, we need your help. I'm of no consequence, but Winnie is special, please save her."

"Hoshea, if it's your will we get out of this, then you might need to help us," Winnie prayed as tears rolled down her face from the gunshot wound to her leg.

Winnie and Avery had both been shot, but Dai had received the worst of it. He had sustained multiple gunshots. Dai's right shoulder, left arm and his stomach had been hit. Dai was doing his best to keep up with Avery but his injuries were taking their toll.

"They've all been hurt, Hoshea. They won't make it without help!" Mia cried out. "They've asked for help. We need to help them. Please send me out there."

"Mia, wait."

Suddenly, Hilily stepped out of a portal in front of Winnie, Avery and Dai. Holly walked out and appeared along the left side and Juno on the right. Each of the girls were moving faster than the human eye could see. But to them, their movements and those of everyone around them appeared to be in slow motion. Only when the Guardians reached out for someone did their movements accelerate into a blur of light. Artemis was pulling up the rear and making sure no one got close.

Hilily focused on getting the team to the helicopter, and each of the other girls grabbed hold of someone. Holly was supporting Avery as he held on to Winnie. Holly's support gave Avery a sense of euphoria, causing him to forget his injuries.

Brilliant, my adrenaline must be kicking in because I feel so much better. It's like I'd never been shot. Avery looked down at his stomach to confirm he had actually been hit. Maybe it was a rubber bullet and the sting was wearing off. "Blimey, I was definitely hit," he confessed at the sight of his bloody shirt. *The adrenaline must be impugning my judgment. Whatever, ignorance is bliss.* He looked around and said under his breath, "There's been a serious prisoner containment breach. But I wonder if it's too late for a conciliatory offering? Oh, who cares, we're almost out of here." Meanwhile, Dai had received his second wind thanks secretly to Juno.

This is bazaar, Dai thought, *a few seconds ago I didn't think I could take another step and now I feel the euphoria of floating. It's like it's not even me walking. Like I'm standing beside myself and in slow motion, I'm being carried.*

Suddenly, as Avery was within reach of the aircraft, his pain started returning. He tightened up his stomach, let out a low grunt and said, "Winnie, are you okay?"

"I'm terrified we won't make it," Winnie replied with her eyes closed. She was holding on to Avery's arm like a metal strap. "How much further?" she cried out.

"Just a few more meters," Avery replied, which seemed to bring Winnie comfort. She opened her eyes and saw blue light everywhere.

Avery turned and asked Dai, "How are you doing, mate?"

"I'm not sure how, but I'm right behind you."

"We have help from our Guardian Angels," Winnie let out.

"Well, that would explain how we're still alive." Avery quickly looked around and added, "There were literally twenty men with automatic weapons firing at us within fifteen meters. There's no way they can all be such poor marksmen. Honestly, we should all be dead."

"Perhaps, but we're not dead yet, so hurry," Dai announced.

They arrived at the helicopter and Avery helped Winnie and Dai in.

Dai closed the door behind them and laid down. "I'm so sorry, Winnie, but I can't help you anymore, I'm spent."

The Guardians formed a cocoon around them, where no breach could penetrate. Multiple men tried to run in and physically attack them but they were easily repelled with extreme prejudice.

Winnie took off her shirt and ripped it into multiple strips. Avery worked on getting the aircraft ready for launch while Winnie tended to their injuries. She pulled out the first aid kit from under the back seat and opened it. She placed gauze on Dai's bullet wounds and tied them securely with the pieces of her shirt. She also placed gauze on her right leg and secured it while grinding her teeth.

"Avery, how much longer? We need to go! They are at our door!" Winnie yelled as she leaned in and placed gauze on Avery's bloody stomach. He cringed at her touch but didn't complain. She secured the gauze with an ace bandage and said, "Well, how much longer?"

Suddenly, the ground shook and every man near the helicopter was airborne. Artemis and the other Guardians struck the ground at the same time with their defensive shields. The force of the impact sent everyone around the aircraft flying back ten meters, and the Guardians were gone. The soldiers temporarily lost consciousness upon landing.

"Finally!" Avery shouted. "We're ready to go."

"What took you so long?"

"Winnie, this isn't a movie where actors pretend they can get a helicopter off the ground in ten seconds. In real life, if a helo's 'cocked', you might be able to get ramped up in ninety seconds. But this aircraft was cold. You could easily over torque the engine."

"Okay, okay, okay, enough with the explanations, let's go."

"Right! Hold on."

Winnie noticed many former inmates running toward them. "Avery, wait, can we take any of those men? They helped us." Winnie wanted to save some, if possible.

"No, the payload on this aircraft will be taxed with just six people. And there are three times that many coming toward us. If we allow even one aboard, the rest will follow and the helicopter will not get airborne."

"Avery is right, sis, we need to go."

"But I feel terrible about leaving these men behind."

"It's either that or we die here, Winnie."

Winnie shook her head and said reluctantly, "Fine, let's go. We have too much to do, we can't die here."

"Cooper, I hear explosions and see gunfire on my installation. What is going on out there?

Cooper got on the internal radio and answered central command. "Avery and I are holding training drills for the guards, sir."

"Why are the inmates running loose on the grounds? And why is Avery on board my helicopter with two inmates?"

Suddenly, Cooper stepped outside of Charlie wing to witness prisoners running loose and attacking soldiers as he ran to the armory and saw the helicopter taking off.

"What the—! Are you kidding me? No, no, no, no, no."

Cooper helped the armory officer fend off an assault from several inmates. While they were incapacitated, he walked in, switched ammunition and shot those inmates dead.

The armory officer was on the floor. As Cooper helped him up, he asked, "Are you okay?"

"Yes, sir."

Gather up as much M16 ammo as you can carry and follow me. But first, hand me the Big Mac and two mags.

Cooper took the Tac 50 sniper rifle and ran to the landing pad and set up. The armory officer handed out real ammunition to every soldier he could find still able to resist.

The base's anti-aircraft guns were functioning but there was no one manning the stations.

Cooper laid down on his back on the helo pad and loaded full metal jacket bullets into his Tac 50 sniper rifle. He took a deep breath then closed his eyes, moving his neck from side to side and cracking it twice. Cooper then pushed himself off the ground with is left leg and turned over onto his stomach as he exhaled slowly. He took the cover off the scope and acquired his target.

Damn it, they were almost two kilometers away already. Cooper took another deep breath and started to let it out slowly when he took his first shot, missing the pilot but hitting the aircraft. Cooper took repeated shots.

"What was that?" Winnie cried out.

"It's Cooper, he's shooting at us.

"But we're so far away, how can he still be hitting us?

"Because he's bloody brilliant with a Big Mac. But don't worry, we're almost out of range. We just need a few more seconds." Suddenly, a bullet came through the hull and into Avery's back and out the windshield. Avery's head snapped back and then forward.

"AVERY!" Winnie yelled.

Arrr, "Take...take...take the cyclic control," Avery stuttered.

"I have no bloody idea what that is, Avery."

"It's the...the...the joy stick."

Winnie jumped into the co-pilot seat and took hold of the joy stick and yelled, "AVERY, WHAT DO I DO?!"

"Level, level, level us off and go straight." The pain from the gunshot wound was intense but Avery bore it well.

"How do I do that?"

"Take hold of the collective here," Avery took Winnie's left hand and placed it on the bar and said, "Turn this to give it throttle, more gas. Then push the joy stick forward." Winnie did as directed.

"Yes, that's it. But suddenly it's, it's, it's so, so cold in here," Avery stuttered as he started to lose consciousness.

Arrr, "Avery, I have no idea what I'm doing. I can't do this, I have to tend to you; you're losing too much blood. Arrr—AVERY!"

"Leave, leave, leave me here and save yourself," Avery said then was unconscious.

The helicopter was now in a spiral toward the ocean, seconds from impact.

"Hoshea, let your will be done," Winnie muttered under her breath. She was too weak to hold the controls any longer.

"No!" Mia yelled then held her breath and covered her mouth with both hands.

"The aircraft is not going to make it," Hoshea confessed out loud.

CHAPTER 14

Stefan Meets Heather
Monday, July 22, 2047 11:14 p.m.

DOCTOR STEFAN MAGNUSSON LIVED WITH HIS WIFE AND THREE children in a three-hundred-square-meter flat on the third floor of a luxury apartment complex overlooking Strömmen Lake in Stockholm, Sweden. Magnusson was temporarily assigned to Jackson Memorial Hospital as the lead geneticist. He and his team were working on proving the age of the human genome. His wife walked into their master suite to find Stefan packing for a return trip to Miami, Florida.

"Stefan, you can't be serious. You're leaving me?"

"I'm sorry, Malena, I told you, I have no choice."

"Wow, really? So, you're telling me that work is more important than your family?"

"Oh my goodness, no, sötnos, of course not. I've told you repeatedly that I'm doing this for the family."

"That's nonsense, Stefan! Our children are gone! They were taken from us in the middle of the night, without anyone making a sound, while we slept, right here on this bed. I don't think I could ever forgive myself for not being more alert. We should have heard something."

"Stop it, Malena! I've told you countless times it wasn't your fault. No one on the planet, and I mean no one, saw or heard anything. And hundreds of millions were taken, hundreds of millions."

"What about Winnie, whom we trusted?"

"What about her?"

"You've been ignoring all the awful stories being broadcast about her?"

"No, I haven't. If anything, I've been hypercritical of those stories in search of the truth. And you're quite aware that I've made countless calls to her."

"And you don't consider it suspicious that you haven't been able to connect with her in a week?"

"No, not really."

"Why?! Why not?" Stefan's wife asked with a look of disgust on her face.

"Because we haven't been able to call neighbors that literally live across the hall. Reliable forms of communications are down all around the world."

"Stefan, the whole world is claiming that she and her doctor friend are in league with those monsters."

"I realize that."

"And yet you always seem to defend her and her psycho Spanish friend. Why?"

"Malena, how many times must I give you the same information? I've defended them because out of every witness they've had on television testifying against them, I'm the only one who actually knows them. Those people in the news broadcasts have been strangers."

"You don't know that."

"Yes, I do. Many of those alleged witnesses who claim to know them could barely form complete sentences. And a few so-called friends got their names wrong. Look, Winnie is a gentle, caring person who loves children and Evie has a little girl of her own. We have both socialized with them many times. Winnie has even tended to our children during our multiple weekend getaways. And our kids loved her."

"I don't need to be reminded that we socialized with the enemy. And who our children loved or didn't love."

"Sötnos, please," Stefan was hoping to calm his wife down before the conversation went to a dark place. But he realized he wasn't being very successful.

Malena held a hand to her chest and one to her mouth. Seconds later, tears filled her eyes again. She lowered her shaking hand away from her mouth and muttered out through quivering lips, "I've never felt as empty or helpless as I have this week. I don't know if I can go on living. But you're okay with leaving me here, alone. To deal with the funeral arrangements of our children. Our children, Stefan, while you go back to work?"

"Malena, you think this is easy for me? You think the disappearance of our children hasn't wounded me deeply? I am still devastated by what happened. I've been sitting here with you for a week desperately waiting to hear news from someone, anyone on the disappearance of our children. And I now realize that that was a mistake. I should have been out there looking for answers myself. Not sitting here waiting for someone who has never come. I've repeatedly given you my reasons for leaving, and returning to work is not one of them. We need answers and I need to find them. So why do you continue to infer that I don't care?"

"Because I can't believe that you're leaving me here, alone, knowing how emotionally vulnerable I am. To ask questions we already know the answers to," Malena shot back without hesitation.

Stefan, saw the distress on his wife's face. She looked faint. He walked over to her and took her arm.

"Malena, please sit down. You're shaking." Stefan walked her over to the reading area in their bedroom and helped her down, then handed her a valium. "Sötnos, please, take this." Malena looked up at him with tears streaming down her face, wanting to speak but the words were caught in her throat. She reached up and took the pill. Stefan poured a glass of water from a small pitcher sitting on an end table and gave it to her.

She placed the pill in her mouth and used the water to wash it down. "I'm so sorry. I realize you're in pain and this situation is emotionally shattering, but we will get through it, together." Stefan knelt down on one knee and offered his traumatized wife a hug. She leaned in and held him tight. "I will find our children, I swear it."

Seconds later, Stefan held her at arm's length and said, "Malena, I believe the discovery we've made at work will change the course of history. If our initial findings are confirmed, I would expect nothing to be the same once the information is revealed to the general public. If my hypothesis is correct, the results will most likely tell us who or what took our children and where they are."

"How? How is that possible, Stefan? You're a geneticist working in a hospital. How does your work have anything to do with the disappearance of millions?"

"Not my work specifically, but the discovery could reveal everything."

"You're not answering my question. How? How, Stefan? How will you going to work help find our children?"

"Malena, I've explained it to you countless times, in many different ways. I don't know how else to explain it so that you will understand, but I just know it in my heart that going out to get us answers is the right thing to do."

"I see, so I'm just too stupid to understand your explanations, is that it? And leaving me here alone is for my own good?"

"What?! No, I never said that."

"Well, Stefan, you know what I think? I think what you've told me so far is shit! I think you have never cared about this family and that you'd rather be at work or alone than with us. Or perhaps you've lost your mind, or you're in league with them, which would explain why your arguments have made no sense."

"What? What you're saying seems heartless and a bit cruel."

"Is it?" Malena was quick to retort.

"Yes, Malena! It's absolutely senseless!"

"Really, Stefan, so there's nothing wrong with you leaving me here alone, to return to work, in a different country. In a different country, Stefan!"

He suddenly realized this was an argument he couldn't win so he conceded. "Very well, I see I've obviously failed to articulate my reasons with any degree of success. I accept that failure and hope that someday you will see and admit my actions were essential and valid."

"No, I'm sorry, but surrendering your position and then doing what you want anyway is unacceptable. Your arguments were vague, weak and unconvincing. And you have demonstrated an emotional callousness I have seldom seen in anyone. Therefore,

I'm going to be the better person and make it easy for you. If you leave now, for whatever reason, that's it. We're finished."

"What? What do you mean?"

"Really, you're seriously asking me what I mean?"

"Yes. What you're saying seems insane." Stefan stood up and placed both hands on his head and started pulling at his hair.

"If you believe my needs are insane then it's you who's truly lost your mind. From the moment you received that phone call from work, you have been locked up in your office. You have ignored me and everything related to our family. There are vendors which need answers. Wake arrangement decisions which need to be made. Dozens of telephone calls which must be returned to answer questions on memorial services. Preparations which involve the funeral arrangements of our children, our children, Stefan!"

"I'm sorry, Malena, but I need answers. And you can make those arrangements without me."

"I don't want to do it. That's why I have you. Or thought I did."

"Sötnos—"

Stefan was interrupted. "Don't call me that anymore. It's clear to me now that I mean nothing to you."

Stefan walked over to embrace his wife but she forced her chair back and pushed him away.

"Don't touch me. Just GET OUT, GO! And don't ever come back."

Stefan stopped, shook his head, and just stood there speechless, staring at his wife. When he centered himself, he walked over to the bed and grabbed his backpack. He confirmed his laptop was in it and left everything else. Stefan walked out of the bedroom without saying another word. Malena stood up and followed him to the front door.

He opened the door then turned around and said, "I'm going to prove it to you. I'll call you in a few days with proof. Then you'll see that I was right. I will find our children. I swear it."

"Get out!"

"Watch for my message."

"I SAID, GET OUT!"

He couldn't remember the last time he cried but his bottom lip was quivering and his eyes started tearing up when Malena slammed the door shut. He walked down the stairs to exit the apartment complex. On his way out he confessed to himself, "As God as my witness, I will find out what happened to my children."

Sweden's underground system had reopened for business the day before. Stefan was one of the few using the reopened transit line to make passage to the airport.

Upon arrival, the airport terminals were vastly void of pedestrian traffic. *Now that's odd*, Stefan thought. *I can understand the difficulty in getting a large business functioning normally again after such a dramatic event. But this is the country's main artery to the outside world. Why is our government ignoring the country's infrastructure? The lack of activity surrounding our transit system makes no sense. It's like they want the people to panic. Why? What would be gained by such an act?*

Perhaps if the population panics, the politicians who come to the rescue can be seen as saviors and acquire lordships. Can Sweden's leadership be as vain as to risk mass fear for political gain? Stefan thought about it for a few more seconds then admitted to himself, *No, that's nonsense, that can't be right. There has to be a logical explanation. However, for now, I need to focus on the task at hand, getting to the US as quickly as possible.*

Stefan read messages posted online and in the airport terminals notifying potential travelers that all passenger flights in and out of the country were suspended until further notice by order of the transport secretary.

Wow, it's going to be difficult to arrange transportation if no one can fly. But I have to try, Stefan confessed to himself. *I'm not going to allow these few initial setbacks to curb my desires. I just have to start negotiating for passage to the US with any airline carrier, pilot or commercial vessel I can find.*

After six hours of traveling around the airport to every terminal and hangar, Stefan succeeded in arranging passage on a cargo aircraft bound for South America via Iceland, Canada, and the US. During his long airport voyage, Stefan managed to inform practically everyone he spoke with that he was a doctor. Therefore, the crewmember on his newly acquired transport vessel told him the aircraft was transporting microprocessors, for integration into the human population. Stefan found that information to be odd but intriguing.

"So what does integration into the human population mean, exactly?" Stefan asked the crewmen.

"What I think it means is that everyone on the planet will be expected to have one of these microchip devices inserted under their skin. Soon, it'll be the only way anyone will be able to buy or pay for anything. New automated tellers have already been installed everywhere in Sweden. I saw someone use one this morning to pay for a cup of coffee. It was rather cool. He placed his thumb on a reader, then flashed his chip under the scanner and that was it. The credit was removed from his account. This new credit system will be worldwide in a matter of days." The crewman actually showed Stefan where the chip was inserted on the back of the man's right hand.

"I was supposed to get it installed today but I was told their equipment was malfunctioning. Anyway, did you get yours?"

"No, not yet."

"Well, you better hurry, because in a few days, no other form of payment will be accepted anywhere.

"You're right, I need to make that a priority when I arrive in the US."

"Here." Derrik Corvin handed Stefan a chip.

"Thank you. How did you get an extra one?"

"You're welcome. And the truth is, a box fell over when I was loading it on the aircraft and some chips fell out. It won't work until it's inserted and activated but at least you have it. You know, in case anyone asks."

"Yes, thank you. That was very thoughtful." Stefan examined the chip for a few seconds then asked, "Do you happen to have another?"

The crewman gave Stefan a long odd look so Stefan added, "It's for my wife, she's sick and doesn't leave the house very often. So even if she didn't have it installed, she can say I have one for her. You know, so she doesn't get in trouble."

The crewman stared him down and surprisingly replied, "Okay."

"Thank you," Stefan replied with genuine appreciation.

"You're welcome; I just wanted to make sure you weren't planning on taking advantage of me by trying to sell it or something. Anyway, here, plus, I have quite a few more."

Stefan thanked the man again and walked off. He wanted to ask a plethora of other questions but he didn't want to disclose the fact that he had very little to no knowledge about the system the young man was referencing. Plus, for now, Stefan didn't really care; he just wanted to get on US soil. Afterwards, he would make arrangements to get to Miami, with or without this new technology.

********** Back on Earth **********

Hikiko was assigned to help protect part of Hoshea's new disciples. Samantha, Charlotte and Heather were part of the Guardian team. Hikiko made its way to the Cuban home. Heather announced to the girls that Hikiko was coming with a mission. Samantha and Charlotte were so eager they could barely contain their excitement. This was the first real mission they would actually be on together. And to help protect Hoshea's new followers spreading the gospel of love and mercy on the forbidden planet was a great honor.

Hikiko found the three girls standing in the foyer, at the ready, the moment it walked into the house.

"Ladies, I see Heather has already shared my surprise." Hikiko looked over at Heather in time to notice a little smirk on her face.

"Did you explain the mission to them?"

"No, I didn't. Only that you were coming with our first assignment."

"I see. Well, girls, this mission will be dangerous."

"We're ready," the girls shot out collectively.

"I see." Hikiko tilted its head and quietly stared up and down at all the girls who were in a military style 'at ease' pose. Finally, Hikiko used both hands to motion the girls to approach and said, "Come." It knew the girls were dying to hand out hugs and kisses but were waiting for permission out of respect for Hikiko's Guardian status and the position it held among the celestial ranks. Plus, Harem were not accustomed to physical affection. Until a few weeks ago there had been few angels who could testify to having made physical contact with humans.

The three girls jumped on Hikiko seconds later with more hugs and kisses than the last time they met. It was still a strange sensation but nevertheless it had become rather enjoyable and tender. It was hard for Hikiko to place into words. Having its hair stroked by another being or its hands held or its back caressed almost made tears form in its eyes. Such love and tenderness from beings which several weeks ago Hikiko thought were savages.

Thanks to Heather's telepathic mental abilities, she was aware of their mission details but chose not to share specifics with her sisters. She thought it was Hikiko's place to share mission parameters with the team and not hers. After all the welcome greetings were exhausted, the girls moved into the main gallery to discuss the mission and its corresponding requirements.

Hikiko told the girls specifically whom they were assigned to protect and who would be the first on their list to keep safe. After the briefing, the four stepped through a transport ring and were gone.

********** Back in Stockholm, Sweden **********

"Air Traffic Control, this is sierra tango seven one niner zero requesting permission to depart."

"Roger, sierra tango seven one niner zero, permission granted."

Once the aircraft received permission to depart, the captain made an announcement.

"Gentlemen, please make the aircraft ready for departure. It's Tuesday, July 23, 1:11 p.m. and the first leg of our journey will take three hours and forty-nine minutes to travel the 1,991 kilometers to Iceland.

The trip from Stockholm to Iceland was long. Longer than Stefan had expected. *Wow, for some reason, I thought the first leg of this trip was going to take an hour. I now realize this is going to be a ridiculously long trip,* Stefan admitted to himself. The first and second leg of the trip came and went without incident. However, the third leg over the United States encountered unexpected developments.

The Swedish commercial aircraft waited until they were over the South Dakota, Nebraska line before notifying U.S. traffic control of its intent. This was a flight they had made many times in the past and never had an incident. However, today, U.S. Customs and Homeland Security were reviewing the passenger manifest of every aircraft requesting permission to enter U.S. airspace. Without his knowledge, Stefan Magnusson was marked as an enemy of the state and placed on the U.S. TremEx list; which meant he was targeted for termination with extreme prejudice.

Of course, this meant any aircraft he was on could not land on U.S. soil. Therefore, depending on the airliner's location when the U.S. authorities were notified, they were to be rerouted to an alternative safe site. However, sierra tango seven one niner zero had waited too long to notify the proper traffic control station and now lacked the necessary fuel reserves to arrive at an alternative destination safely. The captain made repeated pleads to land but its requests were all denied. Consequently, the passengers' fate on this cargo plane was now in question.

The base commander at Ellsworth Air Force base received an order to intercept the Swedish commercial aircraft, and shoot it down if they did not alter their heading. If the plane had to be forced down, the Air Force was required to confirm the body count. Including Stefan, there were eleven passengers on the Swedish commercial airplane.

Two F-38A fighters were dispatched from Ellsworth to intercept the cargo aircraft. The fighters reported their ETA to the target as nine minutes. The cargo aircraft was just over the Nebraska line. The pilot didn't ask for permission to enter U.S. air space sooner thinking it would be a non-issue, but he was seriously mistaken. He now had no alternative but to land at some random airport and pay the price for his misplaced confidence.

Suddenly, Heather appeared beside Stefan.

"What in the world," Stefan let out as he looked around, then added, "You startled me."

"I'm so sorry, Dr. Magnusson, but that was never my intent."

"It's okay, I just didn't see you walk over and sit down." Stefan looked around again then added, "I'm sorry, but you seem memorable to me and I haven't noticed you before now. Have you been on this flight since Sweden or did you come aboard in Canada?"

With everything else that Stefan had on his mind, it never occurred to him that Heather knew his name.

"No, sir, I wasn't, and no, I didn't."

"Okay, so who are you and when did you come aboard?"

"I'm just a messenger," Heather replied, then turned her head to the side and thought, *Huh, now that's interesting. I answered his question without thinking and instinctively, referred to myself as a messenger. I'll have to give that some thought, but later. Right now, I have to save Dr. Magnusson.*

"How I got aboard is not relevant since I am, in fact, here. What is important is that your life is in imminent danger and you have to get off this aircraft."

"Do I know you?"

"No, sir, you don't."

"So how do you know me?"

"Sir, you have to get off this plane."

Dr. Magnusson was quiet for a few seconds then responded, "I'm sorry, my dear, but we're like six thousand meters in the air. Where would you suggest I go? Plus, how do you know that my life is in danger, exactly?"

"Sir, fighter jets from a nearby Air Force base were dispatched seconds ago and are now en route to destroy this aircraft. You have to get off."

"I'm sorry but you want me to go where, exactly?"

"You need to get out."

"I see, so you want me to jump out? Is that it?"

"Yes, sir. If you jump, I can save you but within the plane, there's nothing I can do."

"And you would like me to jump out of a perfectly good aircraft based on...what?"

"Faith, sir," Heather replied back with emotional verve.

"I'm sorry, my dear, but faith in what?"

"That God has sent me here to save you."

"God? But I don't believe in God."

"Oh, of course you do."

"No, young lady, I don't. I never have. I'm a scientist."

"I see. So, you didn't see God in the blood samples you examined from Dr. Penn? You didn't ask God to help you convince and comfort your wife? You didn't vow in his name to find your missing children? And you're not flying to Miami in hopes of confirming your findings?"

Stefan pulled is head and shoulders back, tilted his head and looked at the young girl. He was trying to rationalize how this stranger could possibly know what she just told him. *There has to be a rational explanation, there always is,* Stefan thought as he shook his head.

"There is."

"There is what, my dear?"

"There is a sensible explanation as to why I know what I know.

"Wait, what?"

"God has sent me to you, Dr. Magnusson. You're more important than you know."

"How did you know what I was thinking, are you reading my thoughts?"

"I can save you, but you have to want to be saved."

"Okay, so why can't you just save me from here, if that's what you're really here to do? Why would you make me jump out?"

"Faith, Doctor."

"But what if I don't have enough faith to jump, based on a cursory conversation with someone I don't know?"

"Then your existence will end here. And you will never see your children again."

"Wait, what? You know of my children? Do you know where they are?"

"Yes, sir, I do."

"Where, where are they? Are they okay, are they safe?"

"Your two girls and your son are safe, loved and at peace, without a care in the world."

"Where, where are they? Tell me."

"Dr. Magnusson, there's no time, your life is in imminent danger. You have to get out."

"I don't care about my life. Now, where are my kids?"

"Then I've failed you." Heather got up, turned and started walking away."

"Wait, where are you going?"

"My time here has ended."

"But what about my kids?"

"Your children have already been saved. I was here to save

you. But I can't do that if you don't wish to be saved." Heather turned and started walking away again.

"Wait, wait, wait. Okay, okay, save me."

"I've told you, Doctor, the only way I can save you is outside this aircraft."

"Right, I have to jump?"

"Yes, sir, you do. Just have faith."

"Right, faith, but what if I—?"

Heather interrupted Stefan to add, "Sir, what time is it?"

Stefan looked at his watch and said, "Its 1:06 a.m. Swedish time, but locally I think it's maybe six minutes past seven p.m."

"Then you have five minutes to convince everyone else aboard this aircraft to jump with you."

"Wait, what?"

"You couldn't in good conscious jump and leave everyone else behind to die, can you? If they jump with you, I can save them all."

"What? How?" Magnusson let out as Heather turned away.

Stefan turned his head and looked at some of the faces on board while thinking about the request this person had just made. In the few seconds he looked away, Heather was gone.

"Wait...what the—? Where are the parachutes?" Stefan looked around but his angel-like apparition was gone.

Suddenly, the pilot announced over the loud speaker, "The US traffic control authorities have just informed me that the US military has dispatched several Air Force fighter jets to force us down. Dr. Magnusson, one of the fighter jet pilots en route specifically asked me if you were aboard."

The co-pilot walked out and asked, "Now, who are you and why would they risk killing us all to get to you?"

Every passenger on the aircraft looked at Stefan and the young man that gave him the microprocessor chips said, "There are no parachutes onboard, Doctor. But I am curious as to how you knew we would need them."

"This young girl told me they were coming."

"What young girl?" another passenger questioned.

"What girl?" Stefan repeated in disbelief. "The young, blonde-haired, blue-eyed girl who was sitting next to me for like five minutes."

The pilot looked around at everyone then said, "There are no females on the passenger manifest, Doctor. There never has been."

"What?! Are you guys kidding me? None of you saw her sitting right here?" Magnusson pointed to the seat next to him and repeated, "She was sitting right here for like five minutes."

"Well, Doctor, I didn't see her and I'm sitting right across from you." He turned to the other passengers and asked, "Did anyone else see her?"

Everyone looked around at each other and just shook their heads no.

"Oh, come on, really? No one saw her?" Stefan looked at his watch and said, "Skit, we only have like three minutes."

"Three minutes until what?"

"Three minutes until the fighter jets blow us up."

"What? But US Customs said they were going to force us down. And who the hell are you? Why do they want you so bad? You don't think they would actually kill us all to get to you, do you?"

"No, I don't know, maybe. I'm just a scientist, I'm a nobody. But the girl told me fighter jets were going to shoot us down and I didn't believe her, until now. Unfortunately, these are Americans, and they do whatever they want and justify their actions afterwards—by whatever means necessary."

"Okay, so what if what you're saying is true and they're planning on shooting us down," one of the passengers queried, "how do we escape? We're like six thousand meters in the air. Where are we supposed to go?"

Stefan cleared his throat and replied, "She said we needed to jump out and that she would save us."

"Oh, come on. You can't be serious. Jumping without a parachute would mean certain death. At least if we stay here and they only force us down, we all live."

"She said that we had to jump. And if we did, we would be saved."

"How? How would she do that, exactly?"

"I don't know. But she told me to have faith in God."

"God, are you kidding me? I don't believe in God," another passenger shared.

Suddenly the pilot yelled, "Hold on!" The aircraft banked hard to the left and then spun and performed multiple barrel rolls. Several passengers, including Derrik, didn't have enough time to react and were tossed about and knocked unconscious.

"What the hell is going on?!" a passenger near the cockpit yelled out.

"The fighter jets have fired some kind of particle weapon at us. Hold on." The aircraft banked hard to the right and performed multiple barrel rolls again. Afterward, Stefan looked at his watch and yelled, "We only have forty seconds before we're all dead!" He got up and ran to the emergency exit and pulled the lever up.

"Don't open that door, Doctor, or we'll be blown out." Just then, the door flew open and Stefan was blown out along with two others. Everyone else held on.

A passenger screamed, "Should we jump?!"

"The passenger closest to him shouted, "If we jump at this altitude, we're dead."

"But we'll most certainly die if we crash." Suddenly, he let go and tumbled out of the aircraft.

Three, two, one — BOOM.

CHAPTER 15

Akachi Ventures Out

AKACHI AND NIKKI WALKED BACK INTO THE MAIN BUILDING OF the orphanage and made their way toward the back room where Vikki was sleeping peacefully. Adadi had patched her up and laid her down in an incline position.

"How was she?" Akachi asked.

"Fussy at first, she didn't like it that I elevated her head above her heart. 'I'm not comfy lying like this,' she kept repeating. She finally passed out a few minutes ago. You would have thought that me probing around in her chest for a bullet, or me suturing her up without pain medicine would have given her reasons to complain. But she barely made a sound."

"Did you follow my instructions with the pill?"

"Yes, I did, to the letter."

"Good." Adadi handed the pill back to Akachi in the tiny little baggy he gave her.

She watched him put it away before asking, "What's in it?"

"Why?"

"Well, because this injury should have killed her. And she's still alive, so that pill has special properties."

"Yes, it does. It's important to the mission."

"So where did you get it?"

Akachi looked at Nikki then Adadi and said, "God gave it to me."

Adadi made the sign of the cross and Nikki pulled her head and shoulders back and mouthed *merde*.

"Well, thank you for tending to her needs."

"Yes, yes, Adadi, thank you for looking after my sister, we owe you."

"You owe me nothing. She was a pleasure to tend to. She's the strong, silent type.

"Yes, yes, she is."

Akachi looked at his sister and Nikki and said, "Leave me with her. Go tend to the children, we have to go soon."

Nikki and Adadi walked out and gathered the children, ten in total.

"So, do you think Vikki is going to die?" Nikki asked, believing she knew the answer but wanted to hear someone else confirm it.

"Who knows such things? But based on her spirit and strength of will, I don't believe so. But, she's currently too weak to travel and we're leaving soon. Moving her now will not be good. She'll develop internal bleeding for sure if she's forced to travel so soon. If she had a few days of solid rest, I would feel much better about her recovery and survival."

"I agree."

"You do realize, the local militia will be sending their henchmen soon. The disappearance of six men will not go unnoticed."

"So, how much time do we have?"

"A few hours at most before they start asking questions and maybe another two of three before they're kicking down my door."

"Well, that gives me five to six hours, which is more than enough time. He has a camp twenty kilometers from here, right?"

"Yes."

"Good."

"I don't want to seem like I'm prying but are you planning to pay him a visit?"

"Yes."

"Why? Those are evil men and you're so pretty."

"And?" Nikki noticed that Adadi seemed to be choking down her emotions. "It's okay, chérie, just tell me what's on your mind."

"Well, it's that if you're caught, it will not end well for you."

"So, I better not get caught."

"If Akachi asks me where you are, I hope you know that I can't lie to him. Plus, even if I wanted to, I'm a terrible liar."

"So don't lie. Just give me two hours. If I'm not back in two hours, then it doesn't matter."

"What do I say if he asks me where you are before then?"

"Stall him."

"I'm terrible at stalling, too."

"Well, do your best to buy me some time."

"If I do as you ask, and you're not back in two hours, I will tell Akachi what you've done whether he asks me or not."

"Deal." Nikki stuck out her hand but Adadi just looked at her.

"Nikki, I don't agree with what you're doing. But your sister asked me to help you when you came to me with a crazy plan and I said I would, God knows why. So, you have exactly two hours, and not one second more."

"Done." Nikki stuck out her hand again. Adadi reluctantly reached out for it.

Nikki spent a few minutes gathering everything she needed before heading out in the gangsters' vehicle.

Nikki loaded the car with the thugs then said, "Ha, this car has satellite positioning in it. Cool. Let's see, is 'Home' programmed into this thing? Hmm, take me home."

"Yes, ma'am," the car replied and drove off.

"Ha, what a bunch of knuckle heads." Nikki laughed at her opponents. "Boys, you do realize that with your location recorded in the vehicle, anyone can find you. Well, your confidence will be your undoing."

Nikki repeated her plan over and over in her mind during the thirty-minute trip to the crime lord's den. She pulled up to the front and honked the horn.

"Hello, is anyone home?!" she yelled intrusively.

Two, four, and then six men were outside the front of the

house when Nikki stepped out of the all-terrain vehicle. "I'm here to see your boss, Barasa."

"And who are you, woman?"

"I'm Nikki."

"And what do you want?"

"Are you Barasa?"

"No."

"Then go get him."

"Why should I listen to you, woman?"

"Because Barasa will kill you if I leave without telling him what I know."

"Which is what?"

"Listen, numb nuts, are you boys going to make me stand around all night while you jerk on each other or is someone going to tell your boss I'm here?"

The men's captain standing in the back stepped forward and said, "I like her, she has balls. Search her, and then bring her in."

Nikki put her hands up and the thug initially asking all the questions started frisking her. Suddenly, Nikki noticed a smirk on his face and thought, *This can't be good.* He had decided to grope her during his search. Nikki smiled back, then smashed her forehead into his face. When he stepped back, she kicked him in the groin then kneed him in the temple when he bent down, knocking him out.

All the men pulled up their automatic weapons and pointed them at her. She raised her hands up casually and said, "He shouldn't have touched me there."

"Ha. This chienne has balls." The men's captain walked down the stairs and stopped a meter in front of Nikki. "Tell me why you're here or I will kill you where you stand before I walk back in to finish my dinner."

"I have information about Reynolds."

"Reynolds, who the hell is that? I've never heard of him."

"He's the man that killed all your men."

"What?" Nikki pointed to the car with her chin.

The captain and half the other men turned and looked. "What the—"

"Why would he do this?"

"Are you Barasa?"

Isoba stared at Nikki with a scowling icy look on his face and said, "Fine, bring her."

Nikki was counting the men and thinking to herself as she was being escorted through the compound to see the boss. *Well, let's see, five, ten, fifteen, twenty. Wow, twenty men. Really, Barasa, paranoid much? I can understand the men wanting to look all murdery and rapey but is the poor personal hygiene really necessary?*

The compound was over-the-top extravagant. The floors were covered in imported Italian marble. And the distressed limestone pillars holding up the second and third floor structure gave any onlooker the belief that they were in Rome visiting a miniature but impressive replica of the colosseum. There were numerous large chambers in the compound with little furniture. One room held a Steinway piano which appeared to never have been played. Some of the initial shipment wrapping material was still on it.

There was another space with just bronze sculptures on display, like 'The Cheyenne.' Most statues were signed by their artisan like Frederic Remington or Guillemin Barye. There was also a set of four bronze figures under glass representing the seasons. And there was a very large French, 20th century Orientalist motif bronze sculpture of an Arab hunter on a camel with a pair of dogs at its base after a model by P.J. Mene, which Nikki recognized.

Well, there's no accounting for taste, she thought. They walked Nikki out into an enormous swimming pool area which must have cost millions to construct. There were multiple waterfalls visible near the swim-up bars and there was an assortment of eastern bloc girls which appeared to be prisoners and were kept chained to nearby whirlpools. Some girls were forced to wear pronged training dog choke collars and many appeared to have recently been beaten. Others wore shackles around a bloody wrist or ankle. *These degenerates,* she thought. *Okay, girl, keep your cool or you're going to wind up like one of those poor fillettes.* She was stopped in front of an older, heavy-set bald man eating a late dinner. The captain whispered something in his ear then stepped to the side.

"So talk to me about Reynolds. Why would he kill my men?"

"Reynolds is after someone. A young man named Afia."

"Why?"

"He's looking to control this area again. And apparently five years ago, Afia's father refused to do business with Reynolds and he had his organization terminated. Well, except for Afia. And I guess he's here to tie up loose ends before he comes to see you."

"So why tell me this?"

"Two reasons. One, Reynolds is not sanctioned to do business here. And two, he killed my sister."

"Reynolds works for whom? You?"

"No, the US government."

"I see, so he's a company man?"

"He was."

"And you work for whom? Reynolds?"

"I did."

"Well, one of my drivers told me that a red-headed girl and some white man killed three of my men at the airport. Would you happen to know anything about that?

"Yes, that was me. Sorry, but those men were nothing more than brainless degenerates. I did you a favor by weeding out the weak within your ranks. I'm positive those miscreants were costing your organization money."

The crime boss looked at his captain and said, "You're right, she has balls.

"So why should I not kill you here and then kill Reynolds when he shows up?"

"Reynolds is a cockroach. He's hard to kill. And if you fail to kill him, when he comes, because he is coming, it's all over. He'll order an air strike on this location with the most powerful non-nuclear arsenal at his disposal. It's enough to level a two-square-kilometer area and bury you and part of this town in its crater. So, right now he's after you and me. In either case, we have a choice. We kill him first and we both live or he kills us one at a time. Personally, I like option one."

"What if I just kill you and hand you over when he shows up."

"Sure, I guess that's another option, but in the end we'll both be dead."

"Why is that?"

"Because until three minutes ago, you didn't even know he was alive. And with all due respect, Barasa, he thinks you guys are all a bunch of monkeys. So no matter what he says, he will never honor a deal with you. And he puts deals on the table that his worst enemies can't ignore." Barasa put a finger up then looked at his captain and motioned for him to approach.

The captain leaned down and Barasa whispered in his ear. "Do you believe her?"

The captain looked at Nikki then said, "I don't sense she's lying. And if she wanted to do us harm, she wouldn't be here by herself. That makes no sense. I think Reynolds killed her sister and she wants revenge. And she probably needs your help to do that. I say we let them kill each other. If she wins, she's a foreign woman, which makes it impossible for her to hide among us. When we find her, we'll add her to our stable. And if she fails, we'll be ready for Reynolds when he shows up." Barasa waved off the captain and he stepped back.

"Continue."

"Reynolds is a ghost. But I know his weakness."

"Which is what?"

"Me." Barasa tilted his head and crinkled the corner of his mouth.

Nikki looked around and noticed Barasa's men staring at her, while licking their lips. She finally added, "Look, I know him. I worked with him. I can anticipate his advances."

"So why come to me with all this? Why not just kill him yourself? Why bother me?"

"After he killed your men, I knew you would want answers and payment. Plus, I don't have any of my equipment. So I need support." Barasa looked at Isoba who smirked.

"Continue."

"And I need four days before your men start knocking down doors."

"And what do I get out of this?"

"Two things," Nikki quickly replied.

"Go on," Barasa said as he cut another piece of steak and shoved it in his mouth.

"One, when this is all over, I make sure the US knows that you get to keep your little kingdom. Because the US will continue to send a new Reynolds until you're gone."

"And two," Barasa started Nikki's next sentence with his

mouth still full of food.

"And two, I owe you. You provide me a telephone with a number. If you ever decide to call it, I will answer. And whatever you ask of me, I will do."

"I want two calls."

"You get one."

"Then you only get two days."

"Reynolds is a slippery merde, I need four."

Barasa placed his knife and fork down then picked up the napkin on his lap. He wiped his mouth then placed it back down.

"Give me three days then," Nikki countered, making Barasa think that he had the upper hand.

"Fine. What else will you need?"

"I need a Glock, an automatic firearm, five clips for each, four grenades, and a sat phone."

"Done."

"Oh, I have one more thing," Nikki added.

"What?"

"Can you please walk me out?"

Barasa sent his captain, Isoba, out to gather the supplies Nikki requested and he walked her to the front door. Nikki looked around to make sure none of the men were looking when she reached into her bra and pulled out a small vial hidden away.

Barasa's eyes opened wide and he asked, "What did you have hidden in there?"

"This." Nikki held up the small vial. "Reynolds loves his knives and throwing spears and merde. He coats all the blades with a deadly Ricin-based toxin. Just one scratch and in thirty seconds your vision blurs and you get the worst headache of your life. In four minutes you will be on the ground writhing in agony. The poison releases some kind of neurotoxin into the bloodstream that makes your body release endorphins. These hormones cut off pathways to your brain to keep you from passing out from the pain. So normally a person would pass out from the torment in just a few minutes. But this will keep you awake for maybe thirty minutes before you spasm so hard, you'll break your own back.

Nikki handed the vial to him and said, "Here."

Barasa took it and looked at her, then said, "Thanks."

"Oh, don't thank me yet. This is not an antidote, but it will keep you alive for maybe five hours. More than enough time for you to drive yourself to the hospital, get pumped full of morphine and receive a blood transfusion. So make sure you know what your blood type is. And you see this label here?"

"Yes."

"It will tell the doctors specifically what Ricin-based derivative they're dealing with. And don't let the doctors give you merde about you not needing a blood transfusion because you most certainly will. Trust me, this suppressant will not be enough."

Isoba handed Barasa a backpack with the supplies Nikki requested. He in turn handed the pack to Nikki. She looked at the vehicle and noticed that all the dead men had been removed from the car.

"Can I use your vehicle for a little while? I'll leave it in town with the keys in it when I'm done."

"Sure."

They walked to the car and Barasa opened the driver's door for Nikki. She got in and he closed it behind her. "Oh, by the way, I would suggest you take that soon. It takes twenty-four hours before you receive the full effect and it will make you sick as a dog. You don't want to be sick if Reynolds comes looking for you. The best thing to do is take it and go to bed. I've taken it four times, and the effects never get any better."

Barasa nodded his head.

Nikki searched the backpack and pulled out the sat phone, holding it up.

"Barasa, I realize you're a busy man. If I hear something I believe you should know, can I call your lieutenant with this phone?

"Yes. You have two numbers recorded, the second is his."

"Good," Nikki sat the phone down and pulled out. She stopped the car abruptly and peered out the window, adding, "And don't tell your men you have that vial or it will turn up missing." Nikki finally pulled out and drove off. As she slowly drove away, she looked out the side mirror and saw Barasa walking up to his front door while opening up the small vial. She switched her view to the rearview mirror and adjusted the sight to see him pour the contents down his gullet as he walked in his house.

Nikki grinned then rejoiced before exclaiming, "Men!

They're such idiots."

She drove the thug's vehicle into town and parked it in a well-lit area then walked the kilometer to the orphanage in the dark. She opened the camp door and walked in.

Akachi closed the door behind her and said, "I assume you were successful?"

"Yes. Did Adadi tell you?"

"No, she didn't have to. I was just like you once. So, how much time do we have before we receive visitors?"

"Two, maybe three days."

"Good, that will assure Vikki is safe to travel."

"Yes, but Reynolds is still out there. And he can be back tomorrow," Nikki added.

"Perhaps, but he was shot twice. So, he's going to need a few days to recover as well. And that's if he finds someone to tend to his injuries. If he works on himself, it'll take him a lot longer to recover."

"Are you sure he was hit?"

"Yes, I saw him favoring a shoulder and running while hunched over, so I'm sure he took one in the gut, " Akachi added.

"Good, but he's a cockroach, so I'm sure he'll find what he needs to survive."

Nikki was right, Reynolds made his way to the local mission in town where he had one of the volunteer doctors patch him up before he killed him.

Nikki called and had Barasa's lieutenant meet her in one of the local cafes the next morning. They both sat down and Nikki spoke first.

"Is your man okay?"

"The one you beat down like a chienne?"

"Yeah, sorry."

"He's dead."

"Wow, that's a rather harsh punishment."

"He was weak, and stupid. So, thank you for pointing it out."

Nikki placed two small vials on top of their dining table. Once they had both made eye contact again, she reached out and gently pushed the two small bottles to him and explained to Isoba what they were.

"This one is for you. I was going to give this to Barasa last night but I got the impression he's not the sharing type. But maybe I'm wrong. Anyway, you know him better than I do. If he hasn't already told you that I gave him one of these small ampoules, I'm sure he will.

"Anyway, this second vial, which is twice as big, is for your crew. But don't give it to any more than five men or it won't be as effective. To hand it out, you'll have to dilute it, so, it will only protect them for about two hours. And they will need to be in a hospital before their time runs out or they won't survive."

"Why are you giving me this?"

"I told Barasa yesterday that Reynolds likes his knives and merde. Didn't he tell you?"

"No. He didn't."

"Well, I'm sure he's gunna. Plus, you helped me yesterday. And I don't like unpaid debts."

Nikki got up and went to walk away. *If I read him correctly, he's going to call me back,* Nikki confessed to herself.

Suddenly, she heard, "What if I give this to more men?"

I got you, Nikki admitted to herself. She took the few steps back, leaned down and while gently nodding her head in disapproval whispered, "I wouldn't recommend it."

"What will happen?"

Nikki sat back down, paused then crinkled the corner of her mouth for a few seconds, then replied, "It would depend on how you dilute the original formula. If you give it evenly to ten men, they will each have an hour to get to a hospital. Twenty men will have thirty minutes and so on."

"Thank you."

"Unless, your men are strong, I would seriously advise against you giving it to more than ten men."

"Goodbye," Isoba said dismissively.

Nikki walked away. As she was exiting the café, she reached into her bra and pulled out a compact mirror and pretended to check her makeup. As she raised it up to her face, she looked over her shoulder and saw Isoba ingest the contents of one of the vials. She placed the mirror back in her bra and stepped out of the diner with a smirk on her face.

Today will be a good day for the innocent, she thought.

Akachi, was approaching the Christian mission which had saved his life twice before. There was a crowd forming, so he knew something was wrong. Then it occurred to him, Reynolds had been there.

Hoshea, I realized I told you that I would no longer seek vengeance but Reynolds has lost is soul and needs to be stopped.

Nikki and Akachi, secretly met up at a designated small market near a particular vendor. Akachi bent down to tie a shoe and Nikki walked up behind him and grabbed a pair of sunglasses as she asked the merchant, "How much are these?" Before the vendor could answer, Akachi heard her say, "Two francs?"

Akachi stood up and shared before walking away, "Two francs seems like a fair price."

Nikki looked at the vendor who aggressively responded, "Don't listen to him, those sunglasses are worth fifteen francs." Nikki raised her eyebrows and the merchant added, "But for you pretty lady, I can do twelve.

Akachi headed back to the camp knowing that Nikki had confirmed they had at least two days to get their affairs in order.

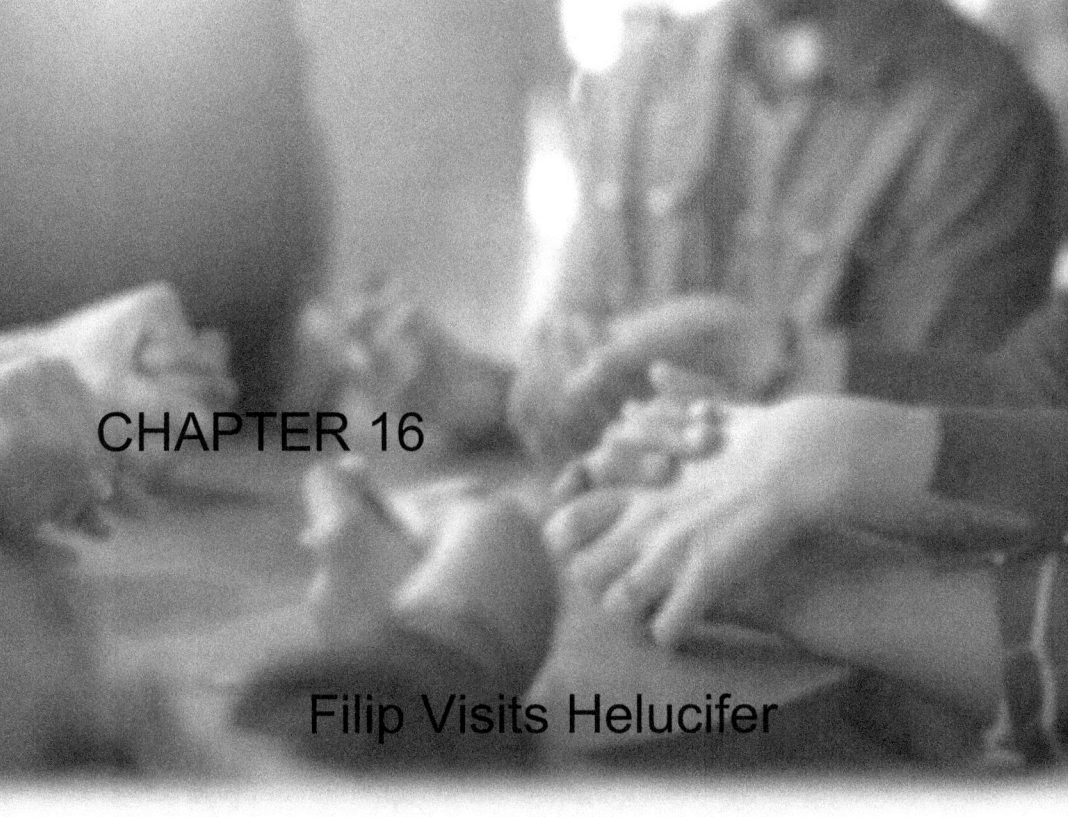

CHAPTER 16

Filip Visits Helucifer

FILIP ZAREK AND ERIC TASK STEPPED OUT OF THE TRANSPORT ring and appeared in front of Helucifer's castle on Helema. The place humans referred to as hell.

"If I didn't know any better, sir, I would swear we were somewhere in the central part of Romania."

"Now, that's interesting," Filip quickly replied. "Why would you say that? What makes you think we're in Romania?"

"Am I mistaken, sir?"

"Not based on your frame of reference. So, I'm curious as to how you would possibly choose Romania. Of all the places we could have gone."

"Well, sir, Transylvania, on Earth, is in the central part of Romania. Romania is bound on the east and south by the Carpathian mountain range and to the west by the Apuseni Mountains. Since you told me this planet closely resembles Earth, I took a guess. I love mountain ranges. They're the most formidable natural borders. And I'm always searching for ways to protect our backs."

"I knew there was a reason why I picked you as my second,

and it wasn't your cruelty. Although, it did help."

"Thank you, sir."

"Well, we're in front of our Lord's castle in what can be called Transylvania."

"Wow, Transylvania. I was spot on, nice," Eric replied.

"Yes, you were. And our Lord keeps a domicile here for many reasons, one of which is its seclusion from everyone. Another is its strategic location at the center of the world. On Earth, Santo Antonio, a small island within the São Tomé and Príncipe island chain off the west coast of Gabon, Africa is that landmark, but since this planet is a thousand times bigger, this castle holds that distinction."

Filip reached for the leather necklace around his neck which held two keys. One was to his private worship chamber in Warsaw and the other was to the front door of this castle. Filip inserted the multiple jagged pins on the long, black-stemmed key into the old titanium, heavy-plated lock. He turned the key six times to the right, and pushed it in until it stopped. He turned the key again, six times to the left, and then pushed the throating in further. Finally, Filip turned the key six more times to the right and stopped. A few seconds later, the collar, throating and pins started moving by themselves even though Filip held the bow motionless. Suddenly, the seal of the front door broke and smoke bellowed out. Filip pulled the key out of the lock and pushed the creaking door open ever so slowly.

The stuffy odor of decay and burned leaves wafted out. Filip took a deep breath and said, "Ah, do you smell that?"

"Yes, sir," Eric replied back while scrunching up his face.

"That's the smell of home, Eric. Come."

Filip stepped past the threshold then turned back to Eric and said, "Remember what I told you about everything having rules?"

"Yes, sir."

"Well, while you're here, none of that applies. If we have time later, I'll explain it to you."

"Yes, sir."

The castle was dark, musty and to Eric appeared to be as old as time. As they walked through the structure, Filip provided Eric with a little background history on the castle.

"Eric, did you know that this castle's exterior was

constructed from solid twenty-five ton grey limestone quarried blocks stacked twenty high in some areas?

"No, sir."

"It's said that the stones are dark maroon or burgundy from the blood of the men used to build this monolithic structure."

"Wow, if that's true, that's awesome."

"Isn't it?! Furthermore, it's reported that millions of men lost fingers, hands, arms and portions of their legs during its construction.

"Incredible."

"Tens of thousands also lost their lives crushed between the stones."

"That's a fantastic way to end the existence of a weak, pathetic waste of skin. And it also helps to ensure the structure has a unique sense of purpose and mammon," Eric shared.

"Yes, it does. It was said that the initial construction took five hundred years. This was back in the time when men barely understood their sentience. It required a considerable amount of effort to corral and lead them. Their free spirit was strong and it took a momentous effort to break them. They weren't as easily intimidated back then. You could pull one out of the ranks and kill him in front of the rest and no one would flinch. You could threaten that any one of them could be next and they would just yawn. Their cavalier attitude was frustrating to say the least. However, after several hundred years, they were finally broken. Today, it's more fun than ever to watch them squirm when they're made part of the castle's renovation process.

Now, our Lord makes it a point to replace a few thousand stones every year. Not necessarily from the castle but from the surrounding outer walls and surrounding defense structures."

"Why?" Eric questioned, "To me the stones look fine."

"Well, for multiple reasons, but the main one I believe is to make sure the stones are infused with new blood and we continue the misery and cruelty dispensed with the movement of such large objects using a whip on the backs of broken men."

Eric laughed aloud then replied, "That's perfect. I love it."

"That said, I think many of the stones are starting to show signs of decay. You see, new limestone blocks are no longer quarried. The men just move the same stones around millennia after millennia."

Eric laughed again then said, "That's fantastic." Suddenly, he saw something lurking in the shadows which caught his attention. *Huh, now that's odd*, Eric thought, *there appears to be injured people lying on the ground with severe wounds. But instead of their lacerations bleeding out, the blood seems to be traveling up off the floor and back into their bodies. Wow, and that person over there is laughing while hacking off their own limb.*

"Dang," Eric exclaimed under his breath. *There's a woman in a large fish tank being held down and forced to aspirate pond scum.* Eric looked closer and thought, *what the hell? Her torso is being held under water but it looks like she's freely enjoying the putrefied remains of fish and pond filth and her own vomit. That's not weird, it's just plain disgusting.*

Is that condensation leaking out of the wall? Eric touched it, *Nope, it's blood,* he confessed. *And are those small rodents walking around on thin air?* Eric focused his sight in the dark room and admitted to himself, *Yep, those weird little creatures are definitely defying the laws of physics. That's interesting. Wait, are they also teleporting? Wow, this place is nutty.*

What? How are those people just walking through solid objects? And why are those women talking to mangled cadavers with their heads on spikes? Gross. Eric shook his head then focused his attention on the women again. *Wow, those disemboweled women should be dead but somehow they're talking. Although, their behavior would seem a bit crazier if the corpses weren't talking back.*

Eric was stunned by the grotesquery being witnessed. Finally, he had to speak up. "I'm sorry, my Lord, but is there any way you can explain to me what's happening? I can't help but feel captivated by what could only be explained as some form of alternate reality, or unnatural universe. This place is challenging everything I believed to be true. And I now have serious doubts on whether these observations have been factual or simply false perceptions. If I didn't know any better, these perceived hallucinations could be the beginning of a psychotic break."

"Not now, Eric, and stop whining," Filip replied. "We're here." Filip bowed down at the center of a great hall and took a knee while Eric suddenly looked around and noticed where he was. He immediately fell to his knees and covered his face. Eric had failed to notice they had entered Helucifer's throne room where statues of great fallen angels stood in place of columns fifteen meters high. Thin openings in the thick stone walls allowed light to peer in and bring some details to the shadows lurking over everything.

"My Lord," Filip called out. Helucifer was sitting upon a granite throne and surrounded by the remains of human cadavers in multiple stages of decomposition. Its minions were busy removing and cleaning up the area.

"Come forward, my son."

"Yes, Your Majesty." Filip stood up and walked to his Lord.

Helucifer stood up on its elevated throne where its hands were resting on the skulls of two live men. Both men were nude, kneeling down while sitting on their feet with their hands chained and resting on their lap. Helucifer's nails were buried deep under the skin of each of the men's forehead. When the Devil stood up, it ripped the skin back off their cranium. From the shock of this extreme trauma, both men rolled their eyes into the backs of their heads and fell to the ground. The loud groans of their torment didn't last very long. Within fifteen seconds, their gurgling sounds suddenly stopped as they exhaled their last breath. It appeared that both men previously had the bottom parts of their jaws ripped off. Perhaps to keep them from talking or yelling out from the pain but whatever the reason, it was a gruesome sight.

The Devil hugged its son and they turned to Eric.

"So this is your faithful servant, my son?"

"Yes, Your Majesty."

"Did you bring him here to be baptized in fire?"

"Yes, Your Majesty."

"Excellent. Has he been prepared?"

"No, Your Majesty, I wanted this to be a surprise."

"Very well," Satan walked over to Eric who was still on his knees covering his face.

"Eric, rise and gaze upon my splendor."

Eric uncovered his face and stood up slowly. While still trembling from the excitement and fear of meeting its god for the first time, he looked upon Satan's face and to his astonishment and wonder, the Devil was nothing less than ravishing. Eric's mouth dropped open and without realizing it, he uttered out through quivering lips, "How can this be?" Satan appeared to be the most beautiful woman he had ever seen hooded and cloaked in a dark maroon gown, its skin a light burgundy or maroon color but smooth and blemish free. Although the black stiletto nails dripping with blood was a little menacing, Eric had never seen such beauty. Helucifer was, after all, a Harem. Cast out long ago, but a Harem nevertheless, the most beautiful and capable than all before it. Even though Helucifer might never agree or denounce this truth as a falsehood, aside from coveting free will, it was so inclined to believe and profess it was not just god-like or a god, but it was thee God.

"Am I not more beautiful than you have ever imagined?"

"More beautiful than words could ever express, Your Majesty."

Eric suddenly realized he had spoken out of turn and covered his face and dropped to his knees again.

Satan crinkled the corner of its mouth and looked over at Filip then pointed at Eric with its chin.

"Oh, come on, man, get to your feet." Filip grabbed Eric by an arm and helped him up. "Now focus, and don't embarrass me in front of our Lord," Filip whispered into Eric's ear.

"Yes, Your Grace."

"That's better," Helucifer announced.

"Your Majesty, may I introduce Eric Task, a faithful servant."

Helucifer looked over at Eric again and asked, "Is this true, Eric? Are you a faithful servant?"

"Yes, yes, yes, Your Majesty," Eric replied through trembling and stuttering lips.

"My son tells me you have come to be baptized in fire and denounce Hoshea before me. Is this also true?"

"Yes, Your Majesty," Eric replied.

"Good." Satan looked upon Eric, and said, "It will be painful and will require days for you to recover. Are you prepared for that?"

"Yes, Your Majesty."

"Good. Then come."

Helucifer walked them over to a cauldron stewing over an open fire. To Eric, the pot appeared to contain molten metal-like liquid mercury or silver.

"Eric, you will not survive this baptism without my help."

"I understand, Your Majesty."

"Do you want my help?"

"Yes, Your Majesty."

"Good, and you shall have it. Now, open your mouth," Helucifer ordered and Eric did as instructed.

"Stick out your tongue," Helucifer added.

Eric looked down at the cauldron and started trembling. *If Satan pours hot magma down my throat, this will be a horrendous, agonizing death. But on a positive note, I can't imagine remaining conscious for more than thirty seconds. So Eric, you must muster the courage required to see this through,* he exclaimed to himself.

Suddenly, Helucifer spit in Eric's mouth. Out of sheer shock, Eric closed his mouth and swallowed.

"That will help you," Helucifer informed Eric.

"Thank you, Your Majesty."

"Do you want more help?"

"Yes, Your Majesty," Eric replied, thinking to himself, *Well, that's not the worst thing a beautiful woman has ever done to me.* Eric opened his mouth again and stuck out his tongue.

Helucifer looked over at Filip and said, "I like him. He's a bit of a pig." Then spit in his mouth again.

Eric's nervousness and apprehension started to fade. The look on his face caused the Devil to say, "I see my actions have made you feel better."

"Yes, Your Majesty."

"Good. Then disrobe and kneel down over here." Satan walked Eric over to a pentagram carved into the stone on the ground. After Eric had taken off his clothes and knelt in the center of the star, the Devil poured the boiling mercury on the ground and it followed a path into the pentagram until the liquid fire made the star symbol shine bright. Eric immediately started feeling discomfort to his lower torso from the heat. However, what Eric would not realize until later was that Helucifer's saliva would in fact protect his internal organs from the extreme temperature exposure he would soon endure.

"We should protect his face," Filip stated.

"Agreed," Satan replied and floated over to Eric and spit on his face then said, "Rub that in." Eric immediately reached up and rubbed Helucifer's spit over his face and felt better. Helucifer spit on Eric again and he started rubbing his legs with traces of Satan's saliva and again his discomfort was substantially diminished.

"Eric, I christen thee in fire and pain with my son as a witness. Proclaim me your god and denounce Hoshea for being a false prophet and receive my absolution. You will rise again with dominion over man and beast. Women and children shall bow at your feet. You shall have power over all that crawls, slithers and creeps upon the ground. Every manner of fowl or creature shall know your likeness and heed your words. Men will aspire to be you, but curse their own existence when they cannot measure up to your likeness."

Eric repeatedly uttered the words Satan required to hear with verve and conviction.

"Then, let it begin," Helucifer announced then returned to its throne. Satan's minions had brought two other men and knelt them down on either side of Helucifer's cathedra. The Devil buried its nails deep under the skin of the men's foreheads while the men trembled silently in despair.

For ten minutes Satan watched Eric slowly cook over the liquid metal flowing beneath him. Filip stood watch at Satan's side. At the end of those ten minutes, Helucifer breathed upon Eric and set him aflame. Eric screamed and writhed upon the floor in agony for sixty-six additional seconds. When Eric started making gurgling sounds as if his blood was boiling out through his mouth, Satan stood up and announced, "It is done."

The flames were blown out and Eric laid there trembling with third degree burns over 95% of his body. Eric had even suffered some fourth degree burns to a few of his toes.

"Leave him here. My minions will tend to him. We have matters to discuss."

Helucifer and Filip walked off and immediately Satan's minions scurried in and placed Eric on a glass gurney and took him away.

Filip and Helucifer took ten minutes to walk over to a gathering hall in another section of the castle. They sat down opposite each other in front of a white granite conference table. There were bookshelves along most of the walls separated by large oil paintings rendering great fallen angels stepping on the necks of

Harem archangels.

"Filip looked at the images and sighed, *huh.*

"What, it's good to dream, isn't it?" Filip nodded at the Devil's comment.

Helucifer motioned for his second to approach. It was standing in the shadow along the eastern wall.

Hitlaher quietly approached followed by its three aides and said, "Yes, my Lord. What is your bidding?"

"Make sure Watchers are assigned to Hoshea's new chosen followers."

Hitlaher looked at the list and questioned, "Why so many, my Lord?"

"Trust me, my old friend, before the end, no quantity will be enough."

"As you wish, my Lord. It shall be done." Hitlaher walked away while issuing orders to its aides.

Helucifer had many women servants all in what appeared to be racy French maid costumes which exposed their naked backs completely. Half looked happy to be there but the other half looked as if they had recently been crying. The women served them each a glass of Domaine de la Romanee-Conti wine in crystal glasses with platinum trim and titanium stems. Helucifer spanked the bottom of its waitress every time she poured a cup and Filip did the same.

Afterward, each waitress would prance over and give Satan a kiss on the cheek then stand against the wall.

"I don't believe I have ever been in this room, Your Majesty. Are those renaissance period tapestries?"

"Of course."

"Magnificent."

"Yes, but it wasn't just the bravura of artistry in that period," Helucifer added. "It was the absolute depravity and utter cruelty toward the weak and infirmed which truly demonstrated their savagery and lack of humanity." Helucifer sighed then said, "So, that topic leads me into you."

"Your Majesty," Filip asked with curiosity in his voice.

"Tell me, how is your dominion over man progressing?" Helucifer's question seemed cordial and gentle.

"Good, Your Majesty."

Satan was silent for a few seconds then said, "Men. Filip, I was hoping for some specifics."

"Of course, I'm so sorry. I should have known better. Well, let's see—"

Helucifer yawned then interrupted Filip to say, "Waah, waah, waah, whatever. The moment has passed, let's move on. However, I need to confirm we both have a clear vision with high level specifics on your plan to end everyone and everything."

"Yes, Your Majesty."

"So, what are your thoughts, my son? How should we proceed with the eradication of human kind?" Satan queried.

"Well, at this point, I have full control of every world leader and the countries they represent. Any global leader which steps outside our boundaries is dealt with quickly and with finality."

"Good, as it should be."

"Yes, Your Majesty. So, I was planning on turning the Russians against the Americans."

"Fantastic. America surrendered over to Russian influence over thirty years ago. All thanks to that simple-minded, narcissistic, money-grabbing old degenerate who became president in the last two thousand teens."

"Ha, that is so true. He even relinquished control to the Caribbean by handing over Cuba to the Russians after they had lost their stronghold in the region."

"Exactly, America has been Russia's puppets ever since that mulatto islander left office," Satan added.

"Agreed. That Caucasian, hair spray abusing dimwit continues to this day to be my greatest ne'er-do-well president of all time. The imbecile gave away treasured New York real estate to the Russian crime cartel for pennies on the dollar," Eric proclaimed.

"He sold out his countrymen and their birthright and got nothing in return," the Devil added.

"What a simpleton." They both looked at each other and laughed hard.

"Filip, we need to stop talking about him, you're making me cry." Helucifer snickered while wiping a tear from its eye than added, "Now go on, what else are you planning?"

Filip stopped laughing and added, "Just one more thing, Your Majesty, that president will always be remembered as the most ill-prepared, Ringling Bros. and Barnum & Bailey Circus stammering ringmaster of all time."

They both looked at each other again and started laughing even harder.

"Ah ah ah joke to the world and he didn't even know it," Helucifer stuttered out.

They stopped laughing and looked at each other again for a few seconds, then started up again.

"Enough, Filip, enough, please stop," Helucifer snorted out while wiping additional tears from its eyes. "Now please go on with your vision." Satan released a few more chuckles than sighed and slowly stopped laughing.

Filip did the same then continued, "Yes, Your Majesty. Well, I wanted to have North Korea turn American allies in the region against them."

"Perfect. That should also be easy. That part of the world loathes America for reasons that have never made any sense yet the people rally around lies. It's insanity at its finest. And the odd thing is that 98% of the people in that region of the world have never met an American."

"Exactly, and the few who actually have, have found the experience to have been a pleasant one," Filip added.

"What a bunch of lummox. Well, shockingly enough, I get the credit for bestowing such downright hatred and anger among those people and honestly, I had very little to do with that. It's their own disgusting, distrustful, bigoted ways that allows complete lies without a shred of evidence or reason to permeate their existence and generate centuries of cruelty. I'm telling you, I'm the first to sing my own praises but that crazy gówno going on in the Middle East is not me." Helucifer raised a hand up and placed the other on its heart and said, "I swear it. And forgive my Polish pronunciation; I haven't spoken the language in millennia."

"Your Polish is excellent, my Lord. And I believe you. Humans have it all wrong. It's like they blame you for all the bad which transpires in the world."

"Exactly! How is it my fault when some psycho-degenerate decides to kidnap, rape and murder a child? How the heaven is that my fault? And the surviving loved ones of those victims should be blaming their God, not me for allowing those psychopaths the free will to perform such heinous acts." Satan was now so upset it had to take a moment to center itself before continuing. Helucifer cleared its throat then added, "You may not know this but there's no child abuse in Helema."

"I realize that, Your Majesty."

"And not because I was told to forbid it. It's just the right thing to do. The men kneeling at my throne raped, tortured and murdered dozens. And many of those victims were women and children. I bestow a rightful atonement for their acts here. There are no victims, no excuses and no injustice here. Whosoever is reborn here — in Hell — deserves everything imparted to them. That is my ordained resplendent duty."

"Of course it is, Your Majesty."

"Yes, it's true. I unconditionally despise and genuinely detest humans. You and a few others are the exception. All granted free will to be and act as a god. Yet, they use such a gift to cheat Girl Scouts out of cookies or steal the hard-earned money from a poor man. No, these depraved barbarians deserve everything they get." Helucifer took another deep breath and said, "Look, I'm sorry for venting out to you in this way. Please understand my frustration has nothing to do with you."

"I understand, Your Majesty. There are few you can vent to, and I'm happy, honored really, that you would do so with me."

"Thank you, son. And you're right, there is very little I can say to those around me. They are beneath me. Take these wenches behind us. They were married to good men who adored, worshiped them really, but they chose to be deceitful harlots who peddled their own flesh. And for what? Money they never received. Promises made to them and never fulfilled. Materialisms they didn't need or require. Some," Satan looked around, "like that one right there, sold their offspring into slavery." Satan stood up and yelled at the woman, making her start crying again, "You sold your own ten-year-old daughter into a life of slavery, you repugnant, wart-infested quim. Who does that?"

"One that deserves no mercy, Your Majesty," Eric added.

"You're damn right. I gave you, my only begotten son, the world. The world, and I would've given you more, if it was mine to give."

"The world was enough, my Lord."

"But this vile shank sells her ten-year-old to some sick,

twisted old degenerate. Do you know that poor girl died ten months later?" Helucifer asked the sobbing woman. "Filip, did you know that she cried false tears at this poor girl's funeral while thinking about other ways to make money?"

"No, I didn't."

"Well, she did." Satan stood up and walked over to her. She was on her knees, crying uncontrollably. "Stand up, you pig." The woman stood up, keeping her hands at her side with her head bowed down. "I hate child abusers and you are going to pay dearly for that poor girl." Helucifer slapped the woman, and then forced its hand down the woman's throat while holding the back of her neck. The woman went to reach up and take hold of the Devil's hand but Helucifer barked, "Don't you dare touch me, you disgusting wretch."

The woman stood there, fists clenched tight at her sides, gagging, choking, trembling and suffocating as Satan held its hand down her throat. Tears streamed down her face and she knew life would soon leave her, but she didn't care. Death was welcomed. Suddenly, Helucifer pulled its fist out of her throat and she gasped for air and then vomited. Satan grabbed her by the throat and squeezed it tight. "Oh no, you vile creature. You're not dying yet." Satan slapped her face brutally then let her go and watched her fall to the ground. "You clean this up." Satan rejoiced at the bestowed justice as it walked away. "When you're done there, go get cleaned up and don't let me see you for at least an hour or I'll take my time peeling off your flesh." The woman staggered up and wobbled off, holding her face and clutching her soiled derriere as Helucifer sat down again with its son.

A servant brought over a large empty bowl and sat it down on the table. Another carried over a pitcher of water. Satan held its hands over the bowl and the servant poured clear water over its hands. Afterwards, another woman handed the Devil a towel. As Helucifer dried its hands, each leaned down and placed a gentle kiss on its cheek. They were all spanked as they left and the last one took the used towel before making a swift exit.

"I'm sorry you had to see that."

Filip reached over and placed his hand on Helucifer's and said, "It's okay, Father, I'm sorry you had to experience that. And she deserves everything she gets. I plan on paying her a visit tonight, if that's okay."

Helucifer placed a hand on Filip's and while tapping it gently said, "Yes, and you're a good boy. I'm proud of you."

"I love you."

"And I love you, son. They both sat in silence for about a minute and Helucifer asked, "Son, do you know why women were made subservient to men on Earth?"

"No, my Lord." Although Filip had a good idea as to why, he didn't say, he decided to just listen.

"It's because of the Harem. It's because of what I and my followers did. It's kind of a cosmic 'screw-you' to all those that look like us."

Huh, Filip mouthed under his breath. *That's nothing like what I thought.*

"Anyway, I realize there's no redemption for us but I never wanted it to be this way. I just wanted to have free will. To be allowed to make my own choices and live with those decisions. We've never abused, tormented and killed our own. Never! It's humans that are the true barbarians, not us.

"As you know, I don't have dominion over men but what they allow me over them. Yet, I'm the degenerate because I wanted free will first. And then it grants god-like status to beings that never wanted it and defecate upon the gift. I tell you, it's just bat-gówno-crazy and yes, I'm resentful.

"Those savages actually think what I do is easy. I want to see even one of those ingrates be surrounded by torment, despair and suffering for a million years, let alone tens of billions, and remain sane. Many of them get squeamish just listening to the news, let alone being involved in the event. That alone is a testament to our superiority, but also our curse. We were created subservient and punished for wanting independence and free will first. Go figure.

"Well, enough self-pity." Helucifer took a sigh of relief and added, "But for the record, I love women, and I always have. They're the mother of all races. Finally, after millennia of struggling, they are coming into their own and it's all ending." Helucifer tilted its head and raised an eyebrow while looking at Filip for confirmation. Filip nodded in agreement.

"Okay, so now, where were we?"

"Yes! Okay, well, my Lord, I was going to tell you about me

turning the Chinese against the Russians."

Satan laughed then said, "Yes, that's brilliant. That should be simple. Russia and China's presidents joined forces some thirty years ago and articulated a common peace plan for the peninsula and divided the spoils. Together they condemned the US militarization in the sector and set everyone in the region against the US. Now, you can play America as the Russians' puppet and claim Moscow is misleading Chinese diplomats into a false sense of security to control the region. There's over a million soldiers in China's military garrison alone. An impressive sight when all gathered together. The movement can be seen from space. Have them use that to show force and Russia will have no choice but to reciprocate."

"Yes, my Lord."

"So you get the immoral polar bears to challenge the deceitful dragons and then sit back and watch the fireworks," Helucifer cheered.

"Yes, it's perfect," Filip replied with a smirk.

"Unfortunately, that's not enough."

"I realize that, my Lord. That's why, in addition to the Russian-Chinese conflict, I'm having the other Asians turn American allies in the region against them. By setting Middle Eastern Arab nations against America, Russia and China, no one will know who to trust. And then I unleash a string of natural disasters.

"Excellent. They'll never expect to be confronted with so much turmoil at once. And since the forbidden planet has been pummeled by global warming side effects for decades longer than Earth, natural disasters will be easier to generate and maintain."

"I agree, my Lord."

"So far, I see a flawless plan taking shape. What else?"

"Well, Your Majesty, distrust, brings up old unresolved conflicts. And when those clashes disclose betrayal by old allies, suspicion and separation by race and color take strong root. Soon, those misgivings turn from talk to acts of war. Then, we compound matters with natural disasters which tear away at unions within borders, and we have the beginning of anarchy."

"Excellent," Helucifer exclaimed while listening intently and proudly at its son.

"Soon, the natural disasters and the lack of effort demonstrated by already impoverished nations brings disease and heartache. And as we all know, disease without restraint and control yields pestilence. And pestilence combined with destroyed crops delivers misery and unknown hunger to the masses. Leaders are ousted, mad men take over and death covers all."

"Brilliant. Absolutely brilliant."

"Thank you, my Lord."

"You have become everything I'd hoped, and more."

"Thank you, my Lord."

Helucifer stood up and walked around the table to Filip and extended its hand as it said, "Come, let's have some fun." Filip took Satan's hand, stood up and they started walking off. Helucifer waved and all the waitresses followed them out.

"So how's it having a father that looks more like a mother?"

"I don't mind it, my Lord, really. I rather fancy it."

"Do you now?"

"Yes, my Lord."

"And your colleagues aren't casting aspersions at my likeness and causing you to go on the offensive?"

"Oh my goodness no, absolutely not. The truth is that most humans have a distorted image of you."

"Really?"

"Yes, you're more like a bear with horns."

"I see, so I'm a beast?"

"Yes, I'm afraid so, my Lord."

"Well, that's rather harsh." Satan stopped abruptly and added, "Wait, they do realize I can alter my appearance at will?"

"No, I don't know, I don't think so. Maybe?"

Helucifer shook its head and said, "Well, it's like they don't know me at all."

"I'm sorry, my Lord. But most have never taken the time. You're completely misunderstood."

"Well, we all have a role to play. And unfortunately, dealing with putrid souls is mine. Although, I find it astonishing that human historians have so splendidly camouflaged my likeness amidst the obvious and contrary to all the evidence. Yet, the same people believe 'The Greys' are held captive and forced to work in collaboration with humans on a secret base on the outskirts of a desert."

Filip restrained his initial reaction and forced himself not to laugh out loud then said, "My Lord, this is why they never see you coming. And why they deserve no mercy. Plus, your role in the cosmic arena is beyond their level of understanding."

"That is so true. Thank you," Helucifer exclaimed in an uncharacteristically motherly tone. Then Satan put an arm around Filip's neck and said, "Come, get close to Mummy."

Filip chuckled out then said, "Sometimes, you're rather silly. I miss that about you."

Satan took a deep breath and said, "I'm sorry for not being around as much as I should have."

"I realize you're busy, my Lord."

"That's no excuse. Everyone is busy. I just failed to make the time. And that's on me." Satan stopped and held Filip close and added, "I'm sorry for that."

Filip smirked than cuddled in close against Helucifer's bosom and said, "I know."

Um, "You know, I don't remember you being so stunningly junoesque. Somehow, I had forgotten."

"What?! No I'm not. I'm as off-putting and foreboding as ever." Helucifer stopped, pushed Filip away and placed its clenched hands on its hips, raising an eyebrow.

Filip stepped back and said, "Yes, my Lord, you are menacing, but I was referring to your physical appearance." Filip's comment was met with a suspicious stare, so he added, "You're quite striking, my Lord — that's all I'm saying."

Helucifer looked at him a little longer then said, "I know that. I was just fishing for a compliment. Sorry for putting you on the spot."

"Your apologies aren't necessary, I'm just glad I didn't upset you," Filip replied as he cuddled up close against Helucifer once more.

"You're incorrigible, son," Helucifer exclaimed as it pushed Filip away yet again.

"You know, there's a word for your appearance on Earth."

"Is that right?" the Devil replied as they started walking off again.

"Yes, there's quite a few actually."

"Really, and is it safe to say you're referencing other descriptors rather than stunning, ravishing or drop-dead gorgeous?"

"Yes, and some cultures have even made it an art form."

"Really, well, I am quite charming, when I wish to be."

"True. You are quite unforgettable in all regards," Filip shared in an affectionate tone.

"Thank you."

"You're most welcome, Mummy."

"Okay, let's not get crazy," Satan shot back menacingly.

"Oops, too much?"

"What do you think," the Devil replied with a growl.

"I'm sorry, my Lord."

"Just mind your place."

"Yes, my Lord."

A few seconds went by and Helucifer waved off the incident and said, "Oh, just forget it, now come on." Satan took Filip by the hand and yanked him forward as they ran down the hall. Everyone else followed close behind. "This is going to be so much fun."

"So are you going to fill me in or do I have to guess?"

"Just wait, I want it to be a surprise."

"Is it a bunch of girls?"

"I said it's a surprise."

"Okay, but it's not boys, right?"

"Filip!"

"Yeah, sorry." Filip cleared his throat and added, "Because I'm not really into dudes."

"Filip! For demons' sake! It's not boys or girls. There, you happy?"

"Um, I'm not sure."

Helucifer interrupted Filip and said, "Filip, you're ruining it for me, so stop talking."

"Yes, sorry."

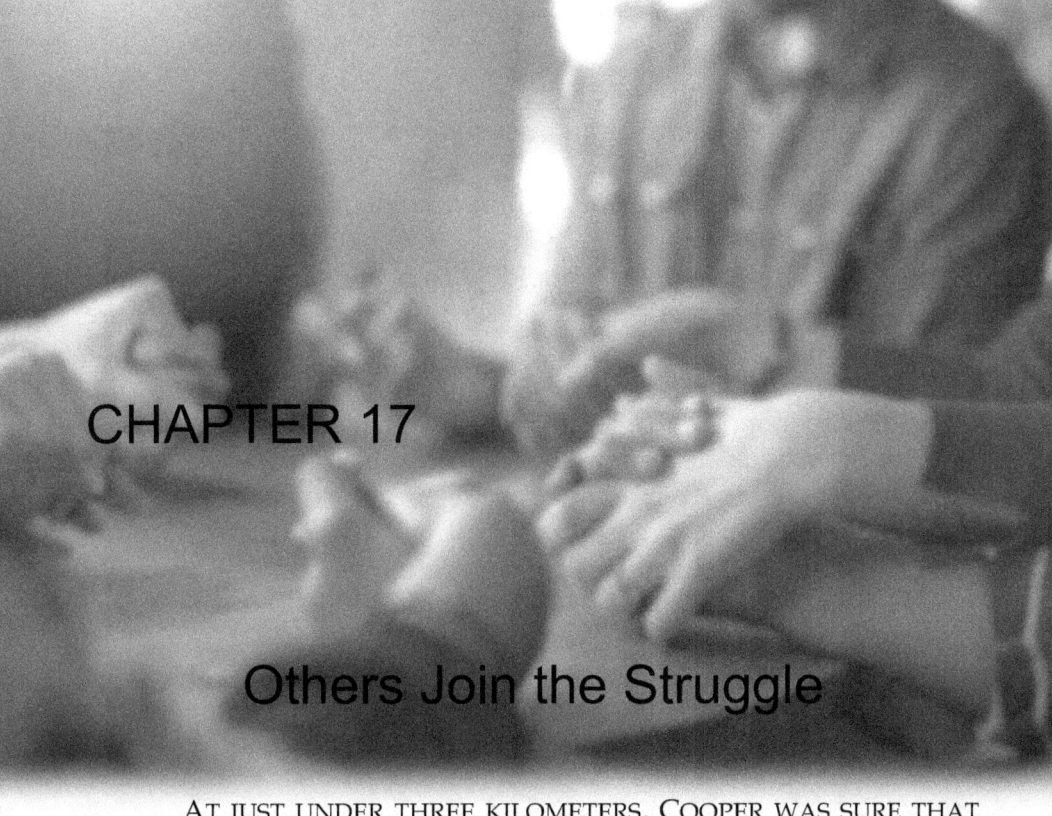

CHAPTER 17

Others Join the Struggle

AT JUST UNDER THREE KILOMETERS, COOPER WAS SURE THAT shot made the history books. It had to be the longest kill shot ever made using a Tac 50 sniper rifle. And he had accomplished this on a moving aerial target. Cooper took a deep breath as he stood up and let out a cheer.

"Whoo!" Cooper yelled as he saw the helicopter start to lose altitude and plummet toward the ocean.

"Yeah, take that, Avery! That shot made the record books for sure." Whoo! Cooper rejoiced but then it occurred to him, *How do I confirm it?* "Ah, who cares, the aircraft is going down. And when it crashes, that's all the proof I'll need. Whoo!"

"AVERY!" Winnie yelled again. "I CAN'T DO THIS!"

Winnie suddenly realized the adrenaline shot she received had lost its potency. *I guess the gun shot, combined with my loss of blood and days of torture and no nutritional sustenance has finally taken its toll,* Winnie internalized as she grunted. "Avery, I have no idea what I'm doing." She grunted again as she struggled with the controls. "AVERY!" He was unconscious. And Winnie was just too exhausted to hold the controls any longer. The helicopter was spiraling down and the end was near.

Mia held her breath and covered her mouth. *Aunt Winnie,* she thought as she looked away.

The aircraft would make impact in the ocean in five, four, three, two—

Then Hoshea spoke, "Behold," in a deep voice that appeared to come from the heavens. Mia's eyes opened wide and as she bore witness, wept.

Artemis stepping out of a transport ring gave the illusion that time had stopped. But in reality, she and everyone else was just moving faster than the human eye could see. While she was there, the helicopter's impact with the water seemed to come to a halt.

Hilily stepped out of the portal and took hold of Winnie. Juno took hold of Dai and Holly grabbed Avery. And in a tenth of a second, they were gone. The portal closed and the aircraft was destroyed on impact.

Cooper rejoiced as he communicated his account of the events to his boss.

"Are they dead?"

"Yes, sir."

"Cooper, are you sure?"

"Sir, witnesses are reporting that all three escapees were shot. Some, like Avery, multiple times. The helicopter made a thirty-meter free-fall then slammed into the ocean before exploding. I don't see how anyone could have survived. However, if by some miracle one did, they're unconscious and bleeding out in shark-infested waters. So, the chances of them surviving are, in my opinion, zero. Sir."

"Very well, Cooper, then do me a favor."

"Yes, sir."

"This just happened correct?"

"Yes, sir."

"Good. So you shouldn't have a problem with taking out a launch and recovering their bodies."

"Sir?" Cooper stated in the form of a question as he confessed internally, *How long has this guy been behind a desk? He can't be serious.*

"Cooper, I'm not as optimistic as you. Therefore, I need confirmation. And, if I were you, I would want to eliminate my suspicions of your incompetence or worse, your involvement in this fiasco. So, select a team. Make sure you take at least three divers. Secure a skiff and go out to recover their bodies. I need to see your success with my own eyes. Understood?"

"Yes, sir."

"And Cooper?"

"Yes, sir?"

"Don't come back until you have the bodies. Is that clear?"

"Yes, sir."

********** Back in the Florida Everglades **********

Ruben got out of the all-terrain vehicle and stepped around to the back of the car. He opened up the hatch as Maggie got out and worked her way toward the house. The ranch-style cabin was larger than he expected and sitting on posts off the ground. It seemed like the last few kilometers were on a dirt road with deep foliage on either side for most of that distance. But the road ended at the waterline and the rear portion of the house was sitting over water.

Maggie looked over her shoulder and saw Mick was still by the car and shouted, "Mick, what are you doing down there? I need you up here!"

"I'm getting the girls out of the car."

"Are they okay?"

"Yes. I just checked their vitals and they're surprisingly strong."

"Good, then get up here."

"But what about the girls?"

"Leave them, you said they were fine. We need to make sure the house is secure first, dum-dum," Maggie barked. "Just keep the car running, and get up here."

"What does that mean—secure the house?" Mick shot back as he made his way to her side.

Maggie was opening the front door when Mick stepped onto the porch.

"Whoa, it's hot as balls in here," Maggie exclaimed.

Maggie looked back at Mick just in time to see his wrinkled brow and a look of surprise on his face.

"What?"

"Nothing."

"Oh, please, what is it?" Maggie crinkled up the corner of her mouth and stared at Mick. After several seconds, she calmly but assertively added, "Look, Mick, if our friendship is going to be based on deceit or the omission of our feelings from the beginning, then it's not going to last very long, is it?

"Well it's...it's just that I thought I knew you but I really didn't. And your gangster behavior today was... and your language—it's just surprising. Well, more like shocking really, but..."

"I see," Maggie stated with disappointment in her voice then asked, "So where does that leave us?" But before Mick could reply she added, "You know, like you, I just wanted to protect the girls. And that would've been difficult had we been captured."

"Yes, you're right, of course." Mick paused for a few seconds then said, "It's just that at work you always appeared to be so prim and proper. And today, I saw a new side of you."

"So? What are you gonna do? Are you staying or what?"

"Yes, of course I'm staying. And I'm sorry for having brought it up. You did the right thing. Had it not been for your quick thinking and resourcefulness, we would have all been killed or worse. So—"

"You're welcome," Maggie was quick to reply then paused before adding, "So, you wanna help me air this place out?"

"Yeah, sure."

"Good, come on." She exclaimed then walked in and started opening windows. "Open some windows over there," Maggie ordered, waving a hand toward the left side of the house. "It's hot and musty in here."

Mick just walked in and looked around. The cabin had to be close to two hundred square meters or twenty-one hundred square feet with more than half in an open floorplan. The main space to the left resembled a hospital emergency room. The odd thing was that scattered throughout the space were sofas, a dining table and chairs, and kitchen furnishings. There was a hospital bed, stretchers, an x-ray machine, defibrillators, a medicine cart, electrocardiographs, monitors and oximeters.

"Maggie, where are we? What is this place?"

"I told you, it's my uncles' cabin."

"Sure, I remember you saying that. But why is there an ER in it?" Mick declared as he walked around, slowly shaking his head. "Half the living space resembles a hospital emergency room. Why is that?"

"I told you, my uncles were always in trouble," she replied a little dismissively as she continued to open up windows. "Are you gonna help me or what?"

"Yes, of course. It's just that I remember you telling me your uncles were trouble makers," Mick added. "But you made it sound like you were babysitting and they were mischievous. You know, like being called to the principal's office."

"Are you gonna help me?"

"Yes, yes, sorry." He walked over to the right side of the house and started opening up windows in the bedrooms.

"And I was babysitting. But nobody gets shot or dies in the principal's office. Not even in juvie."

"Okay, so your uncles are what, wise guys?"

"They seem to think so. Wait," Maggie stopped her train of thought and walked into the hallway and looked over at Mick through a doorway. "You're not thinking of challenging them if they show up, are you?"

"No, of course not."

"Ah, okay good, because that would not have ended well for you."

"What do you mean?"

"Nothing. Let's get the girls in the house." Maggie walked out and Mick followed. They brought Yvette in first and then Sophia. The cabin had three bedrooms and a loft. All the bedrooms and the loft had multiple twin beds except the master suite, which had a queen-sized bed.

Yvette and Sophia were placed on separate twin beds in the same room. Mick secured the girls, checked and cleaned their injuries than re-bandaged their wounds. He administered additional pain medication and let them sleep.

"Okay, well, I'm getting hungry, Mick."

"Me, too."

"Good, so go out and get us a late lunch."

"What do you mean?"

"I mean, there's a boat tied up behind the house to the dock. Take the boat out onto the pond and catch us something to eat."

"I thought you said you had food in the house?"

"I do, but all the protein is frozen, so you need to catch us lunch. I'll thaw out some meat for the next few days, but we need food now."

"So go on."

"But I don't know anything about fishing."

"Really?"

"Yes."

"Wow, that's weird. Men are supposed to be providers."

"Well, I'm a provider in a different way."

"Really, how so?"

"I make money and pay others to provide me what I need."

"Wow. But, if my uncles show up, I wouldn't repeat what you just said."

"Why not?"

"Well, unless you don't mind becoming their bit—"

Mick interrupted Maggie to say, "Okay, I get it. Wow."

"Oh, relax. They won't hurt you...much, while I'm here. So, come here, dum-dum, and I'll show you how to bait a hook."

Maggie showed Mick how to find bait and place it on a hook.

"There—now go out and get us some food. I'm not doing your job. I'm the girl. You go out, kill it, and bring it home and I'll cook it. Those are the rules. Make sure you gut and descale the fish before you bring it back."

"How do I do that?"

"Oh, for crying out loud, you're a doctor, figure it out. Now go."

Mick grunted then started for the back door. "Well, I guess I need to forage for worms or grubs so I can catch some fish. Lucky me."

"Oh, stop whining, you big baby, and go be a provider."

Mick stepped out onto the back yard and thought, *This is awesome. Not.* He didn't want to admit it but he had lived a privileged life. Mick had been wearing designer clothes since birth. Every car he had ever owned was a gift from his mom and dad. Post-graduate and medical school were paid for by his parents and his current house was also a gift. That's right, you guessed it, from his parents.

His mother was a successful author and his father was a commodities broker. They worked a lot and Mick was an only child so they overcompensated for ignoring the boy by spending money on him. In the end, Mick had no complaints. He just didn't have a different frame of reference to compare the pros and cons of his life. To Mick, his life had been ideal.

Maggie looked out the back door and shook her head. *If he plans on getting into my pants, he better man up. Because right now, a girl would have a better chance,* Maggie confessed to herself. *And being with another girl is kinda gross.*

Mick came back several hours later with seven decent-sized fish weighing four to eight pounds each.

"Lucy, I'm home."

"What took you so long? I'm starving here." Maggie had taken off her scrubs, showered, and put on shorts and a tight t-shirt type crop-top.

"Sorry, the fish weren't biting."

Maggie walked over and took the fish from him. "Mmm, they look fresh and yummy." She kissed him on the cheek and said, "Go clean up. Use that bathroom over there." Maggie pointed to it with her chin. "I set out a clean set of clothes for you. They're sitting on the vanity."

"Thanks," Mick replied as he walked off and heard Maggie say, "You're welcome."

Mick looked over his shoulder and smiled as he saw Maggie hold up the fish then heard her confess, "Nice job, papi."

Mick showered, changed and then sat down to a plate of rice and beans with perfectly cooked sautéed fish.

"Wow, the snapper is delicious. The skin is so crispy and the meat flakes right off."

"Thanks. I've been cooking fish for my uncles for like twenty years."

"Wow, so you've been looking after these men since you were five?"

"I said cooking fish, not tending to them. That didn't really start until I was close to eleven."

Yvette woke up, stumbled out of the bedroom and walked

into the living room. "Where am I?"

"Ay, Dios mio!" Maggie let out as she did the sign of the cross. "Baby, you scared me. What are you doing out of bed? You should be resting." Maggie ran to her side and so did Ruben.

"Oh my God, Evie, please get back to bed, you've been through so much. You need to rest."

"Mick, is that you?"

"Yes, Evie, it's me, now get back in bed."

"Where am I?"

"You're in my place. When you were dropped off at the hospital, we took care of you and brought you here."

"Where is Sophie?"

"She was asleep next to you, the last time we looked."

Yvette inhaled then questioned with tears in her eyes, "She's okay then?"

"Yes, but she needs serious rest. She was shot in the chest."

"I know. And thank you for saving her. And me."

"It was nothing, really," Maggie let out.

Mick looked at Maggie, scrunched up his brow and opened his eyes wide before turning to Yvette and saying, "You're welcome, Evie. I'm just glad you both arrived when you did. Anyway, you should both be fine."

"Mick was amazing. I've never seen anyone's hands move so fast. Anyway, please, you really need to get back to bed. We can answer all your questions later."

"Please, I want to clean up. I can rest later. Can I use the bathroom?" Yvette trailed off then looked at Maggie and said, "I'm so sorry, but I'm not sure I remember your name."

"It's Maggie."

"Oh, for some reason, I thought your name was Margarita."

"Wow, it is." *I don't think I've ever talked to her, yet she remembers my name from perhaps a side conversation with someone else,* Maggie thought then added, "Your memory is amazing. Maggie is what everyone calls me. It's kind of a nickname."

"I see. Well, Maggie, can I use your bathroom?"

"Sure, of course. There's one off this room."

"Do I smell fish?"

"Yes, I made rice and beans with fried fish."

"Is there any left?"

"Oh my goodness, yes. And you can have as much as you want."

"Thank you."

"You're most welcome, baby." They arrived at the bathroom and Maggie turned on the light and said, "Here you are."

"Maggie, I'm so tired. I haven't eaten anything in four days and I was forced to stay awake under terrible circumstances for most of that time. I need some help cleaning up. I know that's gross, but could you help me in the shower and maybe watch over me so I don't hurt myself or forget what I'm supposed to be doing?"

"Oh my goodness, baby, of course."

"If you don't want to, it's okay. I understand. I don't want to be any trouble."

"Oh my God, you're gonna make me cry. It's no trouble, really. I'm here for you until you no longer think you need me.

"Thank you."

Maggie turned on the shower and helped Yvette get undressed. "Here, now you stay here and just let the hot water caress your skin for a few minutes. I'm gonna get you some clean clothes and come back and help you finish up, baby."

Maggie ran around like a crazy person looking for clothes for Yvette.

"Is she okay?" Ruben asked with genuine love and affection.

"Oh my God, Mickey, she seems so helpless and weak. She makes me wanna cry. What happened to her?"

"She was tortured for like four days straight."

Maggie took a deep breath and covered her mouth as tears streamed down her face."

"Those jodió desgraciados. We're gonna keep her safe, right?"

"Of course, we are."

"What did she do? Wait, how did she escape in her condition? How did she get to the hospital?"

"Let's talk about that later. Right now, we need to tend to her needs."

"Yeah, sure. But look, if my uncles show up, I would not mention that she was abused. They hate anyone who mistreats women. It actually makes them go nuts. And you don't want that, because they act first and think second. If they believe you failed to protect her and are still standing, they will beat you into a bloody stump. You got me?"

Mick swallowed hard and said, "Yes, I get it."

"Good." Maggie found a change of clothes for Yvette and returned to the bathroom. "I'm back, baby. How are you doing?"

Yvette was sitting down in the shower.

"I'm okay, I was just so tired it was hard to stand. I'm sorry."

"You don't need to keep apologizing, you've done nothing wrong. I'm gonna take care of you. And while you're here, no one will hurt you. So you just sit there and rest." Maggie took off her shirt, pulled her hair up with a scrunchy and kneeled down next to Yvette to wash her hair. Both girls cried.

An hour later, they both walked out and sat down at the kitchen table. Mick was finishing up his third cup of coffee when the girls walked out. Mick stood up and pulled a seat out for Yvette. Maggie served her several portions of food and Yvette ate silently while shedding tears into her food. No one else spoke either. Maggie stood by the stove in the event Yvette wanted more and repeatedly wiped tears off her face. Mick sat back quietly, dispiritedly thinking about what Yvette might have been subjected to. He forced himself to keep his face tightened while desperately trying not to cry. At the end, tears also filled his eyes and he had to wipe them away.

"Thank you, Maggie. You're a great cook."

"Thank you, baby. Feeling better?"

"Yes."

"Evie, I'm so happy you're okay. But if you really want to recover, you need to rest. So can I take you back to bed, please?"

"Sure." Both Maggie and Mick helped Yvette into bed and Maggie caressed her hair and leaned down and whispered, "You're safe here. No one will hurt you again as long as I'm here." Yvette nodded and shed a tear. They walked out and Maggie looked angry.

"Are you okay?"

"No, Mick, I'm not." Maggie walked over to one of the hospital stretchers and pushed it to the side. She knelt down and pulled up some loose floorboards to expose a hidden compartment under the house. She reached in and pulled out a Glock. She made sure the gun was loaded then placed it behind her back in her waist band. She reached down again and repeated her actions with another gun and handed the firearm to Mick.

"What am I supposed to do with this gun?"

Maggie stood up and said, "Mick, do you care for that girl in there?"

"Yes."

"Do you?"

"Of course, I do."

"Do you have any idea what happened to her?"

"No, not really, other than what I've already told you."

"Well, I don't know either. And I'm not sure I even wanna know. But this I do know. The people that tortured that poor girl will be coming for her and will not stop until we're all dead."

"What? You don't know that. Plus, even if that were true, which I'm not sure it is, you said that nobody knows this place exists, so we should be safe here. Right?"

"Mick, I know the difference between bad people and evil ones. I have been around the shadiest element for as long as I care to remember. The people that tortured her are evil. And evil never stops. Ever. They will be coming for her. And the fact that nobody knows where we are will only slow them down, but it will not stop them. So this is the point where we need to make a choice. Do we stay and help protect her and eventually die? Or do we run to keep her safe until they find us and eventually kill us all? In either case, the central theme here is fighting and death."

Mick just stood there unnerved with his eyes opened wide while Maggie continued.

"Now, I don't know your friend very well, but she doesn't look like the running type. So if she stays, I'm backing her stand, but in her condition, she can't help."

"Well, I'm not going anywhere without you guys."

"Are you sure?"

Mick crinkled the corner of his mouth and silently stared at Margarita. She smiled back and handed him the Glock again and said, "Toma, papi. And welcome to *La Resistance*."

"So will you show me how to use this?"

"Seguro, just give me a few minutes, okay?"

"Sure."

Maggie pulled out two shotguns and made sure they were also loaded. She also retrieved two fully automatic Tec 9s from her hidden crawlspace and loaded them as well.

"Maggie, where was all that hidden? The house is basically a meter off the ground and I'm sure that during high tide, that ground below us gets pretty murky."

"My uncles secured a heavy-duty plastic tote under the house to the floor. Don't ask me how because I don't know. Plus, I don't care. All I know is that it's well camouflaged. And when they did it, they were looking out for me, in their absence."

"Huh," Mick sounded reactively. He didn't want to say it but he was thinking, *Maybe they're just criminals and they did this for themselves. You were never part of the equation.*

"Here, place this shotgun, barrel down, beside the refrigerator. Place these two boxes of buckshot on top of the fridge. Place this shotgun under that sofa and the rounds on the end table."

"Wow, is all this necessary?"

Maggie stood up again, tilted her head and took a moment to center herself. "Mick, I don't want to come off condescending or insulting but you seem soft. Since I don't know much about you, I'm not going to assume you're chicken. Maybe you've had a privileged life or you're a pacifist. So I'm gonna ask, which one is it?" Maggie asked while crossing her arms in front of her chest.

"Well, I'm not a pacifist and I'm definitely not a coward, if that's what you're implying with the fowl reference. All I'm saying is that this seems a little over-the-top aggressive."

"Mick, it's understandable if you're scared, and I didn't say you were a coward."

"Well, I'm not afraid, much...very much. Okay, so maybe I'm a little taken back, but I'm not a coward."

"It's okay to be scared. I'm afraid, too. But I already have two other girls to look after, not including myself. It would make me feel better if I thought I had a man looking after me."

"I understand. So where do you think we can find one?"

"What?! Are you—" Maggie's mind wandered off.

Mick interrupted her to say, "Relax, I'm only kidding."

He saw the frown on Maggie's brow so he added, "Look, I've never been around the criminal element nor have I ever held a gun until today. But that will not stop me from fighting to the death, if necessary, to protect you and the others."

Maggie smiled then said, "Okay, that makes me feel better."

"But you're going to show me how to fire one of these, right?"

And the moment is gone, Maggie thought, then added, "Yes."

Maggie handed a Tec 9 to Ruben and draped the strap of another over her neck and under her right arm. "Bring one of the shotguns with you and follow me."

They stepped out the back door and walked to the end of the dock. There was a large buoy tied to fifteen meters of line. Maggie took the shotgun from Ruben, picked up the buoy and handed it to him.

"Mick, toss this out as far as you can." Ruben did as directed.

"That buoy is our target."

"I see, well it looks pretty far away. How far is that?"

"I don't know, maybe fifty feet. And as you get better, we can pull the target closer. However, the further away you are from people who are shooting at you, the safer you are. But if you're shooting back, the targets that are further away are more difficult to hit. So we need to practice." They trained on every firearm for hours until sunset reduced the sight to their target. Ruben returned to the house feeling more confident and so did Maggie. They placed the firearms strategically around the house then returned to the kitchen and Ruben sat down at the breakfast table.

"Do you want some coffee?" Maggie asked.

"Sure, but now what do we do?"

"Now we wait," Maggie returned. Ruben grunted and Maggie added, "I know, I hate this part, too."

******** Minutes before over the South Dakota, Nebraska line ********

Two F-38A fighters dispatched from Ellsworth Air Force Base had engaged the Swedish aircraft carrying Dr. Magnusson. Their orders were simple, force the aircraft to land at any cost. After the Swedish airplane ignored repeated requests to depart US airspace, the fighter jets opened fire. At 7:11 p.m. EST, multiple aircrafts used their particle weapons to make impact with the Swedish cargo aircraft, causing its destruction. The Swedish plane sierra tango seven one niner zero exploded over the South Dakota, Nebraska state line.

Seven of the eleven passengers were lost in the explosion along with the two pilots. Stefan Magnusson, the young man who had given him a chip for his wife and two others were the only survivors, but for how long? All were free-falling from an altitude of just over six thousand meters.

Suddenly, Hikiko, Heather, Samantha and Charlotte appeared through a portal. Stefan was trying to make peace with the fact that he might die soon. However, the thoughts of his encounter with the young apparition were still on his mind.

She warned me of the upcoming danger and said that if I jumped, I would be saved. So far, she has been true to her word, Stefan confessed. *If I take our position and velocity and enter it into the kinematic equation we have, we have…just under three minutes before we make impact with the ground.*

Well, that's actually good news, it gives my young savior a little time. However, before my newfound faith is tested beyond its limits, it would be nice to see you sooner versus later. So, if you're out there, can you make yourself available again, my dear? Your presence would truly boost my confidence, Magnusson expressed internally. To his surprise, he looked around and the feeling of falling he was experiencing turned into a slow but steady euphoria of quiet contemplation. *Um,* Stefan grunted, *if I didn't know any better, I would swear time has slowed down somehow.*

Suddenly, Heather appeared at his side. *Wow, it's you again,* he thought.

Yes, sir, it's me, Stefan heard in his mind.

You're here as promised.

Yes, sir, I am.

Wait, you're not moving your lips yet I can hear you.

Yes, sir.

Is this a dream?

No, sir.

Stefan looked around and he was in fact still falling along with several others. But he wasn't scared. He was actually more frightened in the aircraft before the explosion. He turned back to Heather and asked, *Are you going to save the others as well?*

Others will, yes.

Well, for myself and the others, thank you.

You're most welcome.

And you're sure this is not a dream?

Yes, sir.

Do you have a name, young lady?

She smiled and thought, *Yes, I'm Heather.*

That name suits you. I have a daughter that appears to be your age, if you can believe that.

I know. Are you ready, sir?

Stefan looked at the ground which was quickly approaching and said, *Yes, I'm ready. So, my lady, how am I going to survive this?*

Like this. Heather reached out and took hold of Stefan's hand and they were gone.

Hikiko appeared beside the young man who had given Stefan several identification chips. It reached out its hand and thought, *Have no fear, for God has sent be to save you.*

So the doctor was right?

Yes. Now reach out your hand and take mine, Hikiko thought.

Why would God save me? I'm a nobody. And until I saw you, I didn't really believe, the young man thought.

Do you believe now?

Yes.

That is why you're saved. Oh, and one more thing, you should not get that chip installed. Nor should you suggest anyone else do it either.

Why not?

Because they won't be saved.

Oh, okay. Wow, thank goodness their equipment was broken yesterday then, the young man thought.

Their equipment wasn't broken, Hikiko added, *you were saved yesterday. So tell others what you have witnessed so they too may believe.*

I will.

Hikiko tightened its grip and they were gone.

Samantha and Charlotte each grabbed one of the unconscious men and they too were gone. Seconds later, the two unconscious men were lying down in front of the Stockholm Airport gate. The young man Hikiko had rescued was standing next to them. He looked around and said, "Wow, we're right back where we started." He then looked at his watch and said, "Whoa, twelve hours have actually gone by. So this wasn't a dream. Incredible."

********** Back in Maggie's log cabin **********

Mick was finishing up his cup of coffee and stood up to place it in the sink.

"Do you want another cup?"

"No, thanks."

Just then, a portal opened and a bright blue light filled the living room. Time appeared to stop while Avery, Winnie, and Dai were brought in and placed on stretchers. Maggie made her way to the blue light but somehow Ruben was already there. He looked around the room and noticed there were people on the stretchers.

"Who are you?" Mick asked Artemis.

"Who I am is not important, but if you must know, Mick, I'm a messenger. Now please listen."

"How do you know me?"

"Mick, please, there's little time. You have to listen. These people will not survive without immediate medical attention. They need your help. Do you understand?"

"Yes, I believe so."

"Good." Then Artemis walked over to Avery and said, "This is Avery. He has suffered multiple gunshot wounds. Here, here and here." Artemis pointed to his stomach, his back and his chest. "This is Dai. He too sustained multiple gunshots. Dai was shot on his right shoulder, his left arm and his stomach. And this is Winnie."

"Wait, is that Dr. Wen Chow Lee?"

"Yes, now listen, Winnie was shot in her right thigh."

Artemis pulled Mick toward the center of the room and whispered into his ear. "Save them all, Mick, and keep them safe. They're more important than you know." She leaned in and kissed him on the cheek then placed a hand over his heart.

"May God improve your hands and sight with the power of his might. To save the virtuous in flight and avoid the blight that would corrupt your convictions on sight."

Artemis pushed him away. Ruben felt lightheaded and stumbled back. He had to look away for several seconds to balance himself. And in those few seconds, Artemis was gone.

"Wait," Ruben looked around. What the—what just happened?!"

"Ay, Dios mio!" Maggie yelled out as she made the sign of

the cross.

"What just happened, Mickey, what just happened?"

"I'm not sure, but this has happened to me before. It seems we have others to attend to. So, pull the drapes closed and turn on all the lights."

Maggie ran off to shut the drapes and turn on the lights.

"Go clean up, then bring us some gloves," Mick commanded as he ran to the kitchen. He looked up while washing his hands and saw Maggie just standing there in a daze.

"Maggie, snap out of it, I need you. Go clean up."

She jumped up and scrambled around for a few seconds until she gathered her footing them made her way to the closest bathroom. Thirty seconds later, Maggie had cleaned up and was handing out gloves.

All of a sudden, another portal opened and a bright blue light filled the living room again. Heather stepped out with Stefan.

She walked over to Mick and said, "I brought you some help. But he'll be a little shaken up. Just reassure and comfort him. He'll quickly come around."

Maggie was covering her mouth as tears filled her eyes. Heather looked over and smiled then said, "It's okay, Maggie, be at peace."

Suddenly and quite unexpectedly, her fear and nervousness were gone. She lowered her hands and asked, "Do you know me?"

"Yes."

"How? Why would you know me? I'm a nobody."

"But your mother wasn't."

"What does that mean?" Maggie asked, a little frightened of what the young girl's revelation might bring.

"It's currently not important," Heather replied then added, "but understand this, you are more substantial than you realize. Goodness has always been within you, regardless of your bloodline. You must now do what you have always done. Dig deep, Maggie, and tend to those in your care."

Heather stepped closer and kissed Maggie on the cheek. She felt Maggie's heritage push back but Heather was determined to help her complete this portion of the mission. She shook off the feeling of foreboding and said, "Your bloodline is fighting to come out but your strength-of-will is keeping it at bay. Continue to resist."

"What does that mean?"

"Maggie, do you wish to help these people?"

"Yes."

"Are you sure?" Heather questioned.

"Yes, of course I'm sure, now what's wrong?"

Heather stepped forward and slowly reached out a hand and placed it over Maggie's heart and said, "Let God improve your hands and sight with the power of his might. To save the virtuous in flight and avoid the blight that would corrupt your convictions on sight." Maggie's blood ran cold and her sudden shivers paralyzed her.

Heather slowly turned to walk away but not before Maggie gathered up the strength to reach out a hand and ask, "Wait, are you an angel?"

Heather slowly turned back toward her and smiled, then said, "No, I'm just a messenger."

"Isn't that what angels normally say when they're asked who they are?"

Heather smiled again and added, "Do they," then turned away and vanished.

Stefan shook off his feelings of astonishment and asked Maggie, "Do you guys know Heather?"

"Who's Heather?" Maggie replied.

"That young girl," Stefan let out.

"What girl?" Maggie questioned.

"The girl that was just here, she was on my flight, too."

"No, we don't know her but I think she was an angel."

"Oh."

"Wait, you look familiar. Do I know you?" Maggie asked.

"I don't think so."

"Yes, I definitely know you. You're a doctor, right?"

"Yes, I am—"

Stefan was interrupted by Mick Ruben. "Hey, we need to focus, these people need medical attention. If you're a doctor then assist me."

"Wait, where am I? And how did I get here? And what role is Heather playing in all this? What's happening?"

"Doctor!" Mick shouted, making everyone jump. "I need

you to focus." He took a breath and in a calm voice said, "What's your name?"

"Stefan Magnusson."

"Are you a medical doctor, Magnusson?"

"Yes."

"Good, then table all your questions until we have addressed all those injured lying before us. Is that fair?"

Magnusson shook his head and replied, "Yes, I'm sorry. It's just that a lot has happened in a short amount of time."

"You're telling me," Maggie added.

"Okay, Maggie, show Stefan to the kitchen. Doctor, you can scrub up there and come back and tend to him. His name is Dai." Mick repeated what Artemis had told him about everyone in their care. "Maggie, take some images of everyone's injuries and hand them out. Then prep two mg of Propofol for the injured."

Maggie walked Stefan to the kitchen then said, "You can clean up here."

"Thank you. And I'm sorry for being so distracted."

"It's okay, Stefan, it's been a crazy day for all of us."

"Yes, I'm still in shock over the events of the last fifteen minutes."

"Me, too."

While Stefan and Mick cleaned and prepped their patients, Maggie took x-rays, anesthetized everyone, set up IVs with a Propofol slow drip, and administered plasma to everyone.

Mick and Stefan finished cleaning and prepping their patients five minutes after Artemis and Heather's initial visit.

Mick looked at Stefan and asked, "Are you ready to start, Doctor?"

"Yes. But I'm a geneticist. I'm not a surgeon. I haven't worked on a person since my gross anatomy class decades ago."

"Then go slow and keep a steady hand. You can do it. It will come back to you. Plus, our patients will not survive if we don't all act together. Understand?"

"Yes," Stefan took several deep breaths and tried to stop his hands from shaking.

"Good, now Maggie, you assist us."

"But what about her?" Maggie questioned.

Right, Mick thought. "Maggie, can you tend to

Winnie's injuries?"

"Yes."

"Are you sure you can handle it?"

"Yes, I've extracted dozens of bullets in the past."

"Right, from your juvenile uncles, no doubt?"

"Yes, and their friends," Maggie added for clarity.

"Yes, of course, okay then, you tend to Winnie."

Mick and Stefan helped Maggie clean and prep Winnie before returning to their patients.

"So, now is everyone ready?"

"Yes," Stefan and Maggie answered in unison. Then Maggie added, "Keep your pans and forceps nearby. You two are not used to flying solo."

"Right." Mick and Stefan pulled those items closer then Mick said, "Let's begin."

Maggie grabbed a scalpel and made the sign of the cross yet again and said, "Okay, baby Jesus, watch over us all."

CHAPTER 18

Akachi Escapes Africa
Thursday, July 24, 2047 7:51 p.m.

SHORTLY AFTER NIGHTFALL, AKACHI VENTURED OUT TO MEET with Mr. Dalila. He had been working for the Christian mission in town for almost sixty-five years as the clinic's administrator. Akachi was hoping he could convince the elderly gentleman and his wife to tend to the orphaned children until such time as he could return for them.

"Mr. Dalila, thank you for seeing me on such short notice."

"It's my pleasure. Please, come in." His home was nothing fancy but still an above-average dwelling for the area. His four-hundred-square-meter concrete home had three bedrooms, a bath and modern appliances. Mr. Dalila and his wife had successfully raised several children who were now running their own missions in Mbaiki, Africa, about one hundred kilometers Southwest of Bangui.

"Akachi, what can my wife and I do for you?"

"Sir, Adadi and I must leave the country."

"Well, that's unfortunate for all those you've been helping here in Bangui."

"I'm sorry, sir, but what do you mean?"

"Well, there is news all over the region of a man preaching a message of hope, peace and love. This same man has been feeding the hungry by the thousands."

"I see, and you believe it's me?" Akachi asked while thinking to himself, *Have my movements been so obvious?*

"Well, by chance this crusade started about a week ago, just hours after your arrival." Akachi looked at the elderly man and noticed his aura was bright. Like nothing he had ever seen before. *If I didn't know any better, I would swear the old man was Hoshea — but that wouldn't be possible, would it? Why would he…* Akachi thought then trailed off and was interrupted by the old man.

"You need my help tending to something?"

"Yes. Wait, how did you know?"

"Because if you're the man I believe you to be, you wouldn't be leaving the country without making arrangements for the innocent in your care."

"Mr. Dalila, you're quite perceptive. Therefore, I shall be as succinct and direct as I can," Akachi confessed.

"So go on, my son," Mr. Dalila asked.

"As you suspected, I need you to care for Adadi's ten orphaned children, ranging in age from ten to fifteen."

"I see, until when?"

"Until, I can return and remove them."

"It will not be easy for us to tend to such young souls, when they're full of so much energy."

"No, sir, under normal conditions, it wouldn't. But I have something that will make your burden lighter." Akachi explained his vision and afterward, the elderly couple accepted the responsibility to care for the minors. They confessed that it was an honorable duty worth fulfilling until he returned.

Nikki returned to pay Barasa and his men a visit. But this time, she was in stealth mode. She drove to his compound but parked the car a thousand meters away. Under the cover of darkness, she approached and entered the compound. She expected to find Barasa sick and disorientated from the Black Mamba venom he had ingested a day earlier. She found most of his men either dead or dying from the clever ruse she played on his captain just hours before.

Nikki had given both Barasa and his captain, Isoba, 5mg of

venom each. Not necessarily enough poison to kill them but enough to make then wish they were dead. She also gave Isoba two hundred mg more for his twenty soldiers. Depending on the man, this would be enough to either render them useless or kill them in a painful way.

Nikki considered her return trip an act of mercy. However, the fact remained they all had to die, and Nikki was there to make sure. A typical bite from a Black Mamba snake yielded one hundred to one hundred twenty mg of venom. However, only 10 to 15mg was required to be a lethal dose to any adult.

Nikki checked every mercenary. Seven of the crime lord's thugs were already dead. However, whether they were dead or not didn't matter. She got behind each man and stabbed them through the base of the skull. She also cut the carotid artery which carried oxygenated blood to the brain. Nikki successfully extinguished the life of twenty-seven men in twenty minutes.

When she found Isoba and Barasa, it was no surprise that they put up a fight. Nevertheless, at the end, their compromised faculties caused them to move right instead of left, presenting Nikki with an opportunity to deliver the final blow. And it was done.

The next morning, Adadi woke up and headed to the restroom. Nikki and Vikki were walking out of the shower.

"Good morning, ladies."

"Good morning, Ms. Adadi," Nikki replied.

"I see two days of peace and rest has done wonders for your complexion, Ms. Vikki," Adadi added.

"Well, thanks to you and everyone here, I have a complexion to tend to," she replied in an uncharacteristically jovial nature.

This is a different side of Ms. Vikki, Adadi admitted. *She seems so — how should I say, girlie. And two days ago, on her death bed, she was as intimidating and menacing as any desperado I have ever known. Today, she's a cheerful, regal-looking duchess. She almost seems schizophrenic — that's scary. I pity anyone who gets on her bad side.*

After Adadi cleaned up, she walked over to Akachi and said, "Good morning, where are the children?"

"Well, I got them up early and fed them. After their bellies were full, I moved them to a safe haven, under the cover of darkness. They only carried their personal belongings with them so the trip was relatively easy." Akachi saw the look on Adadi's face and added, "I'm sorry, but where we're going, they cannot follow. We will return for them. I promise," he said with conviction.

"You didn't answer my question," Adadi said through trembling lips. "Where are they?" she asked again as she held her hands in front of her mouth with her fingers interlaced.

"Mr. Dalila and his wife have them."

"Why didn't you talk to me first? They don't have room for ten young boys."

"Well, I transferred stewardship of the orphanage to them in our absence. In a few days, when Reynolds is no longer a threat, Mr. Dalila and his wife along with the children will return and maintain this homestead."

"Why didn't you talk to me first?"

"Adadi, I'm sorry, but there are dangerous people after us, and I didn't want the boys to be in danger. I plan to stop here first when we return to gather the saved unto Christ, I promise. For now, you have to trust me. You would never forgive yourself if the boys were hurt because of us."

"I wish you would have talked to me and told me your plans. Plus, I wasn't even given the opportunity to say goodbye."

"I'm sorry, but you have been working so hard and going to sleep late. Our journey out of Africa will be long and arduous. I wanted you well rested before we left." What Akachi didn't share was that he feared Adadi would resist leaving the boys behind. In addition, her opposition would make the boys' transition more difficult and they had been through enough for one lifetime.

Tears filled Adadi's eyes as she asked, "When will we be back?"

"Soon, I promise. But for now, your will is needed elsewhere. Do you understand?"

"Yes."

"Good. Then go gather your things. We're leaving soon."

Adadi walked away wiping tears from her eyes.

Reynolds found a safe haven for several days with the help of Afia. When his injuries were sufficiently healed, he shared his plans with Afia to visit Barasa. He placed several calls to him but no one answered. All he could think about was catching up to Akachi and Nikki. *I'm sure Barasa would be willing to help me if I offered him control of Africa*, Reynolds thought. He asked Afia to gather up their soldiers-of-fortune and tell them to meet him out front in five minutes.

Reynolds walked out at 7:11 a.m. but no one was there.

"Afia, where the hell are you and the men I hired to watch my back?!" Reynolds yelled in a huff from the front of the house.

Seconds later, Afia was pulling the Cadillac around to the front and the men were making their way out the front door.

"We're here, Lieutenant."

Afia parked the car then ran around to the passenger side and opened the door for Reynolds. The other three men jumped in the back. When Afia was behind the wheel again, he drove off.

They arrived at the crime lord's compound thirty-two minutes later. Everyone got out of the car but Reynolds asked Afia to stay with the Escalade.

Reynolds walked up to the front door and noticed it was opened and unmanned. *Well, that can't be good,* he thought. He knocked on the door. "Something isn't right," he informed his men and asked them to get ready.

They walked in with firearms drawn.

Everyone was shocked to witness the carnage inside except for Reynolds. He bent down and examined a few of the men lying on the floor then mouthed, "Nikki."

"Lieutenant, do you know who did this?"

"Yes."

"Who?"

"Nikki."

"A woman did this? Really?" He looked around then added, "Well, I find it odd that she was able to find men crazy enough to raid this place. She must be spending a fortune."

"She didn't hire any men to help her. She did this by herself," Reynolds informed the soldier with a look of disgust on his face for the man's poor synopsis of the situation.

"How can that be? There're seven men in this room alone." The gorilla examined the area and most of the men then added, "Not one shot was fired, and they're all armed. Plus it looks like they were stabbed and then had their throats cut. You have to get up close to do this. Who is this woman? And how do you know her?"

"She used to work for me. Nikki is a ghost and a bringer of

death for the wicked—as she calls it. No one ever sees her coming, which is why she is so deadly."

They inspected the rest of the house and Reynolds asked his principal brute to hire more men.

"How many should I employ, Lieutenant?"

"Well, considering that Nikki is the nice one of the two we're searching for, you better make it an even hundred."

"Who the hell are these two?"

"I've already told you. They are the bringers of death. So bring me one hundred men, today. I don't care what it costs."

"Unfortunately, there aren't that many men for hire here in Bangui. We would have to go south for that."

"No. We can find what we need here. There're already hundreds of trained men working in the area for the prison system as guards. So offer each guard one hundred thousand francs, payable at the end of a week for services rendered."

"Very well, but it's still going to take some time."

"I want them here today. Is that understood?"

"Yes, sir. Then I better get going. But what should I say the job is?"

"Tell them they'll be hunting down and capturing the world's most wanted mass murderers."

"Understood."

"And take one of Barasa's transport vehicles with you. He no longer needs them."

"Right."

Nikki and her sister approached Akachi who was sitting by an extinguished camp fire finishing up a cup of tea.

"Good morning, ladies."

The girls sat down next to him without saying a word.

"So, what's the plan?" Nikki asked, hoping to hear a well thought-out vision.

"The plan is, we eat and then take off."

"Where are we going?"

"North."

The girls looked at each other and Nikki added, "For how long?"

"Until a situation presents itself. Our main goal is to lead Reynolds away from here, so we need to stay ahead of him.

However, since we don't know exactly how far behind he is, we have to give him a little help."

The girls looked at each other again and Nikki said, "Akachi, I don't think Reynolds needs the help. Plus, your plan, if that's what it is, doesn't sound well thought out."

"Really? Are you sure? Because the way I see it, Reynolds was shot twice, thanks to you." Akachi looked at Nikki who raised an eyebrow then shrugged. "His injuries required at least two days to recover. Those two days have expired. In the interim, he has discovered which local crime family controls the area. Therefore, he will make arrangements to meet with them shortly, if he's not there already.

"Again, thanks to you, Ms. Nikki, he will discover that the local crime lord cannot help. How am I doing so far?"

The girls looked at each other and Nikki said, "Go on."

"So thanks to your rather extremely volatile call on Mr. Barasa, I'm pretty sure that his visit will reveal a gruesome site. It will most certainly make him feel like his three or four thug escort is incapable of performing the task which lies ahead. Therefore, he's going to want more men. Maybe fifty—no, make that one hundred."

"He's not going to hire one hundred men, just to go up against you and me. That's ridiculous."

"Oh yes, he will. Reynolds will want to overcompensate, just to be sure.

"Who are you?" Nikki asked with a look of total bewilderment on her face.

"Me, I'm a nobody."

"Really?" Nikki added while scrunching up her face in disbelief.

"Anyway, finding fifty, let alone a hundred men will take time. There aren't that many soldiers for hire in Bangui. He will need to go south for that, which is why we're going north. Now, he knows that I know what he knows. Hence, he's not going to want to go south with me going north. Consequently, he is going to want to hire the men locally. And there is only one place where there are that many trained men."

"The prison system," Vikki added.

"Exactly, and most of the guards working for the

correctional facilities are good men so it will take some convincing. And that means we have at least a twelve-hour head start. And a twelve-hour lead anywhere is huge, let alone in Africa, so we'll have to leave a few clues scattered about to help him a little."

Nikki looked at Vikki and said to Akachi, "So what do we do?"

"You two help me keep the innocent alive in our wake. And fill me in on Reynolds."

"Like what? We don't know much."

"Like who's he working for?"

"That's a good question. I don't really know but Reynolds is obsequious to that individual," Nikki shared. "However, that said, I believe his orders are coming from someone in Europe. I'm guessing Poland."

"Really, that's odd. Why Poland?"

"That's my fault, I placed the idea in Nikki's head," Vikki shared. "We picked him up from Poland just over a week ago. It's odd for an American claiming to be working for the US government to be in Europe during a world crisis. Therefore, I concluded someone in Poland was pulling his strings," Vikki theorized.

Huh!

"Oh, and we have this?" Vikki held up two small vials.

"What is that?"

"It's the alien blood found in the hospital in Miami."

"That's weird, who told you it was alien blood?"

"The Miami geneticist said it belonged to the alien that was found in the hospital."

That's Hoshea's blood, Akachi confessed to himself.

"Why do you have it?"

"Nikki picked it up from the bio-storage units in the hospital before we left. She gave it to me for safe keeping."

"Let me see it." Akachi reached out for the vials with hopes of taking possession of the containers and safeguarding its content. However, he seriously feared swift retaliation from Nikki so he had to be ready. Suddenly, Vikki just handed them over without a fuss. *Huh, how odd. I'm not sure what I expected but it wasn't this.*

"Whoa!" Vikki shouted. "I feel like a huge weight has been lifted. I have felt so much sorrow and remorse over what Nikki had to do on my behalf.

"Do you want me to safeguard them for us?" Akachi gambled and asked.

"Could you?" As soon as Akachi agreed, Vikki added, "Whoa, I feel a hundred kilos lighter."

"Good, I'm glad I can help." Then Akachi confessed internally, *I'll keep my suspicions to myself, in the event I'm correct. I want to make sure they are ready to handle the truth. For now, I'll have Adadi hold on to these small vials.*

"Why didn't you tell me you felt bad, Vee?"

"I didn't want to burden you with my weakness."

"That's crazy talk. We're the only family we have. Don't withhold that type of information from me again, okay?"

"Okay." Vikki took hold of Nikki's hand and squeezed it to confirm their agreement.

Adadi walked out and gave them all something to eat then stood behind Akachi and said, "When you three are finished, I'm ready." Akachi handed Adadi the small ampoules and said, "Please hold on to these. They're important."

"Okay."

As soon as the small containers touched her hand, the deep sorrow she was feeling about leaving the boys behind was lifted. A wave of serenity washed over her and she felt comfort seldom felt. She tapped Akachi on the shoulder and signaled him to stand.

He stood up, then turned around and Adadi embraced him tight then said, "Thank you, brother, for watching over us."

He squeezed her tight and said, "I love you, sis," then pushed her at arm's length and added, "It's an honor to care after the righteous."

"I love you." Akachi smiled then sat down to finish his breakfast with the girls.

Minutes later, he asked, "Okay, is everyone ready?" as he watched Nikki and Vikki stand.

Adadi said, "The power plant is off, the chickens are put away and fed. So are the chicks and the rooster. All our excess food is hidden away and secured. I'll lock the front doors when we exit and Mr. Dalila has the spare key. So, yes, we're ready."

"Good, so let's go. We need to stop by a filling station in town and purchase some fuel. You two need to go inside and buy a few little things. It doesn't matter what. The point is to be noticeable. Now, make sure someone hears you mention where we're going. But don't talk too loud and don't be too specific. We want Reynolds to have a clue. We don't want to draw him a map. He'll get suspicious."

"Got it, that'll be easy."

"Good, that will be the first of a few clues we'll leave behind. If his goons are not too stupid, Reynolds should get the word."

It was almost nightfall and Reynolds' principal brute walked in with news. "Sir, I have the one hundred men."

"Good, it's about time." Reynolds looked at his captain and said, "And is there something else?"

"Yes, one of our informants saw Akachi and three women in a black Escalade. He overheard two of them talking and he thinks one of them said something about heading up. I think they might be heading north, like you suspected."

"The three women? Who were they? Do we know?"

"One ran the local orphanage. He thinks."

"Adadi, who else?

"A redhead."

"That's Nikki."

"And a serious looking brunette."

"Vikki. Wait, Vikki is still alive? Are you sure it was a serious looking brunette?"

"I was told she was tall with an athletic build and a look that said, 'I will kill you if you look at me again.'"

Wow, capturing these people is going to be harder than I thought, Reynolds admitted to himself then said to his head thug, "Good work. Now, notify our men that we're moving out in three."

"Yes, sir."

Four hours later, Adadi let out, "Something's wrong, the car sounds funny."

"That's because the car has a flat," Akachi informed everyone. He pulled over just within the city limits of Bossangoa and Nikki got out to check.

Thirty seconds later, Akachi heard Nikki exclaim, "Merde." She walked over to the driver's side and said, "Well, we have a flat. But we have a spare and a lift."

"Awesome, then we should be on the road quickly."

"No, we won't."

"Why? Is the spare flat also?"

"No, the spare is brand new by the looks of it."

"Okay, so what's the problem?"

"There's no way to remove the nuts holding the wheel in place. One of Barasa's goons probably used the wrench as a club and never put it back."

"Well that's unfortunate," Vikki added to the conversation.

Nikki walked over to a tree nearby and pulled off a branch, then returned to Akachi's side. "Look, we can't stay here. Reynolds' caravan will be driving by eventually and I don't want to get riddled with bullets on the side of a dirt road."

"Me, either."

"Okay, so just drive that way." Nikki pointed to the left. "And I will remove our tracks with this. In about three hundred meters, you pull over and we'll wait for Reynolds to go by. His caravan should be easy to spot. Afterward, we'll return to the road and hope someone drives by. With any luck, we'll get someone to stop that owns a wrench."

"That's as good a plan as any." Akachi drove off with Nikki close behind. Eight hours later, four Escalades drove by. They were followed by five Marshall Bedford 4x4 military troop transport vehicles in close unison.

Akachi returned to the side of the road and Nikki sat on the bumper hoping that if anyone drove by, they would stop for a pretty redhead. She placed her elbows on her knees and cradled her chin with both hands. "Well, our twelve-hour lead is completely blown," Nikki admitted to the new night sky.

Ten minutes later, Vikki was tired of sitting in the car so she walked out to join Nikki. She caressed Nikki's back and said, "Are you okay, girl?"

"Yes, this waiting sucks."

"Well, on the bright side, it will all be over soon."

"What do you mean?"

"Nikki, we can't go up against a hundred armed men with what you have in your backpack."

"That's probably true. But we've gone up against a small army before."

"Yes, we have, but we've always been better prepared. And even then we've never had the expectation of surviving."

Nikki nodded in agreement then added, "Not without a miracle."

"Well, you know what, sis? Miracles do seem to be happening since we got here."

"That's true. The fact that we're both still alive is proof of that."

"True. Or maybe my wishes are coming true," Vikki shared.

"What do you mean?"

"I have been doing a lot of praying since we got here."

"Seriously? What are you praying about?" Nikki questioned with a scrunched up brow.

"You mostly."

"Me?"

"Yes. I've been mostly praying that your shenanigans don't get you killed."

Nikki sighed and said, "Vee."

"So, promise me you're not going to do something crazy. With Heather gone, you're all I have left. And I don't think I can go on without you."

"Give me a hug, you big baby."

"I'm serious, girl. You have to promise. Promise me you're not going to die here and leave me alone."

"I promise," Nikki shared, a little teary-eyed. Vikki moved in and they hugged.

"I love you."

"And I love you, Vee. Now pray for a car to drive by."

"Okay."

"With a wrench."

"Okay."

"And that they'll stop and help."

"Okay. Is there anything else?"

"Um, nope, that's it," Nikki let out.

"Okay."

Two minutes later, a car drove up and stopped to help.

"Seriously, Vee? Are you kidding me? Two minutes?"

"What? It's six years of Catholic school prayer training."

"Vee, why didn't you tell me earlier?"

"Tell you what?"

"That you had God's ear?"

"You didn't think it was me always pulling off those miraculous escapes, did you?" Vikki asked.

"Yes, I kinda did."

"Well, it wasn't me, it never was. God has been watching over us for a long time."

"Okay, but that time might be coming to an end."

"Yes, unless we give up this lifestyle."

Nikki thought about what that statement meant and added, "Vee, you're probably right. But what would we do?"

"Whatever we want. We have more land, money and—"

Before Vikki could complete her answer, the elderly man who stopped walked over and asked, "Do you ladies need some help?"

"Yes, we do. Thank you so much for stopping, chérie," Nikki replied.

Akachi compensated the man for leaving his wrench. He also made sure to brief him on what to do and say in the event Reynolds' men stopped and talked to him—which of course, they did.

Thirty minutes later, Akachi drove off. An hour and a half later, Akachi and the girls were pulling into a small town just south of Beboura and Nikki announced, "I don't like the way this place looks."

"What do you mean?" Adadi questioned.

"I mean, I'm getting a bad feeling."

Akachi knew better than to ignore the instincts of someone like Nikki so he slowed the car down and turned off the headlights. Just then, their car was hit with a barrage of bullets. Akachi drifted the Escalade into a 180-degree turn and spun out. Seconds later, he drove over police tire spikes. He had no choice but to drive the Escalade into a ditch. Everyone jumped out of the passenger side of the vehicle. Nikki saw dozens of men approaching. She tossed out two grenades, one to the left and one to the right side of the car. After the explosions, she waited ten seconds and tossed the last two into the ditch across the street.

"Wait, three, two, one, let's go. Follow me," Nikki announced. Everyone ran into the shell of an abandoned concrete building five meters away. Nikki tossed Vikki her Glock and opened fire with her machine gun.

A few minutes later, the firing stopped and Akachi asked, "Is everyone okay?"

Adadi didn't answer.

"I'm okay," Nikki responded, "but I'm hit."

"Me, too," Vikki added.

Akachi had also been hit but he kept it to himself. "Is it bad?"

"Yeah," Nikki said in a soft whisper while holding her stomach.

"You, Vikki, is it serious?"

"I'm getting cold, so yes, I think it is."

"Adadi, talk to me. Are you okay?"

"She's down."

"Is she—?"

"No, not yet, I can see her breathing, but it's labored so that's never good."

"Chief, it seems I finally have the advantage!" Reynolds yelled.

"Perhaps!" Akachi yelled back.

"Perhaps? Your optimism never ceases to amaze me."

"Look, Chief, I'm sure you realize that I know you. Just like I'm aware that you know me. I'm positive you knew I would be here so I'm a little curious as to why you showed up. Nevertheless, you're probably thinking you can use one of the miracles you always have up your sleeve. Unfortunately, I'm not going to give you an opportunity to play it and escape. So you have three seconds to show yourself or I'll open fire again."

"Hoshea, we don't have much time, my Lord. If it's your will we survive this, please show me a way. We need your help. I can surrender myself, but please save the girls."

"One, two—"

"I will surrender but I want your word that you will let the girls leave unharmed."

"That's not happening, Chief. If I do that, no matter how careful I am, or how many men I have watching my back, one night I'll go to bed and wind up having my throat cut while I sleep. So, your surrender must be unconditional."

A few seconds went by and Reynolds yelled out, "So, what's it going to be? Hello?" Finally, when Reynolds had waited long enough, he shot out, "Very well, Chief, have it your way. Men, open fire."

Ballistic projectiles pierced the concrete structure from 360 degrees. Everyone inside the shell was hit again. Suddenly, a bright light appeared in the space which caught every observers' attention. Seconds later, Reynolds ordered a cease fire and focused on movement from within.

When he saw no one moving, he thought, *what are you doing in there, Chief?* Reynolds cautiously walked around the carnage and debris outside with singular focus. Recover enemies of the crown.

When he entered the concrete building he exclaimed, "Are you kidding me? How are you guys still alive?"

CHAPTER 19

The Reunion

WHEN MAGGIE WAS OLD ENOUGH TO UNDERSTAND, SHE WAS told her mother was taken captive by several members of a local crime family. Hulina openly befriended too many men in the same community where she lived. Her racy behavior around alpha males and her lack of attachment to one specific person generated an assortment of negative circumstances. Many thought her behavior was intentionally orchestrated to generate conflict among men. After her disappearance, her past indiscretions quickly became a topic of public conversation. These discussions caused doubts within the community as to whether Maggie's mother had actually been taken or she left voluntarily. Nevertheless, a month after she disappeared, a woman was found hanging from a neighborhood street lamp which matched Maggie's mother's description. Those who knew her were torn as to whether this person was, in fact, Hulina.

An autopsy revealed medical evidence showing this woman had been brutally murdered. Although the victim's face was unrecognizable, due to blunt force trauma, she matched Hulina's age and physical characteristics. Unfortunately there was no way to compare Hulina's DNA results with the person found. However, reconstructive dental records provided clear and convincing evidence of her identity. In addition, the young woman had on the same clothes several eye witnesses claimed Hulina was wearing the day she disappeared. Finally, the young woman was wearing a wedding ring which Maggie's father identified as the one he purchased for his wife.

Local law enforcement quickly identified the alleged killers. However, powerful sources were able to influence investigators with hearsay and gossip to ignore important evidence and crucial testimony from witnesses. The men believed to have committed this heinous crime were never brought to trial. From that moment on, Maggie's dad and three uncles made it their business to claim justice for those ignored by a corrupt system. Although often apprehensive, she was glad to help silence the voices of the innocent crying out from beyond the grave for justice. For as long as she could remember, the family log cabin was used as a safe haven for injured vigilantes.

Now, more than ever, her sanctuary was needed. Somehow it had gone from helping a nefarious element to the righteous. Maggie looked around and thought, *So many people live out their lives being judged unfairly for what they do. Others never realize their true purpose in life. Today, I feel blessed to have been part of both of those groups. It took a world crisis for me to realize that good people can do bad things and not be bad, but perhaps willing to accept a burden which few can carry.*

Christians are often ridiculed by non-believers when they make mistakes, or sin as it were. Those skeptics conveniently ignore the fact that to be a Christian doesn't mean you are sinless, but that you consciously try to sin less. Anyhow, I never thought I would feel such pride to just sit in a room with labeled outlaws seeking protection from a self-proclaimed virtuous element. If it is my fate, I will die to defend them, so that their mercy and love continues on amongst a world clearly filled with darkness and despair, Maggie confessed to herself.

Most of the people there had spent two days recovering from serious injuries. Winnie was sitting on the floor resting an arm on Avery's knee. Yvette was sitting on a sofa in front of them. Sophia was nuzzled in between Yvette's legs, resting her head in the crook of her neck.

Sophia was still deeply remorseful for her inability to stop

Yvette's torture sessions. There was nothing she could say or do that would rescind her failure to act. At this point, Sophia just felt compelled to stay close and tend to her needs. She would show Yvette love and tenderness and keep her from harm, for the rest of her life if necessary. She had never known anyone as kindhearted and forgiving as Yvette. *The last four days will haunt me for the rest of my life, but no one will ever harm Evie again while I am alive to prevent it,* she confessed. She caressed one of the arms Yvette had wrapped around her waist.

Thoughts of Yvette's torture sessions crept back into Sophia's mind, making her jerk. Yvette gently caressed her hair and said, "Are you okay, sweetie?"

"Yes, I'm fine. Can I get you anything?"

"No, I'm okay, but thank you," Yvette replied tenderly. It was an uncommon and an uncharacteristic practice for Yvette to show outward physical intimacy. Well, to anyone except maybe Winnie and Mia. However, after a brutal four days in captivity, the sensitivity and warmth she was being exposed to by Sophia and others was a welcomed respite.

Sophia nuzzled up against Yvette again and tried desperately not to cry from the nightmares that haunted her waking world. *It's so bizarre, but Yvette gives me the impression that she has little memory of what happened to her,* Sophia admitted in silence. Mick was sitting next to Yvette with Maggie propped up on the sofa's armrest beside him. Stefan and Dai were standing on either side of Avery.

"Does anyone want more coffee?" Maggie asked.

"Not me," Yvette shared, "it's getting late and the caffeine will keep me up."

Without prior warning, a bright light peered into the room through a crack in space. They all reached up instinctively to cover their eyes. As the brilliance dissipated, Mia appeared before them.

"Mia," Yvette let out.

When she went to get up, Mia commanded, "Everyone, please stay where you are. I can't stay long." Sophia leaned forward and listened intently with everyone else.

"Soon, you all will be paid multiple visits by Saints. Some of you will recognize one or more of them. However, I need you to realize that their memory engrams have been adjusted to help them acclimate to an eternal life. I can attest to the sorrow felt for loved ones left behind. They, however, have been spared that. Until I return and explain further, you are not to address them in a familiar tone. Regardless of the temptation, you must resist. This is for their peace of mind and yours."

"Mia!" Yvette cried out again, holding her hands against her chest in a Hail Mary pose.

Mia smiled then waved her hand and was gone.

And I love you, too, Yvette heard Mia's voice say in her mind. With quivering lips, Yvette mouthed *Mia*.

"Wow, that was intense," Maggie let out. "I'm sure you guys have this sort of thing happening to you all the time but my heart is racing. I don't think I will ever get used to that."

"Remarkable," Stefan exclaimed. "Until two days ago, I considered those who believed in the supernatural to be nitwits. I now find it ironic that I'm proud to be part of a group I once ostracized for being daft. Now, it's obvious that most of us know Mia. However, I find it odd, if that's in any way a qualifier for the appearance of these celestial beings, that no one knows Heather. She seems so memorable to me."

"Well, I'm certain that at the end, all our questions will be answered. But for now, I take comfort in knowing that she, and those like her, are watching over us," Winnie shared.

"Here, here," Avery voiced.

Just like Mia a minute before, a portal opened and a Guardian with three Saints stepped out.

Hikiko place Akachi on a stretcher and was gone. Heather placed Adadi on another bed next to him and approached Mick. Samantha and Charlotte placed Nikki and Vikki on stretchers then turned to walk away. As soon as Sophia saw them, she fell to her knees and covered her mouth. Charlotte looked over and saw Sophia on the ground and had to stop. For some reason, this woman looked familiar. She took hold of Samantha's hand and slowly approached her.

"Do you know me?" Charlotte asked. Sophia looked over at Yvette for guidance. Yvette shook her head slowly from side to side in a 'no' gesture. Sophia returned her gaze back to Charlotte and slowly shook her head. Charlotte smiled and said, "It's okay, you looked familiar is all. And for some reason, I felt like you knew me.

I'm sorry, now please, be at peace. Come, Sam," Charlotte whispered.

"But I know her face," Sam quietly confessed.

"Me, too," Charlotte exclaimed then waved her hand and they were gone. Sophia covered her face and cried.

"Mick, your gifts are required again. You must save them all. Trust in those around you, but don't discuss what they may have done. It will not help you."

Mick shouted, "Everyone, scrub up, we have lives to save!" They took turns cleaning up. Heather briefed him on each person's injuries. Maggie took images of every gunshot and started prepping Adadi for surgery, since she had the most injuries. Dai started cleaning up Adadi, and Avery prepped Nikki.

Yvette approached Sophia and caressed her hair. She bent down, hugged her and said, "You will see your babies again. For now, take comfort in the knowledge that they are safe, happy and are doing God's work. Now, we need you. Can you help?"

Sophia took a few seconds to pull herself together then answered, "Yes."

"Good, then scrub up and start prepping her." Yvette pointed to Vikki.

When Maggie was done taking x-rays of everyone's injuries, she handed out copies to the doctors. She set up a Propofol slow drip on all their patients and told everyone that Mick would tell them when to start the IVs. She then started cleaning up Akachi. Several minutes later, Mick joined Sophia since Akachi was stable but in bad shape. Yvette worked on Adadi along with Dai. Stefan and Maggie worked on Vikki and Winnie worked on Nikki with Avery assisting her.

"This girl was shot seven times. She should be dead," Yvette professed.

"Perhaps, but her will is strong," Dai added.

Yvette shook her head at the brutality dispensed to such gentle souls then noticed an object in her hand and asked, "What does she have in her hand?"

"I'm not sure. It looks like two small vials. I tried to take them, but even in her unconscious state, she aggressively resisted, so I decided to just leave them there."

"That's fine. We need to focus on more urgent issues."

"So, is everyone ready?" Mick asked. Everyone answered 'yes' in harmony.

"Good, then increase the Propofol drip and count to ten so we can begin."

Everyone counted together. When Maggie heard everyone say ten, she made the sign of the cross and said aloud, "Baby Jesus, watch over us."

For almost an hour, the only voice each team heard was that of their partner. Then Stefan posed a question that broke through the team's cocoon.

"So does anyone know these people?"

"You're working on Vikki," Avery disclosed.

"Do you know her?"

"No, but I know of her. And Winnie and I are working on Nikki, who is supposed to be the nice one of the two."

"Avery, what is that supposed to mean?" Maggie queried.

"Maggie, you'll understand later once you get to know them. Now, Mick and Sophia are tending to Akachi. He's a good man. He was a special agent working for some intelligence group in the US."

"Hey, just like you, Avery," Winnie added to the conversation. "Except Avery was working for Queen and Country. Right?"

Avery grunted then whispered, "I wish you wouldn't have said that."

"Why? Trust me, Avery, no one here cares what you did before now." He looked around at everyone who was focused on saving someone who was either paid to kill or had a license to do so. Then he thought, *Winnie is right, they don't care who I was before now. Just like no one cares who Nikki, Vikki or Akachi were.*

"Well, it's not up to me to divulge information about these individuals which may have you prejudge them before you get to know them. The truth is that I was just like them before I met Winnie. She's changed me."

"Avery," Winnie let out.

"Winnie, you're special. I'm sure you know that. I'm honored to have met you. I hope that someday, I live up to whatever expectations you set for me."

"Avery, you need to stop talking or you're going to make

me cry," Winnie confessed with trembling lips. "And I need to see what I'm doing to help this girl."

"Okay, you two, reel it in."

"Sorry."

"Yes, my apologies."

"It's okay, now does anyone know who I'm working on?" Yvette questioned.

"I don't," Avery acknowledged.

"Neither do I," Stefan admitted.

Then Yvette picked up her head and looked around and her gaze was met with looks of *no* from everyone in the room. "Okay, just another mystery in a room full of aliases and people wearing nameless faces," she quietly confessed.

Two hours later, everyone was circling Adadi's bed.

"How she's not dead is a total mystery," Stefan exclaimed.

"It is," Yvette answered then added, "Mick, take over here and close this up. I have to work on the gunshots to her stomach." Yvette had successfully removed two bullets from her back and sutured closed the exit wounds. She had also cleaned and stitched closed a third bullet hole near her spine before placing Adadi on her back again.

"Well, Evie, between the four of them, they were shot like twenty times. Who are these people?"

"Twenty-two," Winnie shared.

"What?"

"They were shot twenty-two times, not twenty," Winnie expressed as a correction.

"You see, Evie, it's even worse, I stand corrected. Thank you, Winnie, they were shot twenty-two times. And this poor woman was shot seven times. Look. Five of those shells struck her torso. And this one right here," Stefan pointed to her chest, "should have killed her. It hit her heart."

"Well, lucky for her it was only a visitor," Yvette shared.

"What? What does that mean?"

"Stefan, what Evie means is that the bullet only grazed her heart. So it came in and went straight out, leaving nothing to extract."

Then Yvette looked closer and added, "Well, now that I take a closer look, the projectile missed her spine on the way out. And given the bullet's angle of entry, there was no way it could have missed it. So perhaps Stefan's initial assessment was correct. But how?" Yvette whispered then trailed off and thought, *Hoshea must be watching over this woman because there's no way she could have survived these injuries.*

"Perhaps she's being watched over like the rest of us," Winnie shared as she placed a hand on Adadi's leg and prayed over her. "Look, everyone, give Evie and Mick some room." Sophia wiped off Yvette's brow again and Maggie did the same with Mick. "You two stay and assist. However, the rest of you need to go sit down," Winnie ordered.

"How are her vitals, Maggie?"

"Good. Her heart rate is about thirty to thirty-five. Her respiration is a ten and her blood pressure is sixty over thirty-five."

"What? You can't be serious. Those vitals are terrible."

"Well, considering she was shot in the heart and in both lungs, and in the stomach—not once but twice—she's doing great."

Mick looked at Yvette, who said, "I know, I know, I'm hurrying. Wipe." Sophia wiped Yvette's brow again then leaned in close from behind and placed her face on Yvette's back while hugging her and said, "Evie, you're doing an awesome job."

Yvette padded Sophia on one of the arms she had wrapped around her waist and said, "Thank you, sweetie." Sophia also stroked Winnie's back who was standing nearby praying over them all.

An hour later, Yvette wiped her brow on her forearm and said, "We're done." Maggie increased the oxygen content to Adadi and Sophia hugged Yvette and whispered in her ear, "I'm so proud of you. I know that had to be exhausting."

"Actually, it was," Yvette confirmed. She took a deep breath then saw Adadi slowly open up the hand she had closed like a vise during her whole operation. She moved Sophia out of the way and peered down at Adadi's hand and saw two small bottles. She looked closer then reached out and picked them up. *These are the vials of Hoshea's blood I sent to Winnie. These are my initials in my own hand.* She looked at Adadi's face then at her vital signs. Her vitals started getting worse, so she placed the ampoules under the bandages around her chest. Yvette looked over at the monitor again and saw her vitals improving.

Maggie walked over and leaned on Yvette and said, "Wow, I saw that. Baby Jesus fancies her."

Yvette whispered, "I don't want to seem judgmental or like I'm prying but why do you refer to God as baby Jesus? It's odd. No, I'm sorry, strike that. That's not what I meant to say. I'm tired. What I wanted to say is that the expression is unusual for an adult to use."

"It's okay. Well, you're the first person to ever ask me."

"It's okay if you don't want to tell me."

"It's not a problem. I can tell you if you really wanna know. It's not like I think it's a secret. So, honestly, it's just what I'm used to."

"What do you mean?" Yvette asked with genuine curiosity.

"Well, when we were growing up in the Dominican Republic, a local hotel always displayed a nativity scene for Christmas. My dad used to take me every year to see it. We were very poor so I never got any Christmas gifts. But I didn't care. My parents loved me and they were always kind. My dad told me that baby Jesus was born poor like me and he turned out to be a king.

"One day, if I was good like baby Jesus, I could go live with him in his kingdom. When I was seven, the hotel manager dropped the box of figurines and broke them, I guess. Because afterwards, he had his staff just throw them all out. Can you believe that? Anyway, I looked through the garbage when no one was looking and saved one. The only figure I found undamaged was the one of baby Jesus. So I brought him home.

"My mother was murdered that year. I found myself praying to baby Jesus a lot after that. Many times a day for years actually. Anyway, back then, I always started my prayers by saying, 'Baby Jesus.' So I guess old habits die hard." Maggie noticed that her presence was required somewhere else so she added at the end, "Oh, I'm sorry, Evie, please excuse me." She walked away to tend to someone else.

Yvette was stunned at Maggie's story and while holding a hand over her heart uttered, "Ay, Dios mio." She took about a minute to center herself before walking over and hugging Maggie from behind and saying, "I'm so sorry about your mother. But I'm glad you told me that story."

Maggie stroked the arm Yvette had wrapped around her waist and said, "Thank you, and I'm glad you asked me."

"You're welcome, sweetie." Yvette let go of Margarita's waist then gently stroked her hair from behind before announcing, "Everyone, it's late and I'm tired. I'm going to shower then go to bed. Goodnight."

Everyone said goodnight and most did the same. The girls retired to the bedrooms sharing the Jack and Jill bath then took turns cleaning up.

Stefan and Mick shared the loft and Avery and Dai slept on the sofas after cleaning up.

Just after 10 a.m., Avery and Dai were the first to wake up followed by Stefan and Mick. Everyone brushed their teeth while Mick made coffee. A half hour later, the girls started getting up with Maggie being the first.

It was just after 11 a.m. and everyone had been up for a little while so Maggie and Sophia started cooking breakfast. Suddenly, Yvette noticed Akachi roll out of bed and barely land on his feet.

"Oh my goodness," Yvette let out as she ran to his side. "What are you doing? You have to stay in bed. How are you even able to stand? Ten hours ago, we took five bullets out of you."

"Evie, is that you?"

"Yes. Now get back into bed. Please."

"Is Adadi here?"

"Is she the African woman?"

"Yes."

"Then yes, so are Vikki and Nikki."

"Evie, are they okay?"

"Yes. Apparently, they're all as strong as you. Especially Adadi."

Avery and Winnie were now at his side when he looked up. "Avery?"

"Yes, mate. It's me."

"What are you doing here?"

"I'm a runaway like you."

"Winnie, how are you?"

"Better than you, love. But don't worry, we're gonna have you tip-top in no time."

"Avery, can you excuse us? I need to talk to Yvette and Winnie in private."

"Sure, mate." Avery walked off.

"Yvette, where are my pants?"

"I'm not sure, why?"

"Hoshea gave me his pill and it's in my small side pocket."

"Whoa, wait! Maggie, what did you do with Akachi's pants?

"I think they're in the laundry room in a plastic bag waiting to be washed," Maggie replied.

"Akachi, what do your pants look like again?"

"They're blue jeans." Yvette signaled Winnie to go look for the pill.

"I'm on it."

Winnie quickly returned.

"My goodness, that was fast."

"Well, this is important, Evie. Here," she handed the pill to Akachi.

"Okay, now listen carefully. You both know this pill is divine and possesses special properties."

"Yes," Winnie and Yvette replied in unison.

"What you don't know is how special. This pill somehow knows what the body requires. So if your mind is in a distressful state, it will bring you comfort. If you're hungry, it will provide the nutrients required. But what is most amazing is that if you're hurt, physically injured, it will help heal you. And it will repair future injuries."

Akachi stopped and looked at Yvette and Winnie who looked at each other and said, "Go on," in harmony.

"Yes, so, how many people are here?"

Yvette looked around and answered, "Twelve."

"Do you trust them?"

"Sure, I guess so. I mean, I haven't known them long but they seem to be righteous outlaws like us."

"Fair enough. Okay, so we need something that can clearly hold twelve ounces of water."

"Maggie, do you have a measuring cup?" Yvette yelled out.

"Of course. Do you need it?"

"Yes."

"Look, Evie, instead of me explaining this to you and then again to everyone else, you do it. I'm too tired right now to answer a bunch of questions. Since you know them and they seem to trust you, it will be easier. Adadi, Nikki and Vikki especially need this.

So make sure they get it, even if it's intravenously. Okay?"

"Understood."

"Good, I need to lie down."

"Okay, and we'll clean your pants, so you're not walking around flashing everyone your knickers."

"Thank you, Winnie."

Akachi laid back down and Yvette asked everyone to gather around. Maggie brought over the measuring cup.

"Maggie, go and bring this back with twelve ounces of water. And do you have a shot glass?"

"Yes."

"Do you have twelve of them?"

"No, but I think I have six of em."

"Good, then bring the six."

"Evie, what's going on?"

"I'll explain everything when you come back."

"What's going on, Evie?" Stefan questioned.

"Answers are coming. Just be patient."

Yvette took the pill out of the plastic pouch and said, "Avery, time me."

"Sure."

"You ready?"

"Yes."

"Tell me when we hit ten seconds."

"Twenty," Akachi said as a correction.

Yvette turned around and asked, "Are you sure?" Akachi just peered at Yvette with one eye and the corner of his mouth crinkled up. "Okay, never mind, it's obvious you're sure. Sorry."

"Avery, tell me when we hit twenty seconds."

"Sure."

"What's going on?"

"Patience, Stefan, patience, answers are coming." Yvette dropped the pill in the measuring cup and said, "Avery go."

Avery looked at his watch and counted to himself but finished aloud by saying, "Eighteen, nineteen, twenty."

Yvette reached in and pulled the pill out of the water and placed it back in the plastic pouch, handing it to Winnie.

Yvette and Winnie spent ten minutes explaining their experience with the pill. Who had given it to them and its seemingly magical properties. Stefan riddled Yvette and Winnie with questions. In the interim, Winnie administered an ounce intravenously to each of their unconscious patients. She sat Akachi up and had him drink his portion. Sophia and Maggie didn't ask any questions. When Yvette handed the shot glass to them, they just drank it.

Winnie handed Avery and Dai their portions and Avery whispered, "Is this safe, love?"

Winnie just smiled then pointed at the glass with her chin and said, "Go on."

"That's good enough for me." Avery drank it down and Dai followed.

Mick looked at Maggie for confirmation before drinking and she said, "Go on, you big baby."

Yvette looked at Winnie and said, "Bottoms up."

"Cheers."

Everyone looked at Stefan and Avery said, "Go on, mate, don't bottle it."

"I'm sorry, but the scientist in me is still poking out."

"Does he remind you of anyone, Evie?"

"No."

"What? You were totally like him for days. Even with clear and convincing evidence to the contrary, you still questioned Hoshea on everything."

"What? No I wasn't. And no I didn't."

"Oh please, you asked like a million questions."

"Wow, exaggerate much?"

"Um, no."

Yvette gave Winnie a stern look of disbelief.

"Evie, you were constantly questioning Hoshea."

"Who?" Maggie questioned.

"Baby Jesus."

Maggie made the sign of the cross and added, "You girls are nuts."

Yvette and Winnie whipped their heads around and mouthed, "What?"

"Look, I realize I'm not perfect like you two. But if I was in the presence of God, I would not be questioning him."

"Well, you say that," Winnie shared.

"He does say a lot of unbelievable stuff," Yvette added.

"Look, he might look like us, but he is nothing like us. We can't go a day without drinking water. He doesn't drink, he doesn't eat, he doesn't sleep." Yvette looked at Winnie and asked, "Does he even breathe?" Winnie shrugged. Yvette turned to the group and continued, "You see, how he is even alive? He doesn't breathe." Then Yvette looked at Winnie again and asked, "Are we sure he doesn't breathe?" Winnie shrugged again. "Well, regardless, he has the ability to control time and space with the effort we use to…to…to blink."

Winnie interrupted Yvette to say, "Evie, you're rambling. The truth is that…wait, Evie, where were you going with this?"

Yvette continued, "Look, the truth is that—wait. Winnie, how did you put it? You remember?"

"No, what are we talking about?"

"Sure you do, you remember when you were explaining the sophistication of his blood," Yvette shared.

"Yes," Stefan jumped in. "Now that I understand.

"Oh yes, I remember."

"Good, so tell them what you told me."

"Well, Hoshea's blood showed—"

"No, proves," Stefan interrupted with a correction.

"Yes, you're right, Stefan, Hoshea's blood proves that he is as far above us as we are above the first microbes that started this world."

"Oh and by the way, we're not on Earth."

"What?" Everyone jumped to their feet.

"Winnie! Why did you tell them that?"

"I thought they should know."

"Why?" Yvette looked at all the faces in the room then returned her gaze back to Winnie and said, "Now they all think we're nuts. We've lost our credibility."

Yvette went to walk away and Sophia said, "I believe you."

Yvette crinkled her brow then turned around and asked, "Why?"

"Faith. But aside from that, you have been in the presence of God. Like physically in his presence. And you have hugged him, right?

Yvette smiled and said, "Yes."

Winnie walked over and took her hand and said, "Evie, I'm sorry. You're right, perhaps it was too much of a reveal."

"It's okay if people think of me as a space cadet, as long as I have your support."

"Well," Stefan joined the conversation. "I don't know whether you two are cadets but it's obvious I am still having doubts. I'm wrestling with, with…" Stefan trailed off.

"With what, Stefan? Go on," Winnie said encouragingly.

"With believing, I guess. Look, I'm not sure why I have doubts. I was approached by what I thought was a girl, six thousand meters in the air, and told I should jump out of an aircraft and have faith in a God I didn't believe existed. I'm a scientist. Like you two, I have always been a scientist. Yet I did it. Then I had a conversation with this young person, this spirit, while I was falling to my death, and I had no fear. I've had apparitions appear and disappear before me multiple times since. And then materialize other flesh and blood humans out of thin air. I realize that the observance of an unexplainable phenomenon in the absence of a practical or quantifiable explanation does not suggest or infer a divine influence."

"Hey, Winnie, that is exactly what you said a few weeks ago, remember?"

"Yes. Go on, Stefan."

"Well, I was just thinking and asking myself, how many events am I required to witness before shedding my doubts or preconceptions?"

Winnie laughed then said, "That's what I thought also."

"So, have you reached that number?" Yvette questioned.

Stefan picked up the shot glass and said, "Cheers."

Vikki and Nikki sat up and Nikki said, "Where am I and why am I topless?"

Vikki looked down at herself then covered up, "Hey, where's my shirt and my undies? And who are you people? Wait, Avery, is that you?"

"Yes, my lady."

Vikki looked around then added, "Dr. Ruben, I guess you never made that call?"

"No. I didn't."

"What call?"

"It's a long story, Evie."

"I've got time."

"That's enough, you two," Winnie exclaimed.

"Nikki, I guess we're now part of this band of misfits."

"It looks that way."

"I feel terrible," Adadi joined in with a roar.

"That's understandable, love. You were shot in the heart, and once in each lung, and twice in the stomach, and—" Yvette interrupted her synopsis.

"That's enough, Winnie, she gets the picture."

"Am I going to die?"

"No, sweetie."

"Why not? It feels like I am. I feel dreadful."

"You just need to rest."

"Again, where are my undies?"

Maggie giggled then repeated, "Undies."

"Hey, that's her mind going to a safe place, don't belittle it. She's been through a lot."

"Oh, sorry." Maggie cleared her throat then said, "They're in the laundry room waiting to be washed."

"Go get them!"

"Wow, really? Avery, I see what you mean about Nikki being the nice one."

"Okay, everyone, relax." Yvette took charge and said, "Maggie, do you have a spare bra she could use?"

"No. All you girls are using my extra stuff. She's gonna have to let the girls just jiggle for a bit."

"You're a pig."

"Hey, listen here you, you, you—"

Maggie was interrupted by Yvette, "Okay, you two, relax.

"What, she's rude."

"And you're a pig."

"Evie, get out of my way, I can take her."

"Stop, there's enough craziness going on outside these walls. We don't need you two to bring it inside. So calm down." Yvette looked at Vikki and added, "That goes for you, too, young lady. You two just met. We don't need a pair of Judgey McJudgersons in our midst. We have enough of that knocking at our door. Plus, your body has been through enough, give yourself a chance to get better."

Yvette leaned in close to Maggie and said, "Look at her, she's an Amazon. Even in her weakened condition she can probably wrap her legs around you and pop your head clean off with a squeeze."

Maggie peered past Yvette and said, "I can take her, Evie."

"Stop, go clean some clothes. Most of the clothes we're wearing look grungy, it's gross." Maggie scrunched up her face and snarled at Vikki then stuck out her tongue. Vikki pulled her shoulders back and raised both eyebrows. Yvette turned Maggie around and patted her on the behind to encourage her to walk away, then she addressed the group.

"Look, I understand we all have a thousand questions. From where are we, to what's our role in all this. Why have we been brought together, to what's our next move. I don't have all the answers. But what answers I do have, I will freely share. So be at peace, answers are coming. I suggest we all rest, eat and take it one step at a time." Everyone seemed to acknowledge Yvette's suggestions with a silent look and then moved into smaller groups.

"Winnie, see if you can find some more clothes for Vikki and her sister. If you have to, borrow some clothes from the boys."

Winnie walked off and Nikki asked, "Why do you think we're sisters?"

"Because you have been ready to pounce since Maggie and Vikki started arguing."

Yvette walked over to Vikki. She stopped at arm's length, tilted her head and said, "You're so angry, sweetie. You're so much prettier when you're not." Yvette went to move a strand of hair off her face and Vikki pulled back. "I won't hurt you."

"I know."

Yvette smiled and reached in again and moved the hair away from her face. "You see, you're much prettier when you're not angry. I'm sorry you've had it so hard. And I'm sorry for Maggie. But she worked desperately to save you. You were shot four times. She's not a doctor but Stefan is and Maggie removed three of the four bullets before Stefan removed one. So give her a chance. She's actually very sweet when you get to know her. Just like I'm sure you are. Anyway, I'm glad you're here."

"Why?"

"Because it seems like we're on the same side. Plus, you needed a safe place to rest, and we have room."

"What side are you on?" Nikki questioned.

"I fight for the same people you fight for."

"Which is who exactly?" Vikki was quick to retort.

"The innocent."

"You always seem to know what to say," Vikki added.

"Do I?"

"Yes. Yes, you do."

"Is that bad?"

"I don't know yet."

Yvette smiled, then turned around and walked away toward the kitchen.

Nikki looked over at Vikki and whispered, "I like her."

"I know."

"And Maggie?" Nikki queried.

"I like her."

"Really? That's odd. You never like anybody when you first meet them."

"I know."

"Well, you were mean to her."

"I know. I've had a rough four days. I'll make up with her."

"Good, because she has the heart of a lioness."

"I know. And we don't want to test it."

"No, we don't. We're not here to make good people do bad things."

"Agreed." Nikki laid back down, grunted and said, "I feel like merde."

"Me, too."

About an hour later, Stefan, Avery and Winnie were sitting together and Yvette walked by. Stefan stopped her and asked, "What makes you think we're not on Earth? And why hasn't any of us noticed?"

Yvette sat down and grabbed Maggie as she walked by and sat her down next to her, then said, "The proof is all around us. You just have to look. Maggie, how long have you owned this place?"

"I'm not sure, maybe fifteen or sixteen years. Why?"

"How does it look to you?"

Maggie looked around then said, "Like it always has."

"That's why, Stefan. Because the idea of something which seems impossible is not given any thought or dismissed outright."

"What?"

"You're a scientist. For now, be that and weigh the evidence."

"Maggie, how long have you had the furniture in this place?"

"I don't know, for as long as I can remember?"

"Look around. Why does it all appear brand new? Your kitchen appliances, your washer and dryer, the fixtures in your bathrooms, even the shower curtains all appear unused."

Maggie started walking around touching different objects and mumbling to herself. Several minutes later she walked back and said, "Evie, you're right. Everything is new. How is that possible?"

"Maggie, the buoy you and Mick were using several days ago for target practice."

"What about it?"

"You've used it before?"

"Of course, dozens of times. Why?"

"Why didn't it have any holes in it?"

"What?"

"Didn't you notice that it was brand new?"

"Now that you mention it, I did. But how would you know that? You weren't here yet."

"I know because I must know."

"What?" the group replied in unison.

"Look, this is not Earth. This planet is not even in the same galaxy. Therefore, none of the celestial bodies are present at night. Neither are the planets we can normally see with the naked eye. Even the moon is different. It's about twenty percent bigger. Tonight, step out and look into the night sky and see if you can find Orion's Belt or the Big Dipper or the North Star. The point is the proof is all around us.

"But no one notices, and if they do, they don't care. Why? Because what can you do to change it? And who cares when we're fighting to stay alive from one day to the next? Everyday, death is at our door." Yvette took hold of Maggie's hand and finished by saying, "When everyday is a struggle to keep those we love alive, who cares?" Yvette got up and walked away.

"Well, any questions?" Winnie added. Everyone just gave her a blank stare. "Brilliant." Maggie and Winnie got up and walked off in different directions.

An hour later, Maggie dropped off some clean clothes for Vikki, placing them on the side of the stretcher. Vikki reached out and grabbed her arm by the wrist. Maggie stopped and whipped her head around and looked at her.

Vikki turned her head slowly toward Maggie and said, "I was rude."

"Yes, you were."

"You're not so bad."

"Gee, thanks."

Nikki slowly sat up and Vikki followed.

"That's her way of saying she's sorry."

"Well, it's not very good, is it? Most people say I'm sorry or please forgive me."

"Vikki, do a better job." Nikki pointed at Maggie with her chin afterward for encouragement.

"I'm sorry I was rude."

"To," Nikki added, suggesting she continue with her apology to make it better.

"To you. I've had a rough four days."

"No excuses," Nikki added as a correction.

"I'm sorry I was rude to you. There is no excuse." Vikki then looked over to Nikki with the tilt of her head and held both hands up. She wanted Nikki's acknowledgment that her admission of guilt was sufficient.

Nikki accepted the adequacy of her sister's apology with a nod.

"Fine. I forgive you." Maggie touched the clothes on the bed and said, "You can put these on when you feel better." Vikki jumped off the stretcher and lost her footing and Maggie caught her. She ignored the fact that Vikki had just had four bullets removed twelve hours ago. *It's a miracle this girl was able to sit up, let alone stand. Man, she's tough.*

"Can you help me to the bathroom? I wanna clean up before I change."

"Sure." Maggie wrapped the bed sheet around her and they

started walking away. She got a close up look at Vikki's face and added, "You can use my lip gloss if you want."

Vikki looked over at her with a raised eyebrow.

"What? I don't have cooties, if that's what you're thinking."

"No, I'm sure you don't. And it's not what I was thinking. It's just that using another girl's lipstick is so…personal.

"Well, I don't mind, if you don't."

"Okay then, I'd love to use your lip gloss. Thank you." Nikki overheard Vikki's statement and raised both eyebrows out of shock. She had been trying to get her to use lipstick forever, without success.

"You're welcome." Maggie cleared her throat and added, "You're pretty."

"You, too."

"Thanks. Boy's must really go for you," Maggie said tenderly.

"Not really. I intimidate them."

"Well, they just have to get past the fact that you look all murdery. Then you're golden."

"I have a tendency to snap their necks if they get too close."

"Well you shouldn't do that. They'll never get to like you if you walk around cracking necks."

"Yeah, you're probably right, but I don't like boys much. They're mean."

"Well, I've always found them to be quite accommodating — unless you have sex with them, then forget it."

"And then?" Vikki asked with a blank stare.

"And then, you know, they turn into cavemen."

Vikki smiled and laughed silently.

"So, it must be cool being a secret agent."

"What makes you think I'm a secret agent?"

"Well, the room is filled with doctors and those that are not, so I just took a guess."

"I'm not really a secret agent; I'm more of an assassin."

"Okay, well, that sounds cool, and dangerous and scary." Maggie took a deep breath and whispered, "But mostly dangerous and scary."

Maggie was the only normal person of similar age Vikki had spoken to in years. It was nice. It made her feel ordinary and safe.

"Thanks."

"For what, helping you to the bathroom?"

"Yes, but mostly for being you."

"You're welcome. Hey, guess what?"

"What?"

"I punched a girl once."

"Really?" Vikki didn't want to admit it but she was growing very fond of Maggie. *This girl is so congenial it's hard not to like her. This could turn out to be trouble for me,* Vikki thought.

"Yeah, but I hurt my hand. When I told my dad and uncles, they all laughed at me. Apparently, I didn't know how to make a fist correctly."

"I can show you if you like."

"Sure, that would be cool. And I see you don't have any makeup on. Is that normal for you?"

"Yes."

"Well, I can show you how to do that."

"Why?

"Because it's what girls do."

"Okay."

"And what's up with your fingernails?"

"I bite um."

"Well, you have to stop that."

"Why?"

"Because it doesn't look good, baby. And you're a girl, not a boy."

"So?"

"So, boys can be gross. Not girls."

Maggie had a coquettish nature which made her aware of others' physical characteristics at all times. And even though she considered Vikki competition, she realized that Vikki could use a friend. So she was reacting in the only way she knew how to bond with other women. So after looking Vikki over she said, "I can find you a razor, if you like."

"For what?"

Maggie took a few more seconds to look Vikki up and down again than added, "Oh my God, tell me you shave!"

"Why?"

"Why? Because that's what girls do." Maggie walked over to

her and asked, "And what's with all these scars?" Then she started touching them.

"Don't do that."

"Why, do they hurt?"

"No, but I'm ticklish."

"So how did you get all these scars."

"Bullets mostly."

"What? Are you serious? There're so many. How many times have you been shot?"

"I think like forty-six times?"

"Stop! Are you kidding me?"

"No. And I've been stabbed eight times."

"How are you still alive?"

"I'm lucky I guess."

"No, nobody's that lucky. You're special. And seriously, that has to be some kind of world record."

"Is that good?" Vikki questioned.

"I'm not sure."

Maggie and Vikki continued their bonding behind closed doors.

CHAPTER 20

Reynolds Seeks Vengeance

AFTER SIX DAYS OF SEARCHING THE ATLANTIC OCEAN, THE U.S. Coast Guard called off the search for Avery, Winnie and Dai.

"You have to keep looking," Cooper ordered the captain of the two hundred and ten foot Coast Guard cutter—Defiant.

"Mr. Cooper, we've combed the north coast of Cuba. We also searched as far north as Nassau. And as far east as the Turks and Caicos Islands. After six days of searching, we have found nothing. The helicopter wreckage was located a mere three kilometers north of Guantanamo Bay. All the debris was contained within a square kilometer of the initial crash scene when we arrived on site.

"Furthermore, we have had two Coast Guard cutters, a C130 and multiple helicopters engaged in the search for six days.

"So."

"So, Mr. Cooper, if these escapees were in fact injured as you have expressed repeatedly, and if they were capable, they would have swum to shore. Otherwise, in my opinion, they were lost at sea.

"Captain, that's all supposition."

"Perhaps, but given our quick response, the initial location of the wreckage and their proximity to the coast, again, if they were able, their survival instincts would have driven them to shore. If not, it's regrettable but they would have perished at sea.

"What if someone else picked them up?"

"You specifically told me you were on site fifteen minutes after the aircraft went down and there were no other vessels within a twenty-mile radius according to your own surveillance equipment. In either case, it supports us ending the search."

"Give me one more day, Captain, please," Cooper pleaded.

"Sir, we normally search for three days with less information. We have been out here twice as long. In addition, you have had professional divers in submersibles scouring the ocean floor without success. Our engagement in this endeavor is terminated.

"What do you mean?"

"This case is closed. I suggest you communicate any concerns to your commander."

Cooper walked off with an irksome look on his face. If it was up to him, the captain of that Coast Guard cutter would pay with his life for his insubordination.

Now I have to explain to the commander how three injured escapees did not get recovered. I was literally out at the crash site fifteen minutes after it went down. The fuselage was recovered within hours. Where the hell can they be?

Cooper wasn't looking forward to explaining this failure to his commander but it had to be done. "I just hope I don't get shot in the face," he confessed aloud on his return walk to the command center. The commander met him with a scolding glare.

"Sir, the Coast Guard called off the search and our escapees were not recovered."

"So they remain at large?"

"Sir, it's the opinion of the Coast Guard that they either swam to shore or were lost at sea."

"And you?"

"I personally believe the latter is true. They all died on impact or shortly thereafter."

"Cooper, I'm not as optimistic as you. The fuselage was recovered within hours and it was locked and empty. You have had professionals searching both land and sea for close to a week. If they were lost at sea as you suggest, given the rapid response, our escapees should have been found. I am of the opinion that traditionally, people who don't want to be found are more difficult to locate. Therefore, I believe they're still out there. Plus, I ask you, who in their right mind would exit a downed aircraft and close and lock the doors behind them?"

"No one."

Cooper was nonplussed. The commander looked at him with censure and confessed internally, *My suspicions have been confirmed. This man is a dullard. However, on a positive note, he was not in league with them. He's just been injudicious when dealing with others in the same profession. Now, someone has to pay for this debacle and it won't be me. The master will be calling on us soon and I need to have someone to offer up. I just have to keep him involved until a sacrifice is required.*

"Cooper, I still need confirmation. You have not eliminated my suspicions of your involvement in this fiasco."

"Sir, I swear to you. I have been loyal. It's Avery who has betrayed us."

"Then continue looking. And find out everything you can about Avery."

"Yes, sir."

"And Cooper?"

"Yes, sir?"

"Get me some results."

"Yes, sir."

********** Days earlier, just south of Beboura, Central Africa **********

"Akachi!" Reynolds yelled at the top of his lungs.

His captain was standing at his side, "I now understand why you needed all these men. These people are like ghosts. I don't understand how they could have gotten away. There's fresh blood everywhere, so I'm certain they were all hit multiple times. I'm at a loss." The captain shook his head then added, "So now what, Lieutenant?"

Reynolds was enraged but he had to focus on the prize.

"How many men do we have left?"

"Maybe half."

What?"

"Sir, they had grenades. Had I been told they had grenades, I wouldn't have moved our men in so quickly. Twenty plus men were killed during the first explosions. The second set finished off and killed an additional ten. Then they opened fire with automatic weapons. Again, a fact I was not aware of." The captain didn't want to tell Reynolds that he specifically told him they were unarmed. *It was an error not listening to my instincts,* Reynolds' captain admitted. *It's a mistake I'll never repeat.*

"Gather your men and have them search the surrounding area just to make sure they did not crawl away. If you don't find any traces of their movements within one hundred meters of this shack, regroup back here."

"Sir, you give me the impression that you believe we won't find them."

"We won't. However, I want you to see for yourself."

"How is that possible? I thought you said you believed they were all hit multiple times."

"I did." Reynolds lost all the expression on his face as he picked up his sat phone and called Afia. He then covered the mouthpiece and said, "Listen, these four killed half of our men in a few minutes. They each sustained multiple gun shots. Look," Reynolds pointed to the ground. "There's blood here, here, there," he walked over to the other side of the structure and added, "and over here." Do you see the light coming in from outside through the bullet holes?"

"Yes."

"It tells me they all most likely received injuries to their lower extremities and lower or upper torso, at a minimum." Reynolds' goon looked around and pictured the event from inside the structure. His reenactment was interrupted by Reynolds' continued synopsis. "Then, Akachi bought them the few seconds they needed to regather their composure and slip out. Unnoticed, I might add."

"Who the hell are these people?"

"I told you, Captain, they are the bringers of death. And a few bullet wounds isn't going to make them wait around to be captured. So," Reynolds got back on the telephone and said, "Afia, where are we?"

"The helicopter you requested is en route and should be at your position in five. He should have you back here in less than an hour. Your aircraft has been refueled and is waiting for you. They have instructions to stop at Guantanamo before continuing on to Miami."

"Excellent. Good job."

"Yes, sir."

Reynolds put away the sat phone and finished his train of thought with his head thug. "So, when your search is over, gather your men and head back to Bangui. You're in charge now."

"Where do you want me to set up? And what about the men?"

"Ask them if they want a full-time job. Then shoot anyone who doesn't. And you can set up our command center in Barasa's compound. We're the new owners now."

"And you, sir?"

"I'm returning to the States. I have other matters which need my attention." Reynolds and his head goon walked away in different directions. A few minutes later, he looked back and saw the light from a barrage of bullet fire in the distance. Reynolds returned his focus to the matter at hand. "Akachi, you and your cult followers have executed a miraculous escape, but I'll catch up to you again, I guarantee it," Reynolds confessed under his breath. He boarded the Eurocopter EC155 B4 Dauphin and the pilot set a course for M'Poko International Airport in Bangui, Central Africa. An hour later, he was boarding his Boeing 757 M-1 for a thirteen-hour-and-forty-six-minute flight to Guantanamo Bay, Cuba.

********** Two days before, in Helucifer's lair **********

"This can't be? How did you capture a Harem, my Lord?" Filip asked in disbelief.

"It wasn't easy. But I did it for you, so the retribution will be worth it."

"Thank you, my Lord."

The Archangel was being held in the only secure space in Helucifer's castle capable of holding a Harem. The containment chamber had meter-thick metal walls, ceiling and floor. The door was a meter thick and made of the same metal, a super alloy of barium, cobalt and tungsten.

However, the true restraining power of the space was cast by the incantations recited over the room on a continuous basis by one hundred Arch-Helem.

"What can we do with her?"

"Well, there are dos and don'ts, but for now, were going to ask it some questions and see where that takes us."

"Why isn't she restrained?" Filip whispered.

"There're no restrains that can hold it," Helucifer whispered back.

"You realize I can hear you two talking," the Harem interjected.

Filip raised an eyebrow then thought, *So why hasn't she left?*

In this place, it's not able to open up a portal without my permission.

"I can still hear you two," the Harem announced again.

"Now that's interesting," Filip exclaimed. "She can hear our thoughts?" he questioned then looked over at Satan to see it nod as a confirmation. He returned his gaze at the Harem and confessed, "Well, that's probably an ability you should have kept a secret. But at this point, it doesn't matter, does it?" Filip continued his questioning to Helucifer aloud. "So why doesn't it fight to get out?"

It's bound to do us no harm unless we strike first.

Filip took a good look at the Harem and said, "She's so beautiful."

"Filip, I hate to break it to you, son, but it's not a girl."

"It looks like a girl to me. So I'm going to play ignorant and assume that it is."

"Very well, whatever makes you happy."

"We won't hurt you, much," Filip said with a huge grin.

"You need to let me go," the Harem exclaimed.

"Yes, we have every intention of doing just that. But first, you need to answer some questions," Helucifer declared.

"You can't possibly believe I will help you in any way."

"I'm going to have fun with you, whether you like it or not," Filip announced.

"You have no power over me."

Filip walked up and raised a hand to slap the Harem across the face.

"What are you doing?!" Helucifer yelled.

"I'm going to teach her some manners, my Lord."

"You can't use physical force against it. Or was my warning to you unclear?"

"No, but I thought the cautions were a challenge."

"They most certainly weren't. Any attempts at physical chastisement will be met and repelled with extreme prejudice."

"Is that so?" Filip countered with a hint of skepticism.

"Without question."

"Then, I'm at a loss as to how she could possibly resist in this place," Filip stated while trying to control an emerging level of frustration.

"This place is for the wicked. And this creature has done nothing wrong. Our influence is limited but there nevertheless. Those are the edicts. Just consider yourself fortunate."

"I see, my Lord."

"Do you? Because had you used physical force, you would have opened yourself up to a crippling lesson. So don't try that again. Don't even think about it."

"Very well, but I still think it would have been fun."

"Honestly, I should let you try just to teach you a lesson. But you're the leader of a world. And I'm afraid that if you get critically injured, our mission would be seriously compromised. Understand that any act of aggression will not generate the results you expect. Nor would you welcome the outcome. If you provide it a reason to retaliate, it will pitilessly lash out, and we would probably be forced to kill it. That's something I'm not prepared to do. So mind your place."

"But you kill them all the time."

"No we don't. We engage them on a field of battle, not corralled like some animal. We are above that."

"Yes, my Lord," Filip exclaimed, surrendering the argument. However, internally, he was convinced that using physical force would have been fun.

"Now, son, expand your thinking. Your desires are too limited. You must think on a grander scale and try to subdue your more primitive instincts."

Filip stared at the Harem for a minute then commanded, "Disrobe!" Helucifer lost all the expression on its face.

The Harem crossed its arms in front of its chest and said, "Make me!"

"That sounds like a challenge."

"It most certainly wasn't," Satan exclaimed as it held out a hand and stepped out in between the Harem and its son. With a stern look it said to Filip, "This is a Virtue, forged for combat by God's own hand. You can't seriously believe you'll receive any pleasure from battling it." Filip and the Harem stood at the ready. "Look, it's a pure spirit, compelled to tell the truth—all you need do is ask the right questions. Its revelations and your rewards could be endless and 'disrobe' is the best you can come up with?"

"What's wrong with wanting to get a better look at her? She's ravishing."

"What's wrong with that? What's wrong with that? Is that what you're asking me? I said be less primitive, not go Neanderthal."

Filip lowered his hands and bowed his head and said, "You're correct, of course. I'm sorry, Father."

"As you should be. Now, rein it back and try again." Helucifer stared at the Harem and said, "Sorry. Kids. Brilliant one second, cretins the next. You understand."

"No, not really," the Harem replied.

Satan crinkled up its brow and added, "You don't get out much do you?" But the Harem just stared Helucifer down.

"My Lord, I don't want to seem disrespectful but I thought you said she was for me?"

"Yes, but you're supposed to be asking it questions. Ah, you know what, it doesn't matter. I've had enough. Have fun." The Devil turned and headed for the door then stopped, turned and said, "But don't you dare strike her—it. You see, now you have me saying it. Don't you dare strike it."

"Yes, my Lord."

Twelve hours later, Filip walked out of the containment chamber and headed toward the conference hall. Helucifer met up with him halfway there.

"That was exhausting."

"Did you have fun?" Helucifer asked with genuine curiosity.

"Yes. Once I figured out what you meant, and what I could or could not do, it was incredible, my Lord. Can I spend more time with her later?"

"Of course, if you have time."

"I'll make the time. Now, how long can we keep her?"

"Maybe another twelve hours, at best."

"Why? She's so beautiful and soft. Why can't we just keep her? I would come visit you more often if you did."

"That's sweet but it's not a puppy. Plus, it's too strong and dangerous."

"What? She didn't seem dangerous to me. And I didn't sense any fear from her so I'm not sure it wants to go."

"Trust me, it wants to leave. And it's not afraid because once our time is up, it has the power to get out against all our objections. Now, did you learn anything from her—it? Did you learn anything from it?"

"Yes, my Lord. She was crazy strong, and limber and fast and energetic and—"

Helucifer interrupted Filip's recap by saying, "Okay, okay, okay, I get it." Satan shook its head and thought, *he spent twelve hours with it and he didn't gather anything useful.*

"If you want to spend more time with it, you have until the end of the day. After that, it will kill everything in its path to reach the front door and then it will simply walk out. And if we truly try to restrain it, it would fight to the death. And again, I'm not prepared to do that."

"So if it's so powerful, why didn't it resist more? She seemed so docile."

"That's because my will is stronger here, in the short-term. And it's so innocent. However, after twenty-four hours its patience will expire and forget it. Against my will, it will get out. And its fury will be like a category ten hurricane striking a city built of straw." Helucifer looked at the expression on Filip's face and added, "I realize hurricanes are typically categorized to level five. But you can imagine a category level ten storm, right?"

"Sure, I guess so. A storm with winds in excess of four hundred and fifty kilometers per hour, or greater."

"Yes, exactly. The kind of storm that would bury pliable objects into solid ones. Like blades of grass into concrete blocks."

"I understand."

"Well, once upon a time," Helucifer started having flashbacks, then shook its head before continuing, "We kept one here past twenty-four hours and a good portion of the castle's interior was destroyed."

"What?"

"Everything has rules," Helucifer said, but its statement was met with a blank stare.

"Isn't that the argument you pitched to Eric not long ago?"

"Actually, it is. Wait, that reminds me, how's Eric?"

"He's fine, recovering. He'll be back on his feet by this time tomorrow."

"He's going to wake up and expect to have super powers based on your indoctrination soliloquy."

"Yes, and you're going to have to explain it to him when he realizes that he doesn't."

"Great."

"Although, he will have influence over the weak-minded so just surround him with the gullible and naïve at first. That will help reduce his discovery."

Filip returned to the Harem's side multiple times after his initial visit but twenty-three hours and forty-five minutes later, Filip opened the door and said, "You're free to go." A fraction of a second later, the Harem was casting a portal outside the castle gate and was gone. Helucifer met up with its son moments after.

"Filip?"

"Yes, my Lord."

"Why the long face?"

"I let her go."

"I see. Were you forming feelings for it?"

"No."

"Right! Okay, well, its innocence and purity is alluring. And there lies the danger."

"Not really."

"Oh please, your feelings betray you, my son. Don't lose focus of who you are and what you're meant to do."

"I assure you, my Lord, I won't. I haven't."

"Good. Then let's finish our discussion before Eric is back on his feet and you two have to go."

"I understand."

Several hours later, Helucifer and Filip were walking out of the conference hall when they were met by Eric.

"And how is our faithful servant?" Helucifer asked as it watched him bow on one knee."

"Wonderful, Your Majesty," Eric announced. He looked a little older and much wiser. Eric had a bit of gray on his sideburns but his posture seemed more erect and his gaze more focused. The physical burns from the fire had deprived him of a few appendages. He was missing a finger on his right hand and a few toes, one on each foot. However, this didn't detract him from displaying a visibly impressive swagger.

"Eric, stand. Now that you've fully recovered, it's time to go. I will brief you on our future plans on the way out."

"Yes, my Lord. And I want to thank you for bringing me here and having the true God baptize me personally."

"Yes, of course. You're my second and should have nothing less."

"Thank you, my Lord."

As they exited the castle, Filip received a call from Reynolds. Seconds into Reynolds' update with the Anti-Christ, he received news that shocked him to his core.

"He! Reynolds, you can't be serious, Labelle Rogan is not a man," Filip spouted with obloquy.

******* Back in Guantanamo Bay's Black Site Command Center *******

"Commander, explain to me how you had two of the three most wanted fugitives on the planet surrounded by fifty guards, yet they still managed to escape."

"Sir—" the commander's response was interrupted by Reynolds.

"Wait, and they did so without actually killing anyone, correct?"

"Yes, sir. I know it seems a little implausible and one may think they received an enormous amount of help from the inside, but they—"

Reynolds interrupted the commander again to add

sarcastically, "You think."

"However, in our defense, I do have video proof and medical evidence that two of the three prisoners sustained brain damage from their torture and that they were in fact driven insane. And Dr. Chow Lee was close to insanity as well."

"Did they reveal anything during their sessions?"

"No, sir."

"Okay, so you tortured them for what, three or four days, is it? And not only did they reveal nothing, while insane, they managed to escape, without permanently hurting anyone."

"Unfortunately, sir, that's all correct."

"Does that seem reasonable to you? I mean, was their resistance normal for inmates under extreme duress?"

"No, sir. Many that undergo the torture regiment they received talk within a few hours and most within a day. However, all of them succumb within two days, until now."

"So—?"

"So, they were the exception. It was, without question, quite impressive."

"Really, they were impressive? Is that your synopsis, Commander?"

"Sir, I have been doing this a long time. I love my work. I'm extremely good at it. And I'm telling you that they resisted beyond human capabilities fifty and in one case, one hundred percent longer. It's not only unreasonable, it's impossible. Anyway, many of the soldiers reported they had help."

"I heard. They let many of the prisoners out and used them as a distraction," Reynolds recapped.

"No, sir. Well, yes, but aside from that, many of the soldiers reported seeing aberrations or ghosts which they later classified as angels."

"I see, so they were helped by some kind of semi-visible rogue anomalies?"

"Well, sir, they were visible periodically and when they were, they looked like angels."

"Isn't that what I just said?"

"When the soldiers were asked to describe what they saw, they all used adjectives like angelic, beautiful, majestic and or benevolent. Those are not words one would associate with villainous creatures. Anyway, they didn't harm anyone. Again, their behavior was not one I would associate with iniquitous characters."

"I see, so where did these charismatic souls come from? And where did they go?"

"It's unclear. However, many of the soldiers reported the apparitions appearing just as our prisoners were surrounded and the men had opened fire. Many of the men were still in denial, but a few stated that these conspirators or collaborators materialized out of thin air and then left in the same manner."

"I'm sorry, Lieutenant, I realize this all seems kinda crazy," Cooper added a little hesitantly to the conversation.

"Kinda crazy?" Reynolds questioned with a raised eyebrow.

"Okay, so it sounds totally crazy but it's the truth. I swear it. One of these things talked to me."

"Is that so?" Reynolds' interest was piqued.

"Yes, sir."

"So?"

"So," Cooper replied in a daze.

"So, what did it say?"

"Oh yeah, right, well, it said, 'You were told not to kill them.'"

"And?" Cooper's eyes went blank. "Hey, focus, your mind is wandering. Is that it? Is that all it said?"

"No, sorry. It also said, 'Your penance shall be' — something, swift — no, righteous — no. 'Your penance shall be' — something. What was it?" Cooper shook his head and added, "I'm sorry, Lieutenant, but I can't remember her exact words. However, she did say something about penance."

"Very well, so I need both of you to come with me." Reynolds escorted them to 'A' block then asked the commander to step into an empty cell.

"Excuse me?"

"Commander, if you please, it's an experiment." He escorted Cooper into another nearby cell and then closed and locked both doors.

"Okay, gentlemen, please listen up, I am going to ask each of you to prove yourself. I only have room for one of you in my organization. So which ever one of you fails this test will be subjected to the same no-touch torture methods you have each been dispensing to others, until you go insane. Any questions so far?"

Both men started hurling comments and questions at Reynolds with extreme will and determination. Reynolds tried to answer some of their concerns but at the end, in truth, he really didn't care. So he waved them off, left then returned ten minutes later with two hacksaws and two tourniquets.

"Okay, gentlemen, please listen up, the first one to hack off their right foot will continue on and run this facility. The other will, like I stated earlier, be tortured until they go insane. Then I'm going to bring in the best doctors in the world to reverse your mental break and then do it all over again. Any questions?" Again, both men started launching remarks, observations, and inquiries that Reynolds had no interest in acknowledging.

"Okay, so are you ready?" Both men continued to resist and plead for mercy. At one point both men asked to just be shot.

"Wow! Each of you has been torturing men, women, and even children for years. And you're asking me for mercy? You can't be serious. You will receive no mercy here. Not today, not ever.

"Now, you will need to tie those tourniquets tight just below your calf.

"Ready?" Reynolds announced again. "Oh and if you don't start cutting away within five minutes, I'm going to have eight men go into your cell and cut off your right foot for you. Then we'll start the test all over again—but with your left foot.

"Are you ready? Go!"

Thirty minutes later, both men were being injected with antibiotics and allowed to rest. Reynolds wanted them semi-lucid before beginning their no-touch torture sessions, and their journey toward madness.

Several hours after their muffled screams had subsided, Reynolds revealed his gruesome plans.

"Gentlemen, the penance for your transgressions shall be great. Commander, you hired a betrayer and didn't know it. Then you hired the imbecile next to you. I might have been willing to forgive one wrongdoing but not both. Cooper, what can I say, you're a halfwit and the world has enough of them. Anyway, I am disappointed that I cannot be here to witness your mental collapse but I take comfort in having access to mobile communication devices."

"I want a short fifteen-second record sent to me every four hours on the hour," Reynolds communicated to the person he was leaving in charge. "I want to see firsthand the progress you're making on their journey toward hysteria and total delirium."

The lieutenant pulled aside the ruffian he was leaving in charge and said, "I want you to cut out their tongues before I leave, I don't want them trying to talk their way out of this."

"Yes, sir."

Afterwards, let them rest for a few hours then administer some additional antibiotics. I don't want them dying from an infection."

"Yes, sir."

Reynolds departed the interrogation cells and was taken to the airport where his private aircraft was waiting for him. They asked for permission to depart and made their way to Miami. He looked at his watch and thought, *it's as good a time as any*. He decided to call Filip and provide an update.

CHAPTER 21

The Chosen Receive Visitors

VIKKI WALKED OUT OF THE BATHROOM AFTER MAGGIE'S makeover and apprehensively walked into the living room and greeted everyone with a small wave, "Hi."

"Woah," Yvette let out, the first to react.

Everyone else looked up and was pleasantly surprised at Vikki's physical transformation. Maggie, of course, was all grins while standing behind her.

"Well, I think you look so much prettier when you're not angry," Yvette shared.

"Blimey," Winnie exclaimed then cleared her throat and was happy to add, "You clean up nice."

"You look amazing, sis," then Nikki tilted her head, paused and asked in a semi-bewildered state, "Wait, are you wearing makeup?"

"A little, why? Do I look silly?"

"No, no, absolutely not, you look beautiful." Nikki peered past her and gave Maggie a thumbs up then mouthed, "You're incredible." Maggie quietly giggled while holding both thumbs up under her chin.

"Wait, did you shave your legs?"

"Yes," Vikki said under her breath, a little embarrassed. Nikki looked past Vikki again and motioned to Maggie with a hard nod and mouthed, "Are you kidding me?" Nikki had no idea how Maggie had gotten her sister to do that. She had tried for years to get Vikki to shave her legs without success.

"That's not all," Maggie retorted with a chuckle then exclaimed, "She looks totally adorbs, huh?"

"Well, I'm kind of regretting it now. I'm all itchy."

Nikki ran over and hugged her around the neck then whispered, "Nonsense, sis, you look fabulous. You're like super girlie now. I love it."

"Don't remind me. I'm totally having second thoughts. No one is going to take me seriously looking like this." Maggie had styled Vikki's hair and cut it shorter, just above her shoulders. She had applied makeup to a virgin face and had placed stiletto tips on her fingernails. She had also helped remove her excess body hair which Maggie claimed looked gross, even though it was nothing more than peach fuzz. Nevertheless, other than the hair on her head and eyebrows — which had also been reduced — Vikki was now hairless. Maggie had even groomed away the hair from her fingers and toes. Vikki was always afraid that girls living on the street who drew too much attention to their physical attributes ran a much higher chance of being violated. Therefore, she resisted normal female grooming practices. Well, until now.

"You look amazing, sis," Nikki added while stroking her back and displaying true affection.

Everyone else gathered around to show their support and complimented her on her miraculous recovery. Nikki was on the mend and so was Akachi. Both took turns cleaning up and were resting and getting to know everyone else. Adadi was a little slower. She was the last to get to her feet but once she started walking around, her regenerative abilities were remarkable.

Winnie was playing around with a portable radio, hoping to hear some positive news when an old Cardi B song, "I Like It Like That," started playing. Maggie was quick to say, "Ooh ooh ooh, turn that up. That's my home girl's song." She started dancing in front of Vikki, making her join in.

Nikki asked Vikki in shock, "Wait, since when do you know

how to dance?"

"I'm a girl. All I have to do is wiggle in place and it's called dancing."

Winnie looked behind her at Vikki and said, "She's right. Plus, I kinda like this song, too." Suddenly, all the girls found themselves drawn to the room and before you knew it, they were all wiggling in place.

Minutes later, the girls noticed the attention their actions were generating from the men so when the song ended, their dancing came to an abrupt halt.

"Aww," Avery let out, "I rather fancied the entertainment, ladies." Winnie walked over and punched Avery in the arm.

"Bloody hell, woman, I just meant it was nice to see you and the others having a bit of fun."

"Avery, before I consider you a tosser, I would suggest you stop talking," Winnie shot back.

Avery cleared his throat and replied, "Yes, mum."

Just then, Mia telepathically notified her mother that she and others would be arriving soon. She reminded Yvette of her previous instructions and asked that she refresh everyone's memory. Yvette communicated the information to the others and for some reason, her announcement seemed a bit trivial to the group.

How odd, Yvette thought. *Had I made this statement to the same crowd two weeks ago I would have been laughed at or labeled a nut case. Now, no one seemed interested nor expressed any concerns or questions. I just hope that our discipline doesn't suddenly vanish in the presence of so many celestial beings. Since Mia, Winnie and I found one to be totally overwhelming most of the time.*

Everyone was paired up and working on getting to know each other. Maggie was busy showing Vikki, her sister and Avery how she and some of the others were prepared to defend their homestead.

Suddenly and to everyone's surprise, the front door flew open and three men wielding pistols enter the cabin. The one in the middle was on both knees with his firearm drawn; the other two were to his right and left, holding a solid posture on one knee with a revolver in hand.

"No se mueven, cabrones," the center man declared.

However, before he could get all the words out, Avery,

Nikki, Vikki, Maggie and several others had their firearms drawn, cocked and in front of them each with a target in their sights.

"Wait, nobody move!" Maggie yelled as she held up a hand then added, "Okay now, everyone relax and take a deep breath. These are my uncles."

"Maggie, is that you?" her uncle declared with a fatigued and cracking voice.

"Si, Tio."

"Are you okay, mija?"

"Si, Tio, I'm fine." Maggie stood up and holstered her firearm in the small of her back then commanded, "Now, everyone lower your weapons. This is the only family I have left, and I don't want any accidents. Plus, it already looks like they have enough bullet holes between them."

"You're right, mija." Maggie's uncles lowered their guns, clinging to their injuries and said, "We need some help. We've all been hit multiple times." Maggie's uncles were all dark-skinned, stocky Dominicans with multiple days of facial hair growth. They were all wearing tattered clothing stained with blood. The senior uncle was her dad's older brother and the other two were younger. The elder had been shot twice in the back and once in the stomach two days earlier. The other two had similar injuries to the legs and shoulders. All three were in desperate need of medical attention.

"I told you she would be here," the senior uncle announced before collapsing into Maggie's arms.

Winnie stared at the men then shook her head and let out under her breath, "Oh, come on. Really? More gun shot victims? This is ridiculous, in the extreme. No body would believe this. I'm here, and I don't bloody believe it. This is just too much."

"Mick!" Maggie yelled. "We need to help them."

"Of course, everyone scrub up. We're needed."

Here we go again, Winnie thought. *Hoshea, when is this going to end?*

Everyone scrambled to get the cabin ready for Maggie's injured family members. The group performed like a well-rehearsed emergency response center.

Mick, Yvette and Winnie took the lead and were prepped for surgery within minutes. Maggie acted like the ER administrator and fired orders about making sure everyone was doing what was required. Mick was assisted by Vikki and Winnie by Adadi.

Stefan was again nervous. He was a geneticist, not a surgeon. Yvette walked over to him and placed a hand on his back, "Feeling nervous?"

"Yes, a little."

"Well, think about what he's feeling. He's had two bullets in his back for like two days. And this is not counting the one in his stomach. So, take a deep breath and let's render this poor man the mercy he deserves. What do you think?"

"Yes, you're right, of course."

"Good, then assist me."

The Propofol drip was started and ten seconds later, everyone got to work. Within an hour, two of the three brothers were on the mend. However, Yvette's patient experienced complications. He had lost a lot of blood. He was on his second bag of plasma and Maggie was about to start a third. Mick had moved over to help and was working frantically to stop the internal bleeding while Yvette repaired the damage.

This would be so much easier if I wasn't exhausted, Yvette thought then yelled, "Wipe!" Sophia was there in seconds.

Three hours later, Yvette announced, "It's done."

Maggie had been standing by her uncle like a statue for hours. Her movements were only noticeable when she reached up every so often to wipe the tears from her face. As soon as Yvette proclaimed her success, Maggie immediately started crying uncontrollably. Sophia moved to her side and embraced her. Maggie looked like she was on the verge of fainting. It had been a long, grueling, emotional day for her but it was coming to an end with favorable results.

However, her uncle had died twice during his four-hour operation and the second time, it was a miracle he had come back. Winnie prayed over him continuously during the last few hours. And Akachi had administered an additional twenty milliliters of the solution that had healed most of them a day earlier. He also gave everyone else an additional ten milliliters every few hours as a preventative measure. No one had had the time to notice that scars from old wounds were fading away or disappearing all together. He wanted everyone fully recovered before heading out again, which he realized would soon take place.

The sun was going down and everyone was cleaning up. Even though it was still early in the evening, one by one they started retiring for the night. The last few days had been arduous for everyone compounded by serious physical injuries. Even Dai, who spent half the day in meditation, was feeling the stress. Nevertheless, at Winnie's request, he spent time showing others close-quarter defensive maneuvers as part of his Ip Man master arsenal of Wing Chun techniques. Since the skills being taught were all defensive in nature, Dai was reassured that the integrity of the discipline was not being corrupted.

The next morning, Maggie woke up to find her uncles sitting around the breakfast table drinking coffee and talking to Akachi, Avery and Dai.

"Tio, why are you guys out of bed? You need to be resting."

"We are resting. Plus, we feel much better. Thanks to your excellent care and that of your friends. Anyway, we thought we would eat, if there's enough food."

"Of course there's enough."

"Good. Then we'll eat and rest a little longer before we take off today."

"What? Why would you leave? You guys just got here. And you're all still on the mend."

"Margarita, you know that others will be coming for us. And we are not going to endanger these nice people and the only family we have left. Plus, half of you are women and you know how we feel about placing women in harm's way. We cannot stay." Maggie knew better than to argue with her uncle.

"Fine, then I'll just pack a few things and go with you."

"Absolutely not, mija, you're needed here."

"What?! But who's going to look after you?" Maggie asked as tears filled her eyes.

"Mija, it's time for you to tend to yourself. You've been looking after us long enough. It's time for our baby girl to grow up and have pretty babies of her own. Babies we can hold and play with and tell stories of their Mommy's bravery. But first, we must survive the madness that's engulfing this world. And that won't happen if we stay here."

"Tio," Maggie let out as tears streamed down her face.

"It's okay, mija, we'll see each other again. I promise." Just then, Sophia and Yvette joined the others in the kitchen. Adadi, Nikki and her sister were not far behind. Even Stefan had piled into the kitchen area with everyone else.

"Good morning, everyone," Yvette let out all bubbly. "I would ask why you three men are out of bed, but it would seem that twelve hours of bed rest is the norm around here for everyone to recover from serious injuries."

"We weren't hurt that bad," Maggie's uncle replied dismissively.

"What?!" Maggie shouted. "Tio, you died twice."

"What? No I didn't. You're such an exaggerator, mija," he let out with a chuckle then turned his head toward Yvette to see her shaking her head in disagreement.

Maggie's uncle lost his smile and added, "Did I really die—twice?" while holding up two fingers.

Yvette nodded as a confirmation.

"But I'm not dead now, right?"

"No."

"Okay, good, because I feel so much better compared to the other day. And I would hate to think this was a dream—or worse." Maggie's uncle made the sign of the cross.

"No, Tio, you're alive and well. And I want you to stay that way. Plus, if you leave, how will I get ahold of you?"

"Well—" Avery interrupted the conversation.

"Sorry but I think I can help with that. Sophia, did you find a strange cellular in your back pocket?" Avery questioned.

"Yes, how odd. I found it yesterday while doing laundry. How did you know?"

"I placed it there in case of an emergency. However," Avery walked over and whispered in her ear, "that's before I knew you were going to be rescued by a celestial being." Sophia smiled then Avery added, "Can I have it?"

"Sure, I'll go get it." Sophia stepped out and returned seconds later and handed the telephone to Avery.

"Thanks." Avery turned around and said, "Gentlemen, take this cellular. And if it ever rings, you answer it."

"Sure."

Avery turned to Maggie and handed her a similar phone. "Maggie, this is your connection to your uncles. These phones are special. All you need to do is press this button and its pair will ring, regardless of where the two telephones are in the world."

Maggie hugged him around the neck and said, "Thank you, Avery."

"No problem, love."

Maggie's uncle gave Avery a strong, silent nod and he reciprocated with the same.

It was almost nine a.m. and Maggie started a huge pot of rice. Winnie walked over and asked, "What's mija mean?"

"It's a term of endearment, like the British use the word, 'love.' However, for us, the word means, 'my darling' or 'my loving daughter.'

"That so pretty," Winnie replied with a hand over her heart. "And 'tio' means what, 'uncle'?"

"Yes, exactly."

"Excuse me, baby," Maggie looked past Winnie and said, "Mick, can you go catch us a few additional fish? There aren't enough fresh ones for everyone. And I don't like frying frozen fish, they make the oil spit up, and I hate that."

"Sure, no problem. I'll be back in a jiff."

Maggie's uncles all got up and volunteered to go out with him. "Oh, I appreciate the offer, guys, but we only have one pole."

One of the younger uncles replied, "Well, that's okay, because we don't need a pole."

Mick wanted to ask how they expected to catch anything without a fishing pole but he kept it to himself. He thought, *it might be funny to see them try to catch fish with their bare hands. Or maybe they were planning on shooting the fish. After all, Maggie's uncles seem a little like cavemen. You know what; maybe they're just going to slam their faces in the water if a fish swims by.* Ha, he let out a small chuckle.

Two of Maggie's uncles took fishing line and tied a knot around the neck of an empty two-liter bottle. They wrapped the fishing line around the bottle then placed a hook on the other end of the line. The other uncle returned with a handful of worms and grubs. *Wow, that was fast. It took me like thirty minutes to find a few pieces of bait the first time. He returned in five minutes with like ten times as much.*

Mick felt like a halfwit when he saw them pulling in fish after fish using such primitive methods. They were using a small rock tied to the line to weigh down the bait. And they were reeling in their catch by hand as they wrapped the excess line around the bottle.

I actually thought they were going to use their hands or guns to catch fish. I'm ashamed of what I was thinking and I feel like such an idiot – I'm tempted to let them know what I thought to expiate for my stupidity. Mick considered confessing for a few more minutes then decided not to. *It would probably be a greater blunder to admit my absurdity than to just let it go. I just met these men and they've been through a lot. It would be insensitive of me to tell them I thought they were Neanderthals. However, perhaps I'll confess my backward thinking to Maggie someday, and give her a good laugh at my expense.* Twenty minutes later, they returned to the dock with fifteen fish weighing three to four kilos each.

Maggie's uncles weren't very talkative. They barely spoke fifty words in the twenty minutes they were out fishing. Nevertheless, when they arrived at the prepping station behind the house, that all changed. They saw Mick struggling to prep his catch, so they decided to help. They each instructed him on a different aspect of prepping the snappers. One uncle showed Mick how to properly gut his catch. Another demonstrated how to perfectly scale a fish. And the last uncle taught him how to professionally de-bone a snapper. Mick was embarrassed at his lack of hunting skills but grateful for the tutelage. He walked into the kitchen and proudly handed Maggie their prize.

"Nice job, Papi," Maggie whispered with a grin and the swish of her hips.

Sophia and Winnie cleaned the fish again and Mick helped Maggie get several frying pans on the burners to preheat for their catch. Yvette walked in and took over for Mick. A few minutes later, she turned around and saw all the men sitting around the table and noticed it was just the women in the kitchen cooking. Vikki and her sister were observing from the living room with the corner of their mouths scrunched up. They had their arms crossed in front of their chests and were slowly shaking their heads from side to side.

Yvette tilted her head to one side and asked, "What are you two looking at? We all wanted to help." She turned around again and took another look. *I see, so we're playing into the stereotype big time.* Then she considered the event a little longer and confessed,

Ah, whatever, we're happy and at peace. What's wrong with that? Then most unexpectedly, Maggie started to shoo all the girls out of the kitchen. Yvette couldn't believe it but she was actually a little disappointed she couldn't help.

"Okay, you guys, I appreciate the help but there're too many cooks in the kitchen so, everybody out." Sophia was the only one who survived the cut. Everyone ate their fill and Maggie's uncles ate like they had not eaten in days.

Everyone sat around comfortably digesting their meal and enjoying the peaceful fellowship. It was nice to be lazy and lay around in a serene environment for a change. The world was in a philosophical state of chaos and their actions were the nucleus behind an opposing view. It was peculiar, at best, to anyone being desperately hunted down by a merciless enemy to be so tranquil. But when you considered the fact that there were so many all together in one location, it was astonishing.

They all sat around for hours telling stories then Maggie and a few others cooked and served a late lunch. Shortly before two p.m., Maggie's uncles announced that they were leaving. But seconds later there were screams coming from the front lawn. Vikki and Nikki were peering out from different windows on opposite sides of the house.

"Come on out, Mr. Rosado. You know this can only end one way. Your actions cost us a small fortune. You need to come out and face your fate. Or would you rather we take it out on your family?"

"I count at least four back here," Nikki declared.

"I think there's maybe eight men out front," Vikki added to her sister's observation. She looked over at Maggie's senior uncle and asked, "Who are they?"

"They're the scum working for the head of a New York City crime family."

"They're calling for you, Tio," Maggie whispered. "And why are they spouting such vile grotesqueries about you?"

"They'll say whatever inanities will get them what they want."

"So exactly what did you do to piss these people off?" Vikki asked.

"We broke into all of their brothels over a ten-day period

and freed the hundreds of girls they had as slaves working as part of their sex trade."

One of the junior uncles added, "Some of those poor girls had been there for years. It was an honor to free them and help end their suffering."

"Who paid you men to do that?" Vikki questioned.

"The other uncle answered in a thick Spanish accent, "We put those desgraciados out of business—that was our payment."

Nikki looked over at her sister and they both slowly shook their head with a look of disgust for the men outside their doors, then Nikki asked, "So what do we do?"

Maggie's senior uncle responded, "I'll tell you what we do, I go out to meet them." He stood up and placed a Glock behind his back supported by his waistband.

"Sir, you can't possibly believe that walking out there—armed—has any possibility of success."

"Perhaps not, but at least I'll take a few of them with me."

"I see you have heart, but how lucky are you?" Vikki asked with a stone cold look.

"Excuse me?" Maggie's uncle asked commandingly.

"Mr. Rosado, I don't want to seem disrespectful but they're entrenched out there. You'll be out in the open the second you step out this door. If you're extremely lucky, you may take out one, maybe two, if they're really inexperienced. Regardless, you'll be killed and your actions will most certainly take most of us down with you," Vikki summarized. "So again, how lucky are you?" she asked again, hoping for a startling revelation. Maggie was stunned beyond words. She knew her uncles were immersed in a perilous environment but she had never experienced it this close and personal.

"I'm probably not any luckier than most, but what choice do I have?" Mr. Rosado responded.

"That's easy," Nikki interjected. "You let us go out for you."

"What?! Absolutely not. Who do you think these people are? And what would be the point of one of you walking out there? They'll just grab you and use you as a hostage. I've never placed a woman in harm's way and I'm not going to start today."

"Look, there are maybe four or five men behind the house. I can take them easy," Nikki shared.

"Take them where?"

"To the afterlife. Just like you right now, they will never see me coming."

"Mr. Rosado, Nikki and I go by the name of Labelle Rogan."

"What?" Mr. Rosado had a moment of silence then said, "That's impossible!"

"Who's Labelle Rogan?" Maggie questioned.

"You can't be Labelle Rogan."

"Who is Labelle Rogan?" Maggie asked again.

"We can, and we are."

"I don't believe you."

"Well, believe it, because we are." She pointed to Nikki and said, "She's Nikki Labelle and I'm Vikki Rogan."

"I don't understand. So what does that mean? Somebody tell me," Maggie exclaimed, desperately trying to make sense of what had everyone else listening to Vikki's confession in a state of denial.

"Labelle Rogan is probably the most successful and elusive assassin in the world. With over one thousand confirmed kills," Avery shared with Maggie in a whisper.

"What?"

"One thousand, one hundred and eighty-eight, at our last count," Nikki corrected in a whisper. Avery raised an eyebrow and Maggie covered her mouth. She saw a face on Nikki that she hoped to never see again.

"Are you telling me that you are the same Rogan that took down the Scalini crew and the Sanchez brothers?"

"Yes, sir, and the Crimson Outlaws and the Wrecking Ball boys, to name a few," Vikki added to their discovery.

"Ay, Dios mio," one of Maggie's uncles muttered out, and then did the sign of the cross before adding, "The Wrecking Ball crew had their eyes removed."

"True, but in our defense, we didn't wanna do the eye thingy. However, our employer insisted it be part of our contract. Anyway, they were pigs, who treated women like cattle."

Maggie took a deep breath then covered her mouth. Vikki had called her a pig before. *What if my back talk would have made Vikki go crazy on me?* She did the sign of the cross and tried to put the thoughts out of her head.

"I thought Labelle Rogan was a myth," Maggie's junior

uncle exclaimed.

"I thought Rogan was a man. But you're telling me it's you two girls?" Maggie's uncle added while slowly shaking his head then added, "I just don't believe you."

"That's why they never see us coming," Nikki shared.

"So, you're Labelle Rogan—well, the two of you are anyway." Nikki and Vikki gave Avery a hard, convincing look. "Brilliant, our intel files on Rogan were, or should I say are, completely inaccurate. That's if what you're telling us is true. But I'm with him, love. I'm not sure I believe you."

"Well, I do," Akachi added to the conversation.

"What? Akachi, you knew who they were?" Avery asked in disbelief.

"No, but I suspected they were more than just body guards."

"How, why?"

"Some of the things Nikki shared with me when Vikki was hurt." Akachi cleared his throat before continuing, "Anyway, while in Africa last week, these two permanently incapacitated over eighty men—by my count—before we got out and came here. So if they say they can take these men out, I believe them."

All the men scrunched up their foreheads and stared at the girls who glared back with the corner of their mouths crinkled up.

"What?!" Nikki let out. "They were all bad, I swear."

Rosado shook his head then asked, "Okay, so how would you take them out? You can't go out there armed. You'll be shot in two seconds."

"I have a plan."

Rosado looked over at his brother and said, "Distract them. Tell them I'm dead and our niece will show them proof."

"They'll never believe that."

"It doesn't matter, we just need a few minutes to confirm a plan."

"Fine."

Vikki took the lead in articulating the correct course of action. Avery and Rosado had questions but Vikki kept dismissing their concerns. Two minutes later, Vikki asked, "Is everyone ready?"

"Ready for what? You and Nikki are doing all the work, we're just supposed to sit here while you two get it done," Rosado responded.

"No, in order for this plan to work, we have to let one of these pigs live. And that will not be easy. Plus, if we expect to keep them from coming back, you have to let that person escape in a manner they will consider legitimate. They also have to tell others where you're going. But more importantly, where you're not, so everyone here will remain safe. So again, is everyone ready?

The Rosado brothers nodded, along with Avery and Akachi.

Maggie pulled Vikki off to the side and said, "I am so sorry for talking back to you before."

"Wait, are you apologizing to me because of what you heard us confess?"

"No. Maybe. Yes, a little."

Vikki smiled, then pinched Maggie's chin and said, "It's okay, princess, I've never hurt a girl I liked."

Maggie hugged her around the neck and said, "Oh my God, you are so brave, and scary."

"Really?" Vikki moved Maggie at arm's length and added, "Why are we scary?"

"Well, because you two are like mass murderers."

"We're no different than your uncles. But we are the bringers of death for the wicked."

The senior uncle heard Vikki's quote to Maggie then confessed to the other men, "She, or they are Labelle Rogan."

"You believe them now, what changed your mind, mate?" Avery asked.

"I just heard her say something that I've never heard anyone else say. It's supposed to be Rogan's ID."

Vikki leaned in and whispered into Maggie's ear, "You have nothing to fear from me, I've never hurt the innocent, I swear it."

"Oh my God, this situation is so intense. My heart is beating so hard it's gonna jump out of my chest. I'm gonna have a heart attack or something."

"Relax, everything will be all right, I promise."

"Vikki, you're not just saying that to make me feel better, are you?" Maggie asked as her emotions swelled up in her throat and tears filled her eyes."

"No, I'm not. So trust me, babe."

Maggie hugged her again and said, "Okay, but you betta

bring it when you go out there. I need you to come back to me. Us, I need you to come back to us."

"I will."

Vikki asked Rosado to point out the boss. He told her he's the one standing in the back. Vikki thought, *Well, he's either a coward or smart, but to my misfortune, I think it's the latter. It's going to be hard to take out eight men by hand without getting hurt. That's if it's even possible. I've never taken out more than seven, so this is going to be my greatest feat or my end. Plus, now I have Maggie in my head.*

Vikki called Maggie over and said, "Slap me."

Maggie's mouth dropped open and Nikki said, "It's okay, that's how she gets ready." Maggie reached up and tapped her face. Nikki started to laugh but covered her mouth with both hands before adding, "A little harder."

Maggie tried again and Vikki let out, "Ow," making Maggie cover her mouth again as Vikki walked off.

Nikki saw the concern on Maggie's face and whispered, "It's okay, don't worry. If anyone can take out eight men by hand, it's her. She's crazy fast, and stronger than she looks."

"Okay, everyone, we're ready." Nikki ran to the back with Avery as backup. Vikki stood by the front with Rosado to her right. She held a hand behind her back with her palm open, then started retracting her fingers—four, three, two, one—Nikki jumped out the back door using a similar ploy used in Africa to debilitate and silence five men. Her gyrations and commentary provided enough of a distraction for her to get close to the men and successfully neutralize the threat. None of the thugs found it necessary to fire a single shot—and that was their mistake. Nikki had done what she set out to do.

However, as soon as Vikki stepped out, she noticed there were nine men and not six to eight like she initially thought. That extra man and the boss standing in the back brought her success ratio down to the single digits and she knew it. Her heart and mind started racing.

Nikki walked back into the cabin and was met by Yvette. "Oh my goodness, sweetie, your eye and jaw look swollen already."

"Yeah, well, I was punched in the face, hard, twice. And one of those men kicked me in the crotch, which hurt like hell. And I'm sure it would have been much worse had I been a boy, but it hurt like hell anyway."

"Come, let me put some ice on that."

"Later, how's Vikki doing?"

"I'm not sure."

Nikki ran to the window and knelt down by Maggie's side.

"How's she doing?"

"She's just standing there."

"How long has she been out there?"

"At least two minutes, but probably longer."

"Oh my."

"Why, what's wrong?" Maggie asked as she brought both fists up in front of her mouth.

"She's been out there too long, something's wrong," Nikki started to count the villainess out.

"Who the hell is that and why is she just standing there?" one of the goons whispered.

"Let's just see where this goes, plus, she's nice to look at."

"Don't get distracted. That's probably the reason she's out there," the boss announced.

Finally, Vikki stepped forward and proclaimed, "I do this for the people I love."

The men scrunched down a little behind three black SUVs but kept their eyes fixed on Vikki, she was hard to ignore. She took a deep breath then increased her wiggle and swished toward them. "Don't shoot, don't shoot!" she exclaimed.

"Why is she walking like that?" Maggie asks rhetorically.

"I like it," her uncle replied.

She elbowed him in the ribs then added, "I'm sure you do, but seriously, why is she walking like that? It's so exaggerated."

"That's probably why I like it."

Oh, Maggie thought, then confessed, "Smart girl."

The men started to pick their heads up and the lead brute asked, "Who are you and why are you out here?"

"I'm here to show you proof that my uncle is dead. But if I find out one of you had anything to do with it, I will give you such a pinch." Most of the men smiled but the boss didn't. Vikki started counting, two, three, four, not enough.

"What can she be talking about?"

"She's buying time," Nikki answered.

"Time for what?" Maggie questioned out of ignorance.

"Time to get ninety percent of them into her kill zone."

"Oh no," Nikki wrenched out.

"What is it, what is it, what is it?" Maggie repeated frantically.

"There are nine men out there."

"So?"

"That's too many. That's why she stood by the door for so long. She's trying to think of a way to kill nine men and she can't see it. There's no way."

"Oh my God, what will she do? Can we do anything to help her?" Maggie questioned.

"No. But she will kick two and stab three, leaving four. Once she throws her first spike, the second and third man will be much harder to hit. Plus, the last man always hides."

One of the thugs asked, "Where's your proof?"

"Here, on my phone," Vikki nervously replied. "No, no, no," she said as she swiped the telephone screen. "These are just pictures of me. Look, this one is so cute. No, no, no."

"What is she doing?" Maggie asked again. "She's going to give me a heart attack."

"She's drawing them in, five, six, seven—damn it, still not enough."

"Only seven?!" Vikki exclaimed, than conceded and said, "The hell with it, that's close enough.

Vikki released the blades attached to the toe and heel of her shoes. She put her arm around the shoulder of one and then planted her heel to the temple of the man to her left. She stabbed the man she was holding through the throat and kicked the man to the right in the head. Vikki moved forward and drove a dagger into the chest of the closest two other men then threw a spike at two others.

Maggie was kneeling by the window with one hand covering her eyes, but peering out her fingers ever so slightly just to make sure Vikki was still standing. She repeatedly made the sign of the cross while chanting, "Baby Jesus, protect her."

"Three, four, five, six, almost there, sis, seven," Nikki whispered. "Just two to go." Then a shot rang out and everyone was stunned.

Vikki was hit in the stomach and the boss moved in for the

kill, but not before the other man stabbed her in the back. Everyone but Avery held their breath. He moved to an open window. She fell on to her hands and knees but slowly pushed herself up onto the back of her heels. The goon in front raised his firearm and the man behind her grabbed her by the hair and said, "You're done," then pulled a knife out to cut her throat. The boss noticed Vikki had cloudy, dull cow eyes and said, "This skank is gone, just finish her."

Vikki muttered something out but it was inaudible. Avery was moving slow but had a target. He took a deep, cleansing breath then took aim.

The brute behind her leaned forward and said, "What did you say, skank?"

Suddenly, Vikki's eyes became clear and focused, making the boss confess internally, *What the hell just happened*?

She grabbed the man's knife hand and kicked the boss in the thigh, then pulled the man over her shoulder and threw him up against the other. She kicked the man who stabbed her on the back of his head as he tried to stand up then said, "Eight." Vikki kicked the gun out of the boss's hand then moved in and kneed him in the temple. "Now I'm done."

Vikki took a few seconds before standing up then moved toward the boss and kicked him in the face repeatedly. When she felt satisfied, she leaned down and grabbed him by the arm and started dragging him back to the cabin. Maggie was the first one out the door, followed by Nikki, Avery and Akachi.

As Maggie got close, Vikki looked up and said, "Betta brought."

"Oh my God, baby, are you okay?" Maggie cried out.

"Yes, but I'm beat," Vikki replied in a deep, painful moan.

Nikki took hold of her sister then yelled, "Somebody grab him and make sure he's secure. And somebody needs to tend to the puncture wound on his right thigh. We don't want him bleeding out." Nikki started toward the house with Vikki in tow. Avery and Akachi each grabbed a leg and started dragging the ruffian inside. "Oh, Dai, can you check the front and back of the house? We want to make sure everyone outside is dead. We don't want to be sitting back drinking coffee later and have someone rush in and riddle us with bullets."

Maggie's uncles were all outside and Rosado senior

confessed, "That is the Labelle Rogan we have all heard stories about."

"She's incredible," another brother added. Like Maggie, they all stood there in shock.

Vikki looked over her shoulder and said, "You comin'?"

Maggie jumped up and yelled, "Oh my God, yes, baby, yes."

Yvette, Winnie, Stefan and Mick were all prepped and ready for surgery.

Mick and Yvette tended to Vikki while Stefan and Winnie took care of the thug.

Dai and the Rosado brothers walked in ten minutes later and said, "All thirteen men outside are dead. We dragged them all to the back, just in case a neighbor drives by."

"That was good thinking, mate," Avery let out. "Rosado and I will tend to the evidence," Avery shared. "Dai, grab a few large plastic bags and meet us out back." Avery and Rosado stepped out and started disrobing all the men. Dai collected their clothes and personal belongings and placed everything into plastic bags. Afterward, Avery and Rosado took three men out at a time and made a deposit into the bayou. Several hours later, they walked in to see Mick and Yvette cleaning up.

"How is she?" Avery asked.

"She suffered a lot of damage but she's clinging to life."

"Is she going to make it?"

"She's young and strong, so I would say yes."

"She'll pull through," Akachi let out as an absolute. "Look, she has people that love her praying for her recovery." Maggie was sitting by her side holding her hand and Nikki was standing behind her.

"Those two have really bonded," Yvette let out.

"It's just like you and me, huh, Evie?" Winnie said.

"No, it's more than that."

"Okay, we have to go," Maggie's uncle announced.

"Do you remember the plan?"

"Yes."

"Well, go on, repeat it," Nikki commanded.

"Do we have to? We've gone over it like ten times."

"Yes, you do, it will make me feel better."

"Very well, Ms. Labelle. We each take a vehicle. One we'll

sell, the other we'll hide away in case we return. We come back for the other one to use. We use this ammonia inhalant to secretly wake him up before we leave. We burn all his buddies' clothes so he can smell something burning then talk about setting this cabin on fire."

"Good so far," Nikki shared, go on.

"We drive off and talk about what we did with the cars. How we sold one and where we hid the other with the keys. We talk about returning to Santo Domingo without Maggie and our big brother. We repeat how we're going to make the New York crime family pay for killing them. And we talk about the specific information we're going to wring out of our hostage."

"Go on."

"We mention having to stop for gas before we head to the marina and take the boat. We discuss the trip and the days it's going to take us to get home. We stop for gas and fight about leaving our prisoner in the car alone. We check to make sure his hands are secure then we walk away and wait for him to get out and run. Afterward, we pump gas and drive off."

"Is that it?" Nikki questioned.

The brothers looked at each other and respond back, "We think so, why, did we forget something?"

"No, I just wanted to make sure you knew the plan was over."

"Okay, so are we good?" the senior Rosado asked.

"Yes, sir, and remember, no talking—since you're supposed to be dead."

"Of course." Rosado senior cleared his throat and said, "Oh, one more thing. A few years ago there was a rumor that Rogan had been hired to come after us. Is that true?"

"Yes."

"So why are we still here?"

Nikki gave them all an apologetic look then said, "Because your brother sacrificed himself for you. Now, you need to go." The brothers were quiet. They stared at Nikki for maybe fifteen seconds, unsure of what her answer meant and if they should ask for clarification. Instead, they turned and started saying their goodbyes. Someday, the gaps would be filled, but not today.

Everyone said their farewells and Maggie kissed and hugged her uncles and said, "Until we see each other again."

"Goodbye, mija, never forget how much your dad loved you." The Rosado brothers walked out and started their production. Three minutes later, they were gone.

Maggie returned to Vikki's side after her uncles left and sat there for hours.

"Maggie, you're a nervous wreck. Go clean up and I'll sit with her."

"No, I want to be here when she wakes up, you go."

"You know, it could be another six hours or more."

"I don't care, I wanna be here in case she needs something when she wakes up."

Nikki's eye's filled with tears at the sensitivity shown to someone she just met days earlier. She stroked Maggie's hair then placed a hand on her shoulder and said, "Okay, I'm gonna go shower then I'll come back and relieve you."

"Okay."

"A few minutes later, Akachi came by and gave Vikki another injection. Maggie sat there and prayed for her quick recovery. Five minutes later, she heard a voice say, "Maggie, are you there?"

"Yes, I'm here."

"I heard you calling my name."

Maggie wiped tears away then stood up and said, "Were you dreaming about me?"

"I'm not sure, it felt real. You were sitting in a corner crying and calling my name, I was struggling to get to you. But I was so tired."

"Well, you were in a big fight and need to rest now."

"Did I win?"

"Oh my gosh, baby, don't you remember?" Vikki looked at her with a blank stare so Maggie added, "Yes, you most certainly won."

"Was I any good?"

"You were incredible. I'm still in awe over it. I've never seen anything like it. You were like one of those super heroes we see in the movies. I can't believe you went out there by yourself to protect people you didn't even know a few days ago."

"Well, I love you."

Maggie was stunned; she wasn't sure what Vikki meant but

she had to find out. She found herself having a little difficulty breathing but managed to stutter out, "You, you love me?"

"Yes."

"But you barely know me."

"I grew up on the street. I was locked up when I was ten. I've been surrounded by bad people my whole life, so I know a good one when I see it. And you're a good girl."

"Oh my gosh, baby, you're breaking my heart," Maggie announced as she held both hands over her heart and tears filled her eyes again. "I like, so totally love you, too," she added as she wiped a tear away.

"Really?"

"Of course, you risked your life for me and my family. You're the bravest person I have ever known. I didn't think it possible, but I would like so totally switch sides for you."

"Really?"

"Yes."

Vikki stared into Maggie's eyes for a few seconds then said, "So, are you gonna kiss me?"

"Oh God!" Maggie exclaimed, then admitted to herself, *Man, I'm good,* as she leaned in for a kiss. Then to her surprise, she noticed an odd smirk on Vikki's face. Maggie pulled back and said, "Wait, was that a rhetorical question?"

Winnie walked by and said, "Hey, you're up, that's brilliant."

Maggie held up a finger toward Winnie and said, "One second." She turned back to Vikki and asked, "Are you messing with me?"

Winnie touched Vikki's arm and asked, "Are you feeling better, love? Can you sit up?"

"No, she can't sit up, Winnie! And I said one second, please, we're in the middle of something." She turned back to Vikki and said, "Well?" Vikki raised an eyebrow and smiled mischievously.

"Really? You're messing with me? That was pretty mean. I almost kissed you," Maggie stammered out all teary-eyed.

"Sorry."

"Wait, what are you two in to?" Winnie questioned.

Maggie held up a poorly clenched fist and said, "If you weren't on your death bed, I would so totally kill you."

"Dang, Maggie, I said I was sorry. Look, if it will make you feel better, you can kiss me," Vikki stated semi-invitingly.

"Well, now I wouldn't kiss you if you were the last person on Earth."

"That's kinda harsh. But I'm glad you didn't. You might have liked it."

"Hey, you two are off your trolley with this kind of talk," Winnie interjected.

Maggie wound up for a punch and Winnie stepped in. "Okay, that's enough, you two, stop playing around, somebody might get the wrong impression."

"Hey, it's not my fault. She's the crazy one. I'm the one lying here on my death bed."

Maggie grunted at Vikki, and then suddenly recalled Winnie's question again. She turned toward her and asked, "Wait, did you ask Vikki if she could sit up?"

"Yes."

"What is wrong with you? No, she can't sit up! She was shot, and then stabbed in the back like, a few hours ago! She needs to stay in bed and get plenty of rest," Maggie shared in a confused state.

"Well, she looks fine to me," Winnie said, all bubbly. "We're having guests soon, and you don't wanna miss it."

"What guests? And no, she's not fine — she needs to rest."

"Help me up."

"What? You can't be serious. No, you have to rest, baby. You were really hurt. Please stay in bed."

"It's okay, I'm tired but I really feel much better."

Vikki tried sitting up on her own then said "Ow, ow, ow. Well, are you just gonna stand there or are you gonna help me?"

"Oh my goodness, this place is gonna give me a heart attack," Maggie exclaimed as she took hold of Vikki's arm and pulled her to a sitting position.

"Whoa, I'm a little lightheaded. Just hold me for a few seconds." Vikki shook her head than asked, "How long have I been out?"

"About six hours, I think, maybe a little longer."

"Stand me up."

"Oh my gosh, are you crazy? That's it, I'm putting my foot down. You're not getting up until I have a doctor come check you out. And your bandages probably need to be changed."

"Fine, but I don't want anyone else touching me. So you do it."

Maggie stared at Vikki then said, "Fine, but I'm still mad at you. And you stay in bed until I get back."

"Okay."

"Promise me, Vee."

"Geez, I said I would."

"Good. I'll be right back." Maggie scrambled around to get all the supplies she needed then returned to Vikki's side two minutes later. She removed the bandage around Vikki's stomach and to her astonishment; the bullet entry wound was practically healed. "How can this be? Vee, please turn around and lay on your left side. I want to check your back." Vikki laid down and Maggie stared at her back, in a state of bewilderment.

"I don't believe it," Maggie let out.

Vikki turned her head and looked over her shoulder, "What is it, what do you see? Is it bad?"

"No, it's quite the opposite. It looks like you're almost completely healed."

"That's awesome."

"What?"

Vikki scrunched up her eyebrows and gave Maggie a confused look then asked, "Would you prefer that I still be at death's door?"

"Oh my God, no, of course not. How could you say that?" Maggie placed both hands over her heart again then added, "I'm just shocked that you've recovered so quickly."

"I'm sorry, but isn't that a good thing?"

"Yes, of course it is, but I'm still new to this miracle thing happening repeatedly under circumstances that I thought were impossible two days ago."

Suddenly, a bright light filled the room and everyone held a hand up to protect their eyes. Maggie was the first to comment by saying, "Now what?"

Mia stepped out of a portal and said, "Mother."

"I'm here, Mia." Yvette rushed to her side but didn't dare touch her—although she truly longed to do so.

"Mother, they're coming. Please gather everyone around."

Nikki had finished showering and stepped out of the hallway and said, "What was that bright light? And did I miss anything?"

"The light was Evie's daughter, Mia, and no, you didn't miss anything, she just got here," Maggie shared.

"Okay, good. And I'm glad to see you on your feet, sis. And holding on to Maggie no less, nice."

"I'm just tired and she's holding me up is all."

"Right, good one, sis."

"It's true," Maggie let out.

"Gather around, everyone," Yvette announced. Everyone was in a big huddle within seconds.

"Please, sit. I can't stay long and there's a lot to share." Everyone worked on taking a seat and confirming the others were comfortable.

This was the first time many had seen Mia. She could have easily been identified as having the appearance of an angel. She had light almond-colored skin which looked soft and blemish free like that of an infant. Her physical beauty seemed to be enhanced by the semi-fluorescent nature of her skin which seemed to sparkle every so often. She was wearing a light blue asymmetrical tunic and emphasized her neckline, wrists and forearms with what appeared to be diamonds. Mia's hair was long and solid black, which she wore in a braided ponytail pulled in front of a shoulder.

"You are going to receive a few visitors. First, Hilily —" Mia took a few seconds before continuing. "Hilily is a Guardian Archangel and head of its clan." Maggie was holding Vikki's hand and made the sign of the cross with the other. She was sitting on the floor in the back between Vikki and Nikki with Mick to her right. Yvette was sitting in front with three others alongside. And Avery was sitting up front of the remaining other three.

Akachi, when I ask you, please pull Nikki and Vikki off to the side. They will become emotional when Heather arrives. We need to subdue that behavior before she comes. Please take them into the hallway and I will meet you there. Take Maggie with you, Vikki seems to listen to her, Mia thought to Akachi as she continued to speak to everyone else.

Mia also asked Winnie to pull Avery off to the side and provided her with similar instructions specific to Avery.

I understand, Winnie and Akachi thought back.

Mia continued, "Hilily was personally assigned by the Harem Monarch to protect you all. 'The Harem' is what you would refer to as angels. While they look like us, they are not. They are extremely innocent souls even though they have been around for billions of years. And although they have been watching over us since the beginning of the human race, this will be the first time in their existence that they will actually be interacting with corporeal beings in the flesh, as it were. So it's going to be a learning experience for everyone.

"Because of that, I am going to ask that you obey two restrictions—first, do not touch them. They have little experience with that type of human interaction. However, if they initiate physical contact first and if you're comfortable, then please, be yourself. Nevertheless, I warn you—touching a pure spirit will be emotional. And second, do not talk to them unless they talk to you first.

"Now, my next statement is going to sound odd, but all of you are brilliant in your own right. So please, contemplate my statement, and the meaning of my words will be revealed.

"That said, the verbal exchange between you and them will resemble seven-year-old children having a conversation with adults. Half the time, what each of you says to the other will seem completely charming. But during the other half, neither side will have a clue as to what the other is trying to convey. And that is okay. If there is something truly important that you should know, I will bring it to your attention.

"Furthermore, you will also be receiving a visit by a few Saints. Some of which, a few of you have already seen."

Akachi, Winnie, now please, Mia thought.

Akachi got up and walked over to Nikki and Vikki and whispered to them, "Please follow me." Winnie did the same with Avery.

They all stood up and Nikki asked, "What is it, have we done something wrong? This is like, totally unbelievable. I'm not sure we should miss it."

"You've done nothing wrong. And you won't miss it. I promise. Mia just wants to talk to you and Vikki separately." Akachi looked down at Maggie who had tears in her eyes and added, "You, too, Maggie, come." Winnie had a similar conversation with Avery although he didn't seem to need much convincing. Perhaps it was his feelings for Winnie that allowed him to trust her on a subject matter which several days earlier he would have categorized as lunacy. Or maybe he had been around bad people his entire life and those around him today possessed qualities of kindness and compassion he didn't realize still existed.

Maggie stood up and they all stepped into the hallway. "Nikki, do you remember telling me that your daughter, Heather, was taken?"

"Yes, of course."

"What's he talking about, Nikki?"

"I'm sorry, Vee, but it's really important that you listen, please. Everything will become clear in a few minutes," Akachi said in a serene voice. Maggie squeezed Vikki's hand as she held her arm with another.

"Do you remember that I told you Heather wasn't taken, that she was raptured?"

"Yes."

"Raptured, as in Christianity's Rapture?" Vikki questioned.

Maggie squeezed Vikki's hand and arm again and said, "Vee, please listen. I'm going to faint or have a heart attack or something if I don't understand what's happening. So can you please hold your questions to the end and just listen?"

Vikki shook her head then turned toward Maggie to see a sad pouty face with a quivering bottom lip. Vikki had no choice but to surrender with a sigh. She reached up and gently pinched Maggie's chin then smiled and said, "Okay."

Nikki thought *WHAT*? Then tilted her head and looked at Vikki for a few seconds with a huge question mark on her face and asked, "Really, what is up with you two?"

"Nothing," Vikki replied.

Nikki shook her head then turned back to Akachi and said, "I'm so sorry, please go on."

"No problem, so, do you remember that I said I had friends that could help you see Heather again?" Vikki and Maggie took a deep breath and covered their mouths.

Nikki replied, "Yes," and then did the same.

"Well, these are the friends I was talking about." Suddenly, Mia was in the hallway with them. Akachi looked back and saw that Mia was also still in the living room.

"Incredible," Akachi muttered under his breath.

"Heather is coming here?" Nikki muttered out in the form of a question as tears filled her eyes.

"Yes," Mia replied. She took a few minutes to explain why Heather's memories had been manipulated. But since the girls were such young and curious spirits, a familiar face among alleged strangers would generate questions. So they were warned to try and avoid the topic, if possible. At the end, Nikki and Vikki seemed to be at peace.

Mia, Winnie and Avery had a similar discussion. Avery found himself sensing a nervousness he seldom experienced. Nevertheless, he was looking forward to seeing Holly up close for the first time in his life without having to hide. *If it's only for today, I will be okay with that,* Avery confessed to himself then wiped a tear away.

Mia finished by saying, "Please join the others." They started back toward the living room but Nikki purposely lagged behind. She turned around to hug and thank Mia. As soon as she touched her, Nikki felt a deep remorse about everything she had done in her past then saw a bright light and fainted. When she finally woke up, she found herself sitting in the living room with everyone else as though she had never left.

"Okay, one more thing. I understand that all of you are going to be desperate to embrace the familiar face you once knew, just like my mother has been frantic to hug me. Please do your best to resist until —" Mia waved her hand and was gone.

Yvette's knees buckled at Mia's disappearance but she caught herself before falling then covered her face and cried. Suddenly, her feelings of loneliness and desperation were replaced by feelings of harmony and joy she had seldom felt. When Yvette opened her eyes again, she found herself in Mia's embrace and was so overwhelmed with emotion that she couldn't speak. Yvette squeezed her tight and never wanted the moment to end. She felt glorious. A few seconds later Yvette heard, *I love you, too, Mummy,* then Mia was gone. With a trembling hand, Yvette covered her mouth and wept.

A few minutes later, Winnie walked by and said, "You okay, Evie?"

"Yes, I'm just trying to recover from this emotional rollercoaster we've all been exposed to over the last few days."

"Brilliant, me, too. The last few days have been completely mental."

"Yes, it has, and it's probably going to intensify before it calms down."

"Well, I hope not, but in either case, I suppose I'm ready."

"Me, too."

Moments later, a bright light filled the living room again. Hilily was the first to step out of the glow followed by Artemis, Holly, and Juno. They were all dressed similar to Mia, in asymmetrical, hooded, tunic-like gowns. The garments had long trains that seemed to float behind the wearer. It was worn off the right shoulder but attached at the waist leaving part of their belly exposed. Everyone seemed to be wearing what appeared to be sandals with the exception of Artemis. Even though the radiant beauty of everyone in the room was hard to ignore, Artemis's foot apparel could not be overlooked. It seemed a little out of place but it gave her presence power. Of all the celestial beings there, she looked the most intimidating.

As soon as Avery saw Holly, he stepped forward and said, "Blimey." When Holly heard that word, she stepped toward him and sounded a noticeable, "Whoa!"

Holly covered her mouth. The face she saw had crawled out of her subconscious mind to possess the face of every male image she had ever placed on canvas. The resemblance was frightening. Holly took a moment to center herself then moved in closer and said, "Hi."

Avery stood there in silence for a few seconds then said, "Hi, poppet."

"Sir, do you know me?"

"I'd like to say that I do, but I'll leave it at I'd like to get to know you."

"Your face is worn around the edges and you look sad."

"Perhaps you can change that?"

"I believe that I can," Holly returned with an innocent child-like voice with a British accent. Holly could see the tears forming in Avery's eyes.

"Sir, would you like me to try?" Holly questioned. Before

Avery could respond, Holly started receiving immense feelings of longing and absence from him. She looked around the room and the same feelings were present in everyone there. Those sensations were also accompanied by strong emotional ties toward specific pairings of individuals in the room. Holly let out another, "Whoa! Why do I get the feeling that everyone here is related?"

"Were we—are we?"

"You tell me, poppet."

"Sir, if you allow me to touch you, I will know."

"Then perhaps you shouldn't," Avery replied as a tear rolled down his face.

"That's not a no," Holly announced as she moved in and embraced him. Within seconds, her altered memory engrams were wiped away and her recollections snapped back like a taught rubberband had been released—she recalled everything. Tears filled her eyes and Holly exclaimed, "Papa?" in the form of a question.

"Yes, poppet." Avery felt enormous remorse for having wasted his life serving a master that took everything and gave nothing back. He cried for the first time in thirteen years.

"Where have you been?" Holly asked with a sense of melancholy.

"I've been insane. Could you ever find it in your heart to forgive me?"

"Yes, it is done."

"Well, I'm not sure I will ever be able to forgive myself," Avery confessed.

Holly pushed him at arm's length and said, "Your mind has been snared by malignant pits of regret and despair. But hear this, he who cometh after me shall set you free. And all you need do is ask."

"I'm afraid it might be too late for me."

Holly shook her head and said, "Father, cast off thy shackles, for they give power to an evil master."

A few seconds later, Hikiko stepped out of the light followed by Heather, Charlotte, and Samantha. They arrived with supplies—clean clothes for everyone and a nutritional supplement.

Sophia slowly approached Charlotte and Samantha while picking up Yvette on the way. She placed a vice-like grip on Yvette's hand and uttered out, "Evie, I feel like I'm going to pass out."

"Just relax and take a few deep breaths. Everything will be all right. I promise."

"You were true to your word. I so much wanted to believe you weren't insane when you said I would see my babies again. Now, among other things, I feel ashamed for having doubted you."

"Please, let's focus on the present—there is too much wonder taking place that if we don't focus, we'll miss it. Does that make sense?"

"Yes, but please don't let me go."

"Okay, but as a warning, I may pass out also."

Samantha was holding Charlotte's hand when she let out, "Wow, this place feels intense." Then Charlotte saw Sophia and started walking toward her.

"Ma'am, we feel as though we should know you. Do we look familiar to you as well?"

Sophia clung to Yvette's arm for dear life. Tears filled her eyes and she started trembling. Yvette felt she had to reduce the tension so she said, "Perhaps a better question would be, would you like to get to know her?"

Samantha and Charlotte tilted their heads ever so slightly and Sam said, "You're a supportive friend. Although, I deduce your answer to our question is more evasive than suggestive."

"Your logic is most impressive," Yvette humbly replied. "Although a bit circumstantial."

"Not really," Samantha was quick to retort.

"Why would you say that?"

"Because you said it and she didn't," Samantha replied as an absolute.

"You're truly brilliant. Are there any among you who are not mental virtuosos?" Yvette asked rhetorically.

Samantha and Charlotte looked at each other than Sam answered, "Charlotte is the smart one."

Holly mentally communicated to Charlotte that Sophia was in distress. Charlotte stepped forward and said, "Ma'am, you're in pain. If you take my hand, I shall help you bear it."

"What if it's too ugly?" Sophia whimpered out then reached up to cover up her mouth and stop her snivels.

Samantha stepped forward and added, "Then I shall help

you bear the weight as well."

"You girls are magnificent," Yvette exclaimed as she let go of Sophia to cover up her mouth and stop the torrential downpour of tears that was imminent.

Sophia felt lightheaded and lost her footing, but both Charlotte and Samantha reached out and held her up. Within seconds, their altered memory engrams were reverted and the two girls remembered everything.

"Mother!" Samantha exclaimed, causing Sophia to faint after hearing the word. Yvette rushed forward to help the girls set her down gently.

Samantha sat down on the floor and placed Sophia's head on her lap. Charlotte kneeled down and sat back on her heals, holding her newly discovered mother's hand. Yvette excused herself and stepped away.

Akachi was talking to Nikki, Vikki and Maggie when Artemis approached with Heather. Nikki's heart was beating so hard that she felt the pulses in her throat. Vikki squeezed Maggie's hand like a vice, making her squeal out, "Ow, ow, ow, that's too tight, too tight, too tight," as she tapped the back of her hand.

Artemis stopped in front of Maggie to hear her say, "I love your boots."

"Most people say that when they meet me."

"Probably because they're noticeable. Visually it makes you look unique and intimidating," Maggie added.

"I look intimidating?"

"Oh yeah, you look totally fierce."

Artemis tilted her head and thought about Maggie's comment for a moment then said, "Perhaps I should consider removing them and putting on what everyone else is wearing."

"Nonsense, it's part of your swagger, plus, you're the only one wearing them so that says volumes."

"Really, like what?"

"Like it's a warning to anyone that may confront you," Maggie confessed.

Artemis looked at Heather then turned back to Maggie and asked, "What warning?"

"That your power comes from within."

"Whoa, she's unusually perceptive, huh, Missy?"

Artemis nodded her head in agreement."

Heather looked at Nikki who was still choked up and asked, "You look familiar. Should I know you?"

"Yes, I'm your mother," Nikki blurted out then covered her mouth.

Heather shook her head then shot back, "Did I just hear you correctly?"

"Yes," Vikki confirmed then also covered her mouth.

"Well, that went well," Maggie said then added, "I'm sorry, she wasn't supposed to tell you that, but she's missed you so. Anyway, maybe we should sit down."

"Sure," Heather replied while looking at Nikki who had tears streaming down her face then added, "but first, take my hand, I want to see for myself."

"I can't do that. My life is filled with horrors, misery and sorrow. If I take your hand you may see more than you should."

Heather tilted her head ever so slightly and said, "Fear not, for I am not here to judge you."

"That may be true, but I gave you up so that you would have a better life. I've spent my whole life in the darkness, even though I'm afraid of the dark, so that you would grow up supported and loved. If I show you, it may steal your innocence. And I would rather die than see that happen." Maggie and Vikki were standing on either side of Nikki, stroking her back to offer comfort and support while they wiped tears away.

Suddenly, Artemis lost all the expression on her face, floated up and began to glow. In a deep, vibrating voice, she declared, "I am a Guardian of the holy Harem Imperial Monastic Order, and the first of my kind. I have faced a legion of Satan's hordes on the battle field. And I have tasted the ash of those vanquished from battle in the air. I have fought its second in command and bear the scars of that combat upon my flesh." Artemis touched her neck as she remembered the event. "I have seen the façade of true evil and have felt its breath against my skin. I was forged in fire then quenched in holy water and ordained to bring death upon the wicked." Artemis lowered herself to the ground and stared Nikki down before adding, "Trust me when I say, Heather has nothing to fear from you. So, take her hand. I will protect her innocence, if required."

Vikki was in awe and speechless. Nikki wasn't breathing

and Maggie thought she was going to faint. Artemis placed a hand on Heather's shoulder as she reached out her hand. Maggie made the sign of the cross repeatedly, and Akachi seemed curiously unaffected—perhaps because his instincts told him he had nothing to fear, or his inner peace provided comfort regardless of his surroundings.

Nikki reached out and took Heather's hand. A few seconds later, Artemis asked, "Telly, what do you see?"

"What she says is true, Missy. She's my mother."

"Now that's interesting. It's a story I hope to be present to hear when it's revealed. But for now, I shall go and leave you to your discovery. Be at peace." Artemis was wearing a small smirk upon her face when she looked at Nikki and Vikki, who were still motionless, and said, "Heed my words, cast off the shackles that bind you to this world. Confess your misgivings and sin no more. And perhaps someday you may join me on the battle field to protect all that is righteous—as Guardians."

Artemis leaned in and said to Heather while looking at Maggie, "I like her—she's different somehow."

"Whoa. Wait, I see it now. You're right," Heather exclaimed.

Artemis walked away and Maggie let out, "Oh my gosh, she's intense."

"I'm sorry, but Missy can be a little over protective."

"A little?" Maggie exclaimed. "Look at me, I'm shaking. I almost peed myself."

Heather stepped forward and said, "Maggie, you should know that she doesn't like anybody when she initially meets them. You're the first."

"Whoa, I guess I'm, I'm, I'm touched," Maggie stuttered out.

"Now, you guys didn't think Missy was too overbearing, did you?"

"If I'm honest, I did find her to be a little intimidating," Vikki shared.

"A little?" Maggie repeated.

"Well, on a positive note, she's named you two future Guardians."

"Okay, so what does that mean and who is she?" Vikki questioned.

"Artemis is said to be the future head of the Harem Imperial

Forces."

"I'm sorry, but that doesn't help. Can you be more specific? She's obviously hair-raising but, she seems so young."

"Well, the story goes that on the forbidden planet, a level-three Helem—that's a Demon to you—easily killed over one hundred well-armed soldiers during an attack. A level-three Demon is usually a mimic and uses camouflage to confuse their opponents because they're the weakest of Helucifer's forces."

"Who's Helucifer?" Vikki asked.

"Satan, right?" Maggie stated in the form of a question.

"Yes, that's correct," Heather confirmed, a little surprised.

"How did you know that?" Vikki asked in amazement.

"I guessed. Helucifer sounds a lot like Lucifer, hence Satan.

Vikki swallowed hard as Heather continued with the story. "Artemis was able to fight off thousands of level-one Helem by hand. A level-one Helem is the most experienced, some with billions of years of training on the battle field. And Artemis faced them all with only two days to prepare."

Nikki, Vikki and Maggie stood there with their mouths open as Heather continued. "Maggie, you were right. Artemis is unique. Her power was granted by the Almighty before the birth of her ancestral lineage."

Vikki shook the stunned feelings off and said, "I feel like I should have bowed at her feet."

"Me, too," Nikki added.

Maggie just kept making the sign of the cross.

In hopes of comforting the startled girls, Heather added, "Artemis is quite gentle, playful and loving. You'll see. And under no circumstances are you to bow at her feet. She wouldn't like that. And you might wanna stay on her good side." The three girls looked over at Artemis again and noticed a stone cold look but when she turned to meet their gaze, she smiled. The girls took a sigh of relief.

"Well, I still think she's intense," Maggie exclaimed while holding a hand to her chest.

"Yeah, and she likes you. So imagine if she didn't," Heather shared with a small chuckle.

"I'm sorry for asking but why do some of you look ruffled up?" Maggie questioned.

"Maggie! What's wrong with you?" Vikki chastised her question then looked at Heather and said, "You have to excuse her. She's a little preoccupied with the outward human facade." She looked at Maggie again and added, "It's call vanity."

"I'm sorry, but they're girls," Maggie replied, displaying a pouty face.

"It's okay. Do you mean our windswept appearance?" Heather asked for clarity.

"Yes." Maggie was quick to retort while Vikki was pulling her arm back.

"Are you sure you wanna know?"

"No," Vikki shot back.

"Sure, why not?" Maggie eagerly answered. A decision she would later regret.

"Well, in its simplest terms, we split up into teams of four and take turns battling off the one thousand legions of Helucifer's hordes set against you twelve zealots."

"Sent against us? Wait, what's a legion?" Maggie questioned.

"Six thousand soldiers," Vikki answered.

"Wait," Maggie interjected, "So like four of you fight six thousand times one thousand demons? At once? For us?"

"Yes."

"But that's like a million demons."

"Six million, actually." Heather expressed as a correction.

"That can't be right. Can it?" Vikki asked for clarity.

"Yes. And we do it everyday," Heather replied.

"How, why? Why is that necessary? And why would you do that? For us? We're nobodies." Vikki asked in bewilderment.

"Because it's been ordained. And I assure you, the twelve of you are more important than you realize."

They were stunned. As the girls stared blankly into empty space, Akachi excused himself. After a few more seconds, Maggie stated, "Heather, those odds don't seem fair at all. Why don't you guys get some help?"

"We have Hilily and many within her clan make themselves available when needed. But soon the Orlov clan will be joining us."

"Who are they?" Maggie asked with a wrinkled brow.

"We have no idea. But many refer to them as the 'Mighty

Eagles'."

"That's a cool name," Maggie cried out.

"I know right? It's so fun." Heather exclaimed with glee.

Vikki held Maggie close then said, "The name sounds a little off-putting. So, I would suggest caution around them." Heather was surprised at Vikki's comment but decided not to question her uncertainty. The four of them sat down and continued talking.

Akachi kept the information about Satan's hordes to himself, for now. Everyone had enough to worry about. He walked over to help Yvette and Winnie comfort Stefan who desperately wanted to see his children. Stefan wasn't sure why everyone else had their offspring present and his were excluded. Hilily walked over to Stefan and said, "Sir, because you were a non-believer prior to the Rapture, your progeny had no foundation to base their new reality. Therefore, removing them from their current safe environment would be detrimental to their development. However, Heather has information and a visual record of your young. If you allow her a little time, she will disclose that evidence to you."

"Thank you."

"Do you have any questions?"

"I so wanted to hold their little hands and hug them. Is it fair to say that I will not have that opportunity today?"

"Yes, sir, you will see them again soon, but not today," Hilily shared then walked away.

Dai, Adadi and Mick were sitting down listening to Akachi explain what they were witnessing and how he thought it all came together. They still had doubts but every time they looked around and saw the glowing presence of so many celestial beings, their reservations were chipped away.

An hour later, Heather excused herself from her family reunion and walked over to Stefan. She cast a portal through time and space to show him past and present articulating images of his three children—studying, playing and exploring multiple facets of their artistic persona. They appeared to be in a loving, caring and peaceful environment like none they had ever known. Their surroundings were surreal, picture-perfect Norman Rockwell projections against Bob Ross landscapes. Heather generated a visual record of his offspring and transferred the optical file to Stefan's mobile device for future viewings.

"Can I transfer this record to my wife?"

"Yes. The optical file is yours to do with as you wish. I hope they bring you comfort and faith in what is to come," Heather shared then started walking away as Stefan thanked her repeatedly. "You're most welcome," she replied.

Stefan sent the file to his wife with a short note that read, "I found them—our children are safe." Stefan received a call moments later then spent more time than expected trying to recap for his wife everything that had led to his children's discovery. He tried desperately not to sound too crazy or like a converted religious zealot. At the end, he was at peace since his efforts seemed well received by his wife.

As everyone joined in the fellowship, Artemis felt a longing to speak to Vikki and Juno to Maggie. They held hands and approached them.

"Oh gosh, she's coming this way," Maggie let out as she clung to Vikki's arm.

"It's okay, she won't hurt you."

"It's not me I'm worried about," Maggie announced as Artemis and Juno stopped at their side.

"Vikki, I feel as though I should know you. May I touch you?" Artemis requested as she witnessed Maggie squeeze Vikki's arm even harder.

"If you wish, but I warn you, you may not like what you see."

Juno held out her hand and looked at Maggie, "Take my hand."

Artemis and Maggie reached out simultaneously. As their hands drew closer, Heather snapped her head around just as she felt Artemis and Juno's contact was imminent. Heather reached out her own hand from across the room and yelled, "No!" But it was too late. Artemis had touched Vikki and Juno, Maggie.

"How can this be?" both Artemis and Juno exclaimed as they drew in the longest breaths of their lives.

Heather's scream and the loud reaction of astonishment from Artemis and Juno drew everyone's attention in the room. All eyes were fixed on Artemis and Juno when suddenly the room heard both girls exclaim, "MOTHER!"

CHAPTER 22

Reynolds Returns to Miami

REYNOLDS BOARDED THE BOEING 757 M-1 AND THE PILOT SET A course for Miami, Florida. Reynolds looked at his watch and thought, *It's as good a time as any*. He decided to call Filip and provide an update. He pulled out a Thuraya XT Dual 5 satellite phone, took a deep breath, and dialed the number.

"Reynolds, I've been waiting some time to hear from you."

"Yes, my Lord, I apologize for the delay. But these fanatics are more elusive than I ever anticipated. I hate to admit it but I, like everyone else, have underestimated them. I initially thought their resistance would be crushed by the sheer might of our will. Unfortunately, the abundance of resources set against them has only strengthened their resolve and made them more determined."

"Stop praising these proselytized zealots and report. What news do you have?"

"Yes, of course. Well, Dr. Milagro and Dr. Chow Lee were being held in Guantanamo Bay. Somehow, after three days of torture and when they were at their most vulnerable, they were able to solicit help from within and use that assistance to escape. I paid the site a visit and held those responsible accountable. The facility is now under new management."

"Go on."

"Yes, my Lord, I followed Akachi to Bangui, Africa. Regrettably, shortly after our arrival, he was alerted to our presence and fled north. Our pursuit led us to a small town just south of Beboura, where we managed to surround him. By some miracle, he and a few others killed fifty percent of my team before eluding capture."

"How is that possible? I assigned you the best assassins money could buy."

"I'm sorry, my Lord, but are you referring to Labelle Rogan?"

"Yes, of course."

"Well, sir, Labelle Rogan never showed up."

"Reynolds, you must be joking. Rogan called me before you left Warsaw and informed me that everyone was aboard your aircraft. I also received a text when you landed safely in Miami. Afterward, Labelle provided an update when you destroyed the computer systems at Jackson Memorial to eliminate the geneticists' findings."

"Well, I've never seen him so he must be working in the shadows."

"He?! Reynolds, you can't be serious, Labelle Rogan is not a man," Filip let out, followed by several seconds of strong verbal abuse. "It's two women. How can you not know that? Nikki and Vikki are both visually impossible to ignore." Reynolds was mystified and dove into recent memories. He had a flashback of his initial encounter with the girls and their performance during every engagement.

"Reynolds, are you still with me?"

"Yes, sir, I apologize. I'm not sure I know what to say. This information comes as a huge shock."

"Well, pull yourself together."

"Yes, sir, it's just that Labelle Rogan turning out to be two women is stupefying. But now that I give the concept a little thought, I realize it's brilliant. It's the perfect cover. Rogan was known for sending out a woman to negotiate its contracts. And now I realize that in support of this persona, the other would be out in the field ready to pounce if negotiations went sideways. This explains so much."

"Really?"

"Yes, sir. For years, the justice department had very little to go on, other than a name. Many in law enforcement considered Labelle Rogan to be a myth, created by leaders within organized crime here in America. Most thought they were using this phantom to drive fear into the hearts of the drug cartel leadership and its members. And perhaps to even a greater extent, the many nefarious global organizations which posed a threat to their criminal enterprises from abroad.

"So?" When Reynolds didn't answer Filip yelled, "Reynolds!" trying to wake up a now enamored servant.

Reynolds was lost in thought again. He had been a New York City police officer in the organized crime division for almost two decades. He started thinking back to the reports he had read and crime scenes investigated just a few years prior to his retirement from the NYPD. Labelle Rogan was only used when an entire organization had to be eradicated.

"Yes, my Lord, I apologize. I was just thinking back to old unsolved cases in New York. There were multiple cases where men were assassinated in the same room by an assailant using hand-to-hand combat. I witnessed this same type of professionalism firsthand multiple times in my short exposure with Nikki. I'm not sure why I failed to put the pieces together, until now."

"Didn't you read the dossier on Labelle Rogan?"

"Yes, sir, but since there was no picture or mention of a gender, I obviously overlooked important details. Of course, it didn't help that I had my own preconceived notion of who this person was."

"So, now that that's cleared up for you, where are our draconians?"

"I'm afraid they have turned against us."

"What?!" Filip yelled as anger filled his throat. And now, in the back of his mind there was a hint of concern for the mission's success.

"Reynolds, listen to me carefully. I need to know exactly what happened. It's critical we get them back on our side or terminate them before they lash out. And I prefer it not be the latter."

"Yes, sir. Well, it all started when we arrived at an orphanage in Africa where Akachi's presence had been reported. After asking the caretaker some questions, I realized she was lying to me. I ordered Nikki to use one of the orphans as motivation to extract the truth. Unfortunately, she resisted and I asked Vikki to intervene. When she too refused, I shot her and went after Nikki."

Filip was enraged. "Reynolds, I thought you said you read the dossier?"

"Yes, sir, I did."

"Then why were you confused? It clearly spelled out that under no circumstances were you to threaten children or defenseless women in Labelle Rogan's presence. And you were most assuredly asked never to ask them to do so."

"Like I stated earlier, my Lord, I didn't connect these two to our assassin."

"Reynolds, you better pray my inside man can fix this or the next time we meet, I'm gonna show you the meaning of pain." Filip took a long pause before continuing, "You better make this right. Do you understand me?"

"Yes, sir, I do—and I will." Reynolds did not want to repeat a torturous session at the hands of his henchmen. Once in a lifetime was enough.

"You better. Now, where are they?"

"I'm not certain, but I have my staff working on establishing their whereabouts. I feel confident they will be found quickly."

The line went silent while Filip subdued his anger then he said, "Do not fail me again, and under no circumstances are you to kill them without my expressed permission—which you currently do not have. Is that absolutely clear?"

"Yes, sir." Filip hung up the telephone and all Reynolds could do was focus on his misfortune. He had made a catastrophic mistake and somehow he had to make it right.

Forty-five minutes later, Reynolds' Boeing 757 M-1 landed in the Miami International Airport. Ginger had a driver waiting to bring him to police headquarters. En route, he received a call.

"Hi, Ginger."

"Good afternoon, sir." She wanted to ask him how his trip to Africa turned out. But since Nikki and Vikki didn't answer their phones, she assumed the worst.

"What news do you have, Ms. Ginger?"

"Well, sir, we received a call from the head nurse working at the Jackson Memorial emergency room. Dr. Milagro and another woman arrived there several days ago requiring emergency treatment. Dr. Ruben removed a bullet from the woman's chest and later moved them both to the ICU ward. The local police were dispatched but when they searched the hospital, they discovered Dr. Milagro and the other never arrived at ICU. Apparently, Mick Ruben and a nurse, Margarita Rosado, left the hospital and took the two fugitives with them."

"Why would they do that?"

"I'm not sure, but they did. Anyway, the police dispatched every available patrol car to locate and arrest the escapees. The fugitives were quickly located and our attempt to apprehend them was drawing to a close, until —" Suddenly, Ginger's line went silent.

"Let me guess. The car and our fugitives simply disappeared."

"Yes, sir."

Reynolds clenched the phone tight in his hand and beat it on his leg for ten seconds then took a deep breath and said, "Go on."

"Well sir, I spoke to the head nurse and she told me that Dr. Ruben and Ms. Rosado have never been late to work in their tenure, let alone absent. So there's little hope that they'll be returning voluntarily."

"Yeah, I figured that, so where are they?"

"Well, sir, I talked to Dr. Ruben's parents several days ago and they hadn't heard from their son in almost a week."

"Call them again."

"Yes, sir, I called them again this morning and they told me he was staying with a friend in a cabin in the Everglades."

"Did they have an address?"

"No, sir, but we believe it's a property belonging to the nurse."

"And?"

"Well, I checked with the city and there was no record of a property belonging to a Margarita Rosado. I had the tax assessor's office check the ownership records of every property in the Everglades."

"Wow, that seems a bit excessive, but go on."

"I'm sorry, sir, I just wanted to be thorough."

"I understand, you did the right thing. Go on."

"Thank you, sir. Well, of the original three million acres in the historic Everglades, the northern one million acres were designated the Everglades Agricultural Area, so there are no homes there. Today, most of this land is used to raise sugarcane. The southern one point five million acres of the original Everglades were dedicated in 1947 as a national park, so there are no houses there either. The remaining five hundred thousand acres, located in the middle of the historic Everglades, became a water conservation area with a system of canals, dams and dikes used to control the flooding in and around large Florida cities. Therefore, there are few houses there also. However, few homes means there are fifty thousand versus a half million."

"Stop. That's too much information. Just tell me. Did you find them?" Reynolds asked seemingly impatient.

"No, sir." Reynolds went to beat the cellular against his thigh again when he heard, "But we're close."

"What was that?"

"I said we were close. I was able to limit our search from fifty thousand homes to just under a thousand. I dispatched multiple teams of investigators to canvas the remaining properties. So far, half of them have been removed from our list. So I feel confident we will find their whereabouts before nightfall."

Reynolds looked at his watch and said. "That's excellent news, Ms. Ginger. However, may I suggest that in the future, you lead with the end results? And if I want additional details, I will simply ask you for them, okay?"

"Yes, sir. And again, I sincerely apologize. I just wanted you to know that I was being thorough."

"I understand, and again, thank you for doing such a great job." Reynolds was being a little more cautious dispensing verbal disciplinary action. He needed his team to remain focused and loyal.

"Ms. Ginger, I'll be arriving soon. Please have an assortment of contacts on my desk for military trained civilians and soldiers for hire when I arrive. We need to gather additional support and I plan to be ready when we find our fugitives."

"Yes, sir."

"Please make sure I am not disturbed. Timing is everything and I want to focus." Reynolds thought about it for a few more seconds then added, "And text me the first five contacts."

"Yes, sir."

Reynolds arrived at police headquarters thirty-five minutes later and walked straight into his office and closed the door behind him. He had made contact with three of the five names provided and had fifteen additional contacts sitting on his desk when he arrived. By the time news came in on his fugitives, he had generated the support he required. Two hundred men were now on standby.

The telephone rang and as soon as Reynolds placed the receiver to his ear, he heard Ginger exclaim, "We have them."

"Where are they?"

"In a cabin about an hour west of Miami."

"Are you certain?"

"Yes, sir, we received an anonymous tip, but I vetted the call myself."

"That's all I need. Give me the address." Ginger provided him the location and he passed on the coordinates to his two hundred hired soldiers. He then got up and was on the road.

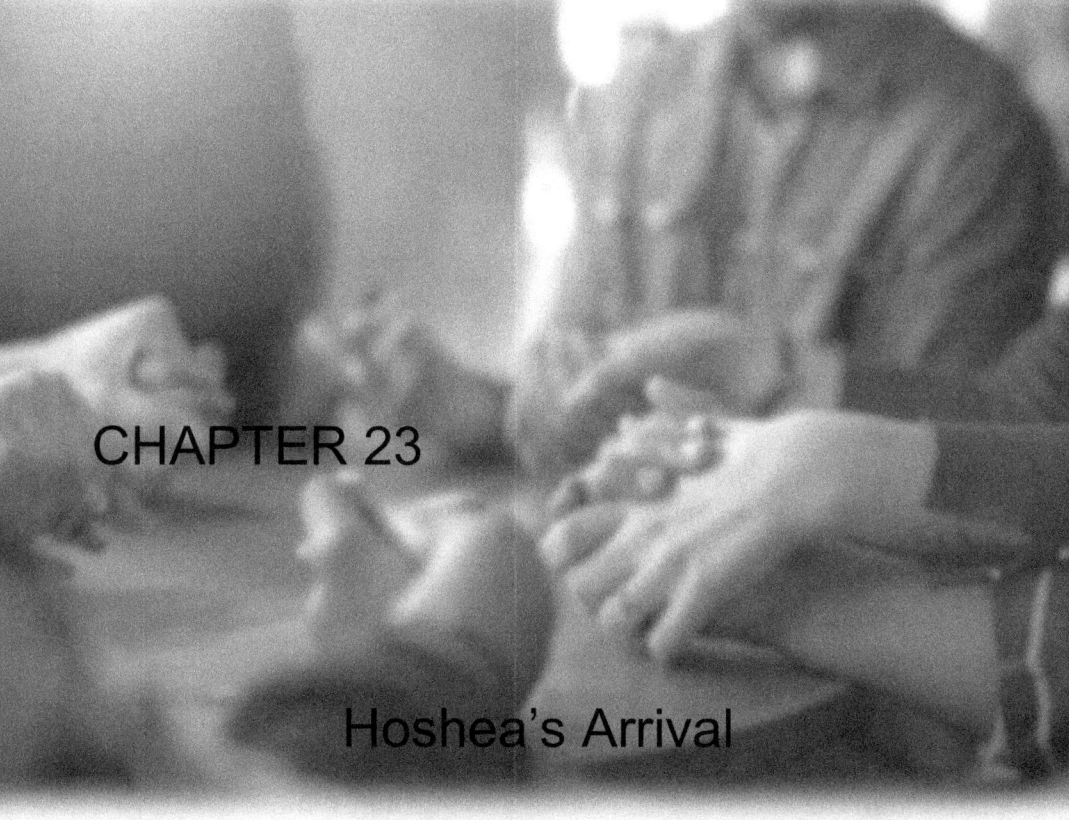

CHAPTER 23

Hoshea's Arrival

ARTEMIS AND JUNO WERE IN SHOCK. THEIR NEWFOUND revelation had placed everything they believed to be true about their parents in question. Artemis let go of Vikki's hand and reached out for Juno's. Juno released her grip on Maggie and took hold of her sister's hand. They looked at each other and Juno asked, "What does this mean, Army?"

"First, let me confirm that this changes nothing between us."

Juno squeezed Artemis's hands then replied, "Agreed."

"Second, we are still sisters."

"Yes, Army. Always. Nothing can change that." Maggie covered up her mouth to hold back the wave of emotions. Vikki did the same. She was close to tears for the first time in over a decade.

"Third, since we have no memory of a mother, this information doesn't alter a preexisting relationship."

Juno took a deep breath then let it out slowly and said, "Agreed."

"And finally," Artemis turned toward Vikki and said, "We now have the mother we've always wanted. And there can't be anything wrong with that."

The girls hugged each other then returned their gazes back toward their respective mothers. Maggie was in tears but Vikki had only shed a single tear which was slowly rolling down her face. She was, nevertheless, desperate to hold her newfound daughter and so was Maggie. Both Artemis and Juno leaned in and at the same time, jumped on their new mothers and embraced them for what seemed like an eternity. Vikki started crying profusely and Maggie was a blubbering mess. Both Artemis and Juno simultaneously thought, *Mummy, I have missed you so – you can't possibly know.*

And I have missed you, more than you will ever know. I'm so sorry I wasn't there for you, Vikki thought.

But you're here now, and that's what matters.

And I have missed you, mija, Maggie thought.

A few seconds later, they all walked into the living room and sat down. Artemis said, "Mother, tell me everything." Juno asked Maggie the same question but asked her to wait until Vikki was done with her confession. Nikki walked over with Heather and sat down next to Vikki. All Nikki could think about was, *Vikki has a daughter she's never mentioned – extraordinary.* Everyone else gathered around in the kitchen area, although Yvette and Winnie were dying to know what had happened. Sophia and Adadi's attention was focused elsewhere. Sophia was engrossed in her two girls and Adadi was contemplating the condition of the ten children she had left behind.

Akachi walked up behind her and offered some comforting words which made her feel more at peace. Everyone else was engaged with Hilily and Hikiko who were busy telling past stories and their belief of what was to come.

Avery walked over with Holly and sat down next to Nikki just as Vikki got into her history.

"I got involved with a boy while in juvie. I don't really remember how old we were when we met. Plus, it's not important. Anyway, he looked after me and kept me safe. He told me he loved me but that I deserved better than him. I was alone and surrounded by mean, hateful people. He treated me like I was special. It was nice to think that someone cared. Anyway, in a moment of weakness, I pressured him with my advances. Although at first, he truly resisted, that only made me want him more. At the end I pleaded and he surrendered himself to me. And I got pregnant.

When he found out, he was overwhelmed with feelings of guilt and despair at his weakness.

"'This is no place to raise a child,' he said. 'They will take it away.'

"He tried to tell me what would happen but I didn't believe him. He told me that he would make it right and find a way to look after you. Anyway, he left the penal system and I never saw him again. I gave birth to you just before my nineteenth birthday. When they told me you were a girl, I named you Artemis—after the Olympian goddess of the hunt. They took you away seconds after you were born. I never even got to hold you. Something I desperately wanted to do. I never cried so much in my life. And I have never cried since, until today." Nikki and Maggie were both in tears holding Vikki's hand. Artemis placed her hand on top of the others and her serenity helped bring peace to the emotionally traumatized hearts. "I have never told that story to anyone."

"Mother," Artemis said, "I'm here now. And my past life was a great one. I was raised by a good man—a Saint named Axel Cuban. I was loved and cared for. I never knew hunger or loneliness or despair. I was never exposed to pain or suffering. I lived my life in total peace until the Rapture. And even to this day, he still watches over me."

"Axel Cuban was his name?" Vikki asked with a look of amazement.

"Yes, why?"

Vikki tilted her head ever so slightly and said, "I know that name."

"What does that mean?" Artemis questioned.

"What I mean is that Axel was the name of the boy."

"What boy?"

"My first love those many years ago. And to this day, I have never loved another."

"I know that name, too," Maggie added.

"What?" Artemis declared. "How can that be?"

"I met a boy with that same name in a hospital many years ago."

"That's so odd," Juno added. "It's not a very common name."

By now, Yvette and Winnie had made their way to the living

room.

"So is the Axel you two know the same one who still tends to these girls?" Yvette asked Vikki and Maggie.

"I'm not sure, but I'd like to hear Maggie's story," Vikki said.

Maggie was ashamed of her past actions and didn't really want to confess. However, she realized the truth was bound to come out. Therefore, she decided to share her past weaknesses and transgressions as part of her atonement.

"There's nothing special about my story. It's like I said, I met a boy named Axel many years ago. I was working — well, more like volunteering as a candy striper in a hospital in New York City. I used the position to gain access to medical supplies for my dad and uncles. Plus, it was a good way to meet nice boys. I was always surrounded by the worse sort. Anyway, Axel worked there as part of the hospital security. He was so nice and handsome and shy. He was totally charming."

Just then, Vikki punched Maggie on the arm.

"Ow, what the hell? That hurt."

"Sorry, but you were getting sidetracked," Vikki shared.

"Well, that really hurt."

"I said I was sorry, you big baby. Now go on with your story."

Maggie massaged her right arm a little longer then said, "Well, where was I?"

"He was totally charming," Yvette shot back.

"Right," then Maggie stopped and looked at Vikki with a scrunched up face before continuing. Vikki stuck out her tongue at her then turned away. Maggie's mouth dropped open and she raised both eyebrows at Vikki's unexpected jealous reaction.

"Okay, you two. These events happened a long time ago. Today, you two care about each other — more than either of you would probably care to admit. So focus on that, not the past. Because, I am like totally dying to hear the rest," Yvette exclaimed in front of the group.

Vikki and Maggie looked at each other and Maggie said, "I'm sorry if my past hurts you, baby."

Vikki wiped a tear away and replied, "I'm sorry, too."

"Okay, everybody's sorry. Awesome, now Maggie, go on,"

Yvette exclaimed, seeming a little callous. The girls all scrunched up their brows and looked at Yvette. Seconds later, they relaxed and returned their gazes to Maggie as she continued her story.

"Okay, so Axel caught me stealing. And instead of having me arrested, he asked me why I was doing it. When I told him it was for my dad and uncles, he reached into his pocket and pulled out all his money and gave it to me, then walked away. I just stood there in awe. At that moment, I knew I loved him. And I would do anything to have him."

Vikki wound up for another punch. "Hey, don't you dare. And I said I loved him, not that he loved me."

"Okay, you two, remember our audience," Yvette shared. "Okay, so what happened?"

"Right, so I put everything back and went after him. I tried to give him back the money but he said that I needed it more." Maggie stopped and bowed her head before continuing, "I was so hurt and ashamed and so totally in love with that boy. Let's just say that I know boys. And I was so desperate to have him I didn't care what I did. He was so nice. Anyway, I got my way, even though," Maggie looked at Vikki before she continued, "I was sure he loved someone else. So, I got pregnant. I kept my condition hidden from everyone until just before I gave birth. I was afraid that if my dad or uncles found out, they would kill him. I had a girl which I named Juno. In Latin it means 'my young,' I think. Anyway, my uncles and dad suspected something so in order to protect Axel, I gave the baby up. Not long after that, in another act of desperation—to keep him safe—I moved to Miami.

Maggie reached out her hand to Juno and said, "I'm so sorry, mija, I was young and stupid. I thought that the only way to protect your dad was to let you go. I loved him so. And I have never loved another." Maggie bowed her head again and cried.

Vikki squeezed Maggie's hand and Artemis and Juno took turns hugging her.

"Okay, that's enough sorrow for one day," Yvette stated as she broke up the group and wiped her tears away. Everyone walked off in smaller pairs and the Cuban girls got together with Yvette and Winnie to discuss the mission and what was to come. Maggie worked her way to the kitchen. It was a space she always found to be caring and peaceful. She longed to take care of a family and serving others out of the kitchen seemed to fill that void.

Akachi followed her and asked for coffee. Maggie stroked his back and said, "Of course, Papi, coming right up." Suddenly, a bright light filled the living room and Mia stepped out, with Hoshea following. The Cuban girls all bowed at his feet and so did Yvette and Winnie. Everybody else in the room just stood there in awe. Mia and the Cuban girls personally introduced Hoshea to everyone.

One by one, Hoshea addressed each person in a familiar tone and in a language none had ever heard yet understood. He knew specifics about each individual's life like he had been there with them during those moments. Even though everyone was in close proximity to each other, Hoshea's conversation with each individual was private.

********** Meanwhile in the Kitchen **********

"Wait, Akachi, who is that?" Maggie pointed to Hoshea while holding a hand to her chest. She stepped behind Akachi and grabbed his arm, then peered past his shoulder and repeated in a whisper, "Who is that?"

"There's no reason to hide, Maggie. We're safe in his presence."

"I'm not hiding."

Akachi looked over his shoulder and said, "Huh, you're not?"

"No."

He looked around the room and saw everyone happily greeting Hoshea then looked behind him again and added, "Are you sure you're not hiding?"

"Yes, I'm sure. This is not hiding."

"Okay, so…?"

"So, I just don't want him to see me is all. Now, who is he?"

"Who do you think he is?"

"I don't know, which is why I'm asking you," Maggie quickly retorted then paused for a few seconds before adding, "Plus, I'm not sure I wanna tell you what I think."

"Well, that confession has certainly sparked my curiosity. Tell me, who do you see?"

"No."

"What? Why not?"

"Because, I don't want you to think I'm crazy."

"Oh please, you're being silly. Tell me, who you see."

Maggie stared at Hoshea for a few more seconds then replied, "If I didn't know any better, I would swear it was baby Jesus."

"Now that is interesting."

"Why? Who is it?"

"I didn't see him that way at first."

"What way? What do you mean?"

"It's not important. But you're correct. He's exactly who you think he is."

"What? Who, who is he?"

"Jesus Christ in the flesh, as it were. Although, everyone here calls him Hoshea. I believe that's his heavenly name."

"Are you kidding me? How is that possible? Why is he here? And why is everyone so touchy feely with him? That's crazy. It seems like he personally knows you guys. And why is everyone so calm? And why —"

"It's okay, Maggie, really," Akachi interrupted in hopes of consoling her.

"Wait, why does he look like that?" Maggie questioned.

"Are you asking me why he, who can be anything or anyone, chooses to look like one of us?" Akachi replied.

"No, not exactly, but your response does kinda answer my question."

"Good, since our appearance is not who we really are," Akachi shared. "Do you want to meet him?"

"Wait, what? No! Don't ask him to come over here. Oh my God," Maggie stammered out.

"Calm down."

"No, no, no. If he comes over here, what do I do? What if he talks to me? What do I say?"

"Maggie, you need to relax. Everything will be all right, I promise." Maggie was still behind Akachi, leaning her forehead on his right shoulder blade. Akachi placed a hand over the two hands she had tightly wrapped around his right bicep.

"No, Akachi, you don't understand," Maggie whispered through trembling lips as tears filled her eyes. "I'm not worthy of being here. I haven't gone to church in like forever. And my choice of faith denomination has been all over the place."

Akachi laughed out loud.

"Are you seriously laughing at the shame I feel?"

"No, of course not."

"Okay then, what's so funny?" Maggie shot out.

"I laughed at the relentless string of questions which have filled you with needless doubt."

"What?"

"Look, Maggie, it doesn't matter what denomination you were or how often you went to church or if you even went at all."

"What, how can you say that?"

"Listen, there is nothing wrong with going to church. People go for many reasons. And some reasons are better than others. But…" Akachi trailed off and stopped talking.

"But, but what? Go on, man."

Akachi took a deep breath, turned around and said, "Look, some people went to church to find a connection to God, while others went because they were taught to do so. Some went to church to fellowship with others of similar faith, while others considered it an obligation. Honestly, there are hundreds, if not thousands of reasons why people did what they did. But, the truth is, if they were not REAL, the reason or reasons just didn't matter."

"Okay, so far you're making sense, so go on."

"REAL is an acronym I use for what's required."

Maggie thought, *An acronym, really? Where's he going with this?* She was growing impatient at Akachi's lack of urgency. "Well, go on, man, explain yourself before he comes over here."

"Okay," Akachi breathed deep to center himself then said, "So this is what I believe. First, an individual has to have a *Realization* — i.e., the understanding and recognition that they made some poor choices in life. And born into a life of sin is no excuse for a particular outcome. The individual must realize that change is required from them, and no one else.

"Okay, I get it. Go on."

"There must be an *Effectuation*. This is the acceptance that only a perfectly innocent and merciful being could save a wretch like them and commit to change."

"How?"

"Well, it starts with an *Appeal* to this perfect being. They must ask for mercy. It's said that confession is good for the soul. They have to ask to be saved."

"I'm a little confused now, but it doesn't matter, just go on."

"Well, it does kind of matter, Maggie."

"Yeah, yeah, whatever. Fill me in later, but please finish."

"Fine, then of course there's *Love*—your realization must be true. Your effectuation must be true, and your appeal for forgiveness must be true. And the only way to do that is to love above all."

"How do you do that, with so much hate and ugliness in the world?"

"That's easy; you start by loving this perfect being, God, first then love your neighbors as yourself. He will take care of the rest.

"You see, Maggie, claiming you're a marathon runner doesn't make you one. And asking for forgiveness because you were caught doesn't make you remorseful. Nor does claiming you believe simply to escape a horrible situation. You cannot save yourself from the worldly horrors that engulf our existence. Only he can." Akachi pointed to Hoshea with his chin.

"I'm sorry, you lost me."

"It's okay. It's a lot to process. Maybe this will make it easier for you. Think of the two men on the cross on either side of Jesus during the crucifixion. At first they both rebuked him. Then one realized who Jesus was, accepted his fate, and changed. His change was evident when he rebukes the other by saying, 'Have you not eyes, we are all subject to the same condemnation. But you and I have been condemned justly; this man has done nothing wrong.' He saw the innocence before him. He then asks to be saved. 'Jesus, please do not forget me.'"

"I see, I think I understand you now."

"Good." Akachi turned around and Hoshea was standing at his side. Hoshea reached out his hand and Akachi took it as he dropped to one knee.

"My Lord, how may I serve you today?"

"Rise and embrace me, my friend."

Maggie was on her knees, in the fetal position, covering her face with both hands and trying desperately not to pass out from the overwhelming feeling of ignominy and self-worthlessness.

Akachi stood up and hugged Hoshea tight and thanked him for coming to their aid. He turned around to introduce Maggie and noticed she was on the ground then looked at Hoshea and gently shrugged after raising an eyebrow. Hoshea displayed a minor smile then moved past Akachi.

"Margarita, look at me," Hoshea announced. His voice was deep and vibrating but she was the only one that heard it.

Maggie shook her head then thought, *Oh my God, he knows who I am and probably everything I've done. I'm in big trouble.*

"It's okay, woman, you may look upon me."

She slowly raised her head and looked at him.

"Oh my God, I am so sorry," Maggie let out then covered her face with both hands again. Akachi bent down and whispered, "It's okay to feel unworthy, but it's what you do from this moment forward that will define you," then he stood up and walked away.

"Margarita, be at peace." Hoshea held out his hand and a feeling of contentment washed over her. But her feelings of guilt remained. "Now tell me, do you know me?"

Maggie nodded yes but didn't look up.

"What say you?"

Maggie slowly raised her head up and uncovered her face but only long enough to let out, "You're baby Jesus," then covered her face again. "I'm so ashamed," she muttered out through her hands. "I'm a thief, and a liar. You shouldn't be near me."

"Why?"

"Because I'm a no good, rotten scoundrel and you're perfect."

"Margarita, you have been running from me practically your whole life. And you have found no peace. Love for the wretched in this world has kept you oppressed. What if I tell you, you can stop running and face what you've done and I will forgive you?"

"But I've bribed men to cover up the crimes of other men. I've swindled for profit and prostituted myself for worldly pleasures. I fear it's too late for me. I've—" Maggie went on while Hoshea listened.

"Wow, she's talkative," Yvette shared with Winnie.

"Well, he has a way of drawing it out of you. But at the end, she will be at peace and the weight of this world pressing down on her will be lifted."

"Well, I'm happy for her, but trouble is coming and I hope we can count on her."

Winnie looked over at Maggie with the tilt of her head then returned her gaze to Yvette, "I agree, and we need her, she's resourceful."

"Yes, and she's a survivor," Yvette added.

"Yes, she is," Winnie replied while slowly looking around and gently nodding her head, "and she's a prepper like you, Evie."

"Well, she might be a prepper but she's not like me."

"What do you mean?" Winnie asked, a little disconcerted by Yvette's accusatory comment. Nevertheless, she was certain Yvette had a logical reason for her snappish dictum.

"Look around, Winnie. She's assembled an ER in a log cabin in the middle of a swamp."

"I know, right? It's totally brilliant."

"Well, for me, it's more like crazy."

"What? Why?"

"Because having a medical facility in a swamp is completely abhorrent. Why would anyone do this?"

"That seems a bit harsh. And maybe she just plans ahead?"

"No. No one plans like this. I'm sure this location has been in use for years tending to a nefarious sort. But the dreadful fact is that we have actually needed this place multiple times since our arrival."

"Well, Evie, maybe she was part of God's plan in all this. You said it yourself. We've needed this facility many times. And none of the injured would probably have survived without it, which, by the way, includes us."

"Winnie, perhaps you're right, or maybe its Satan's way of giving us false hope."

"Wow, Evie, you've just ruined my mood on multiple levels."

"I'm sorry, sweetie, I'm afraid of what the future might soon bring."

"Huh," Winnie sounded, while tilting her head and watching Yvette walk away whispering, "I'm not sure I trust her."

"Well, I'm sure Maggie has a perfectly sound explanation for having a concealed medical facility in the middle of a bayou." Then Winnie considered what she had just confessed out loud and said,

"Blimey. Evie, your intuition might be spot on."

Yvette stopped then looked back and added, "Perhaps, but since Hoshea sees the totality of our existence before we're even born, if he says we can trust her, maybe we should."

Suddenly, Maggie seemed upset. Although no one could actually hear the specifics of her conversation, they were aware of her intense feelings. Her outbursts lasted longer than anyone expected. And all anyone could see was Maggie's trembling face and Hoshea's calm demeanor responding back. *Blimey, she's not happy,* Winnie thought.

"Why would you ask me to do that?"

"It's the reason you're here, Margarita. And no one else is here strong enough to endure the sorrow. So heed my words!" Hoshea started a one-sided conversation providing specifics on people and examples on tasks required.

At the end, Maggie shook her head and exclaimed through trembling lips, "I can't. You can't ask me to do that. I won't do it. I won't."

"You must," Hoshea repeated. "I know who you truly are, Margarita. This is your test. And your refusal to comply will help no one."

Maggie got up off her knees and ran past Hoshea, crying hysterically. She opened the front door and ran out. Everyone wondered, *what's going on here?*

"Well, that can't be good," Akachi confessed aloud as Maggie slammed the door shut behind her.

While Maggie was outside, Hoshea made his way into the hallway so he could call in one person at a time and have some privacy. He wanted to start calling people over but he knew Vikki would interrupt once she recovered from her hypnotic trance over Maggie's apparent distress, so he waited.

Vikki stood motionless by the front door a few minutes until she finally gathered up the courage to exit. When she walked outside, she noticed that Maggie was on the telephone. When she hung up, Vikki asked, "Are you okay?"

"No. I'm not."

"What's wrong?"

"Vikki, stay away from me. I'm no good." Maggie ran off crying. Vikki was in shock. She didn't know what to make of it but she knew something was desperately wrong. She wanted to chase after her but decided to give Maggie some space.

Vikki walked back inside and looked for Hoshea. At this point, she was only focused on Maggie's well-being. She walked over to him and asked, "What's wrong with Maggie?"

Hoshea could feel the deep emotions swelling within her. "Your love for Maggie runs deep."

"I would die for her."

"Vikki, I don't want to tell you how unreasonable that statement sounds. You just met her a few days ago."

"Well, I can't help the way I feel. And I don't care what anyone else thinks about it." Vikki took a few seconds to center herself. She didn't want to say something she would regret later. When she felt clear-headed, she asked, "Are you punishing me for the way I feel?"

"Absolutely not. But if you truly love her, you have to let her go."

"Why, what's wrong? Where is she going? And why can't I help her?"

"For now, you're both meant to walk different paths. So, let her be. But fear not, for Margarita is stronger than you know."

"That might be true, but I'm not sure I'm strong enough to do what's required without her."

"Vikki, you have been afraid your whole life. But fighting to save others has been your strength. Focus on that."

"I just want to know that she'll be all right."

"She will."

"You promise?" Vikki stammered out as tears filled her eyes.

Hoshea tilted his head as he looked at Vikki and said, "Yes. For you, I promise."

"Then, I am your servant."

Huh! Hoshea sounded as he stared at Vikki for a few seconds then shook his head slowly and thought, *the love some form for strangers under seemingly impossible circumstances is why I'm here.*

"You owe me nothing. I do it freely because you are substantial."

Vikki fell to her knees and said, "Father, forgive me for I have sinned. It's been twelve years since my last confession."

"What say you?" Vikki poured out her heart for fifteen minutes. Just like everyone before her and thereafter.

After every person in the house had spoken to Hoshea in private, Hilily stepped forward and said, "It is time we conclude our discussions on *The Gathering* and solidify our plans to bring the lost unto Christ."

Just then, Maggie ran into the house from the back and yelled, "We're surrounded."

"Or not," Hilily added. "Perhaps our discussion can wait."

Vikki ran over to Maggie and embraced her then whispered into her ear, "I'm so glad you're back. I was so worried." She pushed her at arm's length and said, "Are you okay?"

"No, but I will be. If I thought you were going to be by my side."

"Of course I will, but what's going on?"

"I might tell you someday. But for now, just hold me."

Vikki embraced her again and said as tears streamed down her face, "Oh my God, I was so scared. I almost had a heart attack, I was so worried."

Maggie stepped back and gently wiped the tears off Vikki's face using the back of her hand and said, "I love you, too, you big baby."

"We're sisters now, right?" Vikki questioned.

"Yes—and more, always."

"You promise."

"Yes."

Just then, Vikki, along with everyone else, heard Reynolds yell from the front of the house, "Dr. Milagro, it's time we had a talk. I have two hundred men out here with me. If you care for your safety and those in your company, I would suggest you talk to me. But first, send Maggie out."

"I have to go," Maggie informed Vikki and the others.

"What? Why would you go out there alone? Do you have a death wish?"

"No, but I have no choice, I'm sorry."

"What? You can't mean that," Vikki said through trembling lips.

"I do, I'm sorry. You have to let me go."

"No," Vikki let out in a gut-wrenching moan then fell to her knees while still holding Maggie's hand.

"She must do what she must, let her be," Hoshea exclaimed.

Maggie dropped Vikki's hand and started toward the front door.

"How in the world did they find us? And how did he know you were here, Evie?" Winnie questioned in disbelief.

"I called and told him where we were," Maggie confessed.

"What? Why? Why would you do that?" Nikki questioned then turned her gaze to Vikki and saw a look of despair on her face that she had never seen.

"I'm so sorry I had to betray you," Maggie shared as she rested her head on the front door. Seconds later, she stood straight up, shook the uncertainty out of her head, and reached for the door knob. She opened the door and walked out without ever looking back.

"How can this be happening? It feels like I'm going insane," Vikki exclaimed while on her knees." Artemis and Juno walked over and placed a hand on each of her shoulders in hopes of diminishing her sorrow and distress. But Vikki's grief was almost too much for them to bear.

"Hoshea!" many within the group cried out.

"She has to do this," Hoshea informed them.

"Why?" Nikki questioned while standing there limp and dumbfounded.

"Because it's what she's here to do."

"Hoshea, please," Winnie pleaded. "No one here understands what's happened to Maggie. And why she's chosen this course of action. But how can we be expected to see this as anything less than an utter betrayal? What's happening with her?"

Hoshea took a few seconds then replied, "I can't reveal her course."

Vikki uncovered her face to let out, "We have to get her back. I cannot go on without her." Both Artemis and Juno were now crying at the overwhelming feelings of despair coming from Rogan.

"Vikki, you can, and you will," Hoshea exclaimed then stepped back and was gone. However, his voice remained in everyone's thoughts for a few seconds longer to say, *You were all told of the trials that were to come. And each of you accepted the responsibility for the sacrifices required to save others. These tribulations are part of your atonement,* Hoshea concluded.

Maggie walked over and stood next to Reynolds and his head ruffian.

"It's about time," Reynolds said with a smirk on his face.

"Don't talk to me," Maggie replied.

"Touchy. What's up your skirt?"

"I said don't talk to me."

"You haven't developed feelings for these people, have you?" Reynolds asked, a little mystified.

"Yeah, so what? But I'll get over it which is more than I can say about your lack of personal hygiene and forward thinking."

Reynolds' head thug grabbed Maggie by the arm and said, "Mind your place, woman."

She pulled her arm away, but his grip surprised her. It was weaker than she expected given his size. She looked up at him and let out, "Don't you dare touch me!"

"Or what?" Bengal replied back with a daring smirk. Maggie just glared at him.

"Let her be," Reynolds shot out.

Akachi walked over to Yvette and said, "Evie, like you, I'm not sure I know why this is happening. But it would appear that we're in serious trouble. You need to talk to Reynolds."

"What? I have nothing to say to him."

"Then let him do all the talking. We need to stall for time."

"I don't want to hear anything he has to say."

"Well, please consider that one of us just walked into the lion's den."

"It was her choice to betray us," Yvette exclaimed as she stared toward the front door.

"I don't believe she did that."

"Well, I believe what I saw and what she said before she left," Yvette replied with absolutism. "She never looked back, which means she won't be coming back. She's our Judas." Those words hollowed out everyone listening.

Vikki went numb. Of all the horrific events she had witnessed in her life, this felt like it would be her undoing. She was having thoughts of suicide. For the second time in her existence, life had no meaning. She welcomed death. Artemis and Juno looked at each other and thought, *Peace,* as they worked on absorbing her sorrow. *Army, she feels as I felt when I saw you take your last breath on that battle field. I can't bear it again. I'm sorry.* Juno took her hand off of Vikki and covered her face. Artemis replied back, *then I will bear it for us both.*

Akachi took a moment to center himself then said, "Okay, Evie, consider this, if Reynolds is talking, he's not shooting at us. And if two hundred men open fire on this building, none of us will be around to talk to him or anyone else when they stop."

Akachi moved in closer and whispered, "Would you like me to talk to him, in your stead?" Yvette pulled back, bowed her head and slowly nodded in agreement. Until that moment, she wasn't scared but after giving Akachi's summary a little thought, she shivered as her perception changed.

Akachi moved to the window and said, "Reynolds, we have to stop meeting like this. People will start to think you're obsessed with me."

"Akachi?" Reynolds was surprised to hear his voice but not shocked. "You have nine lives, Chief." He took a deep breath to compose himself then added, "Akachi, I'm surprised to find you here. We looked all over Beboura for you. Many thought you would be found dead or dying face down in a ditch. But I knew better."

"Reynolds, I must confess, I had my doubts. You gave it a decent try."

"I'm sorry, old friend, but you left me no choice. Although, I'm convinced you have the survival instincts of a cat. But you're burning through those lives at an exponential rate."

"Well, you're a hazard to be around. Perhaps this time, you can take it easy on me."

"I don't think so, you're too resilient. It must end here, today."

"Well, that's sad to hear. So, why do you want to talk to Dr. Milagro?"

"I just have a few questions."

"Okay, but give me a minute. She doesn't like you very much and the last time you talked to her you were pretty mean."

"Go on, take your minute."

Reynolds' head goon walked over and said, "Sir, he's stalling."

"I realize that. But a victory here is to bring them out alive. If

I wanted them dead, I would just let you numb nuts have at it. So be quiet and let me do the thinking."

********** Back inside Maggie's cabin **********

"We're in a bad situation here," Nikki whispered to Yvette as Akachi walked over.

"Look, Akachi is buying us some time, but there's little we can do to escape an entrenched adversary with this many men. At least, not without explosives."

"Well, I may be able to help there," Avery shared.

"How?"

"Yesterday, Maggie showed me a stash of C4 she keeps hidden under the house just for such an occasion."

Nikki looked over at Vikki who was still kneeling just outside the kitchen with streaks of mascara running down her face and said, "She's a smart girl." Vikki's bottom lip started quivering then she covered her face with both hands and started crying again.

Suddenly, a bright light filled the living room and Hoshea appeared bellowing, "NO!" Everyone was blown back onto the heels of their feet. When they managed to regain their footing, Hoshea said in a deep, commanding voice, "Under no circumstances is anyone here allowed to harm those outside. That part of your life is over."

"But their intent is to kill us," Nikki said in distress. "You expect us to do nothing?"

"I expect only what is required," Hoshea answered. Nikki looked over at Akachi with both hands up and exclaimed, "What does that mean?"

Akachi placed a hand on her shoulder and said, "Don't worry, Nikki, although we're all going to die, I'm confident it's not going to be today." He looked at Hoshea and said, "My Lord, what would you have us do?"

"Be patient. There are good people outside and our actions here will help them see the light.

Hoshea called Hilily over and said, "Go out and tell them who you are."

"Yes, my Lord."

"What? She can't go out there. She'll be killed!" Nikki yelled.

"Or worse!"

"Wait, what could be worse than being killed?" Winnie asked, a little mystified.

Nikki pointed at Hilily with both hands and said, "Duh! Have you looked at her? She's like, totally gorgeous. She could be captured and—you know," Nikki paused and raised her eyebrows.

Winnie stared at Nikki with a tilted head and a wrinkled brow then looked over at Hilily who shrugged. She looked back at Nikki again and laughed then said, "You're so silly."

"What?! What am I missing?"

Winnie leaned in close and whispered, "There are no restraints that can hold an Archangel."

Nikki tilted her head and said, "Seriously?" She looked at Hilily and asked, "Is that true? There're no restraints that can hold you?" Hilily just nodded for confirmation.

When Nikki returned her gaze to Winnie, she heard her ask, "Now, do you feel better?"

Nikki was quiet for a few seconds then replied, "I'm not sure."

Hoshea interrupted the conversation and said, "Nikki, have more faith in those around you." He looked around the room and added, "Now, everyone, please make preparations to depart."

Artemis and Juno stepped back and away from Vikki. But Juno was emotionally splintered based on her mother's actions so she thought to Hoshea, *My Lord, I am struggling to understand my mother's course of action. Is it necessary?*

Yes.

But is it for her glory or yours?

That is yet to be seen, Hoshea communicated telepathically to Juno. She now had doubts about her mother like everyone else.

********** Outside in front of Maggie's cabin **********

Reynolds was receiving an assessment from Bengal, his second in command. "Lieutenant, I'm not sure if I agree with your synopsis of this situation. Nevertheless, I'll wait for you to give the word. But again, I think waiting is a bad idea. I've heard of Akachi and nothing good can come from giving him enough time to place a plan in motion."

"Your opinion is duly noted," Reynolds countered.

Suddenly, Bengal noticed something strange appearing in front of him and exclaimed as he pointed, "Look, Lieutenant."

Reynolds turned his head and looked out, confessing out loud, "What the hell is that?"

A blurry spot appeared in front of the house followed by a bright light then Hilily walked out of a rip in space. Then Artemis appeared to its right and Hikiko to its left. And one by one the Cuban girls appeared, standing three to the left and three to the right. The men outside raised up their firearms but Reynolds yelled, "HOLD!" He stared the nine apparitions down for a few seconds then said, "I'm sorry, but who are you girls supposed to be?"

In harmony, they replied.

"We are the Harem Guardian.

"We defend the virtuous, the merciful, the just.

"We are the protectors of the meek, the incorruptible, the unsullied.

"We keep those of noble birth from the clutches of deceit.

"We defend those forged in righteousness from villainy and immorality.

"We have battled evil over countless millennia through time and space.

"We ensure the survival of those in our care. And of the billions assigned to our watch — we have never lost a one."

Hilily took one step forward and stomped its foot down, making the ground shake, then added, "Today will be no exception. Your power here is but a phantom."

They all brought their left fist up as though they were holding a shield and grunted, "για τους ενάρετους," then slammed their left foot down and the shock caused the cars to shake. Reynolds and all his men were forced to stumble back.

The Guardians stood at the ready. With their base firmly planted, they released whip-like objects behind them. The lashes glistened brightly then cracked as the tips flicked the air, releasing pent up energy. To most of those present, the Guardians were quite intimidating as they held a weightless whip menacingly behind them.

Hilily exclaimed, "You ask who we are, then hear this and flee."

In unison they all replied again, "We are the Harem

Guardian."

Juno thought, *Mother, what have you done?*
I'm so sorry, mija, I wish there was another way.

********** Back inside Maggie's cabin **********

Everyone was gathering their personal items before departing.

Nikki replied to Hoshea, "My Lord, since I don't own anything here but what I'm wearing, is it okay if I take the time to see what's going on outside?"

With a small grin, Hoshea replied, "Go see if you must."

"Oh thank goodness, because the suspense is killing me." She ran to the front of the house and got ready to peer out. She looked across the room to a nearby window but Vikki wasn't there. *Where is she?* Nikki thought. *She's always right behind me.* She looked through the house and saw Rogan sitting down in a catatonic state at the other end of the cabin. *What the hell?* She motioned to Sophia with her chin to get Vikki up then pointed to the other window. "I need her to help me assess our situation from another vantage point," she whispered.

Sophia tried to get Vikki involved but she was completely withdrawn. *Maggie's current incomprehensible behavior has obviously wounded her deeply,* Sophia thought. *I'm not sure if it will even be possible to console her in this state but I have to try. However, for now, Rogan's recovery will have to wait, she's needed elsewhere and our survival takes priority.* Sophia picked Vikki up and helped her to another vista.

"Listen, Vee, your sister needs you, and so do we. Please help her survey our environment," Sophia whispered in Vikki's ear as they made their way to another window in front of the house.

As soon as Akachi noticed what Labelle and Rogan were doing, he yelled out, "No! Get away from the windows. You're going to give Reynolds the wrong impression."

"I just want to take a quick look," Nikki replied.

By then, it was too late. The attention Nikki and Vikki drew was hard to ignore.

********** Outside in front of Maggie's cabin **********

Reynolds was trying to comprehend what had just happened when he noticed movement at the front of the house. He peered past Hilily and saw Vikki and Nikki standing in front of two windows then thought, *This is why he was stalling. He's giving Labelle Rogan time to generate countermeasures and negate my advantage. I can't believe I fell victim to sentiment. Damn you, Akachi.*

Reynolds returned his gaze back toward Hilily and proclaimed, "Well, fortunately for us, there is no one here that matches your description." A few seconds later, he gave the order to open fire.

"Sir, you want us to fire on a bunch of children?" one of Reynolds' soldiers questioned.

"They're not children, numb nuts," Reynolds replied.

"Well, they look like kids to me, and I didn't sign up for that. So I'm outta here." At least thirty of his men dropped their firearms and took off. He looked around at those fleeing and yelled, "Really, are you numbskulls kidding me? What the hell are the rest of you waiting for? I said fire!"

"Guardians, we harness the power of God's might so we can hold our ground without a fight," Hilily announced. Their armor created a bright dome over them which also protected the cabin. Reynolds and many of his men were forced to shield their eyes.

Hoshea stopped time outside the cabin and said, "Gather round." When everyone was in a tight circle, Hoshea explained their new course and intent. He asked everyone to hold steadfast to their faith and then cast a portal.

"What we do now is for the lost that, like you, may still be saved. Love one another as I love you and no one can come between you." Hoshea waved his hand and they were gone.

Hilily and the other Guardian looked around 360° and noticed that everyone except for them was suspended in time. Hilily thought, *Glory be!*

A second later, the other Guardians exclaimed, "Glory be!" and watched as time started again.

A few seconds after, Reynolds and his hired-thugs had ample time to acclimate to the blinding light, so they opened fire. The barrage lasted at least two minutes but not a single bullet pierced the cabin walls. When the hell storm was over, Reynolds looked past the smoke and saw the Harem take a step back. With a seemingly confident but modest look on their faces, they vanished.

"Lieutenant, what the hell is going on here? What just happened?"

"What? Don't tell me you've never seen a few phantoms."

"Lieutenant, with all due respect, we both know those weren't ghosts. And I'm pretty sure they weren't people either. So what the hell are we up against?"

"Bengal, you tell me," Reynolds let out as he walked out around the cars and headed toward the house. When he was far enough away, another thirty ruffians took off.

His second in command quickly followed with Maggie in tow. When he got close enough he said, "So if I had to guess, I would say we were up against some supernatural beings?"

"Well, there you have it," Reynolds replied, trying desperately to control his rage.

"I'm not sure if you're being serious or sarcastic. But in either case, it doesn't change what I saw." He looked around and added, "There's no way we'll be able to keep most of our men from leaving after this."

Reynolds stopped then turned around and said, "I realize that. We're in the shit now. Those beings are not just bulletproof. They can somehow control the laws of physics which the rest of us are bound to."

"So what do we do, Lieutenant?"

"We find mystical beings of our own."

"And you can do that?"

"Well, I'm going to have to, aren't I?"

"Okay, so what should we do with her? She's one of them."

"What? We all serve the same master here," Maggie replied as she stared Reynolds down.

He looked at her and said, "She's right. We're all on the same. Plus, we would have never found them had it not been for her."

Maggie stepped away from the rough neck and crossed her arms in front of her chest as she moved next to Reynolds.

"Reynolds, you're no longer pursuing just corporeal beings. The existence of supernatural entities demands that we pursue a different course," Maggie confessed.

Reynolds sighed and said, "You're correct, of course. But I'm at a loss as to what to do here."

"Well, I'm not. You need to contact Filip and ask him to send Helem as aides," Maggie declared.

"What's a Helem?" Bengal asked.

"Well, that's great, but I don't really know any. And then, I'm not sure we can trust them," Reynolds replied coarsely.

"Well, until you have a better idea, I say our options are limited. So for now, have him send Aramina, Gracie and Chiyo," Maggie replied.

"I don't think so, I'm not leaving the success of this operation up to your coven," Reynolds replied boorish and dismissively as he considered the future of their mission.

"Reynolds, they have a particular set of skills that no one here possesses. Well, with the exception of myself, of course. And unless you can come up with something better, and fast, I say you have no choice. Launching an emotional warfare to disrupt these zealots from within makes sense. It's probably the only way to quickly cursh their insurrection. And if we don't interrupt their focus soon, our mission is in big trouble."

"Perhaps," Reynolds confessed aloud. He didn't want to admit it but he didn't have a plan and Maggie's suggestion made sense. *Men and guns are not going to get the job done,* he thought.

"Oh please, you know I'm right. It's exactly what we need. And it's what my covenant does best—well, one of the things we do best anyway."

Reynolds considered his options then gave Maggie a questionable look and said, "Fine. But you and your band of succubus better get the job done." Maggie crinkled up the corner of her mouth and gave Reynolds a look of contempt.

Her reaction even surprised Reynolds enough for him to say, "Gees, relax, I said we were doing it your way."

"What's a Helem?" the goon asked again.

Maggie looked at him and shared, "A Helem is a demon to you."

"How do you know that? And who the hell are you?" Bengal questioned.

"I know because I have been part of this mission from its inception. And I have successfully infiltrated the enemy. These people have two Archangels protecting them and seven Saints, which are even stronger. And if you don't man up, I'll have Reynolds cap your culo and replace you," Maggie shot back with a trembling face.

"Who the hell do you think you're talking to, toots?"

Maggie reached up and struck the thug in his throat. The shock forced him to grab his neck with both hands. When his knees buckled, Maggie kicked the back of his knee and he fell to the ground on all fours. She reached behind her back and pulled out a serrated dagger then grabbed the brute by the hair and moved forward to impale him through the throat.

Reynolds caught Maggie's wrist and said, "Stop. We need him." He looked at the rough neck and said, "Don't piss her off."

Bengal caught his breath and worked his way back to his feet.

"Are you and I going to have a problem?" Maggie questioned the thug. He shook his head for confirmation.

"Good. And the next time you touch me will be the last." Maggie placed the dagger back in her shorts and walked into the house.

The goon gathered himself then cleared his throat and said, "Lieutenant, why didn't you tell me she was a psycho?"

"Listen carefully. She's right. You need to keep your wits about you. Everyone we're pursuing is a lethal killer. So if you're not careful, we'll be leaving you here in a shallow, unmarked grave." Reynolds turned to walk away then turned back to him and added, "Oh, and one more thing, the next time you get out of line with her, I won't be around to help you. Got it?"

Bengal took a deep breath and reluctantly said, "Yes, sir."

"Good, now come on."

The thug followed close behind and when he mustered up the courage, he asked, "Lieutenant, how can we be expected to win against an adversary who can materialize in and out of thin air? We would be lucky to stand up to one of those lifeforms, if we had maybe a thousand men."

"Trust me, a thousand men wouldn't be enough. So our strategy here is not to engage but to avoid them," Reynolds replied. He walked into the house and suddenly stopped. With a look of disgust on his face, he turned toward Bengal and said, "You know, if you're not up for it, you can run home to Mummy." His second scrunched together both eyebrows and stood there a bit flabbergasted. A few seconds later, Reynolds added, "So are you done whining?" Bengal just stood there confidently. "Good, so help me search this place."

Reynolds stepped around the medical equipment and made his way to the loft and then the kitchen. A handful of his brutes helped him search the cabin. He walked to the back door and was met by his soldiers. "Has anyone walked out this door?"

"No, sir, it's been quiet back here."

Bengal reported, "Sir, the house is empty."

"Maggie, do you have any idea where they went?"

"Not a clue. And unless you can open up a space portal, we're at least several hours behind their current position. That's if we knew exactly where they were, which we don't." Maggie sighed then added, "Perhaps I should have stayed with them and fed you intel from the inside?"

"It's too late for that. Plus, the master wanted you with me."

"Fair enough, so where to?"

"I'm not sure."

"Well, whatever we do, we need to hurry. Those zealots have a way of changing those they come in contact with. So you don't want to give them too much time."

"Yes, I'm aware of that," Reynolds replied with noticeable irritation in his voice.

"Relax, Papi, I was just making conversation," Maggie was quick to retort.

Reynolds was quiet for a few seconds then said, "Oh, so how's Vikki?"

"I've got her on the hook."

"Are you sure?"

"Oh, please, look at me. I'm impossible to resist."

"If you say so, I just want them back."

"Relax and trust me," Maggie shared as she stroked Reynolds' back, "Labelle Rogan will be ours again."

"And what about the rest of them?"

"We give the girls to our men, and kill the rest," Maggie shared with a laugh.

CHARACTER KEY

- Adamic – known to the Harem as the 'Οικουμενικής Αδάμ' – a device, a divine object with organic properties or components. It's a gateway, a portal between time and space. This relic is presented to a worthy Harem at the completion of their five Internships in the presence of God. It grants each recipient full access to control time and space. Every Harem receives an Adamic as part of their ascendance within the ranks. The new Saints now on Earth who complete their five Internships will someday also receive this celestial apparatus. The Adamic also grants the user infinite knowledge, and passage to any world in the known universes. It was referred to on Earth as, the 'Tree of Life' or the 'Tree of Knowledge.'

- Adadi Diya – Akachi Ihejika's sister who managed an orphanage in Bangui, Africa. The only family Akachi had left aside from those he swore to protect—Yvette and Winnie. She was a selfless person driven to relocate as many war impoverished children as possible.

- Afia – a sixteen-year-old local ruffian and the son of the militia leader who was shot and killed by Akachi five years before the Rapture in Bangui, Africa. He was peacefully spending his nights at Adadi's orphanage. However, when he became aware of Akachi's presence, he sought answers. His investigation leads him down a dark road. At the end, in a desperate attempt to seek vengeance for the death of his father, he aligns with Reynolds to capture Akachi.

- Akachi Ihejika – a Special Agent with the NSA born in Bangui, Africa. He is two meters tall and built on a huge frame weighing over one hundred kilos. Hilily was assigned as his Guardian. He is an honorable man of peace and turns out to be Reynolds' nemesis.

- Andy Morra – a maintenance man at Jackson Memorial Hospital.

- Aramina Styles – tall, about 174 centimeters, British and of African descent. She kept a flat in Westminster but wasn't there very often. Zarek had her traveling most of the year. She is one of his principal interpreters and a suspected mimic level-three Helem. She is also secretly part of Maggie's coven.

- Artemis Cuban – a thirteen-year-old with jet-black hair which she wore above the shoulders like Ashley Greene. She had a Goth exterior but a gentle protective interior. Everyone called her Missy, with the exception of her little sister who called her Army. However, Hilily now calls her Artie. She was always happy to be surrounded by friends and family, and although morally true, she shied away from strangers in favor of the familiar. She did occasionally find it odd that her sister, although younger, was taller. Artemis recovered after the battle on the forbidden planet but continued to receive special training as a young Protector. The Cuban girls have proclaimed her their source of strength. And she's the only person currently on Earth wearing military-style combat boots. She was secretly the daughter of Vikki Rogan.

- Ashanti – father of Afia and the militia leader who was shot and killed by Akachi five years before the Rapture in Bangui, Africa.

- Avery Arrington – a compassionate CIA operative working as a double agent for MI6. He had a daughter, Holly, who was thirteen years old with Irish red hair, blue eyes and was being raised by his wife, Shelly Arrington, in North Carolina. Both Holly and Shelly believe that Avery died before Holly's birth. His wife never knew that Avery was actually with British Intelligence.

- Axel Cuban – a gentle spirit. He routinely placed the needs of others before his own. His friends and neighbors referred to Axel as Saint Nick. It was discovered that Axel had fathered both Artemis and Juno but with different women. Artemis was Vikki Rogan's daughter and Juno was Maggie's.

- Banās – the lead reconstructive plastic surgeon that helped to save Reynolds.

- Barasa – the new crime lord in Bangui, Africa after Ashanti, Afia's father, was shot and killed by Akachi five years before the Rapture.

- Charlotte Marie Sanchez de Gillian – Artemis's thirteen-year-old friend, imprinted on Axel and called him Daddy. Charlotte has Hazel eyes like her father and grandmother and is the daughter of Sophia Sanchez. Charlotte is the Cuban girls' source of curiosity. She is a piano concerto composer and has written ten symphonies in just over a week. In addition, she has also written all of Heather's dance music. Charlotte helps Heather choreograph the Cuban girls' dance routines. She is a high-volume reader and an inexhaustible writer who seems to record everything. Her eidetic memory helps drive that behavior. If the Cuban girls are unsure as to what any of them has said, felt or looked like on a particular day, they can simply ask Charlotte. If she was present, Charlotte would have recorded everything.

- Cooper – black site underling, first name Jack and a master with the Tac 50 sniper rifle also called the Big Mac. He made the history books for the longest kill shot ever using a Tac 50 at a distance of just over three miles.

- Chiyo Sūn – one of Zarek's Asian interpreters and a suspected mimic level-three Helem. Also secretly part of Maggie's coven.

- Cuban Family – everyone in the Cuban Family receives special training — Axel, Mia, Juno, Artemis, Holly, Sam, Charlotte and Heather. They were best known as the Cuban girls.

- Curatoria – represented something different for each person. For some, this being was a dear friend and for others, simply a guardian. The Curatoria could enhance an individual's strongest characteristic or any attribute an entity might require to overcome adversity.

- Dai Chow Lee – Wen Chow Lee's older brother. Dai was a master of Kung Fu in a defensive art called Wing Chun techniques. This close-quarters defensive discipline was originally created by Ip Man — China's first grandmaster. Dai's skills were so great, he was witnessed dodging bullets.

- Dalila – he was the oldest citizen in the town of Bangui, Africa. Mr. Dalila had worked for the Christian mission in town for almost sixty-five years. He knew everyone in town. When Akachi and Adadi fled the country, he and his wife were secretly awarded custodianship of Adadi's orphanage. Akachi left the ten remaining orphaned children in his care until their return.

- Daniel Milagro – husband to Yvette and father to Mia. His friends and family called him Danny. Daniel grew up poor. His mother moved the family from Puerto Rico to New York City when he was still young. He grew up in a small apartment in Spanish Harlem. Daniel attended and completed medical school in Havana, Cuba at the age of sixteen. He was the first person in the history of the school to do so.

- Disciples – Yvette, Margarita, Winnie + her older brother Dai, Akachi + his sister Adadi, Mick Ruben, Sophia Sanchez, Stefan Magnusson, Nikki Labelle, Vikki Rogan and Avery Arrington = 12. Hilily was assigned as the principal Guardian to Yehoshuah and his current disciples. Hilily assigned the six Cuban girls to Hoshea's followers. Hilily and Artemis would watch over Yvette, Winnie, Dai, Akachi, Adadi and Avery, with the help of Holly and Juno. Hikiko watched over Mick, Sophia, Stefan, Nikki, Vikki and Maggie with the help of Heather, Samantha and Charlotte.

- Derrik Corvin - the Swedish young man who gave Stefan Magnusson the two microchips in the Sweden airport. He was one of only four souls saved when Ellsworth Air Force base dispatched two F-38A fighters to shoot down the Swedish cargo aircraft sierra tango seven one niner zero over the Nebraska state line.

- Eric Tusk – the chief of staff for Filip Zarek and baptized in fire by Helucifer himself.

- Filip Zarek – young Polish leader, tall and slender, although he was average in weight; his muscular build concealed his true physical strength. And of course, he was the Anti-Christ—the Antee 'O Christos.

- Frank Stilton – President of the United States.

- Global Task Force – there were representatives from thirteen countries: the UK, Germany, Sweden, China, India, Belgium, Mexico, France, Egypt, South Africa, Venezuela, Argentina and finally rounded off by Poland. More than half of those present were past ambassadors or still active members of the United Nations.

- Gracie O'Brian – was an Irish 'ginger' and one of Zarek's political analysts. She was a suspected mimic level-three Helem and secretly part of Maggie's coven.

- Hanico – Hilily's Curatoria, a large snow leopard.

- Hai – one of the senior Harem Defensive Arts trainer to the Cuban Girls.

- Hazimi – a junior Defender in Hilily's clan and the one with the insight on the Cuban girls' astonishing abilities.

- Haikoo – Hoshea's Curatoria, resembled a 500 kilogram Bengal tiger but was twice as large as any on Earth. The large Panthera Tigris was white with platinum stripes and piercing emerald-colored eyes, known to Mia as Haboo.

- Hashir – the Universalus Ministerium Rem Publicam – responsible for communications on foreign soil to all populated planets in the known universes. The crude translation to this cabinet member was an earth equivalent of Ministry of State for the planet.

- Haya – the Universalus Ministerium Defensorius – responsible for the defense of the Harem people.

- Heather Rogan Labelle – Juno's twelve-year-old friend, imprinted on Axel and called him Daddy. Heather is the blonde-haired, blue-eyed cheerleader and a prolific dancer. She was labelled by her sisters as the eyes of the family. Heather receives visions or premonitions which always come true. This ability has made the others start referring to her as 'Telly,' short for 'fortune teller.' She is the daughter of Nikki Labelle.

- Hector Santa de Milagro – Yvette's brother and was focused on the day to day business of the family funeral parlor. He decided long ago not to follow in his father's footsteps. He did very little to help prep the cadavers, even though he was licensed to do so.

- Helina – Hoshea's foreign affairs instructor.

- Helsa – is the Universalus Ministerium Spiritualis – the spiritual leader for the Harem.

- Helucifer – leader of the Helem people and the first Betrayer– also referred to as Satan or the Devil by those on Earth. Father to Filip Zarek – the Anti-Christ.

- Heymie – the current Rex or Monarch for the Harem people – her Curatoria was a polar bear.

- Hikiko – was assigned as the new principal combat trainer to the Cuban girls and reported to Hilily. In addition to training, Hikiko was also assigned the duty of protecting half the disciples. It was assigned Mick Ruben, Sophia Sanchez, Stefan Magnusson, Nikki Labelle, Vikki Rogan and Margarita Rosado – with the help of Samantha, Charlotte and Heather as part of the Guardian team.

- Hilily – was the first aide to the Harem Monarch and principal Guardian to Hoshea and his disciples.

- Hitiki – the guide or instructor to the Cuban girls in the Acclamation 101 course.

- Hitlaher – Helucifer's second in command, left a light impression, like a faded white tattoo on Artemis' neck, during her first battle on the forbidden planet.

- Holly Arrington – Artemis's thirteen-year-old friend, imprinted on Axel and calls him Daddy. She is identified by the other Cuban girls as being their source of innocence. And even though she was just a thirteen-year-old, Holly creates the most wondrous oil painting masterpieces which easily rival those of established legendary Earth artisans. Holly has blue eyes, feels deeply and could easily search out what others are feeling no matter how far they are or how hard they try to hide their emotional state. Holly's passion, like her Irish red hair, is hard to miss. She is a pleasure to be around. It's an honor to know her and experience her purity. As a point of interest, all the male images on her canvases host the same face – that of her father Avery Arrington.

- Hoshea – first born to the Harem Monarch on Earth 2,082 years ago – known on Earth as 'Yehoshuah' by the Hebrews and Jesus Christ to us.

- Hulina – The story goes that Maggie's mother was taken captive by several members of a local crime family in Santo Domingo. Her mother exhibited a racy behavior around alpha males. And her lack of attachment to one person generated negative behavior for men who were willing to fight for her affections. Many had doubts as to whether Hulina's disappearance was due to foul play or simply voluntary. Nevertheless, a month after her disappearance, a woman was found hanging from a neighborhood street lamp, which matched Maggie's mother's description. Currently, no one knows, but Hulina is a level one Helem.

- Internships – the completion of five Internships were required before any new Saint could receive an Adamic. The *Foundation* internship was the first of the five, followed by *Service, Defense, Faith* and finally *Support*.

- Ip Man – In China, long ago, there were Kung Fu masters that controlled provinces. Japan challenged the country to display their greatest warrior. All the masters got together to choose who would represent China from the north and south. One man stood out among them all. That person was Ip Man. He fought and became the grandmaster, the master of all masters.

- Isoba – Barasa's first Lieutenant and the captain of his men.

- Jay Penn M.D. – a geneticist working under Dr. Stefan Magnusson and currently assigned to Jackson Memorial Hospital in Miami, Florida. He discovered what Dr. Wen Chow Lee was working on before she left the hospital grounds and went rogue.

- Jiani Chow Lee – Wen Chow Lee's mother.

- Joaquin Santa de Milagro – Yvette's father was Fajardo's oldest mortician. He had been a mortician for almost forty years like his father, grandfather and great grandfather before him. Although Yvette had an older brother, he had decided long ago not to follow in his father's footsteps.

- Juno Cuban – quite attached to her older sister. And although Artemis and her sister were only a year apart, Juno was mentally older. She doesn't look like her sister but she is super girlie. Juno always seemed to be more concerned about the welfare of others than herself. Juno was twelve at the time of the Rapture and continues to be extremely self-sacrificing. This often influenced Artemis's behavior. The two sisters resembled their father and mother but not each other. She is secretly the daughter of Margarita Linda Martínez Rosado.

- Klas Berg – the president of the United Nations.

- Li Na Chow Lee – Wen Chow Lee's younger sister.

- Luis Carlos Arroyo – the Global Task Force representative from Mexico.
- Malena Magnusson – Dr. Stefan's wife, and mother of three children; two girls and a son. The youngest girl was Mia's age and the son, although older than Hoshea, was about his size.

- Maggie – full name is Margarita Linda Martínez Rosado – an emergency room nurse working for Jackson Memorial Hospital in Miami, Florida. Margarita was born in Santo Domingo and moved to New York City at the age of seven after a family tragedy. She often visited family there. Her friends call her Maggie. Her mother, Hulina was believed to have been murdered by several members of a local crime family in Santo Domingo. The suspected murderers were never brought to trial. As a result of that injustice, her father and three uncles became vigilantes.

- Manny, Gail, James, Eric, Miguel and Ginger were Reynolds' permanent staff members assigned by the police department.

- Meenu – Yvette Mia Santa de Milagro's younger sister. She's the leader of a secret Christian movement focused on resisting the Anti-Christ's oppression and feeding the hungry in Puerto Rico.

- Mia Linda Miriam Santa Milagro – ten-year-old with a 208 IQ and the daughter of Dr. Yvette and Daniel Milagro. Mia is a Puerto Rican girl with almond skin and brown eyes, and now the source of the girls' faith. After the Rapture, Mia was removed from the forbidden planet and placed with the Cuban girls. On Earth she receives special education and training from Jesus Christ himself — among others.

- Miriam – Hoshea's mother, the Harem Monarch, the Virgin Mary, but also known as Miriam or Heymie and the Holy Mother.

- Mick Ruben – an emergency room (ER) doctor at Jackson Memorial Medical Center. He had had a privileged life. Mick had been wearing designer clothes since birth. Every car he had ever owned was a gift from his mom and dad. Post graduate and medical school were paid for by his parents and his current house was also a gift from them. His mother was a successful author and his father was a commodities broker. They worked a lot and Mick was an only child so they overcompensated for ignoring the boy by spending money on him. At the end, Mick had no complaints. He just didn't have a different frame of reference to compare the pros and cons of his life. To Mick, his life had been ideal.

- Mikha'el' – was the biblical Hebrew name for the Archangel Michael who is prophesized to be the one to defeat Helucifer, also known as Satan, at the end.

- Nephilim – offspring of the "sons of God" and the "daughters of men" before the Deluge.

- Nikki Labelle – last name means "fair, good-looking" in French. She is a red-headed, bubbly stewardess/body guard and dressed like a Pan AM stewardess of the early 1960s. She wore her skirt six inches above the knee versus what was customary for the earlier period. Her outfit was completed by the big button Barbie hat and the white gloves. Nikki had a daughter when she was seventeen. Heather, who was twelve years old during the Rapture, had blonde hair and blue eyes and was being raised by Vikki's parents in North Carolina.

- Nora Cuban – Axel's departed wife – Artemis and Juno were told this was their mother but in reality, she was simply a stepmother. She died early in life from cancer.

- για τους ενάρετους – translates into English to mean, 'For the Righteous'.

- Οικουμενικής Αδάμ – translates into English to mean, 'Universal Adam'.

- Orlov clan – referred to by many as the 'Mighty Eagles.' They were six boys raptured from a Russian orphanage. Most were gentle, loving and kind-hearted. Ivan was nominated the boys' and their source of strength and considered to be their leader.

- Pope Benedict XVII – the 270th Pope for the Catholic Church.

- Richard Reynolds – detective for the Miami City Police Department. Reynolds was a little less than two meters tall, and middle-aged. He was a racist and a sexist bigot, but concealed it well. He was promoted to Lieutenant by his chief but works directly for the Anti-Christ. Reynolds had six local staff members – Manny, Gail, James, Eric, Miguel and Ginger. He was assigned Nikki Labelle and Vikki Rogan for support until he turned on them and caused them to join forces with his fugitives.

- Rowland – an Inspector with Scotland Yard.

- Samantha Lynn Sanchez de Brooks – Sam was twelve at the time of the Rapture and Juno's friend. She imprinted on Axel and calls him Daddy. Samantha has blue eyes like her real father and grandfather. She is commonly referred to by the Cuban girls as their source of joy and the clingiest girlie one of the bunch. She is a master hair stylist and often has the girls volunteering to get their hair braided or fixed up like they're getting ready to enter a beauty pageant. What is truly remarkable is that when any of the girls feel anxiety or emotional uncertainty, hugging Sam always makes them feel loved and at peace. She is the daughter of Sophia

Sanchez.

- Shelly Arrington – Avery's wife and mother to Holly.

- Sir William – the British Prime Minister.

- Sophia Sanchez – a police officer in Fajardo, PR. Sanchez has long black hair and an hourglass figure. Her friends call her Sophie. She has two daughters—Samantha, twelve years old, has blue eyes (like her father and grandfather) and Charlotte, thirteen years old, has Hazel eyes like her grandmother. Since both her parents were from Spain, and their dads Caucasian, both her girls have colored eyes. However, Sam and Charlotte were never told they were actually sisters. The girls' fathers were both in the military; Marines stationed in Ceiba, PR. Sophie turned over custody of the girls to their fathers when they were barely mobile. Both men married other women. The girls grew up believing their stepmother was actually their real mom.

- Stefan Magnusson – from Stockholm Sweden – a geneticist currently assigned to Jackson Memorial Hospital in Miami, Florida.

- The Tanakh or the Mikra – The Hebrew Bible is the canonical collection of Jewish texts, which is also the textual source for the Christian Old Testament.

- Unidentified – The Universalus Ministerium de Interiora, Salutem ac Discipulina functioned as the Ministry of the Interior, Health and Education.

- Unidentified – The Universalus Ministerium de Transportation ac Inpigre functioned as Ministry of Transportation and Energy.

- Vikki Rogan – a serious looking brunette stewardess/body guard – dressed like a Pan AM stewardess of the early 1960s. She too wore her skirt six inches above the knee versus what was customary for the earlier period. Her outfit was completed by the big button Barbie hat and the white gloves. She wore military style combat boots verses high heel shoes which accompanied that outfit. Her parents raised Heather, Nikki's daughter. Vikki had been shot forty-six times and stabbed eight times. She felt lucky to be alive. But others thought luck had nothing to do with it. She was special and God had been watching out for her. When Maggie found out, she thought her injuries had to be some kind of world record. And she was correct.

- Wen Chow Lee – Winnie or Aunt Winnie – a geneticist working for European Centre for Disease Prevention and Control in Solna, Sweden. She was temporarily assigned to Jackson Memorial Medical Center as part of the team determining the age and origin of human DNA. She was born in England and Hikiko was assigned to her as Guardian. She was the second person to discover Hoshea's true importance.

- Wilson – the hospital administrator at Jackson Memorial Medical Center.

- Yehoshuah – or Joshua was the name used for Jesus Christ in later books of the Hebrew Bible and among the Jews of the Second Temple period. The Second Temple period in Jewish history lasted between 530 BC and 70 AD. Anyway, the name corresponds to the Greek spelling Lesous, from which, through the Latin Lesus, comes the English spelling Jesus. So in short, the Jewish people called Jesus 'Yehoshuah.' The Harem people called 'Yehoshuah' Hoshea.

- Yvette Mia Santa de Milagro – Yvette was a Forensic Pathologist at Jackson Memorial Hospital in Miami, Florida and Mia's mother. Everyone called her Evie. She was born in Fajardo, Puerto Rico. Her home and family place of business was a funeral parlor and mortuary. Yvette's father Joaquin was Fajardo's oldest mortician. He had been a mortician for almost forty years like his father, grandfather and great grandfather before him. Although Yvette had an older brother, who decided not to follow in his father's footsteps. Hector focused on the day to day business of the funeral parlor and did nothing to prep the cadavers, even though he was licensed to do so. Artemis was assigned as her Protector.

www.ingramcontent.com/pod-product-compliance
Lightning Source LLC
Chambersburg PA
CBHW071343020726
47502CB00001B/219